# Passion Spurned

They lay facing one another. She felt the hardness of his thighs against her and she pressed close to him, tasting the honey of his tongue and whispering his name. Her body throbbed with longing and she wanted him to free her breasts, to kiss and touch her everywhere. She knew that something must happen or she would die of wanting him.

"Please, Desmond," she sighed. "Oh, love . . ."

He ripped himself from her suddenly and lay apart. Mara felt the heat departing from her body and in its place came cold shame. She remembered Desmond's comment about serving girls and she wanted to creep away and hide herself forever.

Desmond sat up, cold-eyed. "Go back to your mother," he said. "Leave me." His voice was flat, without emotion . . .

# *Mara*

## *Kathleen Morris*

A Dell/James A. Bryans Book

Published by
Dell Publishing Co., Inc.
1 Dag Hammarskjold Plaza
New York, New York 10017

Dell ® TM 681510, Dell Publishing Co. Inc.

ISBN: 0-440-04971-7

Printed in the United States of America
First printing—August 1978

# BOOK I

## *The Child-Woman*

## Chapter One

"Come close, Mara. Let me see your face." Mary McQuaid turned her head fretfully on the coarse pillow and stretched a frail and trembling hand toward her daughter. Mara bent over her mother, her shining hair tumbling down around her face like a curtain.

"Here I am, Mamma. Have you slept well?"

The older woman smiled with effort. She was in pain again, the sharp, binding pain which circled her chest in an iron grip and locked her voice between a series of gasps. The ship was beginning to pitch; the room was small and dark and Mary McQuaid did not know if it was night or day. She had been sleeping so much lately, and her slumber was punctuated by strange dreams—dreams of her childhood in Ireland and dreams of the life which lay ahead in America. She reached up and touched her daughter's hair wonderingly.

"So beautiful," she murmured. Her eyes lingered with pleasure on the young face suspended above her. Not for the first time she marvelled at the miracle that was her daughter.

"Hush, Mamma," said Mara. "I'll bring you something to eat now."

"Stay a bit. The sight of you does me more good than food or drink."

Mara McQuaid, one month short of her eighteenth birthday, was her mother's only work of art. Her small, heart-shaped face, framed in the great gleaming masses of her black hair, seemed to light the wretched cabin with its radiance. Her skin was of a luminescent whiteness which seemed too delicate to touch; the high cheekbones and small, pointed chin were moulded with an exquisite clarity of line. She might have appeared totally angelic if not for the promise of sensuality in her full, curving lips and her great golden eyes. "The eyes of a lioness," her father used to say. "Ye've given birth to a changeling, Mary."

Mara lowered her lashes, trying to hide the fear that had washed over her, cold and insistent as the North Atlantic swells that rocked the boat and beat at them so remorselessly.

"What is it, girlie?" Mary stroked the girl's velvet cheek, coaxing and comforting.

"Nothing, Mamma." Mara could not tell her mother, who in her remoteness seemed so far from her already, that she would never live to see the New World. She felt so sure of it now, and the knowledge made her blink back tears. Part of her wanted to shake her mother, to scream at her and will some of her own strength into that fragile body, but she merely held the thin fingers, pressing them in her own warm hands with a peculiar intensity. When she opened her eyes her mother was smiling at her tremulously.

"Fetch your cousin," Mary whispered, caressing Mara's cheek with icy fingers. "I must talk to Desmond."

Mara stood, smoothing her hands along the skirts of her gray lawn frock. Like everything she owned it was of good quality, but it was old and thin, much mended. Shabby, Desmond had said. "Never mind, darlin', we'll buy you all the pretty things a girl should have when we get to New York," her mother had replied. Or, making her daughter blush crimson, "It's lovely enough you are without gilding the lily."

Mara moved the few short paces across the tiny cabin to the door. As she walked she was acutely aware of her body. How could it be otherwise when the gown pulled so across her bosom, emphasizing the thrust of her full breasts, clinging to her burgeoning body so shamelessly? She had bloomed late, but when her woman's ripeness came to her, it came with extravagance. At sixteen she had been coltish, delicate, with long elegant legs and small, bud-like breasts; her long neck had made her feel awkward and crane-like. And then one day she had seen the village boys looking at her with new interest, snickering among themselves when she passed by. Her mirror told her, when she stood naked and trembling in the cold dormer bedroom in Mayo, that she could never again be a child. Almost overnight her breasts had blossomed. As if by magic they had become full, and tender to the touch, and her once-narrow hips had swelled gracefully outward from her tiny waist. Blushing, she had ducked beneath her long nightgown and dived under the covers. . . .

Now, at the door to the cabin, she smoothed her hair with her hands and lifted her black shawl from a peg on the wall. She wrapped the shawl tightly about her and—head held high—stepped into the cramped corridor beyond.

It was warmer here, the air close and fetid. Beneath this deck was the nightmare of the hold where she knew the steerage passengers were packed in as tightly as mackerel on ice. When the sea was rough their moans and shrieks rose up to the McQuaids' ears like the sounds of souls in everlasting torment. Even now the racking coughs of the sick could be heard, but they were spiritless and feeble sounds, the sounds of those who had abandoned hope. Mara shuddered. The tiny cabin she shared with her mother was squalid enough; she could hardly bear to picture what life must be like below.

Desmond had noted her look of displeasure when they boarded the *Alberta* at Liverpool. "You're not traveling like a fine lady," he'd said scornfully, "but you can give thanks you won't be like *them*." He'd nodded in the direction of a family of six, the mother holding a baby in her arms while a boy no more than two clung to her skirts and howled with fear. The father, a small Kerryman with a jutting jaw, had circled the other two children in his arms and stared straight ahead with a dazed and desolate air. They had been sick on the rough ferry-crossing from Dublin to Liverpool, tossing about on the open deck and stumbling into the arms of the unscrupulous "runners" the moment they docked. The runners swooped down like birds of prey on the poorest and most helpless of their countrymen. Even as Mara watched, a runner wrestled a trunk from an unresisting old woman and shouted at her to follow him. "She'll be missing that trunk if she doesn't look sharp," Desmond said in disgust. "Vultures—the lot of them."

The chaos of boarding the *Alberta* was so terrible Mara knew she would never forget it. The cries of the thieving runners mingled with the shrieks of mothers separated from their children in the stampede to board, and the wails of those who had seen the last of Ireland pierced the air like a lament for the dead. Now they had been two weeks at sea, and the wails had diminished to a single long, collective sigh of anguish and hopelessness.

She stumbled along the passageway, bracing her arms against the walls when a heavy swell pitched the ship forward and then held it in a trough, rocking it in the sickening motion she had come to know so well. She must find Desmond. Desmond, her mysterious cousin who held the secret of their fate locked in his unknowable heart.

Above her were the few passengers traveling to New York in the relative comfort of first-class. She had seen them in Liverpool. There was a doctor from Dublin who traveled alone, and a rich barrister's daughter from Cork with her brand-new husband. The bride was not much older than Mara, but what a difference in her appearance! She had been dressed in a bottle-green cloak lined in fur, and everything about her—from her curled and perfumed blonde hair to the fine kid gloves on her plump, clinging hands—breathed luxury. Even so, she had looked bewildered and not a little frightened. She clutched at her sandy-haired young husband like a small animal in a trap looking for salvation. Not until her eyes had lit on Cousin Desmond had her expression relaxed, becoming soft and dreamy. Her little pink tongue flicked at her lips in an unconscious gesture of pleasure and the pale blue eyes widened. Where was she now? Probably lying under a pink satin comforter in her first-class cabin, whining to her husband to bring her a cup of strong tea.

Somewhere on the upper level she would find Desmond, who spent most of his time playing cards with the ship's crew or trading stories with the captain himself. She crept up the gangway, flattening herself against the wall as if to escape notice. She was not supposed to appear in first class or in the crew's quarters. She was so intent on her mission she didn't see the enormous man who blocked the door until he spoke.

"Here—where do you think you're going?"

His words were harsh but his tone was not. He stood, a rough blonde giant of a man with reddened hands as large as hams, regarding her with bleary eyes.

"I am looking for Mr. Desmond O'Connell." She spoke in her firmest voice. "I believe he can be found above this deck." She continued up the stairs, trying to ignore the menacing seaman's presence.

"And what might you want with Mr. Desmond O'Connell?" he said mockingly, putting a hint of brogue into his American voice. Mara stood at the top step now. He was blocking her way. She threw back her head and looked him in the eyes, trying to remain in control.

"He is my cousin," she said with dignity. "My mother wishes to see him."

"Oh," said the huge stranger in a placating way. "And here I thought it was *you* needed to see him. You wouldn't be the first young lady to go looking for O'Connell." He narrowed his eyes and let loose a volley of short, barking laughs. He reeked of liquor, and Mara could see that his eyes were red and unpleasantly veined.

"My mother is ill. I cannot see the humor in it."

He stopped then and examined her carefully. His weathered face slackened as he took in her enormous amber eyes and the luminous skin which, under his scrutiny, had begun to go a dull crimson. "By God," he whispered hoarsely, "you're a beauty, aren't you?" His voice had become more slurred and Mara saw he was even drunker than she had imagined. The deep seams of flesh at his neck were engrained with dirt and the nails of his hands were black as tar.

"If you won't take me to my cousin," cried Mara, beginning to tremble with fright and anger, "then stand aside. I'll find him myself."

She moved as if to push past him, but he remained in her way, swaying like a great, immovable tree.

"Stand aside immediately."

"Ahhhh, don't talk to me like that. I could be sweet to you." His hand shot out and cupped her jaw, holding her steady in viselike fingers. His other hand sifted through her hair, lifting it and then letting it fall again as if he was mesmerized by the coal-black tresses.

"Let me go! Let me go or I'll—"

And then she was twisting in his grasp, thrashing her slender body from side to side in a vain effort to free herself. He gripped both her shoulders, his thumbs biting cruelly into her tender flesh, and only laughed at her impossible struggle.

"Fight! Fight me! You'll tire soon enough."

Mara began to sob with rage and frustration. It was useless; she couldn't hope to twist free of him. Here, on the top step of the *Alberta*'s gangway, somewhere in the middle of the Atlantic, a filthy, brutish seaman stood laughing at her helplessness, licking his cracked lips with anticipation and lust. A terrible red anger flooded her and she whipped her head, sudden as a cobra, and sank her small white teeth into one of the grimy hands that pinioned her.

He howled once, like a wounded bear, and sprang back cursing. "Irish slut! Filthy trash!" His voice raked over her, thick with fury, but she was running now, past him and down the narrow passageway. She heard his heavy, lurching steps behind her, but she rounded a corner and found herself—to her immense relief—at an open doorway.

Inside she could see a group of men playing cards at an oak table. Cigar smoke plumed up thick and blue, and in the center of the haze she could discern the dark form of her cousin, Desmond. Without thinking, she hurled herself into the cabin, panting and flushed with terror. Her shawl was trailing from her arms and her hair streamed over her shoulders. Her breath rose and fell in ragged gasps, but they appeared not to notice her at all. At last, one of the players looked up.

"We've a visitor, gentlemen." He laid down his cards and nudged the man next to him. "Take your feet off the table, Jim, there's a lady among us."

There were five of them in the room. Mara recognized the man who had spoken as the Dublin doctor, a portly fellow with mutton-chop whiskers and contemplative eyes. The others were crewmen. Only Desmond seemed oblivious to her presence. He was examining the cards in his hand, frowning as if they displeased him. At length he placed them on the table and sighed. "What is it, Mara?" His voice was curt, impersonal.

"I—I beg your pardon, gentlemen. I've come to fetch Mr. O'Connell." She knew she was blushing now, but she tossed her hair back and stared straight at Desmond. "Mother is not well. She wishes to speak to you."

Desmond regarded her coolly from beneath his level black brows. "You're discomposed, Cousin. Have you run all the way?" His blue eyes, startling in the dark face, seemed to bore through her. It was as if he knew all about the horrid man in the gangway and found it secretly amusing.

Mara's eyes blazed. "If I'm discomposed, Cousin, it's none of your affair." She turned to a stout, barrel-chested man who seemed a figure of authority. "Some of your crewmen need to learn manners," she snapped.

This produced an astounding reaction. All of the men, except for Desmond and the kindly doctor, roared with laughter. "Bless my soul, dearie," wheezed the stout ship's officer, "I expect you're right!" And then he laughed again, mopping his cheeks with a sleeve that was none too clean. "You're to blame, all the same," he sighed. "You're far too pretty for an old tub like this."

Desmond stood abruptly, scraping his chair against the floor and almost upsetting the glass of brandy at his elbow. "Excuse me, all," he said in tones of icy formality. "I'll be going to Mrs. McQuaid now." He strode to the door and out, leaving Mara to bob her head in the direction of the men and scurry after him. When they reached the end of the passageway he turned and tossed her a contemptuous look.

"A fine sight you are," he grated. "Bursting into the cabin like a serving girl who's been tussling with the boot-black."

Mara gasped at the unfairness of it, but before she could reply he had grasped her arm and was propelling her upward, to the top deck. "You do me wrong," she sputtered, clambering along beside him. Tears of outrage were blurring her vision, but she refused to explain herself. If Desmond wished to think ill of her, so be it. She refused to simper apologies to this strange, barbarian cousin. Let him think what he would.

On deck the North Atlantic wind assaulted them with a force almost evil in its intensity. For as far as Mara could see there was nothing but an endless, heaving mass of gray. The sea was limitless, terrify-

ing in its steely vastness. She shivered to think of
the steerage passengers who had fallen ill and been
sent to their eternal rest in these frigid waters. The
ship pitched into a deep trough and she fell against
her cousin, clinging for an instant to the front of
his coat before she righted herself.

"What are we doing up here?" she asked miserably. "Mother needs you, Desmond. There's no time
to waste."

He seemed not to hear her. He stood staring out
to sea, his brilliant blue eyes gone gray and cold as
the water. He is a strange man, she thought, more
like a Saracen than an Irishman. His skin was dark
and smooth as if it had been gilded by the sun all
his life. His thick black hair grew closely around his
well-shaped skull and curled slightly over his collar.
The brows and lashes were dark as night, making
the light eyes all the more remarkable for the contrast. At present his long, shapely lips were set
grimly, but Mara had seen him smile and when Desmond smiled it set her to shivering. You never knew
what he had in mind, and although his white teeth
flashing in the dark face could set the village girls
to tittering and blushing, there was something cruel
and foreign in it—something she could not name.

Desmond was tall—as tall as the apish sailor
who had tormented her—but his body was long and
lean like a rapier, quick and supple and as strong as
good, thin steel. She touched his arm and he returned to her.

"I shouldn't lose my temper with you, Mara." He
smiled briefly. "You're only a girl, you understand
nothing."

"And what would you know of me? You're arrogant, Desmond. You care only for yourself. I understand a great deal, and what I don't I soon will."

"That's what I fear, sweet Cousin." This time his grin was mocking. He wrapped the shawl more tightly around her, tucking her hair beneath it with an almost fastidious air. For a moment their faces were close together, and it seemed he might say something. His eyes flickered oddly, but then he turned and together they went below.

Mary McQuaid had been sleeping again. Was it night or day? The cabin was always gray and murky, even at noon. She plucked at the thin, coarse blanket covering her wasted frame. Once she had slept beneath good woollens and satin coverlets, her cheek against a pillow of the finest Irish linen. She had had nightdresses worked with cunning blue ribbons at the yoke, and a bed-jacket of apple green sateen. She liked to pass the hours in the tiny cabin thinking of just such inconsequential things—happy days she had spent as a child in the village near Westport . . . happier days yet when she and Padraic had married and gone to live in his lovely house within sight of the sea . . .

The gulf stream had warmed this part of the Mayo coast. Giant fuchsias bloomed near the sea, and the sands were as white as sugar. Even in the heart of winter the gales never blew so cold and deadly as they did further north in Sligo, or across the Aran Islands toward Galway to the south. It was lucky for her, for she had always been delicate. Her own mother had wept when Mary became pregnant for the first time. Nothing would comfort her, not even her daughter's radiant happiness. She was sure Mary would die in childbirth; her fears had seemed foolish to Mary, who was so full of youth and love she felt invincible . . .

When the pains came she called to Padraic that their son was on his way; they were sure she carried a son. And indeed, two days later, weak from the suffering which had surpassed anything she could have imagined, it was a son the midwife lifted from her torn and bleeding body. Padraic Joseph he was called, after his father, and he lived for three days. She was ill for a long time after that, but when she rose from her bed she was determined to try again. She and Padraic could never get enough of each other in those early days—she had only to look at him in a special way of an evening and they would send the servant girl to bed and climb the stairs, weak with longing. Ah, yes, she had been a passionate woman, had Mary McQuaid. And a woman for whom there was only one man in the world. Even when she lost another child, a girl this time, she could not turn away from him. The little daughter had been stillborn and Mary's own suffering not so great this time, but she was permanently weakened.

The midwife crossed herself when Mary became pregnant again, and muttered that this third child would bring her to her grave. She was frail, God had not intended for her to birth healthy babies—didn't she see that God had not created her to be a mother? Mary would never forget the look on the midwife's face when she replied that God had created her for the love of Padraic McQuaid, and whatever the consequences she was strong enough to bear them. This time she lost the child in the seventh month, and during the long winter the consumption which had touched her so lightly in her childhood returned. For three years she could not leave her bed. Padraic read to her and held her hand, caressing her hair and murmuring his love, but she knew a man of his temperament could not be content in this way for long. Her body ached for him, even in the midst of her fevers, and she wept bitterly when the inevitable happened.

They grew apart, and she turned a deaf ear to village gossip. She did not want to hear that Shelagh from the draper's shop was holding her Padraic of an evening in strong, round arms. She could not bear to picture the publican's lusty daughter, Rose, panting with delight in Padraic's embrace, or to dwell on the image of her beloved's strong square hands bringing cries of delight from the servant girl. Yet she knew it was so.

She bided her time, growing stronger and willing the disease to leave her body so she could woo her husband back.

In some ways she knew she was lucky. She had been born in the years following the Great Famine. Because her parents owned their own land—"minor gentry" as they often were called—her family had escaped the horrible fate which had befallen a million of her countrymen. As a child she had shuddered with terror when the old people told stories of the famine years. Her nightmares were populated with grotesque creatures who stumbled about the countryside with bellies distended and swollen from the slow starvation, their skeletal arms no larger than sticks. She knew they had wandered, their children sobbing in pain, until they died in ditches along the roadside. No, no, she had escaped all that. Her childhood had been happy, she had married the man of her heart. And though she had lost three babies, she would live to be lucky again.

Then, when Padraic had given up hope, she became pregnant once more. No one could understand why she went about singing with joy; they thought she invited her death. She knew differently. This child would live, and he would be someone special, someone quite out of the ordinary. This time she labored easily and when the baby was born it gave a lusty howl and settled greedily to its mother's breast. Mary had been right about everything but the child's sex. She had given birth to a daughter, a perfect black-haired baby whose destiny was to live, as surely as the other wee ones had been bound to die.

They named the child Mara, and lavished on her all the love they had been storing for so long. It was expected that they might spoil her, but even the midwife agreed that young Mara McQuaid was the most perfectly gorgeous infant to be born in living memory . . .

Mara? Where was she now? Wasn't she coming with Desmond, or had that been another day? Desmond. She must talk to him, to let him know . . . He must look after Mara until they were all reunited with Padraic in New York. And why was her husband in New York? It was so hard to remember. Just when the details came clear they receded again; a trick, a trick was being played on her.

She was seized with another spasm of coughing. When it had subsided she lay, spent and ashen, worrying about her daughter. Beauty could be a curse. Men, being what they were, would not realize that Mara was still innocent. She had seen them staring at her, wanting her, struck almost dizzy by Mara's amazing beauty. Come to that, she wasn't sure she could trust Desmond. Desmond, whose link to them was so tenuous. She tried to work back through the family ties which bound him to them by blood, but it was too difficult. "Oh, Padraic," she sighed, and then lapsed into a semi-sleep.

"Mamma! We're here. I've brought Desmond. Oh, please . . ."

Mary opened her eyes. Their two young faces hung over her like jewels in the gloom, one dark and one fair. Mara was flushed and breathless, her eyes clouded with worry. Desmond, as always, seemed calm.

"Leave us, Mara dear. Just for a bit."

Mara felt as if she had been banished. What could her mother have to say to Desmond that required such secrecy? From time to time she could hear her cousin's voice raised slightly in indistinguishable rumblings through the ramshackle wall. She was afraid to walk about the lower decks lest she meet the swinish blond seaman or one of his cohorts. She tried to abandon herself to daydreams.

For all her grief at her mother's weak condition she felt the impatience of a healthy young animal confined to close quarters for too long a time. She leaned against the wall, blocking her ears to the dismal cacophony that rose from steerage, and tried to project herself into the marvelous new life she felt sure was waiting for her in New York. She thought first of seeing her father again, of hearing him call her his little squirrel and watching his eyes light with joy and pride at the sight of her. She imagined wondrous new gowns of mauve taffeta and russet velvet—perhaps her mother would allow her to have something cut low at the bosom . . . She was deep in a fancy involving herself, beautifully gowned and coiffed, at a dress ball in New York, when it came to her that her mother might not be there to share her triumphs.

For a moment she hated herself. Her mother was dying, perhaps, and she could think only of frivolous pleasures. Her deepest shame was reserved for something which she normally refused to admit: when she envisioned New York's glittering ballrooms, the man who bowed to her and extended his hand, the man whose eyes glowed with fierce admiration, was Desmond. She shook her head impatiently. It must be that Desmond was the only man she had seen these two weeks, save for occasional glimpses of the unsavory crew. Otherwise how could she account for it? She did not even *like* Desmond, really. He was unkind, impatient, a man whose only thoughts revolved around hunting and card-playing and vain girls like the plump, rich bride in first-class. She had never been able to get along with him. From the first day he had come to their village two years ago, announcing his intentions of settling in Mayo

with the calm arrogance which made her grit her
teeth with annoyance, she had despised him. Always,
his attitude toward her was mocking and contemptuous. Why, then, did his face appear with such reg-
ularity in her secret fancies?

The door opened and Desmond slipped from the
cabin with a furtive air. His gaze was impassive, yet
Mara thought she could detect a subtle softening,
a glint of sorrow in his demeanor.

"How is she?" Mara spoke in a whisper.

"She is not well, Mara." Desmond gave her an
odd look, as if he were measuring her worth, her
ability to listen to the truth. Evidently he found her
less lacking than usual, for he took her arm abruptly
and walked with her a little way up the passage.
"Come with me," he said. "It's time for us to talk,
and after today's little display I'm afraid you should
not be let at large on this ship." She bridled but his
smile softened the sardonic words, and he escorted
her to his own cabin.

"Come in, Cousin," he said, favoring her with
the cocky grin she hated. "I'll not compromise you."

She had never been in his cabin before. It was as
small and shoddy as the one she shared with her
mother, but there was a difference. Desmond's quarters were redolent with tobacco and brandy, and
everywhere his clothing lay strewn about where he
had thrown it. His sea coat sprawled on the narrow
cot, one of his shirts was draped across the single
chair. An open bottle of brandy, half full, stood on
the floor near the head of his bed. The scene was
oddly intimate and Mara averted her eyes.

"What is it, sweet Cousin? Never been in a man's room before?"

His tone infuriated her. "You should be more orderly, Desmond. If the ship begins to pitch you'll lose the better part of that brandy."

Desmond threw his sea coat to the floor and made room for himself on the bed. His long legs, booted and somehow elegant, stretched straight before him.

"I am so pleased," he said gravely, "that you take an interest." He poured himself half a tumbler of brandy and toasted her.

"*Slainte,*" he said roughly, and tossed the drink down in a single gulp. "I am told we're heading into a gale," he continued. "Fortunately, I never become seasick."

"Nor I," replied Mara, "but I hardly think you've asked me here to discuss the weather."

"Why, what should I discuss with my pretty little cousin? Would you have me comment on your eyes, your hair? I suppose you must be used to compliments."

Mara flushed. "I think you're disgusting," she cried. "You invite me to your cabin—presumably to talk of what will become of my poor mother—and then you sit swilling spirits on your bed while I am obliged to stand in your miserable cabin and tolerate your insults." Her voice had risen and she felt she might scream at him in a moment. "She is my *mother*, Desmond, and I love her dearly. It may seem a joke to you—God knows all of life does—but it is not a joke to me." The force of her anger had filled her throat with tears and now they spilled over, tangling her lashes and coursing down her cheeks. She refused to utter a sound, but her body shook uncontrollably.

Desmond's face had drained of color under the assault of her words. He rose slowly and walked toward her. When they were face to face he spoke gently, almost humbly.

"I am not mocking your sorrow, Mara. Your mother is the best of women and I will grieve sorely if she should die. If I seem to you to be harsh, I pray you forgive me. I have my reasons."

She raised tear-stained eyes to him and for a moment it seemed she could see into his soul. A fine vein began to beat at his temple; the blue of his eyes deepened almost to black. They seemed, she and Desmond, to have turned to stone, paralyzed until some greater force breathed life into them again. Her heart was beating wildly and she felt an almost intolerable heat spreading over her flesh and taking root deep within her. Her lips parted helplessly and she swayed toward him, and then he was groaning as if in pain, catching her to him roughly and cradling her against his breast. She laid her cheek on the rough cloth of his coat and felt she wanted to burrow into his very center. She was trembling now as if she had a chill, but the heat persisted and she felt her face go scarlet with it. His hands against her back were hotter still, like burning brands—dangerous and even deadly. Slowly they moved up and caught at her hair, dragging her head back until her lips were inches from his own. Still he hesitated, his breath coming in ragged gasps, and she arched her body like a bow, pressing herself to him.

He groaned again—something between a prayer and a curse—and then his lips were bruising hers, desperate and savage, as if to drink her soul from her. Her lips opened joyously and her body went limp in his arms; she was afraid she was melting with the heat of her desire, yet she possessed a marvelous strength. Her hands ranged over his back with a will of their own—she had to get closer, closer to him. He tore his mouth from hers and planted it against her warm, curved throat. She felt his black hair beneath her fingertips and closed on it, holding him to her with a fierceness she would never have dreamed possible.

Her shawl had slipped to the floor at their feet. His hands sought her breasts, moving in exquisite fashion over them, caressing with infinite gentleness and then crushing them roughly so that she cried out in pain and pleasure, thrusting herself to him pleadingly.

He was trembling violently as he picked her up in his arms and carried her to the bed. They lay facing one another. She felt the hardness of his thighs against her and pressed close to him, tasting the honey of his tongue and crying out his name. Her nipples ached with longing and she wanted him to free her breasts, to kiss and touch her everywhere. She slipped a hand inside his shirt and felt the smooth bare skin burning against her fingers. She knew that something must happen or she would die of wanting him . . .

"Please, Desmond," she moaned. "Oh, love . . ."

He ripped himself from her so suddenly she felt she had been plunged into icy water. He lay apart from her, breathing in tortured gasps. Mara felt the heat departing, slowly, from her body, and in its place came cold shame. Her hair was matted, tangled; it streamed over the pillow and flowed down her breasts. The skirt of her gray gown was up above her thighs and her body still throbbed as if she were in the throes of a fit. She remembered Desmond's comment about serving girls and bootblacks, and she wanted to creep away and hide herself forever.

Desmond sat up, averting his eyes from her. "Go back to your mother," he said. "Leave me." His voice was flat, without emotion.

Timidly, she touched his shoulder only to have him flinch from her as if she had branded him with a white-hot iron. He spoke in precise, measured tones underlined by what seemed to her pure venom: "Get out. I don't want you. Not now—not ever. Christ knows thousands would think me a fool, but that's how it is. Go."

"Liar!" Her voice was thick with rage. She wanted to fly at him, to scratch out his eyes or pull his hair as a child would do. "I know what I felt and you felt it, too. You couldn't feign it—you couldn't!" She was pleading now, although she didn't know it.

Desmond flashed her a grin of pure malice. "Couldn't I, now? Oh, get away, Cousin. Comb your hair and straighten your dress. We'll pretend it never happened at all."

"I won't. I'll never forget it. I'll pay you back,

Desmond. You can't humiliate me so and expect me to forget." She forced herself to walk to the door with a semblance of dignity. "Remember that, Desmond. I'll pay you back."

"You'll thank me one day, Mara. See if you don't."

But she was gone.


Sleep would not come that night. While her mother slept her fitful, tortured slumber, Mara lay rigid in her cot, staring sightlessly at the ceiling. Her body would not relax—it still hummed and seethed with the memory of what had happened in Desmond's cabin. She had never dreamed that desire could be so strong. She had not known it could pluck every nerve in your body to unbearable life and then leave you in a mass of tangled knots. She felt as feverish as her mother. Her body, beneath the thin nightdress, fairly pulsed with life and strength and need—and all for what?

"Damn you, Desmond," she whispered, *"Damn* you." She turned on her side and pressed her lips to one small, clenched fist. It was stifling in the cabin —airless, suffocating. If only she could breathe the open air again, as she had on the deck with Desmond. She would not dare to creep about the ship at night, but perhaps in the passageway outside some breath of air might stir. Anything was better than lying like this, counting away the long hours of the night in misery. She tiptoed across to her mother and saw that Mary was truly sleeping, and then she wrapped herself in the shawl she and Desmond had trampled underfoot and unlatched the cabin door.

The corridor was dark and utterly silent. She crept outside and stood with her back to the door. Better. Merely to be on her feet was better, although it was just as airless here. Nothing moved. The sea was calm tonight; the *Alberta* plowed along on her course and Mara prayed the gale Desmond had mentioned was merely a chimera. Although, she thought with grim satisfaction, she would not care if he were blown away to the farthest corners of the earth.

Her body quickened. Had she heard a sound? It was so faint she could not be sure, but then it came again—a woman's laughter, muffled but nearby. Dizzy with trepidation, she advanced silently along the passageway. The sounds became clearer and she knew immediately that the woman who had laughed was in Desmond's cabin, now, at this instant. And herself? She could hardly bear to think that she had sunk this low—skulking like a thief in the night, a spy, outside her cousin's love nest. There was a horrible fascination to it, and she strained to hear. There it came again—the laugh—and answering it the murmur of Desmond's reply. She put her ear to the wall.

"Ooooh, Des, yes . . ." A giggle. "Des, darling . . ."

Could she really allow herself to stand at her cousin's door, eavesdropping while he made love to a giggling tart? It seemed she could, although her head was swimming with rage and her heart seemed lodged in her throat. How long she stood there she could not tell, but suddenly the sounds were closer and she realized that Desmond's lover was about to take her leave.

She darted back up the corridor on soundless feet, just in time. The door opened cautiously, and from the dim light within Mara could see the figure of a woman, wrapped in a cloak, backing away. She was smothering her giggles in her hands, and then the cloak fell open and Mara could see she wore only a nightdress, open at the neck and generously revealing an abundantly voluptuous body. The girl's hair was unbound, tousled. It glinted dully gold and Mara knew with certainty who she was.

"You're delectable, Des. I could eat you up." She fiddled with the ribbons at her neck, managing to bare one large, pink breast. She stood for a moment, staring longingly into the cabin. There was a brief reply.

"I shall sleep well tonight," the girl said with a sly laugh. She turned to go and for one memorable moment Mara could see her face quite clearly. The barrister's daughter, the blushing bride sailing to the New World with her husband, looked as sated as a cat who had just lapped up a bowl of cream. Her heavy lips had a soft, bruised look and the pale blue eyes were unfocused, half-lidded. She gathered her cloak about her billowing breasts and blew a kiss to her lover.

"Why didn't I meet you first?" she pouted. "It's not fair."

"Ah, but what is?" And Desmond closed the door in her face.

## Chapter Two

Mara moistened bits of bread in tea and fed them to her mother with a spoon. Mary seemed livelier this morning, more talkative, but her eyes glinted with an unnatural brightness and two high spots of color bloomed in her wasted cheeks. She took the bread gratefully, chattering with a feverish vivacity. Mara invented stories, talking encouragingly of the bright future.

"Think, Mamma," she was saying, "just think how warm and safe we'll feel in America. Father will take us to a lovely house on a square. It will be ablaze with lights, and there'll be soft beds with eiderdowns and a maid to draw your bath! We'll have chicken and roast potatoes and perhaps a glass of port. When you're stronger he'll take us out in his carriage and show us the sights! Here—take some more tea now. It will be spring in New York when we arrive. Think of it."

Mary smiled at her daughter's eagerness. "Yes,"

she agreed, "Padraic will take care of us. It was only for that he went away."

Outside in the passageway came the sound of raised voices and the thud of running feet. A clamor of frantic activity seemed to be taking place. A voice rose suddenly above the others and there was the sound of knocking at their door, frightening in its intensity.

"Mrs. McQuaid! Miss McQuaid! Let me in."

The voice was familiar somehow, but Mara could not place it. "Who are you?" she hissed. "My mother is ill; you must not disturb her."

"I'm Terence Quinn," replied the agitated voice, "I'm a doctor."

Mara opened the door a crack and looked out suspiciously. Directly before her, pacing and wringing his hands together, was the small, whiskered card-player who had refused to laugh when she had burst into the cabin yesterday. His eyes, worried beneath the bushy, owlish brows, softened at sight of her.

"Forgive me," he murmured, "but there's no time for niceties. We're heading into rough waters, Miss McQuaid. Mr. O'Connell told me there's a sick woman here. She must not stay." He lowered his voice. "She might be tossed from her bunk— God knows that must not happen. I've come to take her to my cabin."

"But you're in first class, Dr. Quinn, are you not?"

"For God's sake, girl, what difference does that make to you?" He pushed past her and went directly to her mother's bed. "Mrs. McQuaid," he said urgently, "I've come to move you. Are you strong enough to sit?"

Mary turned bright, excited eyes on him. "Are you the ship's doctor?" she asked.

"Sure and I am *not*," Dr. Quinn said disdainfully. "He's a drunken fool. I'm not much better, but I still have my wits about me." He issued several curt orders and Mara flew to obey. She had wrapped her mother in every shawl they owned and was collecting their few possessions together when Desmond appeared at the door. Outside, all was chaos. They were heading into a storm—perhaps they might all perish—and all she could think was *Desmond is here*. She would not look at him, but every inch of her quivered with the knowledge of his presence.

"I'll carry her," Desmond said simply. He crossed the room and picked Mary up as easily as if she had been a kitten. "Now, Aunt Molly," he said in a sweet, teasing voice Mara had never heard from him, "you'll please to give me no trouble while I transport you to more commodious quarters."

Dr. Quinn led the way, looking back anxiously over his shoulder while Desmond strode behind, his fragile burden wrapped securely in his arms. Mara, shivering in her thin dress, hastened after them. Some of the ship's panic had transmitted itself to the luckless passengers below. She could hear a woman shrieking, another praying in a mechanical, hopeless way, chanting her rosary in a voice gone hollow with fear. Above, the crew ran past, heedless of the small party of passengers trespassing in first class. There was something reassuring in their frantic activity, something almost exhilarating to Mara.

She thought to herself that Dr. Quinn's small, comical face and figure epitomized the virtue of simple kindness—it had been so long since anyone had made her feel safe that she wanted to put her arms around his vigorous, stumpy little body and hug him for joy.

They reached the cabin just in time. Mary had barely been deposited in the doctor's bed when the storm hit. There was a moment of breathless quiet when the ship, born aloft on a towering wave, seemed to hang suspended, and then everything turned upside down. Crockery came sliding across the table where the doctor had eaten his breakfast and crashed in shards on the floor; several thick books flew across the cabin as if driven by devils. Mara found herself flung rudely to the deck, the breath knocked out of her. Dr. Quinn was shouting something to Desmond, but the words were blotted out by the awful noise of groaning timbers and the crashing and crackling all around them.

She watched while Desmond and the doctor tied her mother deftly to the bed, and then the ship plunged again and she rolled across the floor, striking her head against the table leg. Twice more the *Alberta* pitched and fell and then Mara discovered there was a sort of rhythm to it. A moment of stillness, followed by several precious instants of calm, and then the dreadful descent. Her mother's eyes were closed. Mary's lips moved briefly—perhaps she was praying—and then she seemed to lose consciousness.

"What is it!" Mara screamed. "What has happened?"

"I have given her a drop of laudanum," the doctor shrieked back. "It's better for her so . . . all the excitement . . ."

Desmond stood, arms braced against the cabin walls, and laughed wildly. "By God you're a strange one, doctor! Listen to him cousin—he calls this maelstrom *excitement*."

"I love a storm at sea," Dr. Quinn said reflectively in the sudden calm, "but I pity those poor devils in steerage."

Mara, mindful of her sprawling position at their feet, clasped the table leg and tried to stand. "No!" the doctor shouted. "Stay where you are, Miss McQuaid—you're safer so."

The ship lurched again and from somewhere nearby Mara could hear a high-pitched female scream trailing off into a series of hysterical sobs.

"Our friend next door does not travel well," the doctor said in the next calm interval. "Young Mrs. Daly did not anticipate such a honeymoon." He had hunkered down next to Mara, and addressed her conversationally. She wondered if he knew that Desmond and young Mrs. Daly had more than a nodding acquaintance, but his little snapping eyes were innocent of complicity. "I wonder," he continued, "if I should go to her?"

"She has a husband," said Desmond flatly. "Kathy will be looked after."

Kathy! His casual use of the buxom blonde girl's name caused Mara to clench her fists. She could feel her nails biting into the tender flesh of her palms and forced herself to look at her cousin's face. Desmond's eyes were blazing with light, his white teeth gleaming in the dark face with a kind of ecstatic joy. It was danger he loved, she thought. The storm filled him with glee, made him come alive as nothing else could do. Grudgingly, she credited him for thinking of her mother and enlisting the doctor's help, but in every other respect he was hateful to her.

"Will you have a bit of whiskey, my dear?" Incredibly, the doctor was offering her a glass, passing it over politely as if they were at a picnic in a forest glade. "I recommend it," he urged. "We're in for several hours of this, you know."

"Thank you, no," Mara said primly. The doctor nipped quickly at his drink and then braced himself as the *Alberta* drove down into the crashing sea, slipping from side to side as she plunged, then shuddering violently as the tons of water slapped her aging timbers. Outside the port hole Mara could see mountains of water rearing up, then slipping away, only to heave up in towering crests and blot out everything as the ship turned crazily, dizzily, almost upside down. She looked away. She felt panic rising when those glassy walls of water were all she could see—somewhere there was a sane world where the earth turned softly, silently, and firm ground lay beneath one's feet, a world where the ocean was something one saw from the window, gleaming and calm. She did not want to grow hysterical like Mrs. Daly—Kathy—and so she accepted the doctor's whiskey when the next calm moment came.

The small sip burned her throat and settled somewhere deep inside, warming her and creating a welcome diversion. She was so bemused that she turned to thank the doctor politely, passing the bottle back, but she had let go of the table leg and when the next wave came she was flung across the cabin floor, rolling in a tangle of arms and legs and coming to land with a vicious thump half-way across the room. She struck her head against the wall and lay, momentarily stunned, her long hair fanned out around her like the points of a midnight star. Her hands reached out to clasp something for support, but they closed on air. She felt the room grow dark and then she lost consciousness for a moment, slipping gratefully away from the chaos and terror of the storm. When she awakened she was not alone. Strong arms held her close, bracing her body against the pitching and rolling of the ship. Her cheek lay against the cloth of a man's coat.

She opened her eyes, feeling foolish and clumsy, and was prepared to see the beetling brows and puckish mouth of Dr. Quinn hovering above her when it came to her: Dr. Quinn's arms could not hold her with such strength. His flesh would not smell of cloves, nor would his body be so much larger and longer than her own. She lay on the floor clasped in Desmond's arms—it was Desmond's heart that beat so close to her own, his hands that held her. She lifted her head slowly.

Desmond's eyes, dark as they had been in his cabin the day before, searched her face. When he was sure she was fully conscious he grinned. His lips barely moved, but she heard every word he said.

"If you won't look after yourself, little Cousin, someone must." His arms tightened around her, holding her so firmly that any movement was impossible. "Oh, well," he sighed, mocking her again, "never mind. It's only until the storm is over . . ."

She shut her eyes again and lay in the circle of his arms. There was really nothing else she could do.

Mara's eyes fluttered open. She was confused, disoriented. For several instants she imagined herself in her own bed, at home in Ireland, but her stiff, aching limbs soon told her where she was. She stirred, moaning slightly at the throbbing pain in her temple, and looked around her. The light filtering through the port hole was gray and weak, but at least there were no monstrous, glassy, sea-mountains falling past, and it was still day. The *Alberta* rocked steadily; the dreadful careening had passed. A few feet away her mother lay lashed to the bunk, peacefully breathing, serene, asleep.

"The worst is over," said a voice behind her. Dr. Quinn was comfortably ensconced at his desk, reading a book and occasionally sipping from the ever-present glass of whiskey at his elbow.

"How long have I slept?" Mara pushed back the tangle of her hair and arranged her skirts more decorously. She had been lying on a pallet made up of blankets and clothing. Desmond's heavy coat had been thrown over her. Unconsciously, her fingers caressed the tough tweed.

The doctor consulted his pocket watch. "It is mid-afternoon," he answered obliquely. "We had rough seas for five hours. I should say you were oblivious for four." He smiled. "I envy you your youth, my dear. To sleep through a gale at sea, safe in your cousin's arms. Amazing!"

Mara blushed. "I slept badly last night," she murmured.

"Mr. O'Connell kept you from harm, at any rate. That bump on your head is not serious, but if you like I will look at it . . ."

"Where is my cousin now?" asked Mara stiffly.

The doctor gestured discreetly. "Here and there," he replied. "It is very difficult to predict the movements of an energetic young fellow like your cousin."

Energetic, indeed! Mara wanted to laugh. If the good doctor only knew how energetic Desmond really was he might be shocked.

"I've looked in on the Dalys next to us," said Dr. Quinn, as if reading her mind. "Poor Mrs. Daly was very ill, very frightened. Her husband was even more seasick than she." He paused, as if to consider his words. "Do you know," he continued, "they seem uncommonly ill-matched. She is such a vibrant creature, while he—" Dr. Quinn shook his head. "I do natter on . . . I'm only an old gossip at heart if I'm not put in my place."

Impulsively, Mara put her hand on his arm. "You are a good, kind, man," she said impulsively. "You have all my gratitude."

"Nonsense. I'm a doctor. That's what doctors are for. I shall insist on looking after your mother for the remainder of the voyage."

"Shall you practice medicine in America?"

He smiled oddly. "No, my dear. I think not."

Mara went to the basin of water in the corner

and bathed her face. The mirror told her she looked refreshed, happy. Incredible; after such an ordeal she ought to be hollow-eyed and pale, but her cheeks were laved with warm color and her eyes glowed with contentment. It was Desmond's doing. He had held her safe while she slept through the storm and for a moment she forgot she hated him.

There was a timid tapping at the door. Young Mr. Daly stood apologetically in the passageway. Mara studied him covertly. He was a thin man, small-boned and reedy. His narrow chest and shoulders seemed so boyish they belied the face above; John Daly's sandy hair was already receding from the high forehead and his thin, rather fussy lips and pinched nose gave him a prematurely aged air. His pale eyes darted from Mara to the doctor and back again. He seemed nervous and ill at ease.

"Your wife is better, I trust?" Dr. Quinn asked civilly.

"That's just it," said Mr. Daly, wetting his lips and wringing his hands anxiously together. "She's in a bad way."

Immediately Quinn was on his feet, but John Daly gasped with alarm. "It's kind of you doctor, but I think——" He whispered something in an undertone.

"To be sure," said the doctor, when he had heard him out. "Miss McQuaid, this young man feels his wife needs someone of her own sex at present. Would you be willing to go to her?"

"Please," cried John Daly desperately, "if you would spend but a moment with her? The presence of another young lady . . . Kathleen would be so grateful . . ." He was blushing, abject. Mara felt sorry for him. Poor little man, so anxious for his wife, so innocent of her wickedness toward him. Would he help her now if he knew she had made a cuckold of him?

"Of course I shall go," she said soothingly.

"I'll stay here," said John Daly in tones of vast relief. "I've ah—cleaned things up, you understand—" His voice bumbled off into an embarrassed little cough.

The door of the Dalys cabin was ajar; Mara could hear the blonde girl's sobs from outside, and she tried to conjure up a charitable pity for the woman who wept so unrestrainedly. She tapped at the door and entered, approaching the bed. There was a cloying odor of cologne everywhere to mask the unpleasant smells of sickness. Kathleen Daly was lying under a pale blue quilt. Her face had been freshly bathed and her fair hair brushed vigorously, until it shone. Mara guessed that her husband had performed these services—probably he had emptied the slop bucket, as well.

Mrs. Daly lay on her back, weeping volubly. Her blue eyes were puffy and red and her large bosom heaved ponderously beneath the blue satin.

Mara was about to ask if she might help when the other girl pushed herself up on an elbow and stared at her balefully. "You must think me such a fool," she wailed, swabbing at her eyes with a lace-trimmed handkerchief. "I have heard all about how brave you were from Terence Quinn and I think I shall go mad if I have to hear it again."

Mara smiled despite herself. "I've not come to

brag about my courage," she said cheerfully. "At any rate, I slept through the worst."

"How could you *sleep?*" Mrs. Daly demanded, incredulous. "I've never been so frightened in all my born days. It was horrid." She shuddered and sat up further. "Horrid! I've always hated the sea ever since I was small and Daddy took me across the channel to school for the first time. I can't imagine why I'm here at all, indeed I can't."

"You were educated in England?"

"In France, my dear. *Vraiment!* Born in Cork, educated in Paris, and destined for a watery grave." She giggled, scrubbing at her eyes like a little girl and sniffling. "I'm so sorry," she said gravely, "I am being so rude. Please do sit down." She indicated a plush chair with a sweep of one beringed and dimpled hand. "I haven't even introduced myself properly. Please call me Kathy—I'm Kathleen Daly, but I *was* Kathleen Moriarty, much nicer, don't you think?—and you are Mr. O'Connell's cousin, Mara McQuaid."

Mara was beginning to be amused. There was something infectious about the girl's rapid, breathless delivery and something very humorous indeed in the rapidity with which she seemed to have recovered from her illness.

"Are you quite sure you are well enough to sit up?" she asked solicitously. "Dr. Quinn seemed to think you were at death's door."

"Ah, Terence is a dear thing, don't you think? I sent John over because I knew you were next door and I was perishing to make your acquaintance." Kathy grinned openly now. "How old are you?"

"Eighteen, next month."

"I am twenty," said Kathy with a worldly sigh. She stretched forth a lazy hand and fetched two long-stemmed glasses from a table nearby. "Let me tell you something," she said judiciously, pouring golden sherry and passing a glass to Mara. "Never marry in haste, *cherie*. It is the gravest error a girl can make." She lifted her glass and toasted Mara. "Cheers—*a tes amours*."

"Mr. Daly seems a fine man," said Mara in embarrassment. Privately she considered him a fool, but Kathy's ready confidence had discomfited her.

Kathy regarded her shrewdly. "I'll not speak ill of John," she said at last. "I can only repeat the old saw: 'Marry in haste, repine at leisure!' She was examining her face in a hand-mirror now, frowning at what she saw. *"Quel horreur*—I look a fright," she moaned, pinching at one round cheek to force some color. The quilt had fallen away and the upper portion of Kathleen Daly's plump body was revealed, thinly covered in a batiste nightdress worked in lace. It was infinitely more chaste than the garment she had chosen for her rendezvous with Desmond. Mara recalled with a start that this was the creature who had giggled and moaned pleasurably in Desmond's arms the night before. She ought to feel only contempt for Kathy, but she could not. It had been so long since she had talked with a girl her age. The warmth of the sherry and Kathy's open hospitality had done their work.

The blonde girl threw the mirror aside petulantly. "I am pretty, am I not? Everyone says so. But you, Mara, are superb! Your eyes alone are remarkable, and your skin!" Her eyes roved over Mara's gray dress. "Do you lace yourself?"

Mara shook her head. "Mamma says it's bad for the health."

"*Mon dieu.* Such a tiny waist! Why do you go about in those mouse-gray costumes? You ought to have lovely things—gowns that would show your figure."

Mara laughed outright. "I cannot afford them," she said simply.

"What a pity." Kathy suddenly thrust aside her coverlets and leaped from the bed in a burst of inspiration. She sprinted to the wardrobe and threw open the doors to reveal a long row of brightly colored frocks. Her plump hands riffled through her treasures, selecting and rejecting a plum velvet walking suit and then a tightly waisted frock of pink and darker rose. "This," she said at length, withdrawing a simple but costly traveling dress of golden cashmere. "This would suit you, Mara. It exactly matches your eyes. It is simple but lovely." She hugged herself in delight. "Try it on, Mara, do! If you like it I shall give it to you."

Mara looked at the dress longingly. She touched it, feeling the infinitely soft folds caressing her fingertips. She was torn between her yearning to accept Kathy's astoundingly generous offer and the fierce pride that warned her to keep her distance. Pride won out. She was not a serving girl who might accept charity from the young mistress—she was Padraic McQuaid's daughter. Her blood was as good as Kathleen Moriarty Daly's any day, perhaps better, and she could not stoop for the sake of a pretty golden frock.

"You are very kind," she said austerely, "but I cannot."

Kathy came to her side and looked at her searchingly. Her blue eyes had widened and she seemed deadly serious now.

"Mara," she began in a low voice, "of all the virtues God demands of Man, modesty is the least important. It is foolish to reject a kindness, and wicked. It is only pride, and Pride is one of the Seven Deadly Sins. You are very beautiful and deserve to have this frock. I have grown too stout for it lately—" Kathy gestured with mock despair at the full breast beneath her nightdress—"and it will only hang in the wardrobe unused."

Mara began to smile. She could not control her lips; in Kathy's presence laughter seemed quite natural and in another moment she and her new friend were jumping up and down and laughing like children.

"*Ma foi*, Mara—you can laugh, after all! I am so glad to see it—I was afraid you would be dignified and poker-faced forever and I couldn't *bear* it!"

Kathy threw her arms around the younger girl and kissed her cheek impulsively. "Let us be good friends," she said. "I've been so bored and unhappy —you can't imagine—and now I shall have someone to talk to. One can't talk to men—not really." A shadow passed over Kathy's face and Mara wondered if she were thinking of Desmond.

"I would like to be your friend," she said shyly.

"Good, then. That's settled. Now try the dress on, if you please. I want to see how it looks on a divine form like yours."

Five minutes later Mara stood self-consciously in the center of the cabin, arms to her side and head held high. She executed a little pirouette and curtseyed before the wardrobe. "How do I look?" she asked breathlessly.

"If you could see yourself!" Kathy's eyes blazed with admiration. The soft folds of cashmere clung to Mara's body like tongues of liquid topaz. The flowing skirt draped bell-like from her tiny waist, hugging discreetly at the hips and tautening over the round, high young breasts. Mara's slender neck arched gracefully from the round collar; her black hair tumbled over her shoulders in a heavy, shining mass of curls.

"Wait!" Kathy made her sit at her dressing table and went to work with brush and hair pins. Her deft fingers lifted the silken tresses and nimbly coiled and sculpted. When she had finished, she held the glass up. Mara gasped with pleasure. Kathy had dressed her hair so that it rose in two smooth wings at either side of her face and piled itself in a graceful cluster atop her small, sleek head. She looked at least two years older, and so much more sophisticated! Her color was heightened with the excitement of their venture and her immense eyes perfectly reflected the answering gold of the lovely gown. She turned this way and that while Kathy offered rapturous comments on the slender curve of her neck, and marveled that Mara's eyelashes should be so thick and black while her own were sandy and sparse.

"You must keep the dress," Kathy said firmly. "I could never wear it again. It's meant for you."

"I will wear it when we dock in New York," Mara replied, kissing Kathy's cheek. "You are very persuasive."

Half an hour had passed and she had to return to her mother. Reluctantly, she undid the buttons of the new dress and let it slide from her body, stepping from the folds like a young goddess rising from a lake of gold. Kathy took the dress from her and folded it carefully, letting her eyes dwell with good-natured envy on the perfection of Mara's form.

The girl's legs were amazingly long. Even in the much-mended cotton stockings she wore it was easy to discern their elegance. Beneath her chemise her hips, gently rounded, curved delicately upward to the slender stalk of her waist; the breasts could hardly be contained by the clean but shabby camisole and thrust ripely out and upward, spilling over the material like twin mounds of pearly, gleaming snow. Her arms were perfectly rounded, her shoulders delicate and smooth. She stood, unconscious of her beauty, touching the unfamiliar coils of hair looped at her neck, and as she was standing like that the door burst open and Desmond entered.

Kathy gave a little shriek of surprise, while Mara froze, immobile as a marble fawn. Desmond's eyes under the black brows grew wide and lustrous with astonishment. He stared at his cousin, drinking in the sight of her as if he could never stop. His lips moved but no words came. The three of them stood motionless for what seemed an age, and then Desmond strode savagely toward Mara. He picked up her old gray frock and threw it full in her face. "Get dressed," he said in a voice so thick with rage that Kathy quailed. His jaw was set and his blue eyes had narrowed to slits. "Cover yourself!" he roared. He turned from Mara and directed the full force of his wrath at Kathy.

"Well, Mrs. Daly," he said acidly, "and what have you been up to? Putting ideas in my simple little cousin's head? And to what purpose?" He was advancing on her, cat-like. "Does it occur to you that she is innocent? Innocent?" He repeated the word with such malice that Kathy's eyes welled with tears. The implication was clear enough.

"Desmond—" she pleaded, "Mr. O'Connell, please. I—I have made your cousin's acquaintance and I like her ever so much. We are friends."

"Keep your friendship for those who know how to use it," he said cruelly.

Kathy began to sniffle and Mara, who had dressed with a speed born of desperation, could bear no more. She lifted her chin and stared at Desmond defiantly.

"How dare you?" she cried. "Mrs. Daly has given me a dress because she is kind and generous. By what right do you burst into her cabin and address us like this? You are not my father, nor yet my brother, and you are *certainly* not her husband."

She had hoped the reference to John Daly might shame him, but Desmond grasped her arm so tightly she winced. "By God," he said coldly, "you give me nothing but trouble." He pushed her roughly before him, wrenching her arm so she cried out in pain, and dragged her out the door. She felt her face flame with humiliation and anger. To be treated like this in front of her new friend was more than she would tolerate. And what of Kathy, who had given herself to Desmond? What must she be feeling? Something heavy came crashing against the door behind them.

"Don't ever come back here, Desmond," Kathy screamed.

Desmond laughed shortly. "Well, Cousin," he mocked, pulling her along the passageway, "you show good sense, do you not? Tussling with sailors . . . choosing a slut for your bosom friend . . ."

She brought her free hand up and slapped his face with as much strength as she could muster. He dropped her arm and stared at her with loathing. For a moment she thought he might kill her.

"If she is a slut," Mara panted, "you are not without blame, are you, Cousin?"

He said nothing but continued to stare at her, eyes black and unreadable.

"A woman may be many things," she said passionately. "Kathy is open-hearted and good and full of fun. That is more than I can say of you."

He grinned. "Aye, Mara," he said, exaggerating his brogue, "Kathy is full of fun. She overflows with generosity." Slowly his hand came up and loosened the pins in her hair, undoing the elegant coiffure so that her long tresses tumbled down around her face. Even in her anger she longed for him to touch her. Would she never again be able to stand near her cousin without this suffocating, breathless pain?

"Desmond," she whispered, not knowing what she wanted to say.

"I wish to God I had never laid eyes on you,"

he said in measured tones. His voice was level, yet the words seemed to have been ripped from him. He kicked fiercely at Dr. Quinn's door.

"Terence!" he shouted. "I've found a little baggage on deck. Please to let her in."

Terence Quinn had never been able to remain impassive in the face of human suffering; it was his great downfall as a doctor and his crowning virtue as a man. Pain enraged him and the simple fact of death still seemed to him a cruel mystery. His professors at the Royal College of Surgeons had commended his intelligence and skill while despairing of his ability to turn them to his profit. They had been right. He readily admitted that he was a failure as a physician and drank more than was good for him. But he drank to dull the pain his failure brought him.

He had never married, understanding that to come so close to another human being would be fatal, knowing as he did how fragile was the thread connecting his fellow creatures to life and how easily it could be snapped. He liked to think of his profession as a mere cover for his abiding passion—the study of human nature. People fascinated him endlessly, and he kept quantities of large, leatherbound books which he filled with descriptions of those he met, speculating on their characters and relationships and pondering their eventual destinies. He took up the volume he had brought on the voyage and turned back several pages until he came to an entry written soon after the *Alberta* had left Liverpool Harbor.

April 12, 1893

There is a most extraordinary group from Mayo traveling in second class. They are the fragments of a
family, for the father has preceded them to New York
on some vague mission and they are going to join
him. The mother is not much more than forty, but
she is thin and wasted. I should guess she suffers
from consumption and the effects of too many difficult confinements. She is simply but well-educated
and possesses the fine sensibilities of those of her
class—the gentlefolk of Western Ireland who have,
despite fine bloodlines and good upbringing, fallen so
lately on hard times. There is a young man in his
twenties who may or may not be her son who is the
perfect image of Irish manhood—he is a handsome
hothead, a ladies' man and gambler, with great
panache and charm who will yet prove to be a wor-
thy man when he outgrows his youthful arrogance.
It is the daughter who interests me most. She is a
raven-haired child of such breathtaking beauty that
even these old eyes revive at sight of her. She can be
no more than eighteen, but there is a disturbing blend
of virginal purity and womanly passion in her demeanor. She is ever polite and well-bred, utterly devoted to her mother, but she suffers from a repres-
sion of the emotions which will explode one day and
ignite everything around her . . .

April 14

I have played whist with young Mr. O'Connell and
some of the crew today. He is a mere cousin to the
exquisite girl, related to her mother quite obscurely
through marriage, and shies from conversation relat-
ing to them beyond casual pleasantries. He has said
only that he travels with them as a sort of escort until
they can be reunited with the father in America.

April 15

Mr. O'Connell has elaborated on the McQuaid's reasons for emigrating. It seems the father received word of a large legacy and went to America to investigate its veracity. Now he has sent for his wife and daughter to join him . . . It is all most secretive and I fear the mother may not live to see her husband again. And what will happen to the daughter? O'Connell speaks of her with the raffish contempt young men reserve for troublesome girl cousins, but his eyes tell a different story . . . He has lately begun a flirtation with the bride in the cabin next to mine. She is a likeable girl, buxom and cheeky, but spoilt by doting, well-to-do parents. She cannot keep her eyes off the dashing Desmond but her nervous little husband is oblivious. Her parents were eager for the match to keep the girl out of trouble, but they have landed her in deeper trouble by thrusting her so incongruously on a man who is both weak and morbidly inclined.


April 19

John Daly has lost £20 at cards to Desmond O'Connell. What a rascal O'Connell is! He has the bride as well as the money, and as for Daly—he is the kind of fellow who fairly begs to be abused. I cannot help but like Desmond, for all his villainy. Life is an unfair business . . .


April 21

Ten days at sea. How fortunate we are to travel by steam ship! One in six of the wretched steerage passengers died on the old coffin ships of the 30's and 40's. Even the *Alberta,* a shameful old tub, is very heaven compared to the sailing ships that have transported so many of my unfortunate countrymen to the New World or to a watery Atlantic grave. We have had only four deaths on this voyage, but I fear Mrs. McQuaid may not last long. She is in the final stages of her disease if I am not mistaken. How life mocks us . . .

Dr. Quinn pushed the bottle of whiskey away from him. He had lately felt the tell-tale pangs along his upper arms; they were still remote, unserious, but they presaged the end. He was going to visit a brother in Baltimore, but he had no plans to die in America. He was from Tramore, and when the end came in a year or six months he would be buried there, and not in exile.

For the rest of her life, Mara remembered the final days of her voyage to America but dimly. Certain scenes flashed upon her with awful clarity, but the time after her mother's death appeared to her washed in a dull, numb grey. She remembered the doctor's kindness. He had insisted on giving up his cabin to her. On the night Desmond had returned her so rudely, Dr. Quinn administered to her mother and then retired to the squalor of second class. All that night her mother slept restlessly, waking and beckoning Mara close so she could whisper to her. It seemed important that Mara hear her out. Mary's eyes burned with zeal as she spoke.

"We are alike, Mara," she had murmured urgently. "We fight for what we want, when we want things badly we fight . . . I wanted Padraic that way—no, don't turn your head away, we must speak of such things—and I wanted children. I tried and tried, though it nearly killed me, and I *succeeded*." Her eyes shone. "I had *you*, darlin'—you are my reward!"

"Hush, Mamma, you mustn't tire yourself so—"

"Don't deny your nature, Mara . . . Oh, there is so much I can read in your face . . . You were meant to fight tooth and nail for what you want . . . You are my brave, beautiful girl . . ."

Mary's frail body was burning to the touch, yet she was racked with spasmodic chills. Mara climbed into the bunk so she could hold her mother close and listen to her impassioned whispering. All night long she embraced her mother, falling into a fitfull sleep near dawn. When she awakened it was full morning. Sunlight glanced from the sea and filtered through the port hole, shimmering on the cabin's walls in myriad, dancing watermarks.

Mary McQuaid lay peacefully within the circle of her daughter's arms; for many minutes Mara did not understand that she was dead.

Of the burial she remembered standing on the windy deck, her hair whipping about her face, while the captain—a grizzled man with a ginger beard—pronounced the words for burial at sea. The wind took the words from his mouth and by some mysterious trick sent them back in fragments: *Our sister departed . . . commend her body to the deep . . .*

Dr. Quinn stood close to her and held her arm. Kathleen Daly sobbed. Desmond stood with his head bent and his arms to his sides, a little apart from the rest of them. When it was over he came to her and took her hand in his.

"I will take care of you, Mara," he said simply. "Whatever happens I will take care of you."

She turned from him. All around the ocean lay, calm and indifferent, stretching to the furthest horizons the mind could imagine and then beyond. She felt she would never see land again. Her mother lay at the bottom of the sea; life would never be the same. She wanted, with childlike desperation, to see her father.

## Chapter Three

The air which feebly stirred the curtains at Mara's window was warm and balmy. New York was a curious place. It was only May, and the springtime she had so eagerly anticipated felt more like high summer. She could hear the voices of children playing in the tiny garden below her window and she looked out. Two small girls were gamboling about the patch of green as happily as if they had been set free in a meadow. She wondered if they were Mrs. Monahan's grandchildren.

Mara's room was on the third floor of Mrs. Monahan's boarding house, a modest but comfortable establishment on East 22nd Street. Desmond had taken the room for her. He, too, lodged here, but she could not imagine where he was. They had been here for two days now and she had seen him only once since their arrival. She stirred impatiently, hoping Desmond would soon return with word of her father.

She was beginning to feel a prisoner. The room

was small and scrupulously tidy. There was a framed
print of Galway Bay above her bed—presumably
Mrs. Monahan decorated her rooms with an eye to
assuaging the homesickness of her clientele. There
was also a writing desk beneath the window, two
straight-backed chairs, a wardrobe, a porcelain
water jug, and the narrow white bed in which Mara
had spent her first night in New York.

Despite her numbed state, she had felt stirrings
of excitement at her first glimpse of the city. She
had never seen so many people crowded together in
the streets in all of her life. Dublin, the largest town
of her acquaintance, was a country village compared
to this place of frantic activity. While the steerage
passengers prepared to sit out another long nightmare at Ellis Island, the newly built port of entry,
she and Desmond and the Dalys, together with Dr.
Quinn, had been discharged with a bewildering
swiftness. John and Kathleen Daly were going to the
Hotel Astor, and the doctor was to stay with an old
schoolmate in Gramercy Square before journeying
to Baltimore. They had arranged to meet again, but
Mara felt a pang of bereavement at the temporary
parting. They were all she had known of kindness
and companionship on the fateful voyage, and she
was being taken from them so suddenly. Until Desmond could locate her father, he would be her sole
companion. She was sure he thought her a burden
and shouldered the responsibility of settling her in
this frenzied city reluctantly.

As they had driven through the teeming streets in
a carriage, she could barely contain her curiosity at
the sights and sounds which assaulted her. She could

feel the city's immensity, as if it had entered her very pores. They had passed through slums where children, barefoot and ragged, ran and played almost beneath their carriage wheels. Old women scurried in and out of saloon doors clutching pails of beer and men sprawled, drunk at midday, in the doorways. Most of the names on the saloon signs were Irish.

"Desmond," she had whispered anxiously, "these people are from home."

"Have you not heard what the native Americans say of us?" He smiled bitterly. " 'It is as natural for an Irishman to drink as it is for a pig to grunt.' " His laugh was without mirth. "They have no love for us. An Irishman must be doubly sober, trebly honest, before he can be thought an equal."

Mara had been shocked at his words. Like everyone in her village she had been taught to distrust the English, even to hate them. But this was America— a democracy where snobbism and bigotry must be unknown. Surely Desmond was wrong!

The mean streets had unfolded before her wondering eyes in a maze of filth and wretchedness. Dogs ran freely in the road, their barks mingling with the din of shouting peddlars and the shrieks of children. The tenements huddled in upon each other like rabbit warrens. She had seen the pinched faces of children at the windows and wondered how they grew and throve in such dark, cramped quarters. The odor of the streets was a reeking mixture of cooking and beer and the smell of horses and unwashed bodies—it was the ineradicable odor of poverty. She wanted to weep for those who had ridden in steerage aboard the *Alberta*. They would find themselves soon enough in another airless hole, scarcely better than the one they had left.

Her attention had been caught by a young girl pushing a cart beside them. She had not been much older than ten, yet her peaked face was etched with deep lines, her eyes hollow and sharp with an unbecoming wisdom. She was barefoot. Even as Mara watched, the child's eyes rose and locked on Desmond.

"Hoy there!" she had shrilled, grinning up at him. "Give us a coin, handsome." Her voice was purest Armagh. Desmond reached down and placed a silver coin in her grimy paw. "Give us a kiss, boyo," the urchin cried, thrusting her meagre little chest out in a parody of seductiveness, but the carriage had passed on.

"She is so young," Mara had said sadly. "Are there many like her, do you think?"

"Aye, and she'll have more like herself afore long." Desmond had lapsed into a broad country accent, as if to ally himself with the wretched Irish thronging the streets through which they rolled. Presently their carriage had veered and the people did not look so achingly familiar, although their condition was equally squalid. They passed into a Polish neighborhood, and then a community of Italians.

"Why do they not mix?" Mara asked.

"They are not asked," Desmond said drily.

The streets began to broaden near 14th, and Mara had leaned forward, raptly studying the fashionable ladies' costumes. They had passed from squalor to luxury in the space of five minutes. The women who strolled on Fifth Avenue carried little sunshades above their elaborately coiffed heads. Their daytime costumes were of the palest hues—jonquil and lilac and ice blue—and they were laced so tightly Mara feared the stouter of them might faint. Their little boots peeped coyly from beneath the swinging skirts. Mara looked askance at her own plain cotton; she felt very shabby by comparison.

"Shall we buy you some pretty things?" Desmond had asked idly. He was scrutinizing a dark-haired beauty who stood chatting with a friend.

"Father will see to it," Mara replied. "It is not of any importance."

Desmond had grinned his hateful grin and Mara was astounded to see that the raven-haired girl bowed to him, smiling flirtatiously. Her gaze followed him in the carriage with the same naked interest she once saw in the eyes of Kathy Daly.

When they had reached the quiet, respectable street of Mrs. Monahan's lodgings Desmond tipped the driver generously. "How is it you are so rich, Cousin?" Mara asked sweetly. "Have you won at cards?"

"I may have done just that," said Desmond, surveying the neat row of brownstone dwellings where they had debarked. "Now, if Dr. Quinn's memory serves, we shall find a clean bed and good, plain food here." His voice clearly conveyed that nothing could be more boring, but he had taken Mara's arm and led her firmly to the door.

Mrs. Monahan's welcome was warm, almost effusive, and there had been a brief embarrassment

when she asked if they would be requiring a double
room. Desmond explained they were cousins only,
and Mrs. Monahan looked roguish. " 'Tis a pity,"
she said. "Ye'd make a lovely couple. Ah, well.
Supper's at seven, breakfast any time a'tall before
nine. Would the young lady like a hot bath? Some
tea?" Her kindness had made up for the brief stab of
emotion Mara felt at the mention of a double
room . . .


The children in the garden were laughing again,
their voices rising irrepressibly to her ears. Mara
tapped her foot. Why had her father not come? She
wanted to be abroad in the city, drinking in the
strange sights, feeling the pulse and rhythmic life
of New York as she had done with Desmond. At
least she could go to the garden; anything would be
better than sitting in her room alone. She brushed
her heavy hair until it crackled and bound a green
ribbon in it to keep stray tendrils from curling onto
her forehead in the heat. It matched the frock she
wore. Briefly, she wished for a costume to rival
those she had seen on Fifth Avenue.

She ran down the stairs and through the deserted
dining room. Brigid, Mrs. Monahan's kitchen maid,
was snapping beans in the pantry. She blew her
cheeks out, complaining of the heat, and said mali-
ciously: "And where's your cousin, Miss? He's not
slept in his bed all night." Mara turned away from
her. What Desmond did was none of her concern;
still less was it Brigid's business. She continued

straight through to the kitchen and out the open door to the garden.

The little girls were running about in a game of tag. Mara wanted to run, too, but she was afraid she might be seen. She turned her face gratefully to the sun and allowed herself a brief turn on tip-toe. It felt so delicious she spun around again, and then she sank to the grass and sat, skirts spread around her in a most unladylike fashion.

There was a small sound, a discreet cough, and Mara whirled around in alarm. Not five feet away from her, sitting on the low wall surrounding Mrs. Monahan's garden, was a young man. He had been sketching, but he set aside his pad and charcoal stick and rose, making her a bow.

"I am so sorry if I've alarmed you," he murmured. "May I fetch you a chair from inside?"

Mara got to her feet, blushing in confusion and alarm. "It is I who should apologize," she stammered. "I thought I was alone with the children." Something made her add impulsively: "I would so like to sit on the grass—please don't trouble yourself."

The young man smiled. "I am called Roger Winthrop," he said. "All my life people have prevented me from sitting on the grass. It must be delightful."

What a strange young man, so casually straight-forward! He was only a few years older than herself, perhaps twenty-one, and he was dressed so beautifully he seemed misplaced in Mrs. Monahan's humble garden. His fawn trousers and waistcoat were custom tailored, his shirt of raw silk, and the boots on his elegant feet shone blindingly in the sun. He was somehow all of a color—his hair and the small, neat moustache were a warm, rich brown, and so were the intense eyes regarding her so closely. Even his fair skin had undertones of brown, as if he spent much time in the sun. There was something so pleasing in his appearance that Mara felt immediately at home with him.

"My name is Mara McQuaid," she said, sinking back down on her heels. "I am lodging temporarily with Mrs. Monahan."

"You are Irish."

Mara remembered what Desmond had said. Surely this man was a native American, and of English stock. "Yes," she said distantly, "I am proud to be Irish."

"I often think the Irish are the most fortunate people on earth."

She was about to ask him what would make him hold such astonishing opinions when one of the little girls hurled herself across the lawn and landed in a pile at his feet. He reached out and tousled her unruly curls. "Clara!" he cried in mock consternation. "You have not said hello to Miss McQuaid." The other child had come to him and he put an arm around each. "These are Mrs. Monahan's granddaughters, Clara and Lizzie. They are five and seven. Aren't they fine little ruffians?"

Lizzie, the younger, edged close to Mara. "Ye're pretty," she said in a solemn voice. "Ye're hair is like a picture."

Her sister yanked her away. "You shouldn't

ought to talk like that, so cheeky," Clara said in officious tones. "It ain't ladylike."

Roger Winthrop laughed. "It's quite alright, Clara," he said. "What Lizzie said was true enough." His dark eyes admired Mara; he seemed unable to take them from her face and now she could see there were green flecks in the brown which gave his gaze a melting, intimate quality. "Run away, girls," he said in a soft voice. "It's time for your tea."

"I know you're not a lodger here," said Mara, trying to make casual conversation. "Do you know the Monahans well?"

For the first time he looked awkward. "Mrs. Monahan was in service with my parents," he replied. "She was my nurse, and her daughter was my mother's kitchen maid."

Ah, that was the way things were! He was condescending to visit former servants and chatting up the little Irish girl in the garden. She thought scornfully of his remark about the Irish being fortunate.

"I am very fond of Mrs. Monahan. I visit her regularly. The children's mother died of typhus. Mrs. Monahan raises them now."

His voice seemed genuinely sorrowful when he spoke of the death. Perhaps he was not a snob after all.

"Are you an artist?" she asked.

He indicated the half-finished sketch of Clara and Lizzie at play with an apologetic air. "This is only a hobby of mine. I am reading law. I come from Boston, but I prefer it here in New York. And you, Miss McQuaid? Do you like the city?"

"I have seen so little of it," she said ruefully. And then she was telling him of the long voyage and of her impressions in the carriage when they first arrived. The words came tumbling out and she feared she was talking too much, but Mr. Winthrop listened eagerly, nodding his agreement when she spoke of the terrible poverty she had seen, and when she concluded, explaining that her father was to come to her soon, he sat forward abruptly.

"You don't mean to say you are *alone?*"

"My cousin is with me, but he's away at present."

"And your mother?"

Mara had not spoken of her mother's death. She twisted her fingers in the grass and said flatly: "She died at sea."

Mr. Winthrop colored deeply, with sympathy and some emotion she could not read, and then he murmured in a hoarse voice, "I am so very sorry, Miss McQuaid. You have had an unhappy time of it. I wish with all my heart I could change things for you."

"Things will be better when Father comes," she said uncomfortably. The man seemed so intense! He made her self-conscious, yet she liked him and wanted to continue their sudden friendship. If only she were more vivacious, like Kathy, she would know what to say.

"I must go now," Mr. Winthrop said reluctantly. "I have an appointment with my sister, Constance. She will have my head if I am so much as five minutes late." He grinned, looking very young. "I'll come again tomorrow," he continued. "I would like so much to see you again. Perhaps your cousin would allow you to dine with me?"

Mara thought of Desmond's probable reaction and bit her lip.

"Look here, I know it seems impertinent on such short acquaintance, but would you permit me to make a sketch of you? I would make you a gift of it, such as it is."

He was so humble about his sketching that she felt a great surge of affection for him. "I would be delighted," she said firmly, taking his outstretched hand. Let Desmond rave and shout—she didn't care. She wanted this attractive and gentle man for her friend, and if Desmond didn't like it, so much the worse for him!

Roger Winthrop held her hand a fraction longer than courtesy required. His eyes, so deep-set and searching, seemed to cling to her face with desperate urgency. "Until tomorrow," he said softly and then he was bounding through the door, calling an affectionate goodbye to the woman who had been his nurse in Boston.

She settled back on the grass, closing her eyes and feeling her hair hanging warm and heavy down her back. For the first time in days, she felt happy.

There were five at dinner that evening. Desmond had not returned. The Kennedy sisters, two maiden ladies who occupied the large room on the first floor, were eating their beef and boiled potatoes with rapt determination to Mara's left. Across from her sat pale, fidgety Mr. Flynn, who worked as a clerk in the financial district, Mrs. Monahan herself, and Desmond's empty chair. Brigid bustled in and out, her face red and perspiring as she slammed the plates down and asked—not very graciously— whether they would prefer tea or coffee at the meal's conclusion. In the kitchen Clara and Lizzie could be heard tormenting Brigid whenever the swinging doors opened.

"Very nice, Mrs. M.," Mr. Flynn said as he did every evening, "very nice, indeed." The elder Miss Kennedy grunted agreement and plunged her spoon greedily into the trifle.

Mrs. Monahan seemed preoccupied this evening. Usually she talked volubly throughout the meal, but she was silent and tense, occasionally smiling in Mara's direction as if they shared a secret. When the others left the table she motioned for Mara to remain with her.

"Well, my dear, ye've met my little Roger," she said as soon as they were alone. "I always call him that, you know, because I cared for him as a babbie —a sweeter child ye'd never see, so quiet and affectionate he was . . ." She beamed happily.

"He seems a very pleasant person," Mara said, carefully.

"Pleasant!" Mrs. Monahan's eyebrows peaked alarmingly. "Why, Mr. Roger is the finest gentleman in all of Boston or New York. The Winthrop family are one of the oldest in Boston. Och, but they live like kings!" She leaned forward conspiratorially. "There's the house on Beacon Hill, and the summer mansion by the sea, and there's Miss Constance married to a millionaire, living in New York." Mrs. Monahan paused for breath. Her color had heightened perceptibly.

"They're ever so grand," she continued. "When I was in service with Mr. Roger's family there was a staff of twenty! Think of it, dear. Them days is gone forever now—families like the Winthrops must do with ten or less."

Mara wondered why her landlady was telling her about the Winthrops. It was possible she thought it her duty to warn Mara of their evident social importance. For all she knew, her lodger was a fortune hunter, an upstart who hadn't the sense to know that girls from County Mayo did not sit upon the grass and converse with a mighty Winthrop.

"I went into the garden without knowing he was there," she explained. "I didn't mean to intrude."

But Mrs. Monahan was lost in reminiscences. "They descend from the first Winthrops of the Bay Colony, but for a' that they refuse to put on airs. Madam used to say to me, 'Margaret, when all is said and done we're both women, and there's an end to it.' They hired me in the days when Irish servants were thought to be lower than curs. Ye'd scan the papers looking for employment, and what would be written in bold, black letters? 'Honest, hard-working female servant required—Scotch, Swiss, or African—NO IRISH NEED APPLY!' " She snorted in disgust. "Madam didn't hold with that. She was as good to me as me own mother, and I loved little Roger and Miss Connie as if they were me own."

Mara realized she had been mistaken. Mrs. Mon-

ahan did not for a moment suspect that Mara might
have raised her sights to Roger Winthrop; it was as
unlikely to her as that Clara or Lizzie might become
duchesses. She simply wanted to share with her the
days when she had been part of a great household.
It saddened Mara that the affable landlady saw her
life in such secondary terms.

"Of course," Mrs. Monahan said proudly, "Mr.
Roger will marry an heiress. The woman who can
match him for sweetness hasn't been born. There's
no one good enough for him."

Brigid slouched into the room. "You've a visitor,
Miss," she said to Mara with ill-concealed amusement. "He's waiting in the parlor and he can't be
over twelve."

"Are you sure he wishes to see me?" Mara asked,
stung by the servant girl's insolence.

"My, how curious," said Mrs. Monahan. "Go
and see, dear."

Brigid had not exaggerated. The boy who greeted
her was a child, an urchin of the sort she had seen
in the slum streets from the carriage. He was carrying an armload of boxes over which his white,
pinched face peered with an air of great importance.

"Please, Miss," he announced unceremoniously,
"these are from Mr. O'Connell." He thrust the
mountain of parcels in her direction.

"Where is he?"

"He says," replied the boy, who had obviously
memorized the message and was struggling to repeat
it without flaw, "he's detained at cards and will see
you tomorrow."

Mara flushed. Detained at cards! She was wondering how she could pay the boy, but as soon as he had completed his mission he turned and scuttled toward the door. Mara gathered her parcels and fled to her room before Mrs. Monahan could come looking for her.

She closed the door and stood motionless for an instant, caught up in fear for Desmond's welfare. He was a stranger in the city and prey to unknown perils. Perhaps he was even now sitting in a low saloon on the waterfront where ruffians and thieves waited to relieve him of his money. She knew he was a gambler, and as for fighting, she knew he could defend himself with skill and ferocity. But of what use would all his fine daring be against a gang of men?

Even more disturbing was the fact that he had not found her father. Somewhere in the city Padraic waited anxiously—her dear father who didn't even know that Mary was dead and buried. How dare Desmond fritter away the precious time at cards when so much hung in the balance? And yet, in the midst of all her disapproval and impatience, something told her Desmond knew what he was about. He was self-sufficient and wily—alarmingly so—and she would simply have to trust him and wait.

She opened the first of the boxes and lifted out a starched cotton shirtwaist and skirt of purest white. There was an indigo velvet ribbon to tie around her waist and the wide sleeves were banded in matching blue. She held the costume to her, gasping with delight at the crisp feel of it, and then she fell on the other packages. Soon her bed was piled high with mountains of the most beguiling garments she had ever seen or hoped to own. There were two day dresses of organdy with leg o'mutton sleeves and belled skirts; one was of the palest, most delicate shade of primrose imaginable and the other a bold stripe that made her think of Christmas sweets. There was a taffeta evening dress high-necked and simply draped, in the exact golden hue as the cashmere Kathy had wanted to give her. Desmond had remembered. She was caught between wanting to laugh in sheer joy at his extravagant gesture and a paradoxical desire to weep because he was not here to share her happiness.

Smaller parcels yielded up white kid gloves so creamy and thin she held them to her cheek in wonder, and—more daringly—a profusion of stockings for every occasion. There were light stockings and dark, and one pair worked in vertical bands of green. A small square box with a Fifth Avenue seal contained a cunning bonnet which sat rakishly atop her head, and when she looked into the glass she saw that the black aigrette was sewn so it could lay the very tip of its trailing feathers in a light caress against her cheek. The last box was the largest, and when she thrust aside the tissue she became almost giddy.

Desmond had chosen a formal gown for her in a shade of green so bright and shocking she knew few women could possibly wear it to advantage, but the mirror told her it might have been designed for her alone. It was cut daringly low at the bosom so that the whiteness of her skin would lie against the green like snow on emeralds, and her hair fairly gleamed

in contrast. Her golden, catlike eyes were accentuated so strikingly by the gown's color she was almost
afraid of the brilliance of her image.

She marveled at the fact that everything fit so
perfectly. How could he have known? He had forgotten only shoes, and she found this so like him she
was once more caught up in a feeling of profound
tenderness. As she hung her new finery in the wardrobe thrilling to the luxurious textures beneath her
fingertips, she felt a wild emotion build in her,
gathering strength until she feared she might burst
with it. She stood on the threshold of her life, in a
new city full of both dangers and the taunting, elu-
sive promise of boundless joy, and what lay before
her she could not know.

She wanted to dance in the moonlight or walk the
streets like a strumpet or shout for happiness. As she
knelt at her window, the warm, scented night air
flowing around her sweetly, she knew a yearning so
fierce it might have been pain. She had forgotten
about Roger Winthrop. Her eyes stared, unseeing, at
the spot on Mrs. Monahan's garden wall where he
had perched that afternoon.

She would not admit to herself what it was she
longed for so terribly, but her heart and body told
her, with an awesome surety, that it was Desmond.

Long before New York had wakened to its clamorous daytime life, Desmond was making his way
wearily back to East 22nd Street. He had walked
ten blocks, from Canal, to clear his head of the

smoke and whiskey and tension of the game, but exhaustion was at last overcoming him. It was dawn, and he hadn't slept for thirty-six hours.

His fingers closed over the roll of money in his pocket and he smiled to himself triumphantly. There was still enough to sustain them for a time, and the gambling men he had met might yet prove helpful to him. The *Alberta*'s first mate had told him about the game. "They're high stakes, lad, but Irishmen all, and fair and aboveboard. All you need is your stake." All in all, he was pleased.

His inner eye filled with images of Mara, laughing in sheer astonishment at the gifts he had made her. He tried to banish thoughts of her, but they persisted. He saw her holding the green gown to her breast, sucking in her breath with pleasure and amazement. Her eyes would be immense with delight, the sooty lashes casting shadows on her fair skin; perhaps she would smooth a silken stocking over one long, slender leg, turning her ankle this way and that to admire the effect—*no, no,* it was only a torment to him to think this way! He shook his head violently and bade her be gone.

In her place he conjured up the pinched-nose saleslady in the Fifth Avenue emporium who had regarded him in his sleepless and unshaven state as she might a toad come down the drainpipe. He had given her a time, making her turn the place upside down as he leisurely selected and rejected garments, asking if there was nothing finer, more delicately sewn, that she could show him. In the end she was livid with rage, but she had taken his money, all right! Money was the key to it all, devil take it, and he had returned straight to the gaming table, propping open his burning eyes and resolving to win back what he had spent on Mara before he quit.

Now he turned onto Broadway, finding himself in front of a great, airy marble temple which confirmed his views. The architecture and gleaming facade proclaimed it fit for a family of royalty, but it was in fact a temple erected for the hoarding of money. It was far too early for the Greenwich Savings Bank to open its massive doors for business, but Desmond saluted it wryly. If he ever succeeded in making a fortune in the New World, he resolved he would store it in this grand bank that now witnessed him stumbling, with his two-days' growth of whiskers, up the avenue.

A middle-aged prostitute returning from her night's work saw the wild look in his eyes and mistook it for interest in her. "Hey, Paddy," she called, "you're the best-lookin' man I've seen all night. I wouldn't charge you nothing, dear!"

He winced at the "Paddy" but realized she meant no harm. "Thanks, sweetheart," he replied, "but I'd be no use to you at all." It was sleep he wanted now. There were no carriages in sight at this early hour, so he planted one foot in front of the other and continued doggedly toward Mrs. Monahan's and bed . . .


Kathleen Daly lay in her sumptuous bed at the Astor Hotel beside her husband, staring at the ornately paneled ceiling in despair. The morning light had begun to creep into their bedroom, illuminating the gilt frames of the cluster of oil paintings on the opposite wall. There was a scene she knew by heart; even though the light was too dim to see it at present she visualized the girl and her lover, hand in hand, tripping through a forest and swinging a wicker picnic basket between them. From the moment she and John had entered the room she had known, with dull misery, that the painting would spoil whatever happiness she and her husband might find in their marriage bed. Something in the tilt of the young lover's head, caught forever by an obscure eighteenth-century artist, reminded her of Desmond.

She could not bear to think of him, yet she could think of little else. She had lost him forever, simply by befriending his cousin. He had never again allowed his eyes to make love to her when others were present, never again put his strong, dark hands on her body or his lips to hers. She could remember so well the feel of his long, lean back under her palms as they made love in his cabin at sea. She could picture the way his black lashes fluttered over the startling blue of his eyes when the passion took him over; the way he tumbled her to the bed, grinning in the glory of his ardor and raising above her, his body as taut as a well-wound clock and as smooth and hard to the touch as marble warmed by the sun . . . She bit her lip hard and turned her face wretchedly to the side.

Now the light picked out John's cravat, resting where he had tossed it on the Sheraton bureau last night. They had eaten a midnight supper of champagne and oysters and he had become amorous with her, but as always his lovemaking was timid and faltering and she closed her eyes and longed for

Desmond. She had known three men before him—two in France, which was why her parents were so eager to marry her off to John Daly—but she had never known what it was to be obsessed with a man until her eyes lit on Desmond, standing on the dock at Liverpool Harbor. The first time he had held her in his arms she had wanted to weep with the knowledge it was now too late to truly possess him; yet he did not love her and never could—of that she was sure. Desmond made love to her so beautifully because he had been created for the purpose of making love to women. A part of him was always withheld, no matter how affectionate he was in the glowing aftermath of ecstasy. She thought she had seen his soul surface only once. The day he had burst into her cabin and discovered Mara, half-naked in her chemise and stockings, Kathy had perceived what the full force of Desmond's passion might be if he loved with his heart as well as his body.

She wanted to see him again. Even though nothing could pass between them, she needed desperately to have him near her. She shook the sleeping form next to her until her husband opened bleary eyes and regarded her curiously.

"What is it?" he yawned.

"We must take little Mara McQuaid to Delmonico's for dinner soon," Kathy breathed urgently. "We could ask Dr. Quinn, too, for a sort of reunion party . . . and Mr. O'Connell, of course." She made Desmond seem an afterthought.

"It's a damned strange time to tell me this," John said balefully. "I'm not made of money, Kathy." He had begun to complain of her extravagance already.

"Nonsense. What you don't have, I do."

"Oh, very well, dear. You arrange it, then." He burrowed back into the pillow and within seconds he was asleep again. Kathy wanted to scream with irritation, but soon her mind began to hum with plans and schemes and she was happier. At least, she would see him soon . . .


Roger Winthrop had asked to be wakened early, but when he heard Annie bringing his morning coffee he had already been half-awake for hours. He was staying in the suite of rooms which his sister Constance kept for him in her Fifth Avenue house; she had given a small dinner party the night before, and although it was late when the last guest departed, and he had sat up reading a text on contract law until well past two o'clock, sleep had not come easily.

The face of the girl in the garden had hovered over his thoughts like a fever-dream. He could not forget her. Her beauty had been so otherworldly in its purity and innocence, and yet what a promise there was in those blazing eyes! It had been all he could do to restrain himself from touching her raven hair, from pressing her soft white hand to his lips when they parted. Even at this early hour he was in a turmoil of eagerness to see her again. He had been smitten before, but never like this, never with such intensity.

He leaped from the bed and threw on a dressing gown. Annie was opening the curtains in his sitting-room and straightening the papers on his desk. She had brought him a silver tray with a pot of steaming coffee and freshly buttered toast.

"Good morning, Mr. Roger," she said cheerfully. "It looks like another hot day, don't it? Shall I draw your bath?"

"Annie, is my sister awake yet?"

She quirked an eyebrow at him. "You know Miss Connie—Mrs. Burkhardt, I should say—is never called before nine," she said reproachfully.

Roger carried his coffee back through to the bedroom and sat on the edge of his bed frowning. Just as well, really, that Constance wasn't available. What would he say to her? That he had fallen in love at first sight? That the object of his heart's desire was a poor, Irish girl—orphaned it would seem— whom he had met in old Nanny Monahan's garden? Connie would smile in her brittle, superior way and dismiss the matter as if he had suddenly expressed an interest in doing settlement work. She would never be the one to help him win Miss McQuaid's trust and affection.

He knew his sister had set her heart on his making a match with her friend, Elizabeth Schuyler. Indeed, Connie had hinted last night at dinner, in front of Elizabeth, that nothing could please her more. It was unusual for her to play her hand so openly—she was past-mistress of the sly allusion, the subtle thrust—and he had been astounded. He loved his sister with a mixture of brotherly affection and no little awe for her manifold perfections. Connie was thirty, eight years older than he, and for as long as he could remember she had dominated him. She was married to Henry Burkhardt, the investment banker, and the merging of their two great fortunes had pleased both families no end. Life was a pleasant business if you were a Winthrop or a Burkhardt, and Connie had never been able to see why a sensible person should want anything more than what she herself possessed.

He tried to remember Elizabeth Schuyler's face. She had been rather lovely last night, her dark gold hair dressed so that tiny tendrils escaped and curled softly on her forehead, relieving somewhat the stark planes of her aristocratic face. Little garnets had winked at her earlobes, and a collar of garnets and diamonds had flashed a reply from above her decorously displayed bosom. Everything Elizabeth did was graceful and understated. Her voice was low and musical. She could discourse intelligently on everything from law to music and the state of politics in Europe. She read French and German exquisitely, wrote copious and amusing letters to her friends, and sang in a modestly pretty soprano when asked. She would certainly make someone a very fine wife, but he could never be the man.

Any image he conjured of Elizabeth gave way to that of a smiling girl, sitting on the grass in a shabby cotton frock and lighting up an entire garden with her radiance and beauty. He felt with a certainty defying all reason that he wanted to marry her, but he knew with equal certainty that all of New York and Boston—all of the world as he knew it—would frown on his choice.

It wasn't going to be easy.

## Chapter Four

It was midday and Desmond, freshly shaven and rested, was pestering Brigid for breakfast.

"But I've the lunch to do now, Mr. O'Connell," she protested sullenly, rattling pots and pans vehemently to show how put-upon she was.

"Ah, Brigid," Desmond murmured coaxingly, "a fine figure of a woman like yourself shouldn't work so hard. Just give me a cup of tea and a crust and I'll be eternally grateful."

Brigid snorted. "And an egg perhaps? Next you'll be wanting kippers and marmalade. Those who stay out all night must expect to go without." All the same she slapped streaky bacon into a skillet and set about making coffee.

"Where is Miss McQuaid?" Desmond asked presently.

"I can't be expected to know everything," Brigid moaned, "now can I?" She turned to look at the extraordinary lodger and clucked her tongue. He was dressed in tight-fitting dark trousers and high

boots; the sleeves of his shirt were loose and flowing.
He looked more like a highwayman or brigand than
a civilized gentleman, but she had to admit it suited
him. The dark curls at his neck and the ravenous
look in the blue eyes as she set his plate before him
softened her. Brigid sighed and fetched a small pot
of honey for his toast. "There," she said brusquely,
"but from now on, eat when everyone else does."

Desmond blew her a kiss and devoted himself to
the pleasurable task of consuming his steaming
breakfast while Brigid went off to straighten the parlor.

When he had finished his second cup of strong,
black coffee, he lit a cigar and strolled out to the
stoop, watching the life of the street with lazy interest. Two little girls erupted into view from the direction of Lexington Avenue; after them, half-running
and clutching a marketing bag bulging with fresh
vegetables, came Mara. She had not seen him yet,
and he watched her approach with an expression
quite different from the one he assumed when others
were present. She spoke to one of the little girls and
took the other's hand—she was scolding them for
running ahead, but her face was lit with a radiant
smile and her voice was happy. She was wearing one
of her old cotton frocks and Desmond was glad.
He wanted to be the first to see her in her finery.
Now she had caught sight of him and came running
up the street, face glowing.

"Desmond, oh Desmond!" she cried happily. "I
thought you were never going to come back." She
hurled herself into his arms, heedless of the astonishment of Clara and Lizzie. "I've been doing the

marketing for Mrs. Monahan," she exclaimed
breathlessly, "and, oh, the things you sent are so
lovely, but you shouldn't—you shouldn't—" She
stopped to catch her breath and discovered she was
still in his arms. "Thank you," she said, disengaging
herself. "You are very good to me."

Desmond took the marketing basket from her
and handed it to Clara. "Come into the parlor with
me, Mara. We must speak."

"It's about Father, isn't it?" she asked when they
were alone. Her face had drained of color and she
sat abruptly on one of Mrs. Monahan's horsehair
settees.

"Yes, it is—but the news is not bad, only dis-
couraging. Your father has gone to Buffalo on business, something to do with the legacy. We cannot
expect to see him for a fortnight."

Mara's clenched hands unknotted and she raised
her eyes to his. "That is all?" she breathed. "Do you
swear to me that is all you know?"

He came to her and pulled her to her feet. "I
swear it," he said cheerfully. "Now, put on one of
your new frocks and we'll go to buy some shoes. I
couldn't for the life of me determine your size."

They found a hansom cab and soon they were
rolling westward, Mara in her primrose skirt and
waist and Desmond wearing a fashionable but flamboyant gray waistcoat which drew glances from
everyone. She pointed out to him the vegetable
stand she had visited and exclaimed over a teashop
which reminded her of one back home. Everything
seemed fresh and exciting to her and she brimmed
with happiness. The cast iron facades on West

Broadway intrigued her, and she was trying to see everything and listen to Desmond's descriptions of the card game at once.

"Some of the lads were political types," he explained. "There was a Mr. Hennessy, late of Tammany Hall, and his son who is standing for Congress. They'll help us, Mara; they know everything that goes on in the city."

"But what if you should get in trouble?" Mara's eyes darkened. "What if someone should shoot you?"

Desmond roared with laughter. "Why would anyone shoot me? You are mistaken if you think I'm ignorant of city life. I've learned so much in these few days, Mara! Trust me."

The new shoes seemed odd to her. She emerged from the Fifth Avenue shop carrying them distrustfully, marveling at the enormity of the New York emporiums. "They are so strange," she whispered to Desmond. "There is so much of everything. The shoes are all pointed at the toe, and ever so high."

He stopped to buy her violets wrapped in a paper cone, and then they rode uptown to gaze at the millionaire's mansions lining the avenue like so many forbidding palaces. The names of the people who lived here rolled from Desmond's lips in a litany of foreign-sounding flourishes: DePew . . . Burkhardt . . . Lauterbach . . .

"They would no sooner receive us," he said bitterly, "than they would Mrs. Monahan or Brigid." But his mood could not stay dark for long. They turned back and rolled through the slums of the Lower East Side where the densely packed inhabitants were

Russian and Polish Jews and the signs above the butcher shops and ironmongers were written in Hebrew. They stopped near Hester Street while an indignant crowd surrounded a man who was beating his dray horse; they cheered when he was pulled away from the wretched animal by an angry old man in a frock coat and flowing whiskers. They strolled along the sea-front at Battery Park, and by the time they were returning to East 22nd Street the sun had begun to slant toward the west.

"You have a visitor, Miss," Brigid said sourly. "He's been waiting in the garden for an hour."

Mara gasped. She had forgotten all about Roger Winthrop.

"It's young Mr. Roger," Brigid continued snidely, casting a knowing look in Desmond's direction. "Him you met yesterday. Mrs. Burkhardt's brother."

Desmond gripped Mara's arm and looked down at her with an unreadable expression. "Upon my word, Cousin," he drawled, using the mocking tone she hated, "you have a habit of gathering admirers. I shall just come along and introduce myself."

Roger Winthrop's expression as Mara entered the garden was one of unmistakable relief and absurd happiness. It was not lost on Desmond, who noted with satisfaction that the other man's face went dull red at sight of him.

"I am so sorry," Mara was saying breathlessly. "I forgot the precise hour of our appointment."

"Quite all right," Mr. Winthrop murmured, his eyes flying from her face to Desmond's with a look of helpless anguish.

"This is my cousin, Mr. O'Connell," said Mara.

She felt Desmond's stormy presence beside her and didn't dare to look at him. "Mr. Winthrop visits Mrs. Monahan regularly," she explained in a sudden agony of embarrassment. "She was his nanny, Desmond."

Roger advanced to take Desmond's hand. His sketchbook lay forlornly on the garden wall; no doubt he had despaired of her ever coming.

"So, ye visit ye're old nanny, Mr. Winthrop, sir? Och, how charmin' ye've not forgotten her." Desmond was affecting the broad country accent he used when he was angry. Mr. Winthrop's eyes widened in astonishment, but he acknowledged the introduction with unfailing upper-class courtesy. Desmond continued the grotesque parody, shuffling his feet and grinning.

"I spy a book for drawins' on the garden wall," he cried jovially.

"Mr. Winthrop sketches," said Mara stiffly. "He was going to make a picture of me."

"Ah, now, sir—me cousin does not sit to artists," said Desmond. "I am her chaperone, you see, and she is far too young to have her little head turned. She is not yet quite eighteen, sir. *I beg you to remember that.*" The last words were uttered with a steely seriousness that could not be misread.

"I will go," said Roger with dignity.

Desmond held his hands up. "No! I'll not hear of it," he said obsequiously. "It is I who must retreat. We have had such a trying afternoon, have we not, Mara? Good day, Mr. Winthrop." And Desmond turned on his heel and went into the house, leaving them alone.

Mara suppressed a terrible desire to giggle. Desmond's behavior had been so strange, no doubt Mr. Winthrop thought him a lunatic. He looked so forlorn now, so utterly at sea, that she began to feel exceedingly sorry for him. "Please pay my cousin no mind," she said. "He is very—high-spirited."

"That is not how I should have described him."

"He behaves strangely now and then, but he has protected me through so much."

"It's only that I expected him to be *older*." Roger paused. "I had hoped to ask his permission to take you to dine tomorrow."

"Oh, dear—I've had a note from my friend, Mrs. Daly, this morning. She and her husband have invited us to dine at Delmonico's tomorrow evening. It is to be a reunion party. We met at sea."

Roger tried to picture the dark young ruffian of a cousin at Delmonico's. The man was insufferable! It wasn't only his rudeness and the uncanny way he had managed to make Roger feel a blundering fool —it was something proprietary in his demeanor toward Miss McQuaid, something far too intense for comfort. He sighed. The afternoon, to which he had looked forward so eagerly, was proving an utter failure.

Now Mara was trying to invite him into the parlor, smiling and stammering in her efforts to put him at ease. She felt dreadfully wrong in having placed this nice young man at Desmond's mercy, and guilty for having forgotten all about him. She sensed that he had never been treated with anything but the greatest respect and her heart went out to his profound discomfort.

"If you would still like to make a picture of me," she said kindly, "I would be delighted to sit for you."

He brightened a bit. "I could never do justice to your beauty," he said softly, "and your extraordinary cousin might challenge me to duel!" They both laughed then and went into the house. Roger's heart was pounding painfully with conflict. The girl was an angel—so sweet and kind that all his tenderness for her had surfaced again. He could hardly bear to look into that lovely face, so intent now on smoothing his ruffled feathers, without feeling a scoundrel for the almost painful desire she roused in him.

In the dim parlor, seated a few feet from her, it was all he could do not to seize her in his arms. Her face was tinged with a faint apricot where the sun had kissed her creamy skin, and her black hair lay like a mantle of silk against the pale stuff of her becoming new costume. When she told him of the delay in meeting her father, her eyes brimming with distress, he felt almost dizzy. How could anyone—even Constance—fail to love her?

"I hope you will call on my sister Mrs. Burkhardt," he blurted rashly. "I am most anxious for you to meet my family—I will ask Constance to leave a card—" He broke off, miserably aware of the folly of his suggestion. Constance would merely laugh at the idea of calling at Nanny Monahan's, and the thought of his sister, stately in her Worth driving costume, bearing down on Mara, card-case in hand, was ridiculous. Even he could see that.

Mara rose and gave him her hand when it was time for him to leave, and this time he pressed it to his lips. The feel of her soft flesh, so young and fragrant, was more exciting to him than anything he could have imagined. He felt half mad with desire. Her huge golden eyes widened under his stare, and then he was catching her in his arms, covering her face with kisses and murmuring her name over and over, drunk with the sound of it. She stiffened with alarm, her body rigid in his arms, yet something in her seemed to give way to him and his heart leapt with joy to think she might return his feeling.

"Forgive me," he whispered raggedly, gently putting her away from him. "I had no right . . . I could not help myself—"

She stared at him in mute amazement, her face bathed in crimson and lips parted slightly.

"Please say you forgive me," Roger pleaded.

Mara saw the deep-set hazel eyes go soft with remorse and despair, and she hardly knew what she felt.

"I forgive you," she said at last, in a barely audible voice.

"And you will see me again?"

"Yes."


Mara sat in her room, struggling to duplicate the coiffure Kathy had once created for her. Silken strands escaped from the pins and tumbled over her shoulders. She worked patiently until she thought she had succeeded. A glance in the mirror told her the effect was not as sophisticated as she had hoped, but it would have to do. She studied herself anxiously. Delmonico's, she knew, was one of the finest restaurants in town and she did not want to appear provincial and quaint to the society people who would be dining there.

The golden dress rustled pleasantly as she walked; the new shoes caused her to be unusually sedate as she descended the stairs to the waiting carriage. Mrs. Monahan was all admiration. "Ye do look lovely, dear," she breathed. "Now mind ye don't lose your head with all them forks and spoons to choose from . . ."

The restaurant on Park Avenue was infinitely more grand than she had imagined. From the moment she set foot in the long, elegant room, her hand on Desmond's arm, she realized that she had underestimated the extravagance of John and Kathleen's gesture. The snowy linen was dazzling; the silver cutlery alone worth a king's ransom! A profusion of waiters bowed everywhere, appearing unexpectedly and making her nervous. Surely it was not necessary to have so many people to serve a dinner! She held her head very high, trying not to notice that she was the only lady in all of Delmonico's who wasn't smothered in jewels.

John Daly, looking unfamiliar in his dinner jacket, rose to greet them formally. Behind him, the irrepressible Kathy was waving and calling out in tones which caused the other diners to look up disapprovingly: "Mara! I've been longing to see you again!"

Kathy wore an exceedingly low-cut gown of cherry-colored taffeta, whose bodice and enormous, ballooning sleeves were shot through with irridescent threads of pink and rose. Her earrings were little clusters of rubies and brilliantes which drew attention to the matching necklace above her pink, ample breasts. Two plumes of aigrette had been anchored in her blonde curls. Mara felt shyly dazzled by her friend's splendor.

"And here is dear Dr. Quinn," Kathy cried unnecessarily, for Terence was rising from his end of the table and clasping Mara's hand, beaming with pleasure.

"Why, Mr. O'Connell," Kathy crooned archly, "your cousin looks so splendid tonight I almost failed to notice you." Her eyes belied the words; in fact, Mara wished she would be more discreet—even Dr. Quinn must notice the naked hunger in her eyes. She was feverishly ebullient, desperately gay. She complimented Mara on the golden dress, her shrewd eyes telegraphing a sisterly message: "You see?" she might have said, "we women get what we want sooner or later." She teased Dr. Quinn mercilessly about his natty dinner jacket and laid her hand caressingly on her husband's arm often and ostentatiously, as if to hint at a new intimacy between them. John Daly seemed not to notice. Mara understood that Kathy wished to appear carefree and happy in front of Desmond, but something in the girl's forced gaiety distressed her. She resented her cousin for having taken advantage of Kathy, and yet, taking the full measure of the blonde girl's open sensuality and frank flirtatiousness, she was not sure Desmond had been entirely at fault.

Two bottles of iced champagne arrived at their table, and there were caviar and tiny squares of buttered black bread to eat. Mara sipped her champagne and felt a deep sense of well-being. She was safe here, despite the unfamiliar grandeur of the restaurant—her friends would not raise eyebrows when she exclaimed at the elaborate chain and keys worn by the *sommelier,* or watch for her to select the wrong spoon. There was a cold, fragrant soup to follow, and fish so white and translucent it melted in the mouth. There were birds roasted cunningly inside of other, larger, birds, and beef and salad and new wines, always, to match each course. She had begun to feel quite gay. Dr. Quinn was lecturing her on the way in which fine wines were aged in France, and she found herself giggling at the way his whiskers bobbed when he talked. When a waiter moved to refill her glass, Desmond laid his hand on it peremptorily.

"You have had enough to drink, Cousin," he said.

His righteous air infuriated her. *He* could drink until the cows came home—drink and play cards and bed with married women, and *she* was expected to behave like a little convent girl.

"How uncommonly rude of you, Desmond," she said firmly. "I should like some more wine, if you please."

Kathy was watching with fervent interest. "Don't be such a bear, Mr. O'Connell," she trilled at him, hunching her shoulders so that the deep valley between her breasts was accentuated. "Don't spoil my party."

Desmond withdrew his hand with an indolent air and the wine was poured. Mara looked at him co-

vertly. The high, white collar of his starched shirt
served to deepen the dark cast of his skin. In the
flickering candlelight his eyes seemed almost silver,
and she thought with an odd twinge of pride what a
very splendid man he was to behold. Their eyes met
for an instant and locked; Mara was the first to look
away, turning to scan the room with feigned absorption.

Everywhere she saw beautiful, distinguished looking women, all of them more richly gowned and
decorated than herself. She studied their clothing
and came to the reluctant conclusion that all the
ladies had been outfitted in Paris and all the gentlemen in London. The women's beauty was stony
and sure—she could not imagine them faltering over
a phrase or behaving gracelessly in any situation.
The very way their slender, jewelled fingers picked
up a fork or held a wine-glass bespoke a lifetime of
privilege and confidence. She envied them. Still,
when she saw the mirrored reflection of the loveliest
woman in the room she was amazed to find the face,
glowing with excitement and blooming like an exotic
flower in a garden of artifice, was her own.

Melons, peaches, nectarines and raspberries now
appeared on a trolley and Mara exclaimed at their
perfection. She was admiring the intricately carved
bed of ice on which they reposed when she became
aware of a presence looming over the table.

She looked up to find a portly, middle-aged man
staring at her with polite but obvious fascination. He
had finished dining and was leaving with a party of
three other men who hovered discreetly in the background. His smooth, heavy face was clean-shaven,

the jowls neatly powdered and gleaming with good health and robust high living. His evening clothes were clearly of the best quality and everything about him spoke of money. It was not Mr. Winthrop's understated, aristocratic air of wealth, but something more immediate and powerful. Several diamond rings winked on his square, large fingers, and his ostentatious tie-pin, fashioned in the shape of a harp, appeared to be wrought of emeralds.

He bowed perfunctorily to the others, but his words were intended for her. His voice was deep and rough, unmistakably Irish and full of the accents of Kerry.

"I like to see my countrymen enjoy themselves," he announced. "So much beauty at one table lifts the heart." He included both women in his compliment, but his bright, coal-black eyes were fastened on Mara. "If there is ever anything I can do for you, I'll be only too glad." He dropped an embossed card on the table, bowed to the entire company, and left.

"James J. McSweeney," Mara read. "Whoever can he be?"

"I believe," John Daly said, clearing his throat nervously, "Mr. McSweeney is active in politics. He was a union organizer for Tammany Hall—most unfortunate business."

Kathy giggled. "My, didn't he look ruthless, though? I thought he would eat Mara up with his eyes. *Quel homme!*"

Desmond had become very alert from the moment Mr. McSweeney had appeared at the table. His long body tensed and his jaw set stubbornly.

While the Dalys and Dr. Quinn speculated on Tammany politics, he plucked James J. McSweeney's card from the snowy tablecloth and ripped it—to Mara's astonishment—in four neat pieces. Then he picked up his glass and saluted her.

"Yet another admirer," he murmured sarcastically. *"Slainte!"*

"Why did you rip Mr. McSweeney's card?" Mara asked idly. "Is he a gangster, do you think?" They were in the brougham John Daly had ordered for them, on the way back to Mrs. Monahan's, and it was nearly midnight. The air was still sweet and warm, and Mara was glowing with the excitement of her evening out. She could not be angry—not if Desmond ripped ten cards.

"You cannot be so naïve as you seem," Desmond replied distantly.

"Why naïve?" Mara was stung.

"Men like that care only for one thing."

Mara turned to look at him. He sat with one leg propped against the opposite seat, brooding darkly.

"And what sort of man are *you?*" she asked daringly. "What do *you* care for, Cousin?"

The blue eyes slowly curved toward her, flickering with amusement. "How bold drink makes you," he said softly. "I wonder if I approve of your boldness, Cousin?"

"You have not answered my question," she said. They were turning into East 22nd Street now; the lights at Mrs. Monahan's were all out and the street was dim and quiet. Desmond sighed and brought his face close to hers, staring at her with what seemed incomprehensible sorrow.

"I will show you," he breathed, and then he grazed her lips with his in a kiss so light and tender it might not have happened. His warm hand cupped her cheek, the fingers stroking her flesh with feathery movements. Once more she felt the slow, deep heat flare up in her and spread over her body like liquid fire. She was paralyzed, drugged, and could only tremble beneath his lips and fingertips while every part of her yearned to be crushed against him, to feel his hands roving her body, rousing the slow, sweet ecstasy she had known on board the *Alberta*.

Her lips opened under his and her hands came up to embrace him, but he put her away gently, much as Roger Winthrop had done, and bade her go up to bed. The brougham had come to a halt in front of Mrs. Monahan's; he helped her out and when she turned and asked if he was not coming he shook his head.

Mara stood swaying on the pavement and watched in disbelief while Desmond leaped back into the brougham and told the driver to go on . . .

The evening at Delmonico's marked the true beginning to Mara's life in New York. The ten days which followed were a revelation to her. Desmond was seldom to be found, and since Mr. Winthrop could not find him to ask permission to see Mara, she willingly granted it herself. After all, she would be eighteen in a fortnight!

Roger took her driving every afternoon when he had finished in his law chambers on Beaver Street.

Together they saw everything of note in the city. He was a great admirer of striking architecture and frequently lectured her on the differences between Renaissance and rococo, the niceties and pitfalls of the vogue for Chinese decor in fashionable houses. They drove to the Church of the Pilgrims in Brooklyn Heights so Mara might see its glories, and to the town chateaux of the very rich along the Hudson. Names like Whitney, Kress, and Astor dropped casually from Roger's lips. They were friends of his parents, or of his sister Mrs. Burkhardt, whom Mara had yet to meet.

He took her to dine at quiet chop houses on Sixth Avenue, or in the financial district; once they went to Delmonico's, but the public atmosphere did not suit him. Mara instinctively realized he wanted her to himself, although he never repeated his ardent and impetuous behavior of the afternoon in the parlor. Occasionally he allowed himself to kiss her cheek quite chastely, but that was all. Only his eyes betrayed his longing.

They went to an afternoon concert at Carnegie Hall, and Mara sat entranced throughout the performance, barely able to speak when they emerged into the still-light street. Beauty stirred her, and she could not react to it lightly. They saw a play on Broadway one evening which was the talk of two continents. It was about an adulterous woman who repented of her wicked life and was redeemed only after three acts of the most heart-rending agony.

"Why must the world judge women so harshly?" Mara asked Roger during the interval. "Men are allowed everything, women nothing."

Roger threw her a look of alarm, and she did not pursue the subject. All the same, it bothered her. Like Kathleen Daly, the heroine had been kind-hearted and full of good instincts. Why must she be tormented on account of her passionate nature, which, after all, was as much the fault of the men who helped her to her ruin?

Kathy herself came to say goodbye one afternoon. She and John were traveling to St. Louis by train to see relations. It was a sad meeting, for Kathy was loathe to leave New York and Mara knew why.

"I shall miss you," the blonde girl said wistfully. "We never had a proper chance to become friends, but I am fond of you, Mara."

"Have you said goodbye to my cousin?"

Kathy's lips trembled then and she shook her head. In another moment she was sobbing in Mara's arms, her body shaking violently. "Please don't think me wicked," she wailed, looking up with tear-streaked eyes, "but I love him so. I cannot help it, Mara. There is no man on earth like Desmond."

"But you are married." Mara spoke gently. "You must try to love Mr. Daly."

Kathy flung herself away and laughed without mirth. "John does not care for me," she said. "He cares for my money and for my standing back home in Cork, but as for the other—" She broke off and regarded Mara evenly. "Your cousin does not love me, either. If he loves anyone, *cherie*, it is you . . ."

"I have scarcely seen him since the night we dined," Mara said. "Desmond cares only for himself."

When Kathy left she pressed a small package on

Mara. "This is for you. Open it when I have gone."
She repaired the damage to her face and tried to
smile bravely. "St. Louis!" she cried in tones of
disdain. "Think of it! *Fin du monde!* There are
probably Indians in the streets!"

When Mara opened the package she found an
exquisite brooch of glowing topaz set in gold. Her
friend's generosity made her blink back tears; she
wished with all her heart that Kathy might yet find
happiness.

Dr. Quinn, too, left the city, for Baltimore. Mara
sat with him in the garden, trying to persuade Lizzie not to pull at his whiskers. Terence told her
Desmond had called on him at Gramercy Square,
and when Mara showed surprise he laughed outright.

"Come, child, don't let on you think your cousin
a devil!" He lifted a hand to stem her retort. "Young
Mr. O'Connell is a very good fellow, indeed," he
said. "He has your welfare at heart. I will own he is
rash and gambles too much, but he has a very great
deal to trouble him. When your father returns from
Buffalo things will be better."

"Why hasn't he written to me? I am sure Father
would write if everything was going well."

"Don't be impatient," Dr. Quinn said kindly.
"You are far too young to brood."

Mara lowered her head guiltily. Far from brooding, she had been running about with Roger Winthrop, absorbing the life of the city eagerly and with
an almost reckless joy. Thoughts of her father had
troubled her infrequently.

"You must help your cousin," he said seriously.

"You have a very great influence on him for the good." He hugged her with surprising vigor as he was leaving; they would meet again, he said, when he returned to the city to set sail for Ireland, and home.

When he had gone Mara felt very much alone. First the Dalys, and now Dr. Quinn. She never saw Desmond, her father was not due to return for a week, and life would have seemed a very lonely prospect if not for Roger Winthrop. He was coming soon to take her to tea at his sister's. She looked forward to the event with an odd mixture of pleasure and dread.

The impression she had formed of Constance Burkhardt had to be discarded as soon as she was ushered into that lady's presence. The butler who admitted them displayed a chilly welcome for Roger, and showed them through a marble foyer as large as the entire first floor of Mrs. Monahan's brownstone dwelling. "Mrs. Burkhardt is in the Chinese Room, sir," he said reproachfully.

"Thank you, Wilson, I'll take Miss McQuaid myself."

As they ascended a long flight of stairs, flanked by ancestral oil paintings, Roger explained that his sister had conceived a sudden passion for Oriental decor. "She's had this room done up," he said, "and whereas ordinarily she'd receive in the—" He broke off, smiling sheepishly. He was as nervous as Mara.

They proceeded along a broad landing and up a hall; Mara had a fleeting impression of rooms more spacious and luxurious than those of Leinster Castle itself, but Roger whisked her along so quickly she barely caught glimpses of them. They came to a halt outside a door and Roger took her hand, pressing it briefly as if for luck.

The Chinese Room was so dazzling Mara felt she might have stumbled into a brilliant dream by mistake. The walls were lacquered a bright red and covered with embroidered silk hangings of gardens and flowers. One whole side of the room was paneled in silk of a creamy white upon which black serpents coiled and menaced in a dizzying pattern. The Oriental carpet was of black and poisonous green; the low chairs and couches were lacquered bamboo, upholstered in crimson and purple silk. An entire cabinet was devoted to *objets*: scraps of Cathay silk and jars and tureens of glossy *faience* and a sword of dull gold. Precious figures of ivory and jade were scattered everywhere. In the furthest corner, like the most expensive *objet* in her room, sat Constance Winthrop Burkhardt.

"Hello, Connie," said Roger breathlessly. "So sorry to be late. This is Miss McQuaid—Mara, my sister, Mrs. Burkhardt."

Constance inclined her head graciously. Her lips curved slightly in a smile, but her eyes remained untouched.

Mara was speechless. She had expected Roger's sister to bear a resemblance to him, and in fact she did, but Constance was cut from another bolt of cloth altogether. All that was soft and pleasant in Roger's face had bypassed his sister; Connie's features were glacially perfect, as if a master sculptor had chiseled her from a block of alpine snow. Roger's hair and brows were of a warm brown hue, tinged with auburn—Connie's were dark as ebony. Both had the deep-set eyes which seemed so eager and intense in Roger but in Connie were flat and impenetrable. If Roger was handsome, his sister was magnificent.

"So nice to see you Miss McQuaid," she murmured listlessly. "Roger has mentioned you quite frequently."

Mara knew she was being watched with more acuity than Connie's indolent gaze revealed. She felt how inappropriate her simple white skirt and waist must look in this splendid room. At least she had put her hair up, but nothing she could do would make her acceptable to this social lioness. She saw it immediately, and having perceived it she resolved not to bother. It was as if a great weight had been lifted from her. She would not have to struggle to make Constance like her, because Constance would never like her so long as she lived.

Roger's sister spoke for some time of the tiresome preparations she must make so that she and Henry might sail to France in a fortnight.

"Of course you have been to Paris, Miss McQuaid?"

"No," said Mara. "I have been in Ireland and in New York. That, I'm afraid, is the extent of my traveling."

"Oh, dear," Connie drawled, "what a shame for you."

She asked Roger about his studies, commented

on the unusual heat for the time of year, and talked at length about a Miss Schuyler whom she and Roger both knew.

"You know Elizabeth Schuyler, do you not, Miss McQuaid?"

"No," replied Mara cheerfully, "we've never met."

"Ah, that must be remedied. Perhaps a small dinner next week?" she suggested vaguely. "Elizabeth is such a charming girl—a great friend of mine—and quite gifted. She sings so beautifully . . ."

"As for myself," said Mara, feeling wicked, "I do not sing at all."

By the time the maid had wheeled in the tea trolley the two women understood each other perfectly. Only Roger was oblivious. Mara thought she could detect a grudging admiration in Connie's glance for her cheerful imperturbability. Constance poured the tea, diamonds flashing from her long, expressive fingers, into Chinese cups so thin it seemed they might crumble at a touch. She gestured at the enormous assortment of food on the trolley. There were candied fruits and scones and jam and three sorts of cake as well as fresh strawberries and double cream, but only Roger ate.

"Shall you return to Ireland soon?" Constance asked, making Ireland sound a fantastically improbable place.

"I have no plans at present, Mrs. Burkhardt. I hope to see my father soon and then I shall know better."

"How very tiresome for you," Connie murmured,

and then, as an afterthought: "Of course you must come see me often."

"Of course," said Mara solemnly.

"She loved you—I'm sure of it!" Roger exclaimed as they drove down Fifth Avenue, away from the Chinese Room and the dragon within it.

Mara looked at him sharply, but she could detect no mocking expression in the soft hazel eyes. How could he be so blind? His sister thought her a fortune-hunting chit of a girl who had got her claws, quite by accident, into one of the most eligible men in New York. She wanted to tell Roger how much she liked him, and how little she sought to gain from their friendship, but he was staring at her in the old, intense way, caressing her face with his eyes, and she did not want to hurt him.

"You are my dearest friend," she said, and meant it.

That night Connie's personal maid was sent to summon Roger to his sister's bedside for a chat. Connie's long hair had been brushed out for the night, and she wore an apricot silk dressing gown. She looked very stern and beautiful and, as usual, Roger felt in awe of her.

"Of course you know it is impossible?" Connie asked without preamble, beckoning him to sit beside her on the bed. "Your infatuation for the little McQuaid girl is absurd."

Roger's eyes narrowed. "I warn you," he said,

"don't speak of her slightingly. I won't let anyone do that, not even you, Connie."

His sister laughed musically. "Darling little Roger! Do you remember the time in Newport when I broke your toy train and you stamped your foot and called me a monster? You look like that same little boy now."

"Stop it, Connie."

"Of course, I won't deny the girl's a beauty—a first-class beauty. She'd turn any man's head—even a man far more experienced than you, pet. I quite understand that you want to make love to her, and why not? But marry her? Shame, Roger!"

Roger stood up, balling his fists in the pockets of his dressing gown. He had to grit his teeth to keep from shouting. "She is innocent," he said in strangled tones. "Nobody has ever made love to her and nobody will unless it is me."

"Oh, my," Connie sighed. *"You're* the one who's innocent, pet. Fancy, thinking she's a virgin! Why, Roger—girls like that *exist* so that men like you can vent your passions. A young bachelor must have some healthy outlets, after all. It's perfectly normal, dear. When Henry and I were engaged he had a little Polish girl he'd visit. They'd make love and then he could come to me without fear of acting . . . inappropriately. That's the way it's done, darling. So have your fun, Roger, but don't weary me with all this preposterous talk of marriage."

"What you've said is disgusting, Connie. I never thought you were so corrupt." He was trembling with rage at the insult to Mara and another, more obscure anger—how little he knew his sister, after all.

"My dear," Connie said, "you don't know the half of it."

# BOOK II

## Innocent No More

## Chapter Five

"Bless me, Miss, why ever would you be wantin'
to know about him?"

Brigid was Mara's source of information about
everything that went on in the city. Brigid read the
tabloids eagerly and could discourse for hours on
Mrs. Whitney's fancy dress ball or the latest anti-
Irish scandal. She would often drop tidbits in Mara's
path about the daring gowns worn by one of the
"400" or the shocking amount of money spent on
flowers at a young girl's coming-out party. More
often, though, she discussed with relish the burning
of convents or riots on St. Patrick's Day during
which Irish infants and mothers were trampled to
death in the streets. Her favorite story involved a
literary hoax which had been perpetrated some dec-
ades ago in New York: *The Awful Disclosures of
Maria Monk*, a fraudulent account of life in a convent, designed to escalate mistrust and hatred of
the Roman church.

"Think of it," she would breathe angrily. "Nuns

and priests having babies together, and when they
was born they strangled 'em and buried 'em in quick-
lime!"

"But Mr. McSweeney?" prompted Mara. "Who is
he?"

Brigid popped a tray of muffins in the oven and
said onerously: "James J. McSweeney is not a name
should be on a young girl's lips." And then she related the entire history of the man who had presented his card at Delmonico's. McSweeney had first
come to the public's attention in the 'fifties, as a
bare-knuckle boxer.

"He was just a lad, then. His da' had gone out to
California during the gold rush, and Jim McSweeney
stayed in San Francisco and made his name fightin'.
When he came back East he'd a pile o' money and
he opened a saloon. All the lads from Tammany
drank there." It seemed McSweeney's customers had
known a good man when they saw him, and before
long the former fighter was a union organizer. In
the 'seventies, Tammany sent him to Congress for
two terms.

"Och, it was a scandal—graft, and booze, and
women galore!" Now he owned saloons in five cities
and part shares in three racetracks and—here Brigid
lowered her voice to a hoarse whisper—a house
where fancy women sold themselves to society men
for a pretty price. "So now ye know," she said
grimly.

Mara was fascinated by the variety of the man's
talents. She didn't approve of his ill-gotten gains,
but there was a certain primitive justice to his saga.
McSweeney, a despised Irish immigrant at the

height of America's anti-Irish sentiment, had refused to accept his lowly status. He had carved a niche for himself, using brute force and wily intelligence. No wonder the man was notorious! She thanked Brigid and went upstairs to change her clothing. Roger was coming to take her for a picnic in Brooklyn.

"How lovely you are," Roger said wonderingly. "I have never seen a face to compare with yours." He lay propped on an elbow beneath a spreading plane tree, staring up into Mara's face. The elaborate hamper he had brought had yielded up a feast of cold chicken, deviled ham, and fresh grapes which Annie had packed for him. He had not spoken much to Connie since the fatal conversation in her bedroom. He was afraid of losing his temper; he rarely became angry, but when he did he could be surprisingly violent. Few people knew it.

"I am thinking of taking a house," he said now, picking up Mara's hand and stroking the fingers gently. "What would you think of that?"

"But why a house, Roger? You have everything you need at your sister's."

Roger's eyes continued to search her face, hoping to see signs of comprehension. At last he sighed. "Mara," he said, "I want to marry you. I want it more than anything on earth."

Her hand convulsed in his and he laid a finger against her lips. "Don't speak," he urged. "Hear me out. I love you more than I thought I could love anything or anyone. I've written to my mother about you. She is an angel—not like Connie at all—and she will love you like a daughter."

Mara remembered what Mrs. Monahan had said about Roger's mother and nodded. "But Roger—"

"Shhh, darling, let me finish. We could be married in Boston, or wherever you like, for that matter. I would take you to Paris, Rome, Cairo—or would you like to go to Ireland? Anywhere you say, dearest. And then we will come back and settle here. I will find your father for you—oh, darling, darling Mara, don't refuse me. I think I would die."

His eyes were pleading with her; his face was bathed in dappled light which filtered through the branches of the tree, and he looked suddenly like a faun. Mara was much moved, but she could only speak the truth. "It cannot be, Roger," she said tenderly. "You must have a wife of high social standing, someone who will be a credit to your family name. Your sister detests me and even though your mother may be quite different, she will not approve of a marriage between us."

"I don't care," Roger cried passionately. "It's my life, not theirs! My life and yours, Mara. I'll love you until the day I die—I could never love anyone else, never." He gripped her hand so hard she winced, and then he was kissing her with a desperate ardor she had not felt from him since that afternoon in the parlor; he kissed her eyelids and her throat, murmuring words of love. "Don't answer me now," he begged. "Only think of what I have said. I know you don't love me as I love you, but that will come in time . . ."

Mara did not believe that love could be summoned, like a recalcitrant puppy, but she could not bring herself to hurt him. His lips were on her own now and she thought for the hundredth time how loving and sweet, how handsome and gentle he was . . . It would be so easy to respond to him if only . . . She squeezed her eyes shut and tried to erase the image and the remembered feeling of other lips, other arms . . .

Desmond came awake slowly, realizing with a sense of bewilderment that the bed he slept in was strange to him. Had he dreamed? He rolled over and saw the girl's tawny naked back where the sheet had fallen from her body, and the spill of glossy black hair on the pillow, and then he remembered. She was part Chinese, and they had met after the game last night in Hennessy's back room. He had drunk too much in a vain effort to forget what he had learned about Mara's father in the course of the day, and the girl had smiled at him and laid her shapely hand on the sleeve of his coat. Before much time had passed he had taken her off, up the stairs to one of Hennessy's rooms. She stirred lazily now and opened her eyes.

"Hello, Paddy," she said teasingly. "How's your head feel?"

"Don't call me that. Not ever."

She smiled. "Ah, sweetheart, I was only joking. I've forgotten your name, but I'd know the rest of you anywhere." Slowly, her hands came up and trailed over his bare shoulders, tracing little circles over his sleep-warm flesh. She pressed her lips to his chest and murmured, "What's your name then?"

"Desmond."

She took him in her arms and twined her legs with his, rocking gently. "Well, Desmond," she whispered, "I'm Anna. I can get twenty-five dollars a night, but for you I'm free." She nipped at him with small sharp teeth and he rolled her toward him and pinned her to the bed. She was small and beautifully made, and her skin was the color of sun-ripened apricots. He let the desire overtake him slowly, deliciously, trying to curtain the vision of Mara's face when he told her about Padraic. By the time Anna was crying out in pleasure and raking his back with her pointed nails, he had almost succeeded . . .

"Mr. O'Connell, I had not expected to see you. Your cousin tells me you've been away."

Roger had taken Mara home and was preparing to drive away when Desmond came ambling up the street, coat slung over his shoulders and looking quite disreputable. Roger frowned. If the man was going to be difficult he would say nothing; if, on the other hand, Mr. O'Connell deigned to be civil, he felt it his duty to declare his intentions. After all, so far as he knew the strange young man was Mara's closest relation.

"I've come back," said Desmond succinctly. "I am never so far away, Mr. Winthrop, that you can expect to lose me."

"I have seen a great deal of Miss McQuaid these past days," Roger said. "I have just brought her from a picnic."

Desmond grinned. "Have you now?"

"I have also taken her to meet my sister, and I've written to my mother. I have the greatest respect for your cousin; I want to do everything properly."

"What is it you're planning to do so properly?"

Roger considered the wisdom of announcing his proposal. He knew instinctively that the cousin hated him. The hatred was quite impersonal—in other circumstances they might almost have been friends —and had to do only with Roger's feelings for Mara. Still, if they were to be married he would have to face O'Connell sometime.

"I have asked her to marry me," he said simply.

Desmond's expression did not alter; his tone of voice was one of polite interest. "But she has not accepted you?"

"I have asked her not to make a decision just yet. She must have time to think." This was how it was always done in Roger's world. He felt sure even O'Connell would approve the delicacy.

"If thinking is required," Desmond replied, "then surely yours is a lost cause."

"I ask your permission as a mere formality—I intend to marry her whether you like it or not."

"It is not whether *I* like, Mr. Winthrop. It is whether *she* likes. It is entirely in her hands."

"I'm so glad you will speak of it reasonably," Roger said. He offered a tentative smile—one gentleman to another.

"And then," Desmond continued airily, "there is

likely to be another problem. If she should accept you, Mr. Winthrop, I do not foresee much joy."

"And why is that?"

"Because," said Desmond, "I will kill you."

Roger sighed. There was no dealing with the man, after all. "We do not go about killing each other in New York," he said haughtily. "You are not in Ireland now." He tipped his hat, gave the order to drive on, and left Desmond standing on the pavement.

"Devil take you," Desmond muttered, "you poor, besotted fool." He did not take Roger Winthrop seriously, and pitied him for his hopeless passion. It never occurred to him that Mara might consider her suitor's proposal. He went whistling into the house and asked Brigid to summon her to the parlor. He had more important things on his mind than the pretensions of love-sick society boys.

Mara sat very still while Desmond told her Padraic was not coming, after all. The words fell all around her but she did not want to hear. She couldn't bear to think her father had abandoned her; still less could she contemplate the dreadful alternative.

"He has left Buffalo," Desmond continued, "or perhaps he never went there. He has gone west and may be in Chicago now."

"But why?"

"I don't know, but I'll find out. I will go West and find him if need be."

"What if he's dead?" Mara's eyes were immense and clouded with misery. "I know my father, Desmond—it is impossible he'd abandon Mamma and me—if he were alive he would have been at the dock the day the *Alberta* landed."

He came and squatted on his heels before her, taking her chin in his hands. "That isn't Mara Mc-Quaid talking," he said. "That sentiment is for the likes of Winthrop, or John Daly. The world is a very large and perplexing place, little Cousin. Your father may have landed in a deal of trouble and be extricating himself at this very moment. But he is not dead—I'm sure of it."

"Shall we go to Chicago?" she asked.

"Not yet. I must have more information. In the meantime, we will celebrate your eighteenth birthday in fine style tomorrow."

Mara blushed. "I've promised Roger Winthrop I would dine with him," she said in a low voice. And then, encouraged by his softened mood, she told him about how kind Roger had been to her, about all the wondrous places he had taken her. She even described the ill-fated visit to Mrs. Burkhardt's, imitating Constance's condescending airs and graces for his amusement. He did not laugh, and gradually Mara's voice trailed away into the silence.

"Have you anything else to tell me?" he asked with a dangerous calm.

She shook her head.

Desmond tightened his fingers painfully around her chin and narrowed his eyes menacingly. "Don't lie to me," he whispered, "don't ever lie to me." Mara's eyes were wide with terror and sudden comprehension. "He has asked you to marry him," Desmond explained as if cueing her, "and you have not replied. You are to have time to think about whether you will accept. *Isn't it so?*"

She nodded.

"I never thought to take it seriously. I thought the man was so beside himself he grasped at straws. But you, Mara—you've given him cause to hope, haven't you? *Haven't you?*" He shouted the last words, his eyes gone black with rage. "A pretty sight," he spat, "to see a young girl contemplate whether she'll sell herself for a house on Fifth Avenue and all the money in the world! When you lied to me I knew. I knew you were thinking of becoming his wife!"

"Let me go," Mara said icily. "You have no right to talk to me this way. I am *not* planning to marry Mr. Winthrop, but if I were you could not stop me."

"Couldn't I?" He grinned hatefully. "Try me and see." He dropped his hands and got to his feet. "I'm leaving now," he said. "The next time Mr. Winthrop presses his lips to your little hand, remember this: the lowest whore on the Bowery has more honor than you do."

"And you remember this," Mara cried, trembling with hatred at the cruelty of his words. "Roger loves me! He loves me as a man should love a woman. What do you know of love?"

"You'll find out one day," he said. "God help you then."

She hadn't told Roger it was her eighteenth birthday. Partly, she kept it secret because she was

afraid he would buy her a costly keepsake if he
knew. She was already more in his debt than she
wished to be. If only they could have continued their
friendship as it had been! If he had not brought up
the subject of marriage she would be a great deal
more at ease. As it was, Roger's proposal hung in
the air between them, charging the festivity of the
evening with a keen tension.

She could not turn her head or laugh in pleasure
without being aware of his eyes following her every
move. Things she said took on new meanings. Once
she cried impulsively. "Oh, I should love to have
champagne every night!" and immediately regretted
it. Roger's eyes said clearly, although no words
were spoken: "You can, my darling. Marry me and
you shall have whatever you want, always."

After dinner, which they had taken in an elegant
inn off Irving Place, they drove idly through the
warm streets. At last Mara could bear it no more.
"I have been thinking of what you said yesterday—"

Roger leaned forward in alarm. "No," he said,
"please don't say anything yet, Mara. You haven't
had time to consider it." They rode for some time in
silence. At last Mara pled exhaustion and asked
him to take her home. Instantly he was all concern,
chafing her hands, inquiring if she had slept well
the night before, peering anxiously into her face as
if to scout out some unknown fever there. Life with
him would be like this, she saw. To be Roger's beloved would mean the loss of her freedom—every
move she made for the rest of her life would be
closely monitored by his adoring glance; she would
never be able to cry for joy, or laugh at something

silly, or walk about unattended for fear of worrying him.

She would grow to hate him.

Her relief when he left her tenderly at Mrs. Monahan's door surged upon her in waves of giddy release. It was all she could do not to skip up the stairs. She was not tired at all. She felt free, her head clear, she felt she could dance for hours, do anything at all . . . She let herself into her room and spun around three times with sheer high spirits, falling on the narrow little bed and laughing at her own dizzy happiness. She was eighteen today, and anything might happen.

She stared at the ceiling idly, wondering what it was that made her feel the room was different. Something was not as it should be. At last she saw it was merely the curtain, which was drawn across the window. Brigid must have come in while she was away. She went to open the curtain and let the moonlight in, and as she stared over the silvery garden she became aware of another presence in the room with her. There—at the periphery of her vision—was someone lounging in the corner chair. Desmond was in her room. She tried to stifle her gasp of alarm but it escaped and hung between them in the heavy silence.

"Good evening," he said. "I have been waiting to wish you a happy birthday."

"You have been here—in my room." Mara had meant to sound accusing, indignant, but her voice emerged thin and slight. For the first time she felt truly afraid of Desmond. "What right have you to come here?" This time her tone was stronger. He made no answer, but sat, one leg thrown over the arm of the chair, watching her with glittering eyes. There was something primitive and wolfish about him in the moonlight. She shuddered. "You must leave now. I'm tired."

He uncoiled his body slowly, like a snake preparing to strike. "Are you?" he asked softly. "Then we must waken you." He stood and walked toward her with the stealth of a hunter stalking its prey. She backed up as he advanced, shaking her head from side to side as one caught in a nightmare and trying to wake.

"What is wrong with you, Desmond? Have you been drinking?"

"No," he whispered, "but I'm drunk all the same. I am drunk with wanting you."

Her fear changed then, shifted into a new emotion which was still fear but laced round with a wild, jubilant feeling she could scarcely understand. Her body jolted against the wall and she sprang away, backing around the foot of the bed.

"Desmond—" She didn't know what it was she wanted to ask, and there was no time in any case because he had trapped her in a corner, and now he stood silently contemplating his prize. The only sound in the room was her breathing, ragged and labored, and then she realized that he, too, was afraid of the enormity of the moment. His eyes bored into her and his lips moved, as if to call her name, and then he leaned forward, bracing his arms against the wall so she was caught. Still they did not touch.

"Have you enjoyed yourself tonight, Cousin?"

His lips barely moved, but the words, poisonous and soft, pierced her through.

"Has your rich suitor held you in his arms and whispered words of eternal love? Has he kissed you tonight?"

"No." She shook her head violently. "Please, don't torment me about him—I care nothing for him, Desmond."

"Ah, but he cares for you. His hands cannot come near you without trembling with desire. And his dreams—shall I tell you what he dreams at night?" Desmond was shaking now, his voice as unsteady as her own.

"Please—leave off, Desmond. I will call for Brigid—I'll wake the house!"

His hands closed round her throat, holding her softly but with a promise of violence. "I think you'll do no such thing," he taunted. "Tell me, Mara. How does it feel to know that I could kill you in a moment? Think of what you would be missing . . . Think of the happy life as Mrs. Roger Winthrop you would never live to lead . . ."

She had begun to shake with terror, but the old anger rose up and she stared at him, her eyes flashing with defiance. "Kill me then, Desmond," she spat at him. "I am not afraid of you."

His hands slid from her neck and upward, over her face, until they were twined in her hair. He pulled the pins out and the heavy silk came tumbling down around her face in a sudden warm rush; he stepped back to admire his handiwork and she moved quickly, darting past him toward the door.

Her hand was closing round the doorknob when she felt a pain so sharp she gasped aloud. Desmond's fingers grasped her shoulders like a vise; he dragged her halfway across the room. She fell against the wardrobe, stumbled, and righted herself. Her hair hung wildly over her face and she had lost a shoe—she was full of the desire to fight him now, and when he came toward her again she raised her hands, arching her fingers like claws, and dared him to advance.

"Cat!" he jeered. "Are you a tame cat or a wild one, Cousin?"

For answer she raked his face as he stepped close. She felt his flesh tear beneath her nails and was momentarily drunk with triumph, but then he was pinioning her arms to her sides, shaking her as easily in his grasp as he might a doll.

"I hate you!" She ground the words out, spitting them into his face over and over, like a litany. The moonlight revealed him perfectly—the weals along his cheek were bleeding slightly where she had wounded him, and his teeth showed fierce and white in the dark face as he laughed at her attempts to free herself.

"You are an animal!" she sobbed furiously. "Nothing but an animal!"

"*Yesss.*" He said it on a long, indrawn breath, and with one thrust of his arm tumbled her to the bed. Instantly she was on her feet again, rushing at him, and just as effortlessly as before he pushed her down again. He bent over her, grinning like a wolf, and forced her head back until she had to look in his eyes. The brilliant blue had darkened until it seemed to her she was looking into the black pits of Hell.

*"Nobody but me,"* he whispered, spacing the words with a chilling intensity. "Nobody will make love to you but me."

"I will make love with anyone who pleases me," she cried desperately, in a last attempt to defy him.

His fist clenched, the knuckles showing white, and then he gripped the neck of her golden gown and ripped it, in one clean movement, in two. She heard the tafetta shriek as it rent beneath his fingers, and then she was lying before him in her chemise and stockings, shivering with dread in the silvery moonlight.

His hand rested on her throat, fingers splaying down so that his thumb lay on the topmost swellings of her breasts. His flesh was burning hot; she felt as if he had branded her.

*"Nobody but me,"* he repeated. "Do you understand?" And then he ripped the chemise, baring her breasts completely and breathing so raggedly the sound came like a sob in the room.

She saw his hand go to his belt and shut her eyes, turning her head aside and whispering, "Please Desmond—please don't harm me—you are insane—Desmond, please . . ." The sound of her pleas was cut short as he gathered her roughly in his arms, bending her body back until she felt she might break. His hands closed hungrily over her naked breasts, fondling them so roughly she cried out, and then she felt his black hair on her arching throat and his lips against her nipples, rough and hurting, bruising the tender buds with the force of his long-ing.

She cried out again, and then his lips covered hers, silencing her, his tongue twining with hers, his hands strong and cruel on her thighs, dragging them apart with brutal purpose. Even as he hurt her, she could feel the violent trembling of his own body—everywhere her hands beat futilely against him they encountered flesh as hard and smooth as rock, with countless tiny muscles quivering beneath as if he were in the throes of a fit.

He raised himself above her with a guttural groan and then lowered his body, and she felt a ripping, searing agony as he battered his way into her like an enraged bull. He was ripping her apart as surely as he had ripped her golden gown. She screamed against his shoulder, but he was relentless, thrusting into her again and again so that the unbearable pain became a red glow behind her eyes that built and spread like a gigantic conflagration. Just when she thought she could stand no more, it burst in a fan-tastic ball of pure anguish, and receded.

He was heedless of her cries and continued his thrusting, gathering his hands beneath her and holding her still closer, as though trying to pierce her to the core. She would die, she knew; he would kill her with his body, but suddenly he slowed his pace, moving more gently within her. Somewhere, deep inside her, she felt a bright, sweet core of pleasure burning, its flames seeking kind with the fiery passion surrounding her, and she felt with wonder how it grew and grew until she felt her body arching toward his.

"No!" she cried, this time at herself, but it was stronger than she had thought, and even while she hated him with all her strength she felt she could never have enough of him. Her hands came up to hold him, roving fiercely over his back and gripping his smooth, tensed flanks; her legs circled him with a tender urgency she could not hold back, and then she was calling his name in fright and ecstasy both, and being bathed in molten fire so beautiful it seemed she could never know paradise more completely . . .

He lay with his head on her breast, his hands in the wild, matted mane of her hair. He whispered broken words, in English and in Gaelic, his eyes closed and lips warm against her flesh.

"*Tá grá agam duit*," he cried softly: *Oh, I love thee*. It was the most formal declaration of love, almost religious, and she felt hot tears spill from between her lashes and then she was sobbing quietly, steadily, as if her heart would break.

"No, no, you must not cry. Forgive me, Mara. It had to be—" He held her, drinking the tears from her cheek, kissing her wet eyes and crooning to her like a child. She opened her eyes and stared at him in amazement. He might have been an angel—he, who had raped her like a cruel savage taking what he wanted, was at perfect peace. His long dark lashes flickered over the blue eyes, which had gone luminous with pleasure; the mocking mouth was soft with love.

"You do not understand," she said in a distant voice.

"I understand that I was born for you and I would die for you."

"Oh, Desmond," she cried in incoherent grief and rage, "you could have had me for the asking! You only toyed with me, and now—now—you are no better than a rutting animal. I would have come to you so willingly—" The sorrow rose in her and she thought her heart might crack with it. She beat against his chest in helpless frustration, wishing she could kill him. "I can never forgive you now," she sobbed. "Never, never . . ."

He knelt beside the bed, pleading with her in the soft, persuasive voice she might have loved so well, but her sobs abated and she felt herself grow as cold and stony as a statue. She made no move to cover her body, but merely lay—regal in her careless nudity—deaf to his words. When she spoke at last her voice was unfamiliar to them both.

"I wish never to see you again," she said. "I do not hate you, Desmond. You are a subject of complete indifference to me."

She saw his face pale under the finality of her words. She might have pitied him, but how could she pity the man who had raped her? She could have loved him more than anything in the world, but that time was past. He had seen to it.

"Go away," she said. "I don't wish you ill, because you are my cousin. But if you were to die tomorrow, I would not shed a tear."

She closed her eyes, and when she opened them again he was gone.

She left Mrs. Monahan's at dawn, before Brigid awoke and began the morning's clatter in the kitchen. No one saw her go. She wore one of the shabby frocks she had brought with her from home and carried the two cardboard valises which had traveled across the sea with her. She left all her lovely new things hanging in the wardrobe of the room she would never see again. Or almost all of them. Some impulse had made her take the splendid green gown which she had never yet worn, and crush it haphazardly into the larger of the two bags. She would take nothing else *he* had given her, but this, she thought bitterly, she had earned the right to keep. The green gown and the brooch Kathy had given her were all she owned of value in the world.

She began to walk west, heading in the direction of an address she had seen only once, printed on an embossed card. She had no money; the thirty blocks would have to be gone on foot. As the sun came up people looked at her curiously; it was not usual to see a young lady of obvious quality, dressed in a much-mended gown and struggling with two cumbersome valises, walking the streets with a determined and grim expression. Men called out to her occasionally from doorways, but she walked on, oblivious to them.

When she arrived at the street she was looking for it was nine in the morning. It was a surprisingly humble street and very unlike the image she had formed of it. A butcher's boy was coming up from the trademan's entrance of a modest dwelling and she called to him:

"Can you tell me which house belongs to Mr. McSweeney?"

He looked her up and down rudely. "Mr. McSweeney, is it?" he said with a meaningful leer. "Well now, Miss, you're early ain't you?"

She stared straight ahead. She would have to accustom herself to the casual insolences which unprotected women endured, but it was difficult to remain impassive. The boy pointed in the direction of the largest of the houses and said, "You'll like it there. It's much grander inside." He went whistling on his way, turning back to grin at her once or twice.

The door was answered by a man who seemed vaguely familiar. His eyebrows lifted in surprise at sight of her, but his heavy body blocked the door and he asked gruffly what her business might be.

"I should like to see Mr. McSweeney."

"Mr. McSweeney's at his breakfast. He don't see callers afore noon. What's yer name?"

"I am Mara McQuaid. I met Mr. McSweeney at Delmonico's."

The man smiled. "That's why y'look familiar to me, then. McQuaid, is it? And from Mayo, are y'not?"

"I am."

The man stood aside. "Wait here," he instructed. "I'll tell Jim ye're here."

She was shown into a room paneled in ivory and gilt. There were oil paintings on the walls and an Oriental carpet almost as splendid as the one in Constance Burkhardt's Chinese retreat. In the midst of this luxury sat James J. McSweeney, attired in a ruby red dressing gown and Turkish slippers, eating what looked to be a breakfast prepared for a regiment. A sideboard held covered dishes of bacon, kipper, and egg; there were mounds of scones and racks of toast and marmalade, honey, and a steaming pot of India tea. Mr. McSweeney was popping a bit of steak into his mouth with one hand and mopping bread into the yoke of an egg with the other. He looked up and nodded.

"Miss McQuaid," he said in the rough voice she remembered, "Will you have some breakfast?"

She had not planned to accept, but he bellowed an order for another place setting, and in an instant an elderly servant shuffled in and deposited plates and silver in front of her. Reluctantly, she sat at the table opposite him. McSweeney continued to eat in silence, gesturing for her to fill her plate. She swallowed the hot tea gratefully and nibbled at a scone. To her surprise she found she was ravenous.

When her host had finished his mammoth repast he settled back in his chair and studied her with shrewd jet eyes. She felt tongue-tied and awkward and submitted to his scrutiny silently. At last he said in a neutral tone, "You've not come here to share my breakfast, Miss McQuaid. I said I would be happy to help you, and so I will, but you must tell me what I can do. I'm not a mind-reader."

And so she told him. She explained that her father had gone to Chicago for reasons no one understood, that her mother was dead, and that her relative who had pledged himself to help had proved to be a scoundrel. "I cannot depend on anyone else," she said urgently. "I must find my father by myself."

McSweeney's dark brows knitted in thought. "You're not asking me to find your da', then," he said. "You're a young thing to go off west by yourself. What if your father has already left Chicago? What if he's gone to California?"

"Then I will follow him," Mara said firmly. "I will search for him until I find him."

He smiled. "I like a female with a bit of daring to her," he owned. "But if you're to do it all on your own, where do I come in?"

"I have no money at all, and I must start out today. I am asking you to lend me the money." She colored slightly, but her voice was level and assured.

"Today, is it? And I suppose it wouldn't do to send you on a milk train, would it?" He chuckled. "Well, well, I suppose it can be arranged. Only tell me this, Missy—" he leaned across the table toward her, his knowing eyes taking in every detail of her face and body with evident appreciation—"What will you do for me in return?"

"I will pay you back your money when I can."

This time McSweeney guffawed. He tilted back in his chair and roared so loudly the old servant peered through the door in alarm. His eyes squeezed shut; his jowls shook with the force of his mirth and Mara poised herself for flight. He wiped at his eyes with the sleeve of his dressing gown and quieted bit by bit, but small spasms of silent laughter still shook his heavy frame as he spoke.

"Let me understand," he said slowly. "You want me to arrange for you to travel to Chicago, today, by reasonably swift transport. You want me to give you enough money so you'll not starve or be driven to the streets when you arrive. In return, you propose to pay me back . . . sometime. Nothing more."

"Nothing more," Mara agreed.

He looked pensively into his teacup. He rubbed his heavy jaw and sighed. Then he smacked one huge hand on the table, making the chinaware jump and clatter, and said, "Done!"

He imposed only one other condition on their bargain, and that was a small one. Mara must let him know if she left the city of Chicago and keep him posted on her whereabouts. He gave her a list of places in cities from Chicago to San Francisco where she might find a warm welcome upon mentioning his name and reassured her when she demurred. "They won't eat you alive," he said. "No more than I have."

She thanked him for his kindness. She was weary and sad and her body ached and trembled with pain and exhaustion, but she set her eyes on the future and tried not to think of the consequences of her sudden flight.

Something in her demeanor made Mr. McSweeney soften with genuine and heartfelt sympathy. "Tell me," he asked curiously. "Do you know who I am?"

"Yes," she replied. "I know your history."

"What made you so sure I would help you?"

"Because," she said thoughtfully, "you are a self-made man. You remember what it is to be penniless and alone." She paused and then said, all in a rush, "Besides, you are my countryman."

"Correct on all counts," said Mr. McSweeney. "You're a clever girl and a brave one. Bad cess to whoever it is has hurt you."

"Nobody can ever hurt me again," she said defiantly.

"I wouldn't lay odds on that," he said, looking amused. "Still, I'm an excellent judge of character, Missy, and I'll tell you a secret. You'll go far." And so saying James J. McSweeney left the ruins of his breakfast and began to arrange for Mara's departure.

It was the simplest favor he had ever granted.

## Chapter Six

"If Madame would like to see something in a larger size?"

The lady who had been trying, without success, to cram her plump fingers into a pair of white kid gloves looked up in surprise. Mara might have been an inanimate fixture of the shop which, by some miracle, had learned the trick of speech.

"Certainly not," she said with distinct irritation.

Mara sighed softly. Patience in impossible situations had never been one of her virtues, and she thought longingly of the twenty minutes she would soon have for lunch. The shop was on Oak Street, near Dearborn, and if she hurried she could walk to the lake and back before she had to take her place behind the counter again.

"I shall have half a dozen of these," the lady said in her loud, flat voice. "Put them to my account."

In the beginning she had found Chicago an impossible place. For one thing, there were not many Irish here, and Mara missed seeing her countrymen everywhere as she had in New York. For another, it was even hotter here than it had been back East and the black, white-collared frock she wore at work made her feel the sultry heat acutely. What tried her most sorely, though, was the lowliness of her position as clerk in a ladies' haberdashery. She did not think herself unduly proud, but she had never known what it was to take orders all day long from women who treated her like a mote of invisible dust. Mrs. Bronzini, the owner, had pinpointed the problem immediately.

"You're far too striking to work in a ladies' shop, my dear," she had remarked shrewdly after Mara's first day had ended. "It antagonizes the older ones and makes the young ones jealous. You'd do far better in a shop patronized by men." And then she'd made Mara a cup of tea and smiled at her. "Never mind," she'd said. "It's not your fault you were born beautiful, is it? I know you need the work. I only wish you weren't quite so *noticeable.*"

It had been a stroke of fantastic good luck, finding this position so close to her lodgings on Division Street. She had seen the card in the window on her second day in the city; that afternoon she was employed, and she began to like Chicago more. Her lodgings were clean and quiet, although a cut beneath those she had enjoyed with Mrs. Monahan, and there was the lake.

Mara loved Lake Michigan. It fascinated her to see a body of water so large and know it was not the ocean. On the sultriest day the lake sent cool breezes her way, and the broad band of blue could be glimpsed through her single window every morning, shimmering under the first rays of the sun. It was not formidable, like the great, gray Atlantic which had been her mother's grave, yet it was magnificent as a sea.

She sat now on a bench near the Oak Street beach, gazing out over the sparkling water. People turned to look at her frequently, but she did not notice. In truth, the simple black dress heightened her beauty, as did her demurely bound coiffure. The passers-by found her loveliness all the more poignant in its lack of pretense.

The broad expanses of the lake made her think of the great distance she had come, of the wonderful variety and vastness of America. Mr. McSweeney had seen to it that she traveled in a private compartment, and from the broad windows she had watched and marveled at the wonderful scenes that slid by. The wooded green hills of New Jersey and Pennsylvania at times reminded her of home; she pressed her face to the window long after dark had fallen and sat up half the night. The next day there had been new vistas to study. The broad, fertile farmland of Ohio and Indiana had stretched on endlessly, almost tiresome in its calm, abundant richness. There were no famines here, only plenty. To the north lay Wisconsin and Minnesota, those places of mystery and primordial stands of untouched timber, foreign with their euphonious Indian names, and infinitely intriguing. She had seen a family of Indians on the train platform in the early morning hours and had stared, bemused, at their coppery skins and bright black eyes. She thought them a handsome people and hoped to see more of them; she wondered if her father had witnessed these same exciting scenes from another train window and shivered with anticipation and a longing she barely understood.

She had one distressing duty to perform. Somewhere in Ohio she wrote a letter to Roger Winthrop, explaining that she had gone to find her father. She asked him to forgive her for decamping so suddenly, and prayed that he forget about her. She thanked him for his many kindnesses and then paused, frowning, as she tried to conclude. At last she signed it, "Yours, in friendship and affection, Mara McQuaid," and gave it to the porter to mail when the train next stopped. The letter was her last tie to New York, a city she could not think of without feeling pain.

Chicago seemed immense to her, because it was so raw and immediate. When she looked out across Lake Michigan she felt she was perching at the last outpost of civilization, and the feeling was not unpleasant. When it was time to return to the stifling little shop on Oak Street she was refreshed and ready to humor any number of plump matrons who insisted on buying their gloves a size too small.

Toward the end of the afternoon, a man came in to purchase some linen handkerchiefs for his wife. Something in his manner made her think of her father, and she smiled at him so radiantly he took a liberty. He announced that he would like to see some gloves, and nothing would do but that she model them for him.

"Such a soft little hand," he said, glancing about

to make sure they were alone. "Will you let me hold it?"

She stiffened and withdrew her hand. He had mistaken her smile, and now he leaned across the counter, his moustaches lifting as he bared his teeth at her. "I wouldn't half mind taking you to supper one evening," he continued, drooping one eyelid in a rakish wink. "You're a devil of a pretty thing, and I have a special fondness for long raven locks."

"If you've quite finished," Mara said icily, "have the decency to pay your bill and go."

His eyes narrowed angrily. "You girls are all alike," he sneered. "Tease a fellow and then get surly when he tumbles." He paid for his handkerchiefs and left huffily, slamming the door. Mara watched him go, wondering why a friendly smile should be so grossly misinterpreted. Were men so eager to imagine lust in innocent gestures that they threw caution and courtesy to the winds, or was she at fault? He had not really looked like Padraic McQuaid, she realized; so terribly preoccupied as she was with wanting to find him, she saw ghostly shadows of him everywhere.

Often, when she would see a middle-aged man from behind, her heart lurched with sudden panic. What if he should disappear before she could see him properly? She would run along until she came abreast of him; always there was the breathless moment when she saw his face, and always he was a stranger. She had gone to the police, but they had sighed and barely covered their looks of amusement. They had agreed to keep a watch for Padraic as if humoring a child's request. One nice young officer had taken her aside and said: "Isn't there more you can tell us, Miss? It isn't much to go on."

She had tried calling in at political clubs with Irish names, but this yielded no more satisfying result. At the Harp Democratic Organization in the southside slums there'd been a brief glimmer of hope.

"McQuaid?" An aging pol had wrinkled his brow and pondered the name. "There *was* a McQuaid who drank at McGinty's down the street. He was a stranger here."

In the saloon she had stood with flaming face while the rowdy men who lined the bar whistled and called their approval in terms she had never heard spoken aloud. "McQuaid's left," the barman said flatly, "and he'd better come round here no more." He saw her trembling lips then and said, more kindly, "A young fellow, he was, about your age. He'd a limp and one cocked eye. That the one ye're after?"

And so it had gone. At last she placed an advertisement in the "personals" column of the *Tribune*, paying for it from the still generously lined purse Mr. McSweeney had given her. Not a day went by but she expected to hear something; she never allowed herself to think that she would not.

When the long afternoon came to a close, Mrs. Bronzini made her the customary cup of tea and paid her her first week's salary—ten dollars. Mara took half of it and mailed it, that evening, to Mr. McSweeney in New York.

She lost the job a week later. Mrs. Bronzini was loath to turn her out, but there was really no alternative. "You see, dear," she said sadly, wringing her hands, "I have had a complaint, and when that happens there's no end of trouble."

A complaint? Mara was astonished. It seemed a Mrs. Gurley had reported that her husband had been insulted in the shop by a rude and insolent salesgirl. Of course. The man who had been partial to black-haired girls. Mara thought she had never heard anything so base in all her life. "The man is an arrogant swine," she said hotly. "I refused to suffer his intimacies and he became angry."

"I know," her employer whispered wretchedly. "But if Mrs. Gurley takes her custom elsewhere, six or seven others go with her. She is part of a coterie."

Mara understood. Mrs. Bronzini was a widow, the shop her only income. *She* would have to leave, and she would even have to console Mrs. Bronzini, who was weeping openly now. It did seem very hard. She left the Oak Street shop with a week's salary and a dim feeling of panic. It seemed she was back where she had started.

At dinner that night she told the assembled group of boarders she had lost her job, without mentioning the reason. They were a curious group; none was above the age of thirty, yet most of them were prematurely bent and aged from a lifetime of work. Miss Schroth, a thin girl who waited on tables in a teashop downtown, Mr. and Mrs. Kubiak who lived above their iron-mongery but took their meals at the boarding house, the widow Obermeier whose only child had died of influenza, and asthmatic Mr. Thorne—all of them were downtrodden and spiritless. Nevertheless, they were kind, and drank in Mara's cheerful talk with patient attention, as if they were wondering at the queer habits of a creature from another galaxy.

They all murmured sympathetically between bites of over-cooked pork and steamed cabbage, and Mrs. Obermeier, who had always been scandalized by Mara's independence, said: "Have you thought of returning home?"

"What? To Ireland?" Mara laughed. They seemed more doleful than she and she wanted to bring some life into the room. "Perhaps," she teased, "I'll go on the stage."

The Kubiaks gasped, but Mr. Thorne suddenly pushed back his chair and cried triumphantly: "I have it! The very thing!" He disappeared and came back with the evening paper, which he unfolded and scanned portentously until he had located the item he wanted. He read aloud: " 'Young ladies are needed to pose for picture postals of the valentine variety. Our master photographer seeks only pleasant, respectable, youthful ladies with well-formed features and abundant hair. The very highest rates will be paid.' " He put down the paper and inquired all round: "Nothing wrong in that, is there? Only respectable ladies, it says."

The others appeared doubtful, but later that evening Miss Schroth tapped timidly at Mara's door. She darted in, clasping a book. "I have something to show you," she whispered, withdrawing a card from between the pages. "This is what they look like," she hissed.

Mara held the card curiously. It showed the face of a pretty and vapid young girl who simpered from beneath a broad-brimmed picture hat. She was surrounded by an immense wreath of roses and lilies upon which two turtle-doves perched. The photograph had been tinted in highly unnatural colors, so that the girl's lips were colored a violent pink and her eyes an inky blue. "Merry Mischief" was the sentiment. "There seems no harm in it," Mara said reflectively.

"I bought it because I thought I might do my hair like hers," confided Miss Schroth.

Mara had seen the photograph of Constance Burkhardt executed by the great Joseph Byron and thought it magnificent; she had a vivid image of the sneer which would overtake Constance's face at the mere thought of "Merry Mischief" and decided on the spot to apply the very next day.

The photographer was much more taciturn than Mara had expected. He was a large, moody-looking Swede with pale eyebrows and a long jaw. He came out from behind a desk piled mountainously high with plates and papers to greet her.

"I have come to see about the job," she explained. "I'm called Mara McQuaid." He stared at her dismally. "I have never been photographed," she continued, disconcerted by his silence. Was it possible he found her so unacceptable he would not even deign to speak to her? He mumbled something she could not understand and brought a chair from the pile of clutter so she could sit. He continued to stare at her, fixing her with his gloomy gaze until she began to fear that he was deaf and mute.

His name was written in peeling gilt letters on the door: Alfred J. Olsen. "Mr. Olsen," she said, "if you find me unsuitable you've only to say so and I will go."

"No!" It emerged as a shout, startling them both. "Please, you must forgive me," he stammered, "but I could not believe you were real."

"I am real," she assured him.

"Young lady, have you any idea what sort of women come here?"

"The notice said 'respectable ladies,'" replied Mara in alarm.

"Indeed, yes, indeed—most of them are respectable enough, but only this morning I have had to turn away two ladies above fifty years of age, and a half-dozen who were not, ah, well-favored. It is very difficult, Miss, to tell women they will not do. Every woman is beautiful in some way or another, but the camera records only what God has seen fit to grant externally. And then there are lovely ladies who do not photograph well . . ." He sighed, as if the sorrows of his work were more than he could bear. "Now you," he continued, "are *uniquely* well-favored, if I may say so. Excuse my bluntness, but you are more than a penny valentine." He spread his hands helplessly. "Indeed, you are so much more I wonder if you will do at all? You ought to have been painted by Botticelli, Miss McQuaid, not photographed in hearts and flowers."

Mara said nothing, and at the end of his diatribe

Mr. Olsen morosely went to set up his equipment.
He explained to her that he would combine natural
light with artificial to eliminate shadows, and begged
her to make herself comfortable. At the rear of his
cluttered studio there was a large table covered with
hats of every description. There were picture hats
and boaters and bonnets and even a hat made entirely of swansdown. She selected a straw boater and
then discarded it for a wide satin confection with
pink rosettes. "Oh please, Miss McQuaid," Mr. Olsen called, "don't trouble yourself with those foolish
hats." He seemed highly embarrassed, and even
more so when he was obliged to ask her to sit before
the worn velour curtain which formed his back-
drop.

"Where are the roses and turtle-doves?" she asked.

"I add them later," he said humbly.

It was a simple business, really. She looked over
one shoulder toward Mr. Olsen, who crouched behind his camera, magnesium flare aloft in one hand.
She remembered the girl in Miss Schroth's picture
and forced a wide, bright smile. "Ah, no, Miss Mc-
Quaid," the photographer called gently, "in your
case there is no need to smile so vehemently. Perhaps if you pictured a loved one?"

She thought of her father, but that was too sad.
She hit upon the plan of dwelling on the village in
Mayo where she had been born, but before she
could do so the image of a face imprinted itself
insistently on her inner eye. Seconds later she had
banished that image, which in fact she hated bitterly,
but in the interim her expression had been one of
rapture. It was then that the magnesium flare went

off in a great cataclysm of blinding light and smoke, and Mr. Olsen had produced the finest valentine postal of his career.

He paid her ten dollars—as much as she had earned in a week at the shop on Oak Street!—and said he would be honored to photograph her whenever she liked. He promised to send her a print when it was finished, and then he ushered her quickly to the door. He was more comfortable with beauty when it had been captured, immobilized, by his camera—the real thing made him nervous and inexpressibly sad.

She posed twice more for Mr. Olsen, but nothing was ever as glorious as his first effort, which he had printed in sepia tones without the indignity of garish tints and called "Hibernian Beauty." She had much free time, but she couldn't summon up the old enthusiasm for wandering which had gripped her in the East. She was afraid news would come of her father while she was away, or that he himself might come to her and find her gone. She continued to sit by the lake for an hour or so each day, and that and the pallid conversation at dinner-time were her sole diversions.

For the first time in her life she was, quite simply, lonely. In the early days in New York her loneliness had been tinged with the realization that soon things would change, but now she began to fear there would be no change. One day she saw a girl who reminded her of Kathleen Daly and felt a longing to see Kathy, to laugh with her over inconsequential things, and then it came to her with peculiar force that she could never see Kathy again after what had happened in New York.

She went to sleep early and rose early. She attempted to talk to Mr. Olsen one day while he was photographing her, and although he tried to be friendly she could see he wished she would be silent. She existed for him as a face only, which was as it should be. Once she went to pay a call on her old employer, Mrs. Bronzini, but that lady was so filled with guilt at having dismissed her the visit was strained. And so she sat, feeling the great, raw energy of Chicago thrumming around her without being moved by it. She knew there were vast stockyards on the edge of town where children toiled from dawn until the late hours of the night—witnessing the bloody slaughter, mopping up reeking entrails from the floor, and breaking their health before they were even as old as she. The world was unjust, and she reproved herself for being so forlorn when countless others knew far more misery, but it was cold comfort.

It was during the days of her darkest depression that Roger appeared in Chicago; long afterward she would understand that if he had come earlier or later things would never have happened as they did . . .

He was posted in front of her lodgings on Division Street, scanning the streets anxiously, his young face alert for the first glimpse of her. People turned to stare at his smart, eastern attire, casting admiring looks at the well-tailored suit he wore with such casual elegance. She saw him but could not believe her eyes. Her throat went dry and her heart pounded alarmingly at her ribs when she saw it was neither a remarkable resemblance nor a trick of the light, but Roger himself. She went almost faint for a moment. He had followed her to Chicago and she knew a blinding, fierce sense of gratitude for his loyalty. She tried to call his name but could not; like a creature in a nightmare she stood frozen in her tracks. He turned and saw her and the expression on his face was one of overpowering joy. If her pounding heart had been caused by surprise and relief at seeing his dear, familiar face, his own reaction was purely ecstatic. He ran to her and then they were embracing in the street. His eyes were wet with tears as he held her close and searched her face hungrily. He was unable to speak and afraid to let her go for fear she'd disappear again.

"Roger, I'm so happy you're here," she cried, unable to restrain herself. It was wrong to encourage him, but she had been so lonely, and now the man who had been kinder to her than anyone on earth was shielding her in his strong arms, and oh, how handsome he was—she had forgotten—and how gentle, and altogether lovable!

They went inside the lodging house and there—a thousand miles from the parlor where he had first kissed her—she felt his lips on hers and heard him say: "I told you I would die without you. I would go to the ends of the earth to find you, Mara." This time she was roused in a new way and felt with a shock of recognition that her body—no longer so innocent as it had been—was achingly alive to his touch.

"We must never be separated again," he murmured with a frightening intensity she had never
before heard in his voice. "Promise me—promise
me you'll never leave me . . ."

They were married a week later. Mara Winthrop,
who had so lately been dismissed from Mrs. Bronzini's and posed for valentine postals, found herself
wife to the heir of one of the largest fortunes in the
East. They stayed at Roger's suite in the Blackstone
Hotel until he could find a house. Her wedding night
set the pattern for all the days and nights to come,
but they had married in such haste she had never
considered all the consequences.

Roger went on his knees before her, circling her
waist with reverent hands and laying his face against
her breast as if she were a holy icon. Her body, beneath the nightdress, was trembling, and he kissed
her hands and begged her not to be afraid. It never
occurred to him that her flesh quivered with eager
anticipation, and so he gentled her, proceeding so
slowly with his chaste caresses that at last she flung
her arms around him and pressed her body to his,
urging his passion. When he carried her to the bed
she repressed a cheer of exaltation, but even lying
beside her on their marriage bed he withheld himself,
touching her with adoring hands as if she might
break. It seemed hours had passed when he entered
her, and she threw her legs around him with abandon
only to feel him withdraw, shocked at her aggression.
She lay then, demure and quiet, until his passion was
roused beyond endurance and he could no longer
restrain himself. Then the lovely stirrings of pleasure
began for her, and she gave herself up to the rhythm

of it—advance and retreat—cherishing the sensation that rose to engulf her so sweetly, crying out softly in pleasure and release. It was not quite as she had remembered; the violent ecstasy she had known but would not allow herself to think of was missing. Still, she was warm and quivering with happiness, and she reached out to touch her husband.

He was lying beside her, silent and motionless, his body rigid with hurt. "What is it, Roger?" Her voice was still slurred and soft; she could not imagine why he drew away from her so sharply.

"Someone has gone before me," he said wonderingly. "I never dreamed—I never thought—"

And then he began questioning, his voice rapping out in sharp, staccato notes which pierced her through. *"Who was he? Who has made love to you? What is his name?"* His face altered until he was almost unrecognizable to her. Already he was less boyish than he had been, and she alone was responsible for the look of suffering in his deep-set, hazel eyes. Sometimes he became silent and looked at her with mute reproach, but then a sullen rage would overtake him and he would repeat the questions, over and over, the light of true obsession in his ravaged face. "Where did it happen? Was it in Ireland? On the ship? *Tell me, Mara, I must know.*" Or again: "Was it McSweeney? How do you think I found you? I went to Mrs. Monahan and Brigid told me you had been asking questions about that blackguard. I went to him, Mara, and I paid him money to get your address . . . Do you think I enjoyed it? To stand in a room with scum like that and humble myself like a bootblack? Was it McSweeney? Did he rob me of my bride?"

Mara had huddled in the furthest corner of the room, away from him. She was shivering with fright and exhaustion. How could she have thought it would make no difference to him? His jealousy was strong as ever his tender love had been. She longed to comfort him, but she could never tell him the truth. When the image of the blond seaman who had nearly assaulted her on board the *Alberta* came to her rescue she grasped at it, lying to Roger with desperate skill, pleading with him to forget that she had been raped. "It is of no importance, now," she said.

He regarded her as he might a lunatic. "What was his name? Only tell me his name, Mara. I will have him killed. What was his name? Did you fight for your honor or were you as eager as you've been with me? Did he take you only once? *Twice?*"

"I do not know his name," she said dully.

"This will always come between us," Roger groaned. "I will never forget, Mara. You will never be the same to me."

In the morning he was all contrition, and for several days she believed the matter was done with. Then she awakened in the middle of the night to find him staring down at her, the terrible light glowing in his eyes, his hands picking distractedly at the cord of his dressing gown. "My sister told me you were not a virgin," he said, with a bitter laugh. "I called her disgusting, but in truth it was you, not she, who was disgusting. I will never see her again, Mara. I could not bear to admit to her that she was right."

In the morning he wept, kissing her hands and begging her to forgive him. "I would die without you," he repeated. "You are my life."

Mara wept too, in pity for him and fear for herself.

They went to live in a house removed some distance from the city. It stood on a bluff overlooking Lake Michigan, and there was no single room in its enormous expanse in which she ever felt at home. It belonged to a railroad tycoon who was traveling in Europe for a year, and all the furnishings and the entire staff of servants were his. The lake, which had always filled her with peace, seemed to overrun the broad windows and terrify her with its vast, impersonal murmur. When autumn came the waters turned gray and she shut the curtains, shivering.

The house suited Roger perfectly. They seldom went out and the solitude of the lonely bluff kept Mara always close to him. They knew nobody in Chicago. Once friends of the tycoon came by to inquire as to the Winthrops' comfort, and Mara felt herself half-mad with relief to see normal, cheerful faces in her drawing room. Afterward Roger insisted she had smiled too much, had flaunted herself shamelessly before the guests. "Did the man at sea look like one of them?" he asked. "Tell me what he looked like, Mara? Was he big? Very strong? Tell me!"

Always, when his fits of jealousy had subsided, he was abject in his apologies. Often at dinner she would find a small, velvet-lined box beside her plate; obediently she would lift the pearls or sapphires or diamonds from their nest and put them on, thanking him with feigned enthusiasm. Dressmakers came to the house, and milliners and, as the winter drew on, a furrier. He saw that she had everything she could possibly need and always he watched her, his eyes alight with proprietary love, in everything she did. She could not read a book without finding him perched on the arm of her chair, peering down at the pages. She could not walk on the bluff above the lake because he was afraid she might fall. Finally, she could not enjoy the exquisite delicacy with which he made love to her, for fear her pleasure would trigger his jealousy.

October passed, and then November, and still she had heard nothing of her father. Roger had continued to insert notices in every paper; he had had bills printed and distributed about Chicago, announcing a thousand-dollar reward for anyone who could give information about the whereabouts of Padraic McQuaid. He had promised to help her, and in this he remained scrupulously fair. Of course, the lure of money brought a deluge of replies, but each of them led nowhere. Mara had been sure one of the letters was legitimate, but the man in question proved to be a Scot named McKay, and the writer of the letter a penniless scoundrel panting after the reward.

In early December there was a snowfall, and Mara momentarily forgot her unhappiness in her wonder and delight. She had never seen such snow, and she threw on a fur cloak and ran outdoors, stooping to gather great heaps of the powdery white substance and hold it to her face. She put her tongue to it and laughed out loud, and then—sure nobody

was watching—she packed the snow into a firm ball
and threw it far out over the gray and frozen lake.
She remained for some time playing like a child,
until her frozen feet and numb fingers prompted
her to go inside. Her cheeks were scarlet and
flushed with cold and exertion, her eyes glowing
and alive. Roger was nowhere to be seen and she
realized with a pang that she was happier thus. In
fact, it had been the nicest day she had known
since their marriage.

It was the night of the snowfall that Roger chose
to commence a new interrogation. Mara was brushing her hair, preparing to slip into bed, when he
entered the room with a preoccupied look. "I have
been thinking, Mara," he began in deceptively bland
tones, "about your unfortunate episode at sea. It
would explain much, set my mind at rest, if you
could answer one question."

She set her brush down wearily and met his
glance in the mirror. She thought she had heard
all there was to say on the subject, but Roger had
hit upon a new set of questions, and these were
more dangerous to her than any of the others.

"Did your cousin know of the rape?"

Mara felt she had been slapped; the shock drove
through her so thoroughly she saw her eyes grow
wild in the glass and was powerless to stop them.

"Because if he did," Roger continued pensively,
"his attitude toward me was quite proper. I thought
him a boor, but he was acting in your best interests, dearest."

The room had become suffocating to her. She

swayed dizzily and caught herself, palms against the glass.

"I should like to thank him," said Roger. "Perhaps I will write to him; although I don't know where he is, do you? Shall we search for him, Mara, as we are doing for your father? *Would it make you happy to see Mr. O'Connell?*"

"He knows nothing," Mara whispered. "Nothing. I do not wish to see him."

"He once said he would kill me if you accepted my proposal," Roger chuckled. "I don't suppose he meant it."

"Leave me in peace," Mara begged. "You will torture me to death, Roger. Please, leave me." She had begun to cry, and instantly he was beside her, kissing away the tears, caressing her flowing hair and allowing his hands to slip lower, beneath her lacy peignoir, to her naked back. He held her gently, his fingers tracing the line of her backbone with feathery movements. His other hand undid the ribbons at her throat.

"Mara, darling," he crooned, baring her breasts and lowering his lips to them with infinite tenderness, "I only want to make you happy."

She watched helplessly in the mirror, seeing her pearl-pink nipples rise to the coaxing ministrations of his lips, noticing absently how the light struck auburn from his hair as he bent to her willing body, the body which was once more betraying her in its eagerness to welcome him. "Yes," he crooned, lifting his boyish face from her throbbing breasts, "I think we must definitely find Mr. O'Connell and thank him."

She screamed, and then screamed again. She flung herself away from him and stood, panting, against the wall. His eyes registered nothing more than a dumb bewilderment; he did not know, after all. Or so she thought when she went to him, pulling him into her arms and trying to explain that she was over-wrought, not herself. He put her to bed then, drawing the coverlets up snug beneath her chin and kissing her forehead.

"I will not mention your cousin again if it distresses you," he promised. "But I understand now what he meant. I, too, would kill if someone tried to take you from me. I would kill him, and then, Mara darling, I would have to kill you, too." His hand rested briefly on her face in a loving caress, and then he left her to sleep, if sleep would come . . .

From that time on she knew herself to be in danger. She longed to confide in someone, to ask for help, but there was no one. On the rare occasions when she and Roger drove to the city he was always by her side, and none of the servants who ran her home so efficiently and well had ever shown any sign of warmth to her. Even if one of them agreed to post a letter for her, to whom could she write? She pitied Roger so intensely she sometimes thought her heart would break for him. He suffered so, and she was the last person who could alleviate his anguish. Once he fell asleep, after one of his jealous rages had run its course as suddenly and completely as a child, and she held him in her arms, kissing his unfurrowed brow and thinking how tranquil and sweet he seemed in slumber. But soon he awoke and accused her of thinking of another while she lay beside him. It was the first day of the new year.

On a bleak day in March she thought bitterly of how she had imagined herself lonely in Chicago before he came to claim her. She was a hundred times more lonely now, and her solitude was the more painful because there seemed no end to it.

"What are you thinking?" He had come silently into the morning room, stalking her, not able to let her out of his sight for a moment. "I remember," she said, hitting on a plan, "you once told me I would love your mother, and she me. Why could we not make a trip to Boston, Roger? I have never met her."

Roger shook his head sadly, as if at the folly of a child. "That is no longer possible," he said. "Once I should have welcomed taking you to her, but I was innocent of your true character in those days. My mother is a lady, Mara."

"I am a lady too," she replied heatedly. For the first time she felt neither pity for him nor fright at the ingenuity of his torture. "If you dislike my character so much, Roger, perhaps we should separate. I cannot bear to live like this."

She saw that he was shaking with a barely concealed excitement. He had not noticed her words, which only a month ago would have thrown him into a fit of despair. Still staring at her, he withdrew a small square of paper and placed it on the table between them.

"See what I've found," he said in a curious voice. "You will accuse me of trespassing on your private effects and I'm certainly guilty of that, but it's all for your own good, dearest." He smiled. "Look at it," he commanded. "A pretty sight, eh Mara?"

She saw her own face looking up at her from the postal card. It was the one Mr. Olsen had called "Hibernian Beauty"—she remembered sitting for it so clearly she might have smiled if not for the sharp pang of loss the image brought her. The rapturous girl Mr. Olsen had captured with his lens was now a stranger. Lonely she may have been, and penniless, but at least she had been independent and free, her life ahead of her. She had sold that freedom for the promise of Roger's warmth and ardor and love, and was much the poorer now.

"That you've allowed yourself to pose for something so vulgar as this," Roger said contemptuously, "comes as no surprise to me. I wonder if you realize what it means to me? Hundreds of men are now free to stare at my wife's face for the price of a penny. Some of them may press their lips to the photograph . . . imagine vile things . . . and this monster Olsen, the man who led you to shame yourself like this . . . did he take liberties with you? Did he touch you, Mara, help you to arrange your hair?"

"Imagine what you like," she said in a listless voice. "I am done with making apologies. I no longer care what you think." And then she turned from him and walked away, feeling numb. His voice, when he called her name, was almost a shriek. She continued to walk away, but when he shrieked again she whirled about in alarm. He was pointing a small and deadly-looking derringer at her, his hand trembling violently. "I must protect you!" he called across the room. "I will always be armed from now on, Mara. God knows how many men will try to find you when they have seen this filthy picture. No doubt they think I'm blind—a weak cuckold who sees nothing—but they'll be surprised!"

She fled to her room and wedged a chair beneath the handle of the door. He did not follow her, but she sat all night watching the door and plotting for her life. Once she caught sight of herself in the mirror and could not recognize her face. The eyes, huge with fear and determination both, seemed demented. She heard him go heavily up the stairs and into his own room, but still she did not stir until the morning came. Then she took her lovely pearls and a pair of diamond ear-clips from the jewel box and went to the servants' hall below-stairs. Here she found Violet, the kitchen maid, who seemed least forbidding of the house staff.

"I would like you to have a day off today, Violet," she said.

"Yes, Ma'am." The girl's thin, sullen face brightened.

"I will require you to do something for me. It will not be easy, but I will pay you well."

Violet's eyes widened with curiosity and distrust. When Mara placed the jewels in her hands she gasped in shock and nearly dropped them into the pot she had been scouring.

"Take these to the city, and sell them. You will get a good price; they are most valuable. Bring the money to me when you return and I will give you fifty dollars for your trouble."

The girl's eyes glittered. She pressed her thin arms

to her sides to keep from trembling at the thought of so much money. "Does Mr. Winthrop know, Ma'am?"

"He must never know," Mara said urgently. "If you tell him there will be a tragedy, Violet. Something dreadful will happen."

Violet absorbed this information, chewing her inner lip contemplatively. "What if they ask me where I got such jewels as these? What if they call the coppers on me?"

It occurred to Mara that she and Violet were probably the same age. She did not want to involve the girl, but it seemed her only chance. "You will have to go some place where questions are not asked," she said evenly. "Do you understand, Violet?"

The girl nodded, beginning to enjoy the intrigue. "One more thing," Mara said hastily. "You will go to a carriage-hire office and order one to come round for me at five tomorrow morning. Tell them your employer must go to a sick friend, and accept any terms they may give you, no matter how dear."

"Is Madam coming back?" Violet inquired shyly. "After she visits the friend?" Their eyes met and held.

"No. For your own safety I must beg you not to let Mr. Winthrop know you have helped me. Not ever."

"No, Ma'am, I won't."

Mara's last day in the house she had come to hate passed more slowly than any she could remember. She began to fear that Violet might disappear with the jewels and never come back, and she felt sick at the stealth and wiliness of the scheme. She hated paying for her freedom with jewels Roger had given her, but he made her a prisoner, and prisoners, she had come to learn, were notoriously inventive in their efforts to break free . . .

She dined with him that night in a state of giddy terror. Violet had returned, and Mara was now two thousand dollars richer. She suspected the kitchen-maid of having earned more than fifty dollars, but one thief could not accuse another. Roger, whose eyes had searched out all her secrets in the past, seemed oblivious tonight. He was courteous and charming, the soul of husbandly concern when she complained of a headache soon after dinner. He kissed her brow and suggested she retire early.

She wondered if the little derringer lay snugly in his pocket, and shivered. What had happened to the handsome boy who had taken her on a picnic to Brooklyn? Had he disappeared forever, or was there a chance that he might yet come back? She wanted to say goodbye to the other, earlier, Roger, and beg his forgiveness for causing him so much pain, but he was lost to her.

Love, she thought, was a dangerous and violent business—mysterious and cruel. She had once called Roger her dearest friend and now—all because she had married him—he was her mortal enemy.

## Chapter Seven

"There! Do you see?" There was a great commotion and a jostling as everyone in the car pushed to the windows.

Mara had been drowsing, lulled by the train's steady rhythm. She thought of the wheels hungrily eating up the distance, churning across the prairies and plains of America, transporting them so easily over the great pathway to the West. Not so many years ago these plains had witnessed the migration of countless families in wagons, had felt the rolling movement over the ancient trail which had been imprinted deep in the earth by wild animals and Indians for a thousand years. The bones of those pioneers lined the way west; their hardships had been unendurable, yet many had survived, even prospered. Those who had not fallen prey to disease or drought, or to marauding parties of Sioux and Snake, Shoshone and Cheyenne, had lived to see the gold fields of Colorado and California.

A great cheer went up from the passengers in

Mara's car. She opened her eyes and saw that they were clustered at the windows, pointing and exclaiming. The missionary's wife who had boarded in Missouri turned excitedly to Mara, crying out: "There! In the distance—the mountains!" Far off across the plains, rising like a ghostly barricade, shimmering unsteadily so that they might have been a mirage or a figment of the fevered imagination—were the Rockies.

She had not thought anything could move her so profoundly again, but as she stared a great emotion stirred in her, and she cheered with the others, tears rising to her eyes . . ..

The train was a branch of the Chicago Great Western, and all along the line—in Kansas City, St. Joseph and Omaha—people had boarded it with an air of almost religious fervor. They were going west, to fulfill the lifelong dream which Mara now saw was the key to the American spirit—a dream of new beginnings which sent them restlessly wandering to the very edges of their continent. Many of them, born too late to experience the excitement and adventure of the gold rush in '49, were the logical heirs of those who had packed children and possessions a decade later in wagons optimistically emblazoned: *Pike's Peak or bust!* Now they had a dream of their own, born of the fantastic rumors that had drifted east about the fortune in gold coming from the camps at Cripple Creek.

Some, like the Presbyterian minister and his wife, were not concerned with wordly riches but with the spiritual decline they brought. The Reverend and Mrs. Hadley had despaired of bringing the Lord to their decadent congregation in Kansas City. Mrs. Hadley confided to Mara that she and her husband planned to educate the Indians, to gently wean them from the old beliefs and bring them to the true God, Who alone could make their lives on the reservations meaningful. "They have been so tossed about, from pillar to post," Mrs. Hadley said vaguely. "I know Angus and I can help them find peace. Superstition is the bane of civilization, dear, and we will cure them of it with love and patience."

Another passenger was an artist who had been commissioned by an Eastern magazine to send back his impressions of life in the gold camps at Cripple Creek. He sketched incessantly, making impressions of the great, barren plains of Nebraska, of the crowds who milled about on the platform whenever the train stopped, or of his fellow travelers.

Only Mara seemed to have no firm purpose to her journey. She did not dream of gold, and as for the Indians, she thought them splendid as they were. She had once hoped to see more of them; now, at every stop, her wish was gratified. At Omaha she observed an aged Sioux, still tall and upright, who stood apart from the others. He was dressed in a broadcloth suit too short for him. The trousers ended comically somewhere between his knee and ankle, and the white man's hat perched incongruously on his head; the two long plaits of iron-gray hair which framed his face made nonsense of the jaunty cap. But his face, which Mara studied with a sense of awe, was the most dignified she had ever seen. The hawk nose and firm lips were proud and untouched by age; the broad cheekbones seemed to thrust through the dark skin like knives. He stared straight ahead, and Mara knew she had never seen eyes so sad, or so wise. No—Mrs. Hadley could bring nothing to this man. It was an impertinence to try. Still worse was the attitude of the Reverend Angus, who often opined that the red man's problem was simply this: He was childlike and simple and could not grasp the superior and complex workings of the white mind.

The artist was sketching eagerly. His pen flew over the paper, but he was dissatisfied with his efforts and crumpled the sketch angrily, tossing it into the aisle with a look of disgust. "It won't come right," he exclaimed. "They are still too far away to capture." He came to sit beside her, looking at her with the admiring and curious air she had turned from before.

"You are a great mystery to all of us," he said without preamble. "Forgive me for being blunt, but it's my way."

"Sometimes it is a virtue to be blunt," said Mara.

"What takes you West? We've all speculated, you know, about who you might be. Mrs. Hadley believes you're fleeing from a great tragedy, but then—" he lowered his voice conspiratorially—"she is a bit of a fool, don't you think?"

"I have given up judging people," Mara replied. "I have been too frequently wrong."

The man looked from her face to the ring on her finger. "Are you a widow?" His eyes took in the gray velvet traveling suit and moved upward to appraise her face, which was pale and composed, dominated by the enormous golden eyes. "If you are," he murmured, "you are the youngest and most lovely widow I've ever seen."

"Yes, I am a widow," Mara said dully, "but I have no wish to talk about myself. I am going West because I have never been—that is the sum total of my mystery."

"I beg your pardon," he said. "I will not disturb you again." He retired to his seat, looking properly rebuffed. When it was time for dinner, Mara went to the dining car alone, as was her custom. She took one glass of wine with her meal and then retired to her sleeping compartment. She was by far the wealthiest traveler, to judge by her clothing and accommodations. She was also the only one who dwelt, not on the future, but the past.

She sometimes dreamed she was in the carriage again, leaving the house she had shared with Roger, speeding away in the early morning hours while he slept, innocent of her flight. In her dreams the air in the carriage was thick with the wavering light of premonition. When they arrived in Chicago she leaped down and began to run, but the driver called after her: "Here, Miss! You haven't paid me!" And always, as the dream-Mara turned, her hands overflowing with dollar bills, the face of the driver melted away and became Roger's face. Then she would wake, her heart hammering piteously, her hands clenched to her breast with terror. She would press her head to the window and let the plains, flat and eerie in the moonlight, soothe and lull her.

In reality, everything had gone smoothly. She had booked her train at the Great Western offices, and wandered the streets of Chicago all that morning.

She had been afraid to linger anywhere too long;
her greatest horror was that Roger might be at the
station, drawing his net around her and carrying her
back to the house on the lake. She was not using
his name. She had booked as Mrs. McQuaid, and
even that was dangerous. She had thought to use a
false name, but something had stopped her. She
had almost given up hope of finding her father, but
if Padraic were alive and still in America the least
she could do was to keep her name so he might find
her.

Her only reason for going west rather than in any
other direction could be laid to a remark she had
overheard once in the streets of Chicago. "Can you
imagine?" a woman had exclaimed to her companion. "He left one day on business and never came
back. They traced him to Colorado, finally. He'd
come down with gold fever!"

They were in the mountains when she awoke,
descending toward Denver. She began to collect her
things together, musing on how incongruous her
cardboard valises must seem to those who covertly
admired her expensive clothing. They were the same
bags she had brought from Mayo and later carried
through the streets of New York when she went in
search of Mr. McSweeney. They had been with her
when she arrived in Chicago, containing only her
few poor frocks and the green ball-gown she had
never yet put on. Now they were packed with costly
garments Roger had paid for, and lined with the
money his jewels had fetched.

When she stepped from the train at Denver, a
cloak lined in sable protected her from the knifing

winds of a Rocky Mountain March. Soon the snows would melt from the high mountains and pour down into the waters of the swollen Platte. The streets would be thick with mud. But for now, she saw with delight, the city lay blanketed in thick, crisp snow. She wanted to bend and scoop it up as she had done that day above Lake Michigan, but she restrained herself. After all, in two months she would be nineteen years old.

She had become used to living luxuriously, but the Windsor Hotel took her breath away with its outrageous opulence. There were five stories of roccoco splendor; diamond-dust chandeliers cast their radiant dazzle on a scene of international wealth so potent Mara scented it before she had even entered the ornate lobby. She took a room, bravely paying in advance and reckoning that at this rate her money would fast disappear. Mingling about in the Windsor's reception halls were a display of characters so diverse she had all she could do not to stare. There were well-dressed, understated gentlemen and flamboyant men wearing diamond stickpins, a brace of titled English, some ladies so heavily painted one wondered if they could possibly be respectable, and an Italian diva who was appearing at the Tabor Grand Opera House in a performance of *Carmen.* There were Frenchmen and Spaniards and half-castes in impeccable costume; there were Irish and Scots and Italians and Poles. She thought she would be anonymous in such a splendid group, but heads turned to examine her with discreet interest as she passed through the crowd, and several gentlemen tipped their hats to her.

In her room she accomplished her first task, which was to write once again to Mr. McSweeney, telling him of her whereabouts and enclosing the remainder of the money she owed to him. She concluded by begging him not to tell anyone where she was. Frowning, she underscored the word *anyone* in heavy black ink, and signed herself. Then she rang for a porter, handed him the letter to post, and set about unpacking. She counted her money, found she still had well over a thousand dollars, and went to bathe and change her clothing.

The warm, scented water encouraged drowsiness, but Mara was busy calculating. She would surely have to find work; even a thousand dollars would not last forever. But what sort of work might a girl like herself hope to find in Denver? Coming from the station she had noticed dozens of saloons and gambling houses and she could not imagine finding employment there. Certainly Denver was too raucous and fun-loving to have much use for such innocent diversions as penny postals, and she never wanted to work in a shop again. She rose from the bath with a sense of determination. She stood for a moment, nude before the glass, and looked at her body. Her flesh was rosy from the bath; she seemed to be blushing in the heat of passion. Her full, high breasts and proud nipples, the small round waist, gently flaring hips and long, elegant legs were the same as they had ever been. And yet what strange things had happened to this body in the last ten months! It had been awakened violently, returned to chastity, only to be reawakened and know a few brief moments of sweetness before it once more became the battleground of conflicting passions. She remembered the ecstatic sensations of love dimly, as if it had all happened long ago, and then she covered herself and set about the long process of brushing and coiling and pinning the heavy masses of her lustrous hair. She was done with men forever, she told herself. Done with men and done with love. From now on she would think only of surviving as best she could.

She selected a violet satin walking suit that fastened with black frogs over her bosom. Underneath she wore a frothy blouse of cream silk. An amethyst brooch winked from her throat; a matching hat-pin secured her velvet bonnet. When she had finished she took a much-folded paper from her personal effects and read carefully.

*Mrs. Underwood, 32 Larimer Street* was written in Mr. McSweeney's bold hand. It was the only name he had seen fit to recommend in Denver. Mara put on her cloak and descended to the lobby. She hailed a carriage and gave the address, quickly, before she could change her mind. "They won't eat you alive," McSweeney had said, "no more than I have."

It was nearly noon, and now she saw the other half of Denver. If the people at the Windsor were impossibly flamboyant, the milling crowds in the snowy streets were ten times as strange. She saw grizzled men with red eyes and wild beards just down from the mountain camps. They were half-frozen and caked with dirt and mud, and yet they capered and roared with glee. There were Chinese and Blacks among them, and once she saw a blond giant of a man with his Arapahoe wife and stared, transfixed, at the beauty of the coffee-colored infant the Indian woman carried on her back. They passed the opera house and turned into streets crowded with saloons and disreputable looking places of every conceivable nature; the door to a faro house stood ajar and she could see the room, thickly packed with gamblers who shouted and drank with demented gaiety. Mrs. Underwood's house stood some way from the most densely crowded part of Larimer Street, and Mara breathed a sigh of relief. The large frame dwelling looked respectable and quiet.

Mrs. Underwood had to be wakened by her maid and sent word for Mara to come to her bedroom. She was propped on a mountainous assortment of pillows, sipping hot chocolate and eating bow-tie pastries. Mara wondered if all Mr. McSweeney's friends granted audiences at breakfast. She took a seat on the chaise longue to which her hostess gestured. Mrs. Underwood appraised her at length with shrewd eyes. "So," she said finally, "Jim sent you, did 'e?"

She was a Cockney who had learned to speak in the flat accents of her adopted country, but it was early for her and she dropped her h's recklessly. She saw the Irish girl's look of alarm and gave a raucous laugh.

"Don't worry, duck. This is America! We don't 'ave to 'ate each other 'ere." She popped a biscuit into her mouth and chewed happily. "I've always liked the Irish," she said with an air of finality. "Jim and me was good friends in San Francisco. I fancy a man 'oo knows what he's after." She dusted crumbs from her ample bosom and pushed her tray aside. "Don't mind me," she said. "I'll just make the old face presentable and you can tell me about yourself."

She went to her dressing table and peered into the glass. "You mayn't believe me," she said wistfully, "but I was once almost as pretty as you." She pulled at her heavy cheeks with mock gloom, and set about rubbing a variety of oils and creams into her face. She was a large, buxom woman——still attractive and possessed of quantities of golden hair which Mara suspected were false. She watched in fascination while Mrs. Underwood began to paint her face.

Over the cream she applied a thin layer of rosy liquid, working with great absorption. When this was accomplished she commenced to color her cheeks, following the curve of the once handsome bones, blending deftly, until some of their original beauty was restored. "Well, go on, love," she said impatiently, taking up a little brush and dipping it in a pot of black paint, "I don't 'ear you talking."

"I'm called Mara McQuaid. I will be nineteen in May. I was born in County Mayo, and came with my mother to America last year. We were to join my father, only——only she died at sea and I have never found him."

Mrs. Underwood clucked sympathetically, holding her eyes wide open so that the black on her lashes would not smear. Mara found it difficult to tear her gaze from the fascinating process.

"I went to Chicago and married, but my husband died . . ."

"No 'e didn't." It was a flat statement. "You've run away, done a vanishing act—isn't it so?"

Mara's throat constricted with fear. "How did you know?" she whispered.

"It's written all over you, duck." Mrs. Underwood reached for a pot of crimson and turned impatiently round. "Have you never seen a woman paint before?"

"No."

Mrs. Underwood sighed. "Oh dear, oh dear," she said, "you'll not be much use to me or I to you. 'Ow did you meet our Jim if you're such an innocent thing?"

Mara explained.

"Delmonico's, eh? Jim always 'ad a good eye." She studied Mara again, missing nothing, from the girl's slender, booted foot to the top of her fashionable bonnet. "It's a pity," she said at last. "You could earn a bloomin' fortune, love, but you're not that sort of girl." She hummed a few bars of a song and put the finishing touches to her face, blotting her crimson lips on a lacy handkerchief and rising briskly.

"I thought you might help me to find work." Mara spoke shyly.

Mrs. Underwood fell back on her stool, laughing so uproariously that her eyelashes began to shed their black. "Bless me," she shouted, "are you taking the mickey off me? Oh, you're a rare one . . ." At last she calmed herself and said kindly, "I run a sporting 'ouse, dearie, that's what I do. Now I suppose you know what that means?"

Mara nodded, face scarlet with humiliation.

"And I don't suppose you want to work in one?"

Mara shook her head.

"It's a pity," Mrs. Underwood repeated.

There seemed nothing more to say. Mara felt a perfect fool. She ought to have guessed that Mr. McSweeney's friends were no better than himself. She knew Mrs. Underwood meant to be kind, and she could never dislike anyone with generous instincts, and so she said, "I've been foolish. It was a mistake."

"Of course," the madame said thoughtfully, "there's always places that can use a pretty girl who don't want to go the distance. Dance halls, or clubs where you've only to look nice and chat them up a bit. There's quite a nice one, ever so popular, on Market—it's a 'urdy-gurdy place, dear, like in the old days. You let me know if that appeals and I'll fix you up straightaway. You're a beauty, though. You don't want to use it up too fast." She stared balefully at her own image. "When it goes," she said, "it's gone. That's the God's own truth."


Mara was spending her money as recklessly as she knew how. The truth was that she felt she had no right to it; the sooner it had gone the happier she would be. She ate elaborate meals in the sumptuous dining-room where Lotta Crabtree, Ulysses Grant,

Haw Tabor, Buffalo Bill Cody, and the infamous Baby Doe had supped in days gone by. She hired carriages to drive 'round Denver by day and caused a minor scandal when she saw *Carmen* at the opera house, unescorted. She knew she was going to take Mrs. Underwood up on her offer—as long as she did not have to "go the distance," as the madame so delicately put it, there seemed no harm in it. She told herself she cared nothing for the company of men, but she was longing to be in the society of lively people once more. She had been so alone in her life as Mrs. Winthrop she felt half-starved for companionship.

The moment Mara set foot in Lillian Hamm's hurdy-gurdy house her rosy fantasies paled. She had imagined a sentimental atmosphere in which strolling, prettily costumed girls rattled tambourines and sang old ballads to an appreciative audience. The noise that blasted upward from the dance hall to Mrs. Hamm's private office was far from sentimental. She had pictured her new employer as a more refined and motherly version of Mrs. Underwood, but here again she was wrong.

Lillian Hamm was aptly named. Her face resembled a joint of meat which had been heavily glazed and embalmed for weeks in a butcher's window. She examined Mara critically through small, reptilian eyes and lit a long, thin cigar. "Too flossy," she grunted. "You're pretty enough, but you'll scare the men off. My girls must look as if they're having a good time." She turned away before Mara could answer her and bellowed a request for someone named Sheila. "I'll have one of my best girls take you

down. If you think you can unbend, you're hired.
Only—" Mrs. Hamm smiled unpleasantly—"because I need a black-haired white girl. The last one
turned to opium."

Mara almost cried out in relief when Sheila appeared. She had been expecting a monster of depravity, but the girl who stood in the doorway was a
welcome surprise. Her pretty face was fresh and
merry beneath a crop of flying brown curls, and
her laughing green eyes took Mara in with honest
admiration. "You'll do well," Sheila said cheerfully.
"Come along—I'll show you the place." She seemed
at ease in her abbreviated costume, and Mara wondered if she would ever have the courage to display
as much leg as Sheila did. The girl was tightly laced
in a low-cut black bodice with tiny sleeves. Her
skirt was a full, flounced crinoline of brilliant scarlet,
which ended just above her dimpled, black-stock-
inged knees. "You're Irish," Sheila said happily. "So
am I. We're a regular festival of nations here at
Lil's. Since I'm the certified Irish girl you'll probably
have to change your name to Arabella. Or how about
Genevieve? We don't have any French girls just
now . . ."

The room they entered was even less to Mara's
liking than Mrs. Hamm had been. It was so densely
packed with people that the heat and smoke were
almost overwhelming. A rowdy group of musicians
played what passed for music—a harsh jangle of
fiddle, banjo, cornet, piccolo, and piano. Men stood
three-deep at the bar, tossing back whiskey as if it
were water. The other hurdy-gurdy girls were scattered throughout the room, some clenched in the

sweaty grip of partners and others posing prettily, tambourine in hand, until someone came and paid the price of a dance.

"It's seventy-five cents for three minutes, a dollar for five. They can pay in coin or in dust."

"Dust?"

"Gold dust!" Sheila laughed without malice at Mara's ignorance. "Five minutes is what you want, but I warn you, it can seem like five hours." She pointed to a heavily bearded man who leaped and twirled drunkenly, treading on his partner's toes and whooping with glee. Another fellow had drunk so much he could only lurch and shuffle, leaning against the girl in his arms so heavily her knees buckled. All the girls were dressed in identical costumes, except for the colors of the skirts. There seemed a dozen or so, of whom several looked Chinese and one, a plump girl in cerise, Mexican.

"The top girls—those who earn the most—are Michele, Diana, Gretchen, Dulayne, and myself. Watch them."

Mara gazed in fascination while Sheila pointed out the finer techniques of the most popular girls. "Do you see the slender blonde girl—the one in blue? That is Gretchen, who comes from Portland. She's the best dancer of any of us—she can dance on her toes like a ballerina. She works here because she's run away from home and nobody would think to look for her in a hurdy-gurdy house. See how she smiles? The girl in yellow is Diana, who comes from England, and there—in pink—is Dulayne. She's a southern girl—she can ride a horse like nothing you've ever seen. And there—do you see?

—in the orange skirts, is Michele. Soon she'll sing for us. She has the loveliest voice—so many Italians do—and she can wring your heart. Michele is very melancholy, but she never shows it at work. Mrs. Hamm would soon dismiss her if she did."

"Why does Diana shimmer so? It's uncanny!"

"It's her special trick," Sheila whispered, "to paste glitter-dust on her eyelids and bosom. Of all of us, she enjoys working here the most." And indeed, the glimmering English girl smiled with what seemed genuine pleasure, enormous eyes glowing, while a frenzied man in a red neck-scarf twirled her around the floor. Dulayne, on the other hand, was shaking her taffy-colored curls angrily at the impetuous little Spaniard who was kneeling in a stupor at her feet and staring up her skirts. She shouted something to one of the barmen who shook his fist at the offender, and all was well. Sheila had glided off onto the floor, shaking her tambourine and strutting in a wonderfully playful manner to the delight of the onlookers. Mara shrank back into the shadows, hoping no one would notice her. She did not think she could ever succeed as a hurdy-gurdy girl. The work was more demeaning than she had thought, and she would doubtless lose her temper too easily.

There was a brief commotion and then all the music ceased. Michele came forward, her dark eyes flashing, and went to stand beside the musicians. And then, accompanied by only the piano player, she began to sing in a high, pure soprano that rang through the clamorous room with incomparable sweetness. It was as if a lark had alit on a rubbish heap, oblivious to its surroundings. The noise at the bar continued, but gradually even the quarrelsome whiskey drinkers quieted as the delicate girl, dignified despite her orange crinolines, lifted her voice in the haunting lament known as *Frail Barrier*. It was about the dreadful dangers and heartbreaks of mining for gold, and when she had finished several of the men rubbed their eyes on grimy sleeves unashamedly.

Mara joined in wholeheartedly at the applause and cheers that followed. The man at the piano had moved her almost as much as the lovely Italian girl. When he played by himself, without the raucous banjo and out-of-tune fiddle, he was magnificent. His sensitive hands had searched out the most poignant chords, improvising brilliantly. Now he moved into a complicated fast "rag" which only a player of considerable skill could attempt. He was a handsome man of perhaps forty years. His face was mobile and singularly alive. Silver lightly touched his temples and his expressive eyes took on the mood of his music. They had glowed softly during Michele's rendering of *Frail Barrier;* now they snapped and glittered with wicked glee.

"I see you've noticed Caleb," Sheila said, joining Mara. "He is the heart and soul of this place. He sees we're treated fairly and protects us if some boyo wants to play rough. He may look gentle, but he knows the Chinese way of fighting. He's a very intelligent man, our Caleb. He knows everything worth knowing—I promise you."

Gretchen had come to stand beside her. "Please come and work with us," she said engagingly. "It's not a bad life. If you tire of it—" she made an exquisite little *pirouette*—"you can leave. No one will prevent you."

"And Mrs. Hamm?" Mara could not get over her unpleasant impression of the reptilian owner.

"Just don't cross her," warned Sheila.

"Don't worry," Gretchen said, extending a hand to Mara in graceful friendship. "We'll show you how to get along."


Mara moved from the Windsor Hotel and into a lodging house near Mrs. Hamm's which was patronized by all the hurdy-gurdy girls. She shared a large room with Dulayne, and set about the business of adjusting to an unfamiliar schedule. From now on she would go to sleep at dawn and rise at noon. To her relief she did not have to see much of Mrs. Hamm. The other girls had hit upon a plan for Mara's costume. Since all the colored crinolines were already in use, and each dancer liked to keep her color as her trademark, it was decided that Mara should appear all in black.

"Think how effective it will be," Diana said rapturously. "With your white skin and black hair—oh, I wish I'd thought of it myself!"

Mrs. Hamm asked to see Mara before her debut night, and Gretchen and Dulayne went with her to the paper-strewn office above the dance hall.

"What's this?" Mrs. Hamm grunted, surveying Mara critically. "Are you going to a funeral?" Gretchen and Dulayne persuaded her that Mara would show to best advantage all in black, and at last the owner agreed. "But mind you don't put on

airs," she said. "You're no better than anyone else!"
Mara instinctively knew that Mrs. Hamm hated
her and she resolved on the spot to keep out of the
evil-looking woman's way; she never doubted that
Mrs. Hamm was just as unpleasant inside as she was
without.

Her first night was more exhausting than she
could have imagined. At first she hung shyly back,
at the periphery of the room, hoping to escape notice. For a time it seemed to work and no one approached her. She lounged uneasily with her tambourine, feeling more naked than ever in her life.
She knew the effect of the black taffeta was to make
her more noticeable than she might have been in
pink or green. Her eyes gleamed in the gloomy room
and the white of her shoulders and bosom glowed
almost incandescently. Then, too, there was the
matter of lacing. Her waist was already so small she
had no need of corsets, yet her breasts spilled from
the bodice exactly as if they had been propped arti-
ficially. It occurred to her gradually that everyone
in the room was staring at her, and that Lillian
Hamm had been right. She scared them off. It would
never do, and so she moved forward boldly, smiling
as she had seen Diana do. Instantly there was a
stampede in her direction. An elderly cowboy col-
lided with a roguish-looking man in his haste to
reach her, and in the confusion she was snatched
away by a third contender who heaped gold dust
into her hands and gave a shout of triumph.

By the time an hour had passed she had lost
count of her partners and felt sure her ribs were
cracked. She danced with drunks and gamblers and

elderly gents who reeked of whiskey; she was pressed in the arms of a young English nobleman she had seen in the lobby of the Windsor, and then hugged to the bony chest of a renowned gambling-house owner, now in his seventies. The variety and station in life of her partners was astonishing, but even more amazing was the unwelcome news, when she thought the evening must nearly be over, that it was just past midnight.

She relaxed gratefully when it was time for Michele to sing, and once more studied the face of the interesting piano player who so subtly controlled the atmosphere of the room. "Caleb has been noticing you," Sheila whispered in her ear. "He told me to see that you escape early—otherwise your feet will be too sore to dance tomorrow."

As Mara limped up the stairs to bed she vowed to quit the hurdy-gurdy house at the end of the week. When she had opened her *chatelaine* bag at the end of her work night there had been over one-hundred dollars in coin and dust; even when she had given half to the barman, who in turn would give it to Mrs. Hamm, she was fifty dollars richer. It was a fast way to make money, but nothing was worth the crippling of her feet. Her entire body felt bruised and battered. She whispered a silent thanks to Caleb for noticing her predicament, tumbled into bed, and was asleep before she could turn out the light. She never heard Dulayne come in, and awakened in the morning still attired in her black costume. Later, she thought, she would seek out Gretchen and learn how to dance all night without suffering . . .

In fact, her job became easier with practice. Gretchen taught her how to pad her shoes and how to hold her body; Diana and Dulayne urged the more exuberant patrons to treat the new girl gently. Michele told her to keep a handkerchief soaked in cologne in her bodice; when she felt faint she could dab it to her temples and be revived. By the end of the week, Mara was almost enjoying herself. Caleb nodded to her regularly from his place at the piano, and one night, when Michele had finished her song, he launched into a medley of Irish airs which stirred her so profoundly she felt tears tremble on her lashes. He saluted her when it was over, holding her gaze a moment more than was necessary. She began to wonder if he would ever speak to her, then reproved herself for caring.

The spring thaw had begun, and the rivers of the Platte were rising dangerously. Ladies picked their way along the streets, skirts held decorously up to avoid the mud, and there was a promise of spring in the air. It was still far away, blowing off the mountains, but it was so tangible that all the girls admitted to feeling restless. Michele became morose, but Diana's gaiety escalated to new heights. "I *love* America!" she would cry. "Things are so raw here! So new!" The dance hall was packed every night with men who had been snowbound and were now eager to spend their money and dance the night away at Lil Hamm's.

One evening there was a fight. Juanita, the Mexican girl, accused Mara of stealing her best customer. Mara never even knew who it was she had stolen, for Juanita came at her in a tangle of flying crinolines and curved claws and began to pull at Mara's hair, screaming in her jealous rage. Mara tumbled to the floor, skirts flying up, and a cheer rose from the assembled crowd. They were laying bets on the winner, and this infuriated Mara more than all Juanita's pummeling could do. She rolled over and over, hitting out at her attacker. Her hair had come unbound and streamed wildly over the floor; she heard a loud squeal of satin as her bodice ripped. Juanita's sharp teeth had fastened on her hand, and she gave a scream of outrage and punched the girl squarely in the jaw. The crowd went wild with glee, and Mara jumped to her feet, panting with outrage and trying to cover her exposed breasts.

Mrs. Hamm had entered the room, attracted by the shouts and cheers, and stood looking at Mara with her little lizard eyes.

"You'll earn nothing tonight," she said venomously. "Cover yourself and get home. We don't hire street-brawlers here."

"Juanita started it," Sheila said, but the look Mrs. Hamm gave her was enough to silence anyone. Juanita escaped unpunished, slinking away to repair her hair and nurse her grudge. Mara felt angry tears well in her eyes but would not give Mrs. Hamm the satisfaction of crying. Defiantly, she pushed forward the masses of her hair to cover her breasts and turned to go.

Caleb rose from his place at the piano and came to her. He gave her his coat, tucking it around her with a courtly, solemn air, and then he took her arm and led her from the dance hall as casually as if they were going for a stroll in the country. They walked along the muddy streets in silence, Mara clinging to his arm and shivering uncontrollably. He stopped in the shadow of a warehouse and looked down at her.

"Tell me," he said gently. "What are you doing in a place like Lil Hamm's?"

"I might as easily ask what you are doing," Mara said. "Your piano is wasted there."

"I am a grown man," Caleb said. "I do what I like. You, on the other hand, need protecting."

"I'm not a child," said Mara indignantly. "I'm as old as the other girls, and I've been married."

"Ahh," he said, "a woman of the world. I should have known."

"Don't make fun of me," Mara said unsteadily.

For answer the piano player kissed her cheek and then continued to propel her toward her rooming house. At the door he said gravely, "You may keep my coat until tomorrow. I'll call for it at three."


"Sheila told me you knew everything worth knowing," Mara said curiously. "What did she mean?"

He had taken her to a chop house called The Gold Standard where he was well known. They were the last to lunch, and had the place to themselves. Caleb pondered her question. At last he said, "I can do a variety of useless things. I can read Latin and Greek, carve toys from wood, teach a dog to beg, build a kite, speak fluent French, Italian, and German and a little Gaelic—*a chailín bhig*. I can ride a horse, play the piano moderately well and the guitar rather badly, recite poetry by the yard, identify wild-flowers, shoot with deadly accuracy, and know a lovely woman when I see one." He paused for breath and Mara smiled. He had called her "my little girl," and the sudden use of Gaelic had made her flush with pleasure.

"Since you are so accomplished," she said teasingly, "why do you not seem happier?"

"That," he replied, "is the one thing I never mastered."

From that day on they became particular friends. It pleased her to walk beside the piano player in the streets, to dine with him and feel him smiling secretly at her in the dance hall at night. There was an affection between them so easy and warm that Mara felt she might have known him all her life, yet he never told her much about himself. Sheila pieced together as much of his life as she knew, and could come up with only three facts: He had been born in the east, studied once at the Harvard School of Divinity, and lost a wife to typhus in California. He was as respectful of Mara's privacy as he was of his own. Only once, when they had hired a carriage and driven some little distance away from the city, he asked: "Have you ever loved a man?"

Mara considered lying, but at last she said, as steadily as she could, "I loved a man very much, but he proved to be a rogue. Now I hate him."

"Your husband?"

Mara shook her head, and that was all they ever said on the subject. Caleb took her hand and held it closely all the way back to town.

The spring was full upon them now; the Platte

had not flooded and the air was warm and sweet. She had not thought of her father for some time, although she had inserted the usual notices in the Rocky Mountain News. Now she asked Caleb if they might make the trip to Cripple Creek together. Mrs. Hamm would no doubt give her several free days; she had earned more than any of the other girls in her month at the dance hall, and Mrs. Hamm could not afford to lose her.

"I don't expect I shall ever find him," Mara said. "But I would like to see the mining camp. All the gold that has paid for the privilege of trampling on my feet has come from Cripple Creek."

She was still flushed and happy from her outing when she returned to the lodging house. A letter had come for her, forwarded from the Windsor Hotel. One glance at the sweeping script which covered the envelope told her the identity of the writer. "My dear Miss McQuaid," it said:

I have been repaid quickly before, but never so unexpectedly. I have some news for you which may distress you, but I think you must be told. Your husband is dead. He shot himself in the head, in Chicago. His body was brought back East and there was a great to-do in the newspapers. You will inherit no money from his estate, since you deserted him. He seemed an unstable boy to me, but R.I.P. I continue to wish you luck and welcome news of you. Have a care —you seem to draw trouble.

McSweeney

# BOOK III

## *Bride of the Cheyenne*

## Chapter Eight

The narrow-gauge railroad which took passengers to Cripple Creek was equipped with large observation windows. Mara sat lost in wonder at the beauty of the mountains they passed through. It seemed to her she had never seen anything to match the grandeur of the Rockies. They were heading south from Denver, through the mountain passes to the far side of Pike's Peak and the site of the gold camps; all around the lofty peaks, some still capped with snow, rose purple and majestic to the heavens.

"I am catching mountain fever," she said to Caleb. "I never dreamed there could be such beauty!"

"It is not all beauty at Cripple Creek," Caleb warned. "Mining towns are short on beauty. Men searching for gold are notoriously unconcerned with the scenery around them."

He told her of the cowboy, Bob Womack, who first discovered gold at Cripple Creek in 1890 and sold his mine for $10,000,000, cash, and of Old Man Stratton and his Irish partners who followed soon after. The richness of the lode was beyond imagining—once a miner named Jones, unsure where to stake his claim, had thrown his hat into the air and, sinking his pick where it had fallen, uncovered a vein worth thousands. "There've been strikes and battles and riots this year," he said. "It's a rough town which has grown so fast it overreaches itself. In the beginning, men blew themselves to bits in their eagerness to dynamite. It was a crude business; no rules or guidelines then. Soon it will all be controlled by huge companies from a great distance away. Cripple Creek may be the last of the open gold camps."

When they stepped from the train Mara sensed the difference in altitude. The air was thin and made her feel heady. Caleb cautioned her to proceed slowly. "We are ten thousand feet high, now. The Continental Divide is to our west and the mountains to the south—do you see?—are the Sangre de Cristo."

"Sangre de Cristo," murmured Mara, enchanted by the sound. *Blood of Christ.*

Cripple Creek itself was a revelation to her. Frame houses, hastily erected and in a tumble-down condition, ringed the town ten deep. Its central streets were given over to a profusion of lumberyards, claims offices, meat sellers, and the inevitable saloons—dozens of them. There was a hotel, the Anheuser-Busch, which Caleb told her had been a tent-boardinghouse a few years ago. The noise and confusion were exhilarating and somewhat frightening. People milled in the streets, dogs barked, rowdy music spilled from open doorways, and everywhere Mara saw grizzled, frenzied-looking men who might be the same as those who came to roister away a weekend at Lil Hamm's. She understood their primitive exuberance now and wished she had known, that first night in the dance hall, from what they had come.

Her rose-colored velvet traveling costume drew many stares from the ragged, hard-looking men and women who thronged Bennett Avenue, and she held Caleb's arm tightly, wishing she were less conspicuous. Caleb took her into Nolan's Saloon, where Womack had once got roaring drunk and staggered out to the corner of Third and Bennett, thrusting dollar bills at every child who passed. At Nolan's and everywhere they went they distributed the notice Mara had had printed, appealing for news of Padraic McQuaid.

Outside the Bon Ton Casino, sitting in a camp chair and sketching intently, was a man who seemed familiar to Mara. A small crowd was gathered round him, watching his deft strokes make magic on the paper. He turned slightly and she saw it was the artist who had traveled with her on the Great Western line from Chicago.

"Why," he drawled, catching sight of her at the same instant, "it's the mysterious widow. What brings you to Cripple Creek?" He had not forgotten her rebuff and was prepared to make her pay, but Caleb asked him a number of intelligent questions about labor disputes and assayment, and soon he was friendly and eager to talk. He laid his pencil aside and gave them all his attention, occasionally calling or waving to people he knew.

"The winter has taken the usual toll," he said. "Many were dead of eripipelas or black vomit when I arrived. There've been the usual shootings—but what life here, what energy! I've sent dozens of drawings back East. I sketch all day and half the night and never run out of subject matter." He showed them some of his drawings, filling in the story accompanying each.

"This child was born here in 1891. She's three years old now and has never been away from Cripple Creek. Her mother mines right along with the rest . . . Here is a man who gambled away his claim playing faro and then shot the winner dead . . ." He shuffled through his portfolio and tapped one sketch with particular affection.

"Here is a sad case," he said. "This poor girl, Irish like yourself, Mrs. McQuaid, came here alone at Christmas time, half-frozen and about to give birth to a child. The baby was born dead, and when she recovered her strength, she left us. She was a likeable little thing. She'd been through a great deal, but she was very cheerful. Made everyone laugh with her stories."

He held the picture up and Mara felt her knees give way. A tide of shock and disbelief passed through her, leaving her unable to speak. Caleb held her up, searching her ashen face anxiously.

"I knew her," Mara whispered. "Her name is Kathleen Daly."

"Why, yes," the artist agreed, "Kathy! But her surname was Moriarty. I always felt she had run off from her husband." He looked at Mara shrewdly. "How did you come to know her?"

"We sailed on the same ship from Ireland. She was my friend." She wanted to weep, but tears would not come. The artist had sketched Kathy in a characteristic pose, looking over her shoulder and laughing with wicked glee. He had drawn her hair in disarray, so that the fair curls appeared to be blowing in the wind of a Rocky Mountain winter, and if one looked very closely it was possible to guess that the girl's laugh concealed a sadness as much a part of her as the merriment.

"The baby?" Mara inquired. "Was it a boy or a girl?"

"A boy, stillborn."

"Did she name him?" Mara dreaded the answer.

"I do not know." He looked at her with a glimmer of sympathy. "No one knows where she has gone, or anything about her. The midwife who attended her has gone back to Colorado Springs. But look—would you like to have this sketch? I'll gladly give it to you."

He refused payment, and Mara thanked him and took the picture of Kathy. Poor Kathy, who had thought St. Louis the end of the world, had truly found it now . . .

At dinner that night she was quiet and—as usual —Caleb refused to pry. The food was badly cooked, their forks and spoons were spotty and stained, and the noise from the casino next door made conversation nearly impossible. She had lost her appetite for the gay life of Cripple Creek, and asked him if

they could find a quiet place. They had separate
rooms upstairs in the hotel, and he came to her in
hers. "We can talk here," he said. Nicety dictated
that she balk at this arrangement, but one of the
loveliest things about Caleb was that she never
needed to be arch with him. He did, as Sheila had
once assured her, know everything worth knowing.

*"Cad tá ort?"* he asked gently. "What is wrong?"

And so she told him, beginning with her mother's
death at sea and the disappearance of her father.
She told him unflinchingly that her cousin had taken
her by force—here, in this elemental place, it did not
seem so shocking to speak of rape—and that she
had married a man who made her life a torment
with his insane jealousies. "I have had a letter," she
said. "My husband killed himself after I left. He
used to swear that he could not live without me, and
now I see he was in earnest." She closed her eyes
briefly and then continued, explaining about Kathleen Moriarty Daly. When she had finished there
was a long silence, punctuated only by the bawdy
shrieks and sounds of bottles smashing in the riotous streets below.

"Darling girl," Caleb said, "you are not to
blame for anything that's happened. Surely you see
that? Your poor husband would have found another obsession to break himself upon if you had
not come along. I know what it is you fear—that the
child born to your friend was your cousin's."

"Yes," Mara whispered. "He ruined her."

Caleb laughed mirthlessly. "We ruin ourselves,"
he said. "No one can do it for us. Your friend will
take care of herself and no doubt outlive us all. No,

*a chailín,* what is eating at your heart now is only partly pity for the girl. The rest is jealousy, and you must own up to it. For your own good, you must."

"Jealousy? I *hate* Desmond! I hope he is dead." It was the first time she had pronounced his name in almost a year, and as she did so a vivid image of his face, luminous with love as she had once seen it, came to her. She shook her head violently and shouted: "I hate him, Caleb—I swear it!"

Caleb came to her, drawing her onto his lap and caressing her hair with infinitely gentle fingers. "Ah, yes," he sighed, "you hate him. I'll tell you one thing more, and then I'll be silent. You trust me so because I am the only man you've ever met who wants nothing from you. Your guard drops; you are at peace."

"Yes," she said, pressing close to his warm and solid body, "I admit it's true. But why is it so? Do you find me unattractive? Foolish?"

Caleb smiled. "A bit foolish, perhaps. But far— oh, very far—from unattractive. In two years' time I might crawl on my hands and knees across Pike's Peak to find you. But for now you're unfinished— incomplete. To love you now would be like drinking wine before it has aged properly. It would make me sick."

"How disgusting." Mara giggled drowsily. "No one has ever said I was sickening before."

"It would be the end of me," Caleb said. "I wouldn't suffer a broken heart with grace."

He held her in his arms until she had fallen asleep; the noises from the streets of Cripple Creek reached him dimly, as if from a great distance, and

then he too slept, his cheek against the silken spill
of Mara's hair . . .

The return trip on the little narrow-gauge seemed
all the more beautiful because Mara knew it soon
would end and she would be back in the smokey
dance hall. "I don't want to go back," she confessed
to Caleb. "I should like to ride on this train forever, watching the light shift on the sides of the
mountains."

It was balmy and mild—a perfect April day. The
pungent smell of spruce and mountain bracken
drifted in from the open windows and made her
feel almost dizzy with happiness. She had been
in America for a year; she closed her mind to the
awful things that had happened and thought only
of how much she had seen . . . New York, Chicago,
the Rockies . . . It was a boundless land, full of sur-
prises and beauty, and she felt she might grow to
love it as she had once loved Ireland. They were descending to the plains now, leaving the high mountains and crossing the fertile valley of the Platte.

"This was all Ute country once," Caleb told her.
"We've driven them to reservations now—I sometimes think we will have much to answer for."

"Why have they gone so willingly?"

"They haven't. Ask anyone who lived in these
parts twenty years ago! No, Mara, they were far
from willing. So long as the Indians had buffalo to
hunt they ranged freely and despised the way we
lived." His face took on the zealous look she had
come to know so well. "We have broken treaties,
disturbed their land with our railroads and tele-
graph poles, infected them with our diseases, shot

their buffalo for sport, and—as a final solution to
what *we* have done—shoved them onto reservations, out of our way."

Mara thought of the old Sioux warrior she had
seen in Omaha. "Surely a few still live free?"

"Some. Not many. And even those who refuse to
settle on reservations know their way of life is coming to an end. The Cheyenne are the last to cling
to the old ways here in Colorado, but even they are
succumbing. They are a proud race."

She stared out the window at the golden plains
and pictured them as they must once have been,
covered with herds of bison, disturbed only by the
ceaseless winds, innocent of the sure thrust of
progress which would one day change them so utterly. She was so saddened she turned away and began to divert herself studying the other passengers.
A few seats down from them sat a young, well-
dressed couple, newly married and more interested
in each other than in the scenery. Across from her
an elderly woman in *pince nez* made eager notations in a leather-bound volume. She was keeping
a journal of her trip; a schoolteacher perhaps, or a
naturalist. Two small boys pointed and exclaimed
at everything they saw. Their mother hushed them
constantly, to no avail. The only passenger she did
not like the looks of was a red-faced, middle-aged
man dressed in the costume of a retired army colonel. His face was a study in impatience—he tapped
his fingers angrily as if to urge the train along.
Looking at his arrogant, unpleasant face, Mara
guessed he was the sort of man who could never
get where he was going fast enough. He would never

notice the beauty of the land, or give a thought to the Indians who had once roamed it. He would ride through life seeing nothing, understanding nothing . . .

She was musing on the oddness of such people when she found herself thrown roughly against Caleb without warning. The car shuddered and groaned, the train ground to an abrupt halt. The schoolteacher was thrown from her seat and remained on the floor, looking dazed. The two little boys chortled with excitement. The colonel was on his feet, rushing to the front of the car, and bellowing angrily before the rest of them had recovered from the sudden jolt. She heard voices calling: "What is it? . . . A boulder on the track? . . . Have we derailed?"

And then the door of the car opened and three figures came swinging up into the compartment with effortless grace. For a moment she thought she was dreaming, because the three men who had commandeered their car couldn't possibly belong to real life. There was a thick, suffocating silence, a silence of horror and disbelief, and then one of the women screamed. It was real, after all.

Caleb's hand tightened convulsively on her arm. "Cheyenne," he breathed. "Don't move. Don't draw their attention in any way."

The schoolteacher's voice, thin with hysteria, cried: "This doesn't happen anymore . . . it cannot be happening . . ."

Mara watched the men from beneath her lashes, scarcely daring to breathe. The oldest, a powerfully built man of fifty years or so, seemed to be the

leader. Behind him were two braves. They were all
dressed in buckskin leggings and vests; their hair
was braided in two long plaits and hung forward,
tied at the ends with scraps of red ribbon. Each carried a rifle, and the leader leveled his weapon on
the little group, surveying them dispassionately.

She had a wild hope that it was all part of some
extravagant entertainment—a Wild West Show or
a traveling circus—but the steady pressure of Caleb's fingers on her arm told her it wasn't so. The
danger was real. The Cheyenne, whom she had so
recently pitied, looked quite capable of killing them
all without the least remorse. What had once
seemed beautiful to her now took on the look of
cruel savagery. What she dreaded most was the
black, impassive eyes—they seemed somehow less
than human, and hypnotic in their unflinching gaze.

The mother of the little boys had begun to sob,
gathering her sons, one in each arm, and wailing
over their heads. The Indians ignored her, but when
the young man down the car tried to shield his wife
in his arms, the Cheyenne leader calmly swung his
rifle in their direction.

"Don't move," Caleb repeated in a barely audible
voice.

The colonel, who had shrunk back against the
door from the beginning, now stepped forward. His
face was bright crimson; his little eyes snapped with
fury. "Drop those guns," he cried out in a contemptuous voice. "This is not 1860, you know. I am
a colonel, late of the United States Army. If you
don't leave us in peace I will see you're all hanged!"

For answer, one of the braves unsheathed a knife

and calmly held it to the colonel's throat. His dark
eyes remained impassive, but the eyes of his victim underwent a startling change. The colonel's entire face seemed to balloon in an apoplexy of rage;
the chords of his neck stuck out as if to meet the
knife's sharp blade and his hands clenched and unclenched helplessly. The leader grunted out a command, and the other brave came forward, moving
softly and deliberately up the aisle in the direction of
the two small boys. The mother screamed again,
lifting her head piteously and struggling to keep a
tight grip on her sons, but the Indian plucked the
older child from her arms and, lifting him easily
into the air, carried him to the door. The boy had
gone rigid and white with shock and terror. He huddled against the colonel's knees, shrinking as far
from the red men as space would allow.

All eyes were on the two prisoners. Mara thought
she understood. The Indians intended to take the
colonel and the boy as hostages. Would no one come
to help? She glanced out the window and saw, with
heart-stopping finality, a mounted party of twenty
braves along the railroad grading. Twenty rifles
were aimed in the direction of the train. The horses'
manes were tossing slightly in the wind; otherwise
all was unmoving, and silent. The Cheyenne might
have been figures in a painting.

There was a slight commotion as the two hostages were pushed from the train. The leader and one
of the younger men followed. The brave who remained fixed each of the passengers with his black,
unreadable eyes, as if he wanted them to remember
him forever, and then he spoke. His voice was soft

and curiously flat. The words were Cheyenne and no one understood, but what followed required no understanding.

He lowered his gun and walked up the aisle slowly, his moccasined feet making no sound. Mara felt him come closer and closer; although her eyes were cast down she sensed him at her side. He stopped, holding out his hand to her in a gesture of command.

Caleb gave a strangled cry and rose in his seat, but instantly the Cheyenne whipped his rifle up so that the barrel aimed at Mara. The meaning was clear enough, and Caleb sank back. Again the Indian extended his hand and Mara, the gun at her breast, lifted her hand and placed it in his. He pulled her easily to her feet and forced her to walk backward, back, away from the others and from safety, toward the door. Toward the unknown. At the final moment Caleb rushed forward, heedless of the danger to himself, but the Indian brought the butt of his rifle up and felled him with one brutal stroke.

The last thing she saw on the train was Caleb, crumpled in the aisle, unconscious. Blood was beginning to well from the side of his head. Behind him she could hear the schoolteacher's voice rise in a keen of despair and disbelief: *"These things don't happen anymore . . ."*

And then she was standing on the warm and wind-swept plain, too terrified to cry out or move, wishing with all her heart that it had been a nightmare, after all, and she could awaken.

She clung to the brave's back, twining her arms around him to keep from falling from the horse. It seemed they had been riding for hours, and she felt at any moment she might let go and slip down to the ground beneath the flying hooves. She had ridden often at home, in Ireland, but never at such breakneck speed, saddleless, and under a baking, merciless sun. The unseasonably warm day, which had pleased her so when she and Caleb had set out from Cripple Creek, now seemed a curse.

They were riding at the head of the party, just behind the leader. The colonel had his own horse and an escort of two braves who rode beside him, rifles pointing at his head. The little boy sagged, half-conscious and deathly pale, in the saddle of the brave who had taken him from the train. The others thundered along behind. She couldn't tell in which direction they were heading. At first it seemed they were going back toward the mountains, but then they curved in a great wheeling circle and fanned out across the plain to the west. She lay her cheek helplessly against her abductor's back and smelled the strange, alien odor of his flesh through the warm buckskin. It was an odor compounded of roots and earth, and of something oddly fragrant and sweet.

He had simply tossed her onto the horse like a heap of light clothing, vaulted on, and ridden off without ever looking at her again. She would not allow herself to think of what might happen when they reached their destination; she would deal with one thing at a time, and right now she desperately craved water. Her lips were dry and cracked and her head ached with the heat and pounding of hooves. Her traveling hat had long since fallen off and rolled away across the plains like a fantastic tumbleweed of satin and velvet. Her hair was unbound and streaming down her back; she had lost a shoe and the hem of her rose-colored skirt was torn and stained with mud.

A small stand of alder trees appeared ahead, and Mara longed for the comfort, however brief, the spreading branches would provide. They plunged into the grove, brambles raking at her arms and catching in her hair, and stopped abruptly. She could see a small stream glimmering between the tree trunks. All around her the Indians were dismounting and kneeling by the water, drinking from their cupped hands or from hollow gourds that hung at their belts. Her abductor leaped down and motioned for her to stay.

"Please——" she cried desperately, "I must have water."

She lay slumped across the horse's back, panting with thirst, and watched while her brave drank his fill. Then he dipped a gourd and brought it to her, holding it up. She reached for it, afraid to move too suddenly, and then she was gulping the cool, sweet liquid, spilling it over her parched face, opening her throat greedily like a wild creature. She handed the gourd back to him and saw that he was looking at her with curiosity. It was not a look to reassure her, but it was not wholly unkind.

"Thank you," she breathed.

Still he stared, and then—to her amazement—he said, "More?"

She nodded, wondering how much English he understood. "Yes, please—more. Very good water! Yes, more. Please."

When he returned the second time she tried something else. "May I get down?" she asked respectfully. "My legs are stiff. I would like to walk."

But he merely vaulted back onto the horse and they were off again, he riding with the born horseman's ease, rifle in one hand, while she once more clung for her life. They passed through the cool grove all too quickly and coursed over the endless plain, mile after mile of it. When they had gone for what seemed hours more she saw, far in the distance, the shadow of a mountain range.

She couldn't imagine what mountains they were, and she was past caring. She wanted only to stop, to rest, to be out of the sun. She had never fainted in her life, and for the first time she thought she might. She began to weep softly, and then more loudly, since nobody would hear her. She had known many kinds of despair in her year in America, but none could match this. She caught sight of the little boy, to the left of her. He was crying too.

In late afternoon she saw plumes of smoke rising in the air and knew they were approaching the Cheyenne settlement. A group of women waited to take the horses, and the party of braves proceeded on foot to the village. Mara found she could not walk at first; her legs had become so stiff from the long ride she stumbled and fell to her knees twice. The brave hauled her to her feet each time—he was

neither rough nor gentle, but picked her up as one
might lift a package which had fallen to the ground.
There were children running about underfoot, and
dogs, and the closer they came to the village the
more she dreaded to arrive. The little boy seemed
blessedly unconscious now; his arms and legs swung
limply from the grasp of the man who carried him.
Ahead of her the colonel stumbled along, his body
bathed with sweat and his eyes starting wildly from
his head. It occurred to her that he was the only
prisoner likely to understand what was happening,
and his demeanor of utter terror brought little comfort to her. Now that she was free from the discom-
forts of the long ride she could dwell on something
much more horrible—her fate.

The cluster of tepees was large and brightly decorated. Stylized figures of elk and buffalo and eagle
were painted on the hides which reached some twenty feet into the air; the great conical structures
seemed something from another age to her, yet she
realized they could be dismantled and carried from
one site to another easily. Her captors were nomadic,
which made it almost impossible for anyone to
come to her rescue.

She was shoved into one of the largest tepees unceremoniously, and stood blinking in the sudden
darkness, clenching her hands until the nails cut her
flesh, trying to keep from crying out in terror. She
thought it important not to show her fright, but her
body was strung tight with anticipation. She thought
of the sudden blow, the thud of the war-club, the
horror of the knife slicing away her tender scalp
like a translucent cutlet and holding the long hair

aloft while she slid, bleeding to death, to the dust beneath.

The face which loomed in the dusky, twilit shadows, coming closer, was that of a woman. She was perhaps thirty and something in her bright black eyes was infinitely reassuring. She took Mara's hand and led her to a pile of buffalo robes, pushing her gently down. She brought a bowl of water and washed away the dirt and grime from Mara's face, and then she held her hands repeatedly to her lips, making encouraging noises. Mara realized the woman wanted to know if she was hungry, and she nodded vehemently.

Her benefactress busied herself at the fire and then returned with a bowl full of hot, steaming, unidentifiable mass. Mara dipped her fingers in and licked hungrily—soon she was lifting whole chunks of fish and lumps of pulpy, fibrous vegetable and devouring them ravenously. The woman nodded and smiled, approving Mara's appetite. Occasionally she drew in her breath in a long, hissing sigh of pleasure.

"Thank you," Mara said, wondering if the woman would reply in English as the brave had done. But she merely giggled and pushed her charge down on the pile of robes, closing her eyes and holding her hands to her cheek in a pantomime of sleep. Mara was to sleep now.

She lay rigid and wakeful, afraid of what would happen if the hospitality of her hostess was merely a ritual preceding the inevitable murder. Gradually the warm, close darkness and the voices close at hand gabbling away in their soft, alien tongue, produced an illusion of tranquility, and Mara fell into an exhausted, dreamless sleep as if she had tumbled over a cliff into an abyss.

When she awoke it seemed to be night. Now there were two women at her bedside—one the kindly bringer of food and another, younger woman who was pulling her to an upright position. She had obviously taken pains with her appearance. Two white feathers were plaited into her long braids, and a belt of blue beads and bone circled her slender waist. She was handsome, but her dark eyes were sullen and her lips quirked distastefully as she looked at Mara. She produced a comb of the sort that could be bought at trading posts, and began roughly to dress Mara's hair. She dragged the comb through the heavy, tangled masses, exclaiming with irritation when bits of twig or bramble halted her progress. Gradually the silken hair flowed easily under the comb, streaming down and shining blue-black in the firelight so that the older woman clapped her hands in admiration. They consulted briefly, and then Mara was pushed out the tepee's flap and escorted along a narrow path which ran between the Cheyenne dwellings.

The village was wide awake. Children ran about a large, central fire, leaping and calling shrilly to one another. When they saw Mara they came to line the path, stretching out their hands toward her and laughing. The path was also lined with women. Some had babies strapped in cradleboards on their backs and giggled shyly as Mara passed. One smiled at Mara in direct greeting; there was something in her face which set her apart from the others, but how or in what way Mara could not tell. Her escorts were leaving her now, melting back into the shadows. Mara was alone, standing before the largest tepee, which she presumed to be the chief's. Before she had time to wonder about the etiquette of such a situation, the tent flap opened and strong arms pulled her inside.

A dozen men lounged about the fire, smoking and talking. At a little distance from the others the squat, powerfully built man who had led the raiding party on the train sat in state on a heap of robes piled into a throne. Tonight he wore quantities of silver bangles on his thick arms, and a vest of porcupine quills. Red ribbons had been braided in his hair. Beside him, on either side, the two braves stood, arms folded on their chests. All the men except the chief had removed most of their clothing and wore only breech cloths and moccasins.

The chief signaled for her to approach and she walked slowly, head held high, painfully aware of the scores of black eyes that watched her, glittering with anticipation. She had lost both shoes, and the hem of her rose-colored skirt trailed across the earthen floor, whispering sibilantly. She stopped within a foot of the chief, mesmerized by his features and the intensity of his gaze. There was something fearful in the implication of his withheld strength, something brutal and yet not altogether evil. His eyes were hooded but intelligent, and the long, thin lips hinted at cruelty and humor both.

With stunning abruptness, he pointed to her throat. Involuntarily her hands flew up and discovered the object of his interest: the amethyst brooch.

She had forgotten she was wearing it. He barked out a sharp command, extending his hand to her, and she unfastened the brooch as quickly as she could and gave it to him. He snatched it up greedily, holding it so that the firelight could strike myriad glancing sparks from the violet depths. Then he nodded his approval and pointed to her velvet jacket.

The chief rubbed the material between his fingers and then threw the jacket to one of the braves, who instantly ripped the arms from the garment and forced his own brawny shoulders into it, wearing it as a vest. Her skirt was next to go, and it was added to the pile of hides and robes which surrounded the chief's throne. The cream silk blouse interested him less, and Mara began to fear she had run out of valuables. If only she had her trunk with her she could buy her freedom! She stood trembling in her chemise and ripped stockings, scheming for her life and almost unaware of the fact that she was now half nude. Modesty was something which belonged in another world—it would not do to remind herself of what happened to naked women in a room full of savages.

As if reading her mind, the chief now pointed again. She removed the shredded black stockings and watched while he pulled and twisted at them, gauging their strength and usefulness. She dreaded the moment when he would order her to take her chemise off, and pulled her hair forward to give some covering to her bosom.

The finger pointed again, and Mara stepped from her chemise, shivering with cold despite the fire. The nipples of her breasts rose helplessly with cold and fear; she clasped her hair about her desperately. Again he beckoned, and when she came closer he reached out suddenly and grasped her thigh, squeezing it as if testing for strength and resiliency, and then motioned for her to turn around.

She submitted to the poking and prodding of his fingers, feeling his dry hands slide over her buttocks and belly, thighs and waist, with deft, searching movements. He parted her hair and held a breast in each hand, displaying them to the room as he had done the amethyst. The men watched, rapt and appreciative. Finally, the chief lifted her hair, sifting it through his fingers like so much silken treasure, and beckoned the braves to approach.

One by one they filed past, looking at her naked body with keen interest. Some of them touched her lightly as they might a rare treasure or object of great fragility. Some laughed softly.

The only men who stood aloof from these proceedings were the two braves who guarded the chief. She decided they must be his sons and thought with wonder that she had ridden behind one of them all day, clinging to his body, inhaling the odors of his flesh, drinking the water he had given her. She wanted to appeal to him, but somehow he frightened her more than any of them.

At last the chief clapped his hands and the men withdrew to a respectful distance. Mara stood swaying, eyes closed, while the chief spoke to them at length, his voice rising and falling hypnotically in mysterious exhortation. His words were punctuated by an approving chorus.

"*Iyahe-yahe-e Ahe-e-ye!*" the braves shouted each

time their leader paused. Mara did not want to guess at what they were saying. She wondered what had become of the little boy and the colonel, but those thoughts led only to horror. Everything her mind could conjure was bloody and awful—Caleb lying senseless in the aisles of the train, bleeding as Roger must have bled when the bullet entered his temple . . . bleeding as she would bleed if she made one false step . . . She pitched forward on her knees, catching herself with outspread hands, fingers scrabbling in the earth in a desperate attempt to get to her feet again. She could not, try as she might, and she fell forward on her face. The chief's voice stopped and there was an abrupt silence. Mara waited for the blow which must follow, but then strong hands were raising her up again and she leaned against warm bare skin almost gratefully.

The brave wrapped her in a buffalo robe and picked her up in his arms, throwing her over his shoulder like a sack of grain. Then she was being carried out into the dark and starry night, back along the path to the tent where she had slept earlier, back to the ministrations of the women and the pallet of robes. She lay back, looking up at him with gratitude and terror; she couldn't tell which was the stronger emotion.

His coppery face glowed in the firelight, leaping from shadow to light like a figure from a nightmare. He had unbound his hair and it fell dark and straight over his shoulders. His powerfully muscled chest gleamed with almost supernatural brightness, and the eyes—so black and impenetrable—fixed her to the pallet as if she were a butterfly impaled on a pin.

"Who are you?" she whispered senselessly.

For a moment it seemed he might answer, but then he turned and left her, disappearing through the tent-flap like a ghost. Once again she fell into sleep so suddenly it was as if she had been clubbed unconscious . . .

The horror commenced at sunrise. She was wakened by the sullen young girl and given a dress to put on. It was a simple garment made of two long pieces of soft buckskin which tied at the sides. Moccasins were placed on her feet and once more her hair was combed so it flowed sleekly down her back. When she stepped outside the tepee she saw that the whole village was preparing for some momentous event. They were grouped about a long pit, five feet deep. The women and children sat along one side, the men on the other. At one end the chief and his two sons sat in state; the opposite end was open. Mara scanned the rows of children looking for some sign of the little boy who had been taken hostage, but he was nowhere to be seen. She was escorted to the ranks of women and made to sit in front, where she had an excellent view of the empty pit. Her stomach had begun to churn and she felt the bile of pure fear rise in her throat, but no one seemed to be taking any notice of her.

The chief rose and delivered a short, violent address and then, in a changed voice, began to pray. Mara needed no words of Cheyenne to know that it was a prayer—the God he addressed was called *Maheo*. There was a moment of profound silence and she could almost feel the air charged with the electricity of anticipation. When the great cheer burst from the throats of every man, woman, and child assembled she stared wildly from face to face trying to determine the cause of their fierce joy. And then she saw.

The colonel was being dragged from a tepee, bound hand and foot, across the ground. Two men trundled him along toward the pit, their faces expressionless. The colonel's red face was drained of color; he writhed and convulsed in his bonds and Mara could see that his mouth was open, screaming, the sound lost in the general din. His escorts cut the ropes that bound him, holding him between them upright and directing his attention to the chief's sons. Both had taken up bows and were fixing arrows in position; both drew their arms back until the bow was stretched to the uttermost. The arrows aimed at the colonel's heart. The crowd gave a great hissing sigh of expectation, and then the two arrows shot over the pit, landing harmlessly in the earth some fifty yards beyond. This performance was repeated twice more, the arrow landing further each time, and then the colonel was dumped unceremoniously into the pit. The chief walked to the brink and spat upon him, and then Mara's brave and his brother followed suit. They returned to their places and a faint, insistent drumming began.

A woman walked into the rectangle, carrying a large wicker basket on her shoulder. She placed it on the ground with great care and then, taking a long stick, she knocked the cover from the basket and sprang back. In the silence Mara heard a familiar, almost cozy sound—that of a tea kettle approaching the boil. The sound came from within the basket, growing in intensity, and then the woman took her pole and tipped the basket over.

Instantly the long, coiling bodies spilled out in a knot of hissing, venomous fury. The snakes were dull and brown, patterned with diamond shapes and tapering to flat, wedge-shaped heads which darted ceaselessly. She could see the rattles from where she sat, and shrank back involuntarily from what seemed to her a manifestation of pure evil. The snakes slithered over and into the pit, and the colonel's voice rose in scream after scream of primal horror.

It was the trick of a fiend, and Mara was sick with pity. If he stayed in the pit he would be dead in minutes, the snakes swarming over his thrashing limbs and striking him everywhere—if he clambered out he would be shot in his tracks. She saw his hand rise in the air, heard his strangled shrieks, and then he was scrabbling for his freedom, clawing his way from the pit like a drowning man trying to rise from the surface of the water. One of the rattlers was coiled around his ankle as he heaved up and over onto the grass; he was weeping now, blubbering like a small boy as he stumbled to his feet and began to lurch piteously away from the rectangle in a sad parody of a run.

At every moment she expected the arrows to lodge in his retreating back, but they let him go quite a distance first. He was fifty feet away when the first brave lodged an arrow in his leg. He pitched forward and fell, then got to his feet and trotted on hopelessly for a yard or two before the next arrow caught him in the shoulder. They were playing with him, wounding him but not allowing him to die.

She wondered if the venom in his veins would kill him before the next arrow could, but then her brave stepped forward, arched his bow, and sent an arrow cleanly through the colonel's neck. The impact sent him whirling round, so that Mara saw his face quite clearly before he fell for the final time. His eyes were rolled back so that only the white was visible, and the tip of the arrow protruded from his throat. Then he fell forward, and Mara thanked God that his suffering was over. She was sobbing in great, ragged gasps of dumbstruck horror and she could not stop. One of the women tapped her playfully and called her a name: *"Tse-ne-gat."*

She found out much later that it was a Ute word. It meant "cry-baby."

## Chapter Nine

"You are almost well, but you must rest." The voice was disembodied, soothing. Mara opened her eyes. Bending over her pallet was the face of the Indian woman who had impressed her as being somehow different. Her features were softer, less clearly defined. Perhaps she was of a different tribe. And then Mara realized that she was being addressed in perfect English, and wakened fully.

"How long have I been lying here?"

"A day and a night. You have had sunstroke, from the long ride here. You were taken ill after the ceremony."

The ceremony. Mara remembered the colonel's horrible death and shut her eyes again with a moan of despair. Her head throbbed slightly and she was weak and shaky. The woman bathed her face and then fed her soup from a ladle; her eyes were so calm and tranquil that Mara began to feel at ease with her.

"You speak English," Mara said when she had

finished the soup. "Can you tell me where I am?"

The woman looked amused. "As for speaking English," she said wryly, "I was born speaking it. I am not Cheyenne, though doubtless I look like one now." She took Mara's hand and pressed it reassuringly. "You are in the Cheyenne village of Chief Standing Bear, near the Arkansas River. We are twenty miles from the Sawatch mountains."

Mara stared at her wonderingly. She could see now that the woman was white, but the sun had permanently darkened her skin and her hair was plaited, Indian style. "How long have you been here?" she asked.

"I have been with the Cheyenne for fifteen years. I am married to the chief's brother."

Mara shuddered.

"I am called Yellow Deer. When I was your age my name was Lucinda Phipps. I was taken in a raiding party near Durango; my father was killed and my mother and I were separated during the fighting. The Cheyenne adopted me—took me with them wherever they migrated—and I am one of them now. I could never go back."

"But they're cruel, despicable people!" Mara cried passionately. "I have never seen anything so savage as what they did to that poor man. How can you live among such beasts?"

Yellow Deer laid her cool hand on Mara's forehead. "Hush," she said, "you must not excite yourself. Lie still and I will tell you a story. When I have finished you will understand why the colonel suffered as he did, and why you and the little boy were taken."

The woman folded her hands, arranging herself in a formal position, and in the chanting tones she had learned from her captors related the story of the Sand Creek Massacre . . .

"Thirty years ago the great Cheyenne chief, Black Kettle, was assured by the United States Army that his people might camp in safety at Sand Creek, thirty miles from Fort Lyon. Seven hundred tepees were pitched there. Some were Arapahoe, but most were Cheyenne—women, children, and aged men. They dwelt in perfect peace, disturbing no one. In November of 1864 a colonel named Chivington led a raid on this harmless band. He attacked before dawn, and before he was done he had slaughtered nearly four hundred women and children. Scalps were taken and bodies mutilated. Fetuses were cut from the bodies of pregnant Cheyenne women. Scalps were displayed proudly as far away as Denver. It was the act of a mad dog—the white men at Sand Creek so far exceeded any cruelties recorded against the Indians that the world rose up and called them infamous!

"The Cheyenne were not disposed to trust the white man after that, and they declared war on the whole race of whites, making their names known and feared from Colorado to the Powder River country in South Dakota. Black Kettle still hoped for peace and urged his braves to lay down their weapons, but fate had marked him for a terrible end. He was hunted down by George Armstrong Custer in 1868, and murdered, with his wife, on the banks of the Washita River . . ."

"They have been wronged terribly," Mara said

slowly. "I can understand their hatred, but how can they seek vengeance for something that happened so long ago?"

"Standing Bear's memory is long, and he has more cause for grief than most. His own mother and two of his wives were murdered at Sand Creek. The brave who brought you here was spared. He was two days old when his mother was killed. He lay strapped to the dead woman's back in his cradleboard, overlooked by the soldiers. The shamans say he must bring us women and children to compensate for what was done—not to kill, that is white man's work—but to raise and adopt as our own. White men are a different matter. He will kill one every year until he dies. That cannot be altered."

"His name?" Mara asked. "What is he called?"

"Satanta," was the reply. "When he was a child they called him by a Ute name: *Tse-quit*. It means 'Man Who Never Cries.' That is what the white men call him still."

"The little boy who was taken from the train—he will not be harmed?"

"He will be taught the ways of *Tsistsista*—the People. That is what we call ourselves. He will be raised as a Cheyenne."

Mara could not bring herself to inquire as to her own fate and asked merely who the women were who dwelt in the tepee. "There are two of them," she explained. "One is kind, the other young and pretty, but sullen. She does not like me."

"They are Satanta's wives," the woman said. For the first time she looked evasive. Her brown eyes clouded over slightly, as if in discreet embarrassment. Mara saw how she must once have looked, in the days when she was still Lucinda Phipps, but then the mask of tranquility returned and Yellow Deer said, "Rest now. There is a feast tonight and you will need your strength."

"What sort of feast?" Mara felt her pulse quicken with forboding. But Yellow Deer, having said enough, slipped away, leaving her alone. At least she was not to be killed or tortured. When she was strong again she would use all her intelligence and guile to understand her captors fully. Only then could she hope to escape. Surely they must realize that people were not abducted from trains with impunity in the year 1894? That someone would organize a search party and come looking for the hostages? Her greatest fear now was that the Cheyenne might pull up stakes and decamp for a new location before she could be found. She hoped with all her heart that Caleb had not been killed. She felt sure the blow had been intended only to stun, but why would a man who had pledged himself to killing the enemy act with such comparative charity? It was all a great mystery to her . . .

Satanta's two wives came to her when it grew dark, annointing her with a sweet, fragrant oil which they poured from a vial and rubbed into her skin until it gleamed in the firelight. They combed and plaited her hair in two long, thick braids and dressed her in a garment of the finest white antelope skin. She was given a necklace of shells which had been dyed a bright crimson, and when they finished the younger girl stepped back and said, with

a trace of scorn: *"Mah-hah Ich-hon.* Big eyes, you."
Both women departed, giggling softly.

Mara stood in bewilderment in the center of the
tepee. Her naked body, beneath the soft antelope
hide, felt strange to her. She had never been nude
beneath a garment before, and there was a lovely
freedom to it which both pleased and frightened
her. Her legs were sleek with oil and she could smell
the musky fragrance everywhere. She touched her
braids wonderingly, fingered the scarlet necklace.
Was this her official adoption into the tribe? There
was a muffled, intense drumming from somewhere
outside which seemed to work its way into her blood-
stream, echoing the beating of her heart, quicken-
ing her pulse and causing her to move restlessly
about the tepee in a sort of dance. She told herself
she wasn't dancing, merely exercising her limbs after
not having moved freely for so long; first there had
been the nightmare ride, then the hours lost to sunstroke. She was seized with a fierce yearning to leap
and run, to dance with the others in firelight, to feel
the earth throbbing under her feet. She stretched
her arms high over her head, curling her toes in
the moccasins, aware of the crimson necklace swinging over her breasts as she swayed hypnotically. She
heard footsteps and told herself to stop, but her body
was slow to obey.

Satanta himself stood before her, filling the
tepee with his immense, glowering presence. He was
dressed, like herself, in pale antelope hides. He wore
a breech cloth and loose vest which left his smoothly muscled chest bare; the contrast of the white of
the skins against the coppery tones of his gleam-

ing flesh was startling. He held a magnificent robe in his arms which had been pieced together with the feathers of innumerable birds so that it flashed irridescent in the firelight. He offered it; she took it from him and held it to her body like a shield. When she looked into his eyes they were as she remembered—black, unreadable, of a depth impossible to plumb. He stared at her expectantly.

"What is it you want of me?" she whispered.

He moved toward her, striding easily, his anklets of bone and bead rattling with each step. He seemed to Mara to be a man one moment and a savage the next—like some fabulous, mythical beast, he possessed the qualities of man and animal both. She could smell the sweet, musky oil rising from her body, or was it from his? He was so close now she could hear him breathing. He took the robe from her and spread it on the pallet.

"What is it you want?" she repeated. Her heart was pounding almost audibly now. She wished to move from him, but there was no place to go. She lifted her eyes and looked into his face. What she read there was easy to understand. "No," she said. "No—I cannot."

A shadow crossed his face then and he removed his vest, stripping it from his powerful body and throwing it to the ground. There were two hard, ridged scars in the muscles of his chest, as if he had been run through with twin spears; otherwise he was smooth and gleaming as bone. He sat on the pallet and beckoned to her to come near.

"No." She said it firmly. She thought he understood some English—more than he let on—and she spoke persuasively, choosing her words with care: "Yellow Deer has told me you are brave and good," she said. "She says you do not harm women or children. My people have never done wrong to you. I am not American. I come from across the sea. Please leave me in peace."

He listened patiently, but she saw to her despair that he did not understand, after all. She tried sign language, indicating the great distance she had come and the friendship she bore his people, clasping her hands together in supplication. He sat, humoring her as if she were a child, and then with a sigh he caught her by the wrist and dragged her toward him until she stood between his knees. He looked up into her face and said, distinctly:

"You are my wife."

His hands reached for the ties that bound her dress together, working with sure, swift motions until the pieces of soft hide fell apart and slipped to the ground. He appraised her naked body much as his father had done, but where Standing Bear had handled her like a horse trader, with playful lechery, Satanta was neither playful nor quick. His strong, square hands moved over her lightly as bird's wings, covering her breasts and thighs with restrained but obvious pleasure, moving over her back and down to clasp her buttocks, drawing her closer so that his face rested against her belly.

She was trembling violently, her muscles rigid with outrage and fear, and when she felt his teeth graze her flesh she cried out, bracing her hands against his shoulders and trying with all her strength to push him from her. It was like trying to move a rock, and she sobbed in despair and beat her hands against him, crying out "No—no—you *will* not!"

The inky eyes narrowed with anger, although he didn't feel her blows, and he rose, pulling her up with him and pressing her body to his so she could feel the power of his manhood and know how useless it was to fight him. She hung against his body, feeling the knotted muscles of thighs that could grip a horse's flanks for hours on end and never tire . . . the chest and massive arms which could pull a bow back to the breaking point and send an arrow a hundred yards into the neck of a fleeing man . . . the rocky bulk of his loins which would no sooner admit defeat than any other force of nature. She could neither plead with him nor struggle; what he wanted he would take. He threw her down on the pallet roughly and stood looking down at her, hands on his hips and legs spread. With a deliberate motion he brought his hand to his breech cloth and stripped it away in one quick movement. For the first time he smiled, grinning at her with a proud lust that seemed so evil she turned away to keep from screaming. She lay arched across the pallet, thighs tightly pressed together, her hands covering her breasts in a vain gesture of protection.

"Wife," he whispered victoriously, and then he fell upon her in a movement of fluid and terrifying grace. He ripped her hands away from her body, pinioning them above her head, and thrust a leg between her thighs, parting them effortlessly. He forced her to look into his glittering black eyes while his free hand roved her body. Mara grit her teeth and stared up at him in defiance. She would give

him no pleasure, at least; she would never allow him
to enjoy what it was he sought to take from her.

He grinned again——it was to be a contest and he
understood such games very well. He altered his
tactics, exploring her body with masterful gentleness now, his hands moving cleverly over her nipples, fluttering soft as bird's wings in an expert
arousal of woman's flesh——snaking between her obstinate thighs with the delicacy of a butterfly, turning her soft and compliant where moments before
she had lain rigid and cold, hating him.

Her eyes drooped shut and she bit her lip, turning her head from side to side to keep him from sens-
ing his victory, but he was cleverer than she and
seized the moment of her weakness. With a muted
cry he thrust into her body, impaling her, making
her cry out in pained surprise, crouching with his
knees on either side of her, driving into her savagely
again and again, taking his pleasure so quickly it
was over in a matter of seconds. A quick tremor
passed through him; his muscles quivered and he
shut his eyes briefly, but he made no sound.

She lay vanquished beneath him, eyes wild and
breath coming in strangled gasps. Her body trembled with a strange sensation which passed over her
like heat lightning. She could hear the drums again,
pulsing in the night outside the tepee where they lay,
and as she listened he entered her again and she
felt her body throbbing to a strange, primitive
rhythm. He remained within her. She could feel him
gathering strength, beating with her, until in a great,
violent motion he pulled her to him, rolling her
over so that she sat facing him, still joined to his

body, her cheek against his shoulder and her legs clasping his back. He moved gently, then more urgently, holding her fast to him, wrapping his arms around her so that she could not fall away, and she felt all resistance slip from her.

Only the sinuous movements of his body mattered. He searched for her pleasure as ardently as he had taken his own, and she surrendered to him, to the pure sensation of it. She melted into him as if they were one and not two, exploding into a million fragments of ecstatic light and crying out in helpless joy at the wonder of it . . .

She was obsessed with him. There was no other word for it. She lay beside him on the pallet, her lips pressed to his dark, smooth chest, her hands caressing him everywhere with an agonized tenderness. She touched his black braids wonderingly, finding his thick hair supple and soft to the touch. When she tried to press her lips to his he laughed and turned aside.

"You are my husband," she murmured. "May I not kiss you?"

If he understood he did not show it, but drew her back into his arms and held her close. She traced the high, ridged scars on his chest and thought with sadness that there was much she could never know of him. It did not occur to her to question that they were married now: Satanta had said she was his wife, and so it must be. In the most secret recesses of her heart she knew who it was he had come to replace; she had lost the man whose name she never spoke and yet he had come back, disguised in the form of this strangely beautiful savage. She resolved to learn Cheyenne from Yellow Deer so she could speak to him, and fell asleep in the circle of his arms, murmuring his name.

He left her before dawn, and she protested, clinging to him and begging him to remain with her. He put her away from him gently, and said only: "I do not sleep here."

In the morning she felt only shame and thought miserably that she had been mad to imagine herself in love with him. The wanton pleasure he had made her feel was the base reaction of a woman who had lost all claim to virtue. It was not possible to love such a man as Satanta—a man who killed with cold premeditation and kidnapped helpless women so that he might vent his lust. She shuddered with self-loathing and vowed to plot her escape this very day.

And then came fresh humiliation. His wives, who entered the tepee when the sun had risen, looked at her knowingly. Where had they been sent to pass the night while she writhed and moaned in Satanta's arms, and which of them would he choose to bed tonight? It was clear she was supposed to live here with them, to be joyously ready at his beck and call, whenever he should want her. The older woman was kind and pleasant as always, her inquisitive little eyes sliding from Mara's with discretion and delicacy. The young girl did not disguise her scorn and stared at Mara with open dislike. She was jealous, thought Mara, and then she shuddered as she realized what torments lay in wait for her. How would she feel when *she* was sent away?

"It is madness," she said to herself, and when the

older woman lifted her brows inquiringly Mara merely shrugged and turned away. She would have to see to it that escape came quickly; otherwise she would turn into an unrecognizable beast, tortured by the needs of her body and descending into savagery with the lot of them.

The women took her with them down to the banks of the river, where they indicated that she might bathe. The morning was cool and clear and the waters of the Arkansas lay calm and undisturbed beneath the bending branches of the birch and alder. Mara slipped into the water, first gasping at the shock of it, then relishing the purifying cold. She would wash every trace of Satanta from her body, and emerge refreshed. The girl loosened her robe and came to join Mara, her slender body sleek and lovely as a doe's. She arched her neck and raised her face to the sky and for a moment, as the sullen look melted away and was replaced by simple joy, Mara saw how lovely she was. "What is your name?" she asked, bidding for friendship, but the girl made no answer.

"Running Deer," replied the woman on the river bank. "Me—" she placed her hand on her breast— "Little Fox."

"What is my name?" Mara asked, but Little Fox looked down demurely. "Satanta," she said. Gradually Mara understood. Satanta would choose a name for her.

Later they showed her how to help them in the preparation of acorns. She saw she was expected to join in the women's work now that she had been accepted by a husband, and meekly took their instruction, her mind whirling with plans and schemes for escape. She would ask Yellow Deer to help her, and she would take the child with her . . . For the life of her she could not imagine how she would run away, but it was important to plan. She sat in the warm, April sunlight, grinding the meats of the acorns with a mortar and pestle. The work was strangely satisfying. The village was fully awake and busy women nodded to her, their faces curious but friendly, and Little Fox came to crouch beside her, encouraging Mara's modest efforts with many cries of delight and extravagant praise. A small girl-child ran from her mother and came to watch. She was so solemn and round-cheeked it made Mara smile simply to look at her, and when the child edged forward boldly and touched the soft skin of the white face she had been admiring, Mara laughed aloud.

When the acorn meats were ground fine, Little Fox took her to the river and placed the acorn meal in a shallow basin. Then she ladled water over and through the meal, repeating the process so that the bitter tannic acid would be washed away. Mara took over from her instructress, and once more the simple, repetitive motions soothed her, producing the illusion of happiness and content. She felt it was dangerous to allow herself such tranquility, but her mind could not hold to plans of escape when the morning was so beautiful and the light on the distant mountains burned from mauve to red to gold.

She became aware of him gradually, seeing only his moccasins at first, and then the long, strong legs beside her. Satanta had joined her silently and watched with grave, proud eyes, while his new wife performed the duties of a squaw. It was all she could do not to reach out and clasp his legs, and the trembling, feverish joy that overtook her in his presence was so intense it was like pain. She gave him no sign, but continued at her work. She would have to erase the memory of their ecstatic lovemaking if she was to survive. He remained standing on the river bank for some time, silent, at his ease, and then he went away. Some of the loveliness of the morning had faded for her: she had to press her lips together hard to keep from calling after him . . .

In the afternoon she saw the white child playing in the company of two boys his age. Already he was less pale, and when one of the Indian boys touched his shoulder in their game of tag, he laughed. She stared, unable to believe her eyes. The boy looked robust—happy, even. When she came closer he looked up, squinting his blue eyes in the sun, and said: "They're going to let me ride one of their ponies!"

"They are good people," Mara said uncertainly. "You mustn't be afraid."

"No, ma'am."

"What is your name?"

"Billy Armstrong—but I'm getting a new name."

"How old are you?" asked Mara gently.

"Almost five." A shadow passed over the child's face, as if in telling his age he had recalled something, but then he turned away, eager to return to his game. He had not witnessed the colonel's death —all he knew of the Cheyenne was the kindness of Yellow Deer, in whose tepee he stayed, and the

promise of ponies. Only three days had passed, and
he could laugh. Childhood, Mara thought, was a
remarkable, an enviable, state.

The unseasonably warm weather could not last.
For several mornings there was frost, and a cold
wind swept down from the mountains. When Mara
rose each morning she wrapped herself in a red
blanket and went briskly about her chores, moving
to keep warm. There was a rhythm to the days. Little Fox saw to the fire and the preparation of meals,
while Mara and Running Deer went to the river
and lifted the weirs which had been set to trap fish.
It was also Mara's duty to feed the horses, grind
acorns, and—when it was nearly midday—to hoe
the small patch where winter onions and parsnips
grew. Her hands were no longer white and smooth,
and one day she bent over the river and saw her
face reflected in the water, framed by two dangling
braids. It was the same face she had looked at in
countless mirrors—still white and smooth, still dominated by the enormous eyes Running Deer had
noted, and still beautiful. But there was a haunted
look to it now, something melancholy and bereft
had touched her features, and Mara shuddered as
if someone had walked on her grave. She knew what
ailed her, but she could not admit, even to herself,
that she was pining for Satanta.

He had gone, with his brother and three others,
on a hunting party. She had not seen him since the
day by the river bank when he had stood silently

observing her at her work. At night she lay in the tepee, hearing the soft breathing of the other two women, sleepless with longing. Every cry of pleasure he had wrung from her echoed in her ears, making her sick with shame, and her body quivered at the mere memory of his touch. Running Deer became friendlier in his absence. It was as if she guessed at Mara's thoughts and, made charitable in sisterly compassion, sought to comfort her.

One day she placed her hands on her slender belly and indicated that it would soon grow. She pantomimed an infant at her breast, and smiled. Mara understood that Running Deer was carrying Satanta's child and asked Little Fox when it would be born. "Moon of Flying Snow," replied the older woman. Mara thought of the child born to Kathy, and turned away.

When Satanta and the others returned there was a great feast. They had killed two deer and innumerable prairie rabbits and were greeted with enthusiastic cries of pleasure by everyone. Mara helped in the preparations, learning to dress the venison under the capable instructions of Yellow Deer.

"Did you never think of running away?" she asked.

"Yes. I thought of little else at first, but gradually I realized it could not be. It is impossible. They are expert trackers; they could have found me, no matter where I went." Yellow Deer was calm, cheerful. "It is not a bad life," she said. "You will learn not to miss—" she paused, searching for the right words — "the outside world."

"I will never learn to accept what I haven't chosen," Mara said. "Here there is no freedom, and that I cannot tolerate."

Yellow Deer looked at her shrewdly. "You are like my children," she said. "You say one thing and mean another."

The chief wore Mara's amethyst on his head band. It winked in the firelight, mocking her; it seemed that the brooch, symbol of her past life, was destined to ornament Standing Bear just as she was destined to be an ornament to his son. She sat with Satanta's other wives, queen of the pride, at the long feasting table. Courtesy dictated that Little Fox, the oldest of the three, be served her portion first, but the choicest bits of venison and rabbit were handed round to Mara. Satanta was openly courting her now; he sat talking and laughing with the men, but his eyes flew to Mara often, and once he strode the length of the table to see that her bowl was full. She did not return his glances, but when the dancing began she could not keep her eyes from him. He wore three anklets on each leg and a heavy necklace of silver and turquoise hung against his bronze chest. He moved with extraordinary grace, his sinuous body turning and rippling as he performed the ritual dance to the drum and the insistent, high shrilling of the turkey-bone whistle. The others chanted, urging him on. When it came to an end he consulted briefly with his father, and then—standing, in the center of the clearing—he made an announcement. The words were Cheyenne, but Mara knew he was speaking of her. He had acknowledged her as his wife. And something else.

"He has named you," said Yellow Deer softly.

"What is my name?"

"Burning Heart."

Satanta held his hand out to her and Mara, walking as if in a trance, went to him. He led her away, toward the meadow where the horses were kept. It had grown colder. The stars were so large and bright they seemed to wheel across the black sky in the limitless heavens above. Before them the vast plains stretched away toward the mountains. He took his horse, leading him from the paddock, and lifted Mara up. Then he vaulted on the horse's back, gently urged him with his heels, and they sped off into the night. As a captive she had ridden behind him; as his wife she rode in front. His strong arm circled her, his hand upon her breasts, and she leaned against his body, glorying in the swift surging of the beast beneath her, trembling to find herself so close, once more, to the object of her desire. She did not know where he was taking her, nor did she care. It was enough to streak through the night with him, to feel her heart beating against the palm of his hand. She was complete, alive again.

They stopped when they were several miles from the settlement. The moon had come out from behind one of the mountain peaks and shone down on the tall grass of the plains, gilding it like a sea of silver. Satanta lifted her from the horse and carried her a little way in his arms. She clasped his neck and leaned her head against his chest and felt she might die of happiness.

He lowered her to the grass, and before he could lie beside her she was pulling him to her hungrily, winding her arms around him and murmuring his name. His face as he bent to her was clearly revealed in the moonlight, and she thought she had been mad to think his eyes impassive, dispassionate . . . They glowed with desire and something more, some hint of terrible bewilderment that made her want to reassure him. There was much she longed to say to him, but they could not speak to each other.

His hands stroked her gently, arousing her as they had done before, but this time there was no anger, no contest. They both wanted the same thing. She arched her body so violently that words were forced from him; he murmured to her, heedless of the fact she could not understand, and buried his face against her breasts, shuddering with the power of his feelings. She welcomed him into her body with a glad cry, raking his back with her nails, feeling her very soul pour from her like molten lava. The pleasure was so agonizing that she found herself sobbing with amazement and ecstasy. He regarded her wonderingly, stroking her face with gentle fingers and shaking his head slowly, with the look of bewilderment she had seen earlier.

"Oh, my love," she whispered, "you make me so happy. I thought I would never be happy again . . ." And then she put her hand to his cheek and said: "Man Who Never Cries."

He smiled at the words, and then they slept, awakening in the first cold light of dawn. He wrapped her in his blanket and they rode back to the village. This time they went slowly, allowing the horse to walk at his own pace, and she leaned against Satanta's breast, feeling she had been caught in an exquisite dream . . .

She was never again jealous of his wives, but she wished with all her heart that she could live with Satanta himself. She felt only half alive when he was not within her sight; she could never have enough of him. He loved her too, of that she felt sure. One day they bathed together in the river and he actually laughed aloud when she paddled about him in circles. "No," he protested, and then, showing her how it ought to be done, he swam to the far bank, cutting through the water like a seal, and back. When he rose from the water she thought how beautiful his body was in its bronze solidity and went to him, touching the scars on his chest and looking at him questioningly. He turned away, signifying that it was not something he wished to explain, even if he could. Then he knelt beside her, laying his head against her belly, his strong dark hands covering her white breasts. Her hair hung dripping down, like a mantle, covering them. She said, "I love you," and he shuddered, closing his eyes.

She asked Yellow Deer about the terrible scars, and Yellow Deer seemed reluctant to answer. At last she said, "They are from the Sun Dance. We do not speak of it; it is the highest religious act, the most sacred."

"How am I to become one of you if I cannot understand?"

Yellow Deer gazed at her solemnly before she said, "Very well. I will tell you. All great warriors—Satanta, Standing Bear, my own husband—have performed the Sun Dance. It is a quest for the truest form of life; a sacrifice to *Maheo*. The warrior who emerges from the Sun Dance is never the same—he has been purified. He dances all day, looking into the sun, without food, without water, following it from the time it rises in the east to when it sets in the west. He is attached to a pole, by leather thongs, and all day he must blow a whistle made of eagle or turkey wing."

"But the scars?" Her voice was hushed.

"An incision is made in the muscles of the dancer's chest, and hooks are passed through his flesh. He must dance until he has ripped them free from his body."

Mara felt a pang of revulsion, then a wave of pure anguish pass through her at the thought of her beloved's suffering. "How could he allow it?" she whispered. "How could he hurt himself so?"

"You do not know him yet if you can ask," said Yellow Deer. "White men are seeking to outlaw the Sun Dance. Our people will perform it in secret, then." When Yellow Deer said "our people" she meant the Cheyenne. It became more difficult every day for Mara to remember that Yellow Deer was white . . .

It grew warm again as true spring descended on the plain. Wild flowers grew in the pastures where the horses lived—cowslips and columbines and tiny, early poppies. The air was balmy and scented at night, and she went with Satanta far out on the plain, or to the rushing riverbank, to make love. She understood that this was not the rule, and that he broke the rule for her. One night she lay in his arms, plaiting wild flowers into his long braids, and said to him, her voice shy with emotion:

"Tomorrow is my birthday."

He did not understand. She held up the fingers of her hands, then showed him eight more. Then she pointed to the place where the sun would rise in the morning, touched her breast, and held up one finger. "I will be nineteen," she said.

He understood, and held his hands up three times. "In Moon of Bare Branches," he said. Thus she knew he would be thirty years old in November. She had been his wife for a month, and it was May.


Satanta spent the afternoon of her birthday hunting for rabbits. He would give the pelts to Little Fox and have her make a jacket for his new wife. He rode effortlessly, as always, his body so much a part of the horse's that he never had to think what to do. The sun was bright and hot and he felt its nourishing touch on his shoulders and back with joy. Yet he was troubled, and for the first time in his life the trouble had to do with a woman.

He had made love to many women from the time he was thirteen years old. His people thought it right that young boys and maidens should indulge their bodies, although they were strict about matters like adultery. No woman had ever refused him, or complained that he was cruel. He had married Little Fox when he was seventeen. She was gentle and comely and he had great affection for her still. He respected her; she was the mother of three of his children and she was thrifty, loving, and intelligent. He loved his children by Little Fox, and his son who had been born of a second wife, now dead. Running Deer was another matter. He had taken her as a wife only two years ago. He had been smitten by her beauty, beguiled by her slender, quick body and dark, smoldering eyes. But Running Deer was petulant and selfish. Her heart was not good, and even now that she was expecting his child he regretted having made her his wife. He never reproved her; indeed he had tried to be tolerant, hoping she would grow out of her sullen ways as she matured. He had never beaten a wife nor a child; he scorned such tactics as white man's vices.

It was Burning Heart who caused him to be troubled. From the moment he had seen her on the train with the white man beside her he had wanted her. Never had he thought it possible for a white woman to be so beautiful to him; but her midnight hair and the immense eyes like liquid gold had laid a hand upon his heart. Her white skin fascinated him. He had never liked the skin of the white people—it had seemed pallid, unhealthy, and he much preferred the warm bronze hue of his own people, but Burning Heart was soft and like the bark of birch trees to his touch. When he had taken her by force she had stared at him so defiantly, with the courage almost of a warrior, that he had resolved to give her pleasure. And what a tempest he had uncovered—what passion there was in his new little wife! Indian women took their pleasure more silently, accepting it as their due. Burning Heart seemed almost to die in his arms each time, and he, too, felt himself grow weak with passion. He feared she would take his strength from him, reduce him by claiming so much of his life. He could not think of anything but her, and this bewildered him. More than anything, he wanted to have a child with Burning Heart, and here it was that his greatest shame surfaced: He was afraid that she might die. He had never feared for any of his Cheyenne wives, but white women were mysterious; he knew they sometimes died in childbirth and if Burning Heart should die he would be ruined, finished as a warrior and a man. Already he was diminished, because he was afraid. He had never been afraid of anything before . . .

Running Deer knew the penalty for black magic was death or banishment, but she was prepared to take the risk. If she could not make the others see how evil the white girl's influence was, she would turn to darker ways.

"You are being spiteful," Little Fox reproved, the first time she had told her that Mara was an evil woman. "You will only harm yourself." Even her best friend, White Crow, had looked doubtful. She did not dare to approach Satanta himself; it was clear her husband was besotted with the white-whore. It made her sick to see such a man make a fool of himself. And for what? A pale, simpering turnip of a girl with yellow eyes like an owl.

Even the children liked Burning Heart. She
would see when *her* child was born that Burning
Heart never came near the baby, even if she had to
go to the chief himself. But then, thought Running
Deer with a thrill of pleasure, if all went well her
rival would not be with them when the snow came.
She would be gone, long, long before that. Her
fingers trembled with excitement as she dug the
little shallow grave by the river bank. Into it she
placed the claw of the dead crow, smoothing the
earth away carefully. Then she took from the small
pouch she wore around her neck the long, dark
strand of hair she had cut so silently from Burning
Heart's head as she lay sleeping. She tied it around
the claw, her lips moving in a forbidden prayer, and
then quickly scooped dirt over the hole, packing it
carefully back so no one could see the earth had
been disturbed.

If her medicine was strong enough, then the girl
would sicken and die. If not, she would go to the
shaman and convince him that Burning Heart's presence was dangerous to them. She had heard an owl
call the night before, and all the world knew that
owls were ghosts, restless and vindictive spirits. The
silly big-eyes had brought them trouble, of that she
was sure. Wolf Voice, the shaman, was returning to
them soon. He had been away all winter in the
mountains, replenishing his powers, but when he
came back then Burning Heart would see what it
was to cross wits with an expert!

She passed Satanta on her way to the village. She

smiled at him most winningly, but he was absorbed in thought and barely noticed her. He inquired formally if she were well. "Oh, very well," she replied, showing her teeth and looking at him in the way that he had once found so captivating. "I am glad," he said, and passed on.

Mara knew they could not stay in the village forever, but when Little Fox told her they would soon be going to a new settlement, closer to the mountains, she felt a pang of loss. She had come to love the site by the river bank and knew she would miss it. The shaman had returned to them, and she supposed it was his influence that forced them to move. She never allowed herself to think that it was on her account they pulled up stakes and packed their belongings; she no longer dreamed of search-parties coming to find her or the little boy. The world she had once lived in seemed as remote to her as the mountains of the moon.

The tepees were dismantled and packed up, strapped to *travois* along with cooking implements and blankets, and dragged behind the dogs. She saw the white child, on his own pony, in a group to her left. He was sunburned and hardy-looking now; he had learned many words of Cheyenne and chattered happily to a boy his age. Mara walked behind Little Fox and Running Deer, beside their *travois*.

She could see Satanta far ahead, riding beside his father. He was not allowed to ride with her in public; he had already suffered taunts because of his attentions to her—only a man as great as Satanta could escape the outright ridicule of the other braves because they respected and feared him. One night, after they had made love, he had asked her a question which made her blood run cold.

"Do you want to go back to your people?" He had spoken in English, haltingly but with an intensity that deepened her chill.

"No," she whispered. "No . . . I have no people now. Only you."

## Chapter Ten

Summer in the village at the foot of the Sawatch mountains was a time of enchantment. The days were hot and gloriously clear, and at night the stars hung as if impaled on the crags of the mountains, huge and bright. There were berries to eat, and ripe nuts, and the children went nearly naked to help gather sweet grass. Mara tasted chokeberries on the lips of Satanta—always she would remember the wild sweetness of chokeberry kisses throughout the summer of their love. She sensed that he had tried to turn from her, but the force of his passion for her was greater than his desire to remain inviolable.

It was in the early autumn that Standing Bear became ill. He lay in his tepee for two days and would see no one but his sons and Wolf Voice, the shaman. He was spitting blood, the women said; he had sung his death song and was prepared to leave them. Wolf Voice announced that soon he would put himself into a trance and seek out the reasons for the chief's mysterious illness.

Mara feared the shaman. He was a figure of primeval terror, but this was a calculated effect and it was not his wild glance or pierced ears, clattering with bones, that made her fear him. It was his ability to read the minds of all around him that made him dangerous. He was a man of great natural guile and—she felt sure—no affection for anyone save himself. It was impossible to tell how old he was. His skin was finely wrinkled, as if it had been crumpled and then spread out tautly over his sharp-boned face, yet he was vigorous and his sunken, glittering eyes seemed young. When he turned the power of his gaze on Mara she felt he knew all her secrets and was amused.

One day when she was mending a blanket he came to her, squatting by her side, and drew a picture of a tortoise in the dust. The turtle was sacred to the Cheyenne. She looked from the drawing to his face and saw how like a turtle he was himself. He smiled and nodded, leaving her to ponder the significance of what he had shown her.

That night Standing Bear was carried on a litter and placed near the central fire. The entire village was present to watch while Wolf Voice called for a frying pan and placed chips of fragrant cedar inside. He began to pray, sitting on the ground beside the fallen chief, and as he lifted his voice Standing Bear coughed and a trickle of blood seeped from his mouth. His lips fell open and the rivulet became a torrent; he gasped and choked.

Wolf Voice produced a black scarf from the pouch bag he wore at his belt and held it out so all could see. Then he tied a knot, and the chief's breathing quieted. He tied three more knots and as each appeared Standing Bear's labored breathing calmed; the hemorrhage had ceased and the chief slept peacefully. Mara did not know if she had witnessed a miracle or a clever ruse, but her fear of the shaman had increased a hundred-fold.

Satanta did not come to her that night, and her sleep was fitful. She dreamed of great tortoises swimming in a lake of blood, and awakened to find Running Deer hovering over her bed.

*"Teocote!"* the girl hissed. Owl.

Mara heard the echo of the owl's shriek hanging in the still night air, dying away like the memory of sorrow. Running Deer's eyes were large with terror and she shrank from Mara, backing toward her own pallet and murmuring to herself. Her pregnancy had begun to show, and Mara was well aware that Running Deer's hatred for her was growing as steadily as the unborn child . . .

The village had to be purified so that the shaman could cure Standing Bear completely. Stones were heated and placed in a pit, and when water poured over them steam rose in great clouds to drive away any evil spirits.

"What is going to happen?" Mara asked Yellow Deer.

"There will be a ceremony tonight. Wolf Voice must put himself into a trance to determine what is killing our chief. We will all be given visions—even you."

"How can you be sure? How will I receive a vision?"

"Through peyote," said Yellow Deer with an air of finality.

The button she was given to chew was bitter and harsh to the taste. Wolf Voice withdrew the peyote from an ornate, rectangular box inlaid with silver. Feathers and rattles hung from the box, and a fan of turkey feathers. She stared, fascinated, while the shaman placed four of the buttons before Satanta and the other high-ranking braves. The steady beat of the drum had a different quality tonight—more measured and solemn—and they stared into the fire as they had been instructed to do. The muffled throbbing sound and the leaping flames had a hypnotic effect, and before very long Mara was afraid she would fall asleep, pitching forward and disgracing herself. Visions seemed very far away. There was only the feeling of foreboding which had come to her when the owl had cried in the night, and the steadily growing belief that the chief's illness would, in some mysterious way, separate her from Satanta. She wanted to look at Satanta, to find reassurance in his well-loved features, but she was afraid to take her eyes from the fire.

Presently the sleepy feeling fell from her and she became alert, her body taut as if the skin had been stripped away, leaving the bare nerves humming and sizzling on the surface of her flesh. She was sensitive to the nuances of the drum now; it seemed each throbbing beat melted into the next without pause. If she listened carefully she could hear that the drum was one long, continuous voice calling to her from the past, tying all the threads of her life together and circling, circling around her like a silken ribbon of pure force and spirit. The shapes in the fire also had meaning—she could see a band of wild ponies galloping among the flames and escaping into the night. Once, to her horror, she perceived a rattlesnake in the center of the conflagration and wondered if it were one of the snakes used to force the colonel from his hiding place . . .

Suddenly Running Deer was on her feet, writhing in the throes of a fit, leaping grotesquely in the firelight, forcing air through her teeth in a long series of grunting sighs. Words poured from her in a shrill stream, chasing around the circle and echoing with eerie cacaphony. Mara could not understand more than a few of the words, and those she knew were drowned by the rushing in her ears. She did not want to know what it was Running Deer was saying, but later, when Wolf Voice achieved his trance and spoke in a long, windy rush of hollow sound, she thought she understood it all perfectly. There was a presence among them which called down the wrath of the spirits of the dead and sucked the life from their chief. It had been among them for some time now, coming in the shape now of a bird, now as a beast, going about in the dead of night, working evil. They must destroy the presence or be destroyed themselves.

She sat motionless until the fire had burned away and it was nearly dawn. One by one the others left the circle and she could feel the presence of the shaman somewhere nearby in the darkness. She was no longer afraid of him, only amazed that she ever could have doubted his power. She waited to see what he would do, but when a hand fell upon her shoulder it was not the hand of Wolf Voice but of Satanta, her husband. She took his hand and felt the current which flowed between them, entering her and making her strong again. She stood to face him and looked long into his face. They never touched, yet it was as if he had entered her body. She felt him deep inside her, in her blood and bones, and it was as if he struggled to be free . . .

Their last ride together was the longest. She lay against his breast as she had done the time they rode out to make love in the long grass. He did not urge his horse because neither of them wanted the ride to end—both Mara and Satanta prayed for a miracle, but with a difference. She knew no miracle could happen, while he believed until the end that a compassionate God might turn them into another form, so that they might be together forever.

The shaman had declared that it was Burning Heart's presence which caused the evil. It was she who made the chief sicken, she who was laying a curse on the unborn child of Satanta's second wife. Satanta did not believe any of it, but from the moment Wolf Voice had spoken it was no longer safe for Burning Heart to live among them. He had sworn to his people that he would take her far away from them, and he had ridden off with her, his rifle slung across his shoulder. If they wanted to believe that he would kill her, so be it, but he would as soon cut his heart out. He would return her to the world where she belonged, and then he would go back to his dying father and wait to become a chief. He knew he might well be the last free Cheyenne chief, the last who did not live his days out on a reservation. It was fitting that he, whose heart was grieving so sorely, should end the once-glorious saga of his people. He had wrapped his beloved in his red and blue blanket, to keep the sun from her, and now he held her fast and sang:

> It is bad to live to be old.
> Better to die young—
> Nothing lives forever.
> Only the earth lives forever,
> Only the mountains live forever.

When he left her in a deep, grassy grading beside the railroad tracks she stretched her arms out to him one last time, but he turned swiftly and rode off, never looking back.

"You must be gentle with her, doctor. She is in a sort of trance."

Elsie Willison had bathed the girl and put her to bed in her daughter's room. She had lain there for a whole day now and never registered by the slightest sign that she was aware of what went on around her. She did not speak, and Elsie's husband said the girl was a mute. Elsie thought differently, but she had summoned the doctor and begged him to examine the poor creature.

"You found her lying beside the railroad?" he asked incredulously.

Elsie nodded. "The children found her, and they came running to tell us. She was wrapped in an Indian blanket—unhurt, so far as we could tell—and she couldn't talk. She's young, no more than twenty, perhaps not that. She's not an Indian, but she was dressed as one."

The doctor looked down at the face on the pillow and understood Mrs. Willison's agitation. The girl's eyes were open, but there was no light of comprehension there. He looked at her curiously. Her skin had been tanned to a warm, honey-colored hue by constant exposure to the sun, but when he lifted her arm to take her pulse he saw that she was creamy white above the wrist. The long hair, braided Indian style, was shimmering jet and the unseeing eyes seemed to him like sun discs—golden and blazing, yet blind.

Mrs. Willison had clothed her in a nightdress, but around her neck lay a long necklace of red shells which was obviously Indian. Her little hands were roughened by work, the nails short and blunt, but otherwise she seemed well cared-for. Her skin glowed with health and the heart-beat and pulse were strong. It was warm in the room, but the Cheyenne blanket had been drawn up tightly around her; she seemed to flinch when he touched it, or was it his imagination?

She submitted to his examination listlessly, never

looking at him or responding in any way. He discovered a bite-mark on her left shoulder which he thought was several weeks old. It was a mark of love, and he turned his eyes quickly away and drew the blanket over her again.

"Can you hear me?" he asked in a low voice. "Do you understand what I am saying?"

She did not reply, but he had discovered what he wanted to know. She was not deaf.

"You have been living among Indians," he said. "Have they harmed you?"

Again there was no answer.

He sighed and went back to the front room. "She's in a state of shock," he said to Mrs. Willison, "but she's healthy enough, bodily. My guess—" he lowered his voice—"is that she's been forced into—ah—unnatural acts, so to speak. That is what has put her into such a state."

Elsie was not satisfied with the doctor's explanation, but she said nothing. If the poor girl had suffered at the hands of the Indians, then why had she clutched her blanket so fiercely when Elsie tried to take it from her? It was the only sign she had given of being alive at all . . .

Mara lay for another day in the narrow little bed, hearing the sounds of the family as they went about their normal routine, trying not to disturb her. Once the child in whose bed she had been placed came tiptoeing in to retrieve a book. The little girl looked at her questioningly for a while and then left. Mara wanted to be alone, lying beneath the blanket which still seemed to carry some aura of Satanta. The odor of his flesh—sweet and redolent of spice—

still lived there. She knew it would disappear soon, leaving her with nothing of him but the necklace. She could not bear to go on living without some little part of him close to her.

She knew she would never again see him, understood and forgave him for leaving her, but she felt her heart had cracked in her breast and wanted merely to be left in peace forever. Speech seemed useless, profane. To utter words to the kind people who had rescued her would only drive his spirit further away . . .

"I think I know who she is," George Willison announced that evening. "Do you remember—about six months ago it was—when three people were taken from a train by Cheyenne? By the time we saw it in the newspaper all Denver was up in arms!"

Elsie remembered very well. The *Rocky Mountain News,* which reached them here a week late, had trumpeted the affair in bold, black letters: SHOCKING ABDUCTION ON TRAIN FROM CRIPPLE CREEK—CHEYENNE TAKE THREE PRISONERS! There had been a retired army colonel, a young girl, and, worst of all—a little boy, no older than her Joey. And something else. A man who had been traveling with the girl had been injured, hit over the head and left concussed in the aisle of the train. At the time of the reports he was still unconscious.

"But wasn't the girl from a dance hall? *She* doesn't look like that sort of woman, not at all. She seems so innocent."

George smiled. One of the things he loved best

about his wife was her abiding faith in appearances. "It's the same girl, sweetheart. The papers said no one knew much about her, but they did mention she was a beauty. Have you ever seen such eyes?"

Elsie bit her lip. As usual, George was right.

The sheriff was able to add to their information. If it was the same girl, he said, she had no family and no one to go to. Her traveling companion had recovered from his concussion to find that all the search parties had been unsuccessful, and he had gone looking for her himself. Nothing had been heard of him for months; perhaps he had left Colorado altogether. The colonel was presumed to be dead. He was an old Indian fighter and it seemed unlikely the Cheyenne would allow him to live. There was still a reward offered for news of the little boy. His mother had broken down totally, made mad by grief. A sad business, said the sheriff. But when the girl came 'round perhaps she'd be able to help. Certainly, she'd want to do everything she could to see that her captors were punished.

On the third day the girl sat up and took some soup from Mrs. Willison's daughter. She no longer clutched at her blanket, though it remained close to her, and she nodded in thanks when the child took the bowl of soup away.

"You're feeling better?" asked the child.

"Yes," said Mara. "Thank you."

The little girl ran jubilantly from the room, flinging herself out the front door and hurtling up the town's main road to the small general store her parents owned. "Ma!" she cried breathlessly. "She can talk. She's sitting up in bed, and she spoke to me!"

When the Willisons arrived with the sheriff, the doctor, and a retired lawyer who wrote small, colorful pieces for the local newspaper, Mara was subtly changed. She had unplaited her long hair so that it hung about her shoulders. Her voice was faint, but she answered their questions politely.

"My name is Mara McQuaid," she told them. "I thank you for all you've done for me."

When the sheriff asked if she felt well enough to give him a deposition she looked uncomprehending.

"Well, Miss," he said deferentially, "anything you can tell us about your experience would help us. How did you manage to escape? Not one of the search parties was able to find hide nor hair of the people who took you. Now, you must have some idea of where you've been, even if it's just a guess?" Then he repeated what he had said to Elsie. "We know you'll want to do everything possible to see that your captors are punished."

As he spoke Mara's fingers returned to the blanket again. She caressed it, her fingers moving over the brightly patterned wool with infinite tenderness, as if searching for something. At last, she said:

"I'm sorry. I'm afraid you don't understand. I remember nothing. Nothing at all."

She stayed with the Willisons for a week, working in their little store to help repay them for their kindness. People came in to stare at her, pretending they had forgotten to buy an article the day before and regarding her with lively curiosity. Once a little boy whispered to her, when his mother had turned away, "Is it true the Injuns took you? My ma says you *lived in sin with a savage!*" His eyes were shining.

The minister's wife dropped by one afternoon to say she would be only too happy to talk with Mara in confidence. "Sometimes it helps, my dear," she said timidly. "Another woman can understand—*so much.*"

The men were the most difficult. Old and young, polite and insolent, they flocked to the store to have a look at her. She knew what they were thinking when their eyes took the measure of her face and body, and she didn't care. One offered to buy her red necklace for ten dollars, and the look in her eyes when she refused him was enough to send him scuttling out the door as fast as his legs would carry him.

At the end of the week she bade goodbye to the Willisons and thanked them for their kindness. She had no way to pay them for the dress she wore—an altered cotton frock of Elsie's—or for the battered satchel they had given her to travel with. She vowed to recompense them one day, telling them she was going to make her way back to Denver to reclaim her possessions. Only the first part of her statement was true; as for Denver, she never wanted to see it again. She wanted only to keep going, to head where she had never been before, to forget. In the satchel she carried the clothing she had worn when the Willison children found her in the grading, and the blanket. It was all she owned in the world now.

The man who had promised to take her part-way

to Canon City was elderly and taciturn. She trusted him and did not question his reasons for going; alone of all the men in the Willisons' small village, he had never asked her a question or stared at her with speculation. She sat beside him in the rickety carriage, nodding when he pointed out a blackbird or remarked on the beauty of a cloud formation. Only once did he make a personal remark.

"If I was young again, and starting all over," he said contemplatively, "I think I'd head for California."

"Perhaps I will, at that," she replied, and then they were silent.

Canon City had no dance halls, or none worth the name. There were plenty of saloons, but Mara could not imagine herself working in one of them. For one thing, she had forgotten how to laugh. Nobody here knew of her odd past, and when she presented herself at the mission, inquiring for work, they took her in without question. The West was full of misplaced people, lost souls, and wandering adventurers; it was big enough to accommodate them all.

She worked for a while scrubbing vegetables in a cafe, and then in a draper's shop, but she wasn't able to save much money from her meagre salary. She boarded in a single room with a widowed schoolmistress, who asked her no questions, and kept to herself.

When she stared up at the mountains girdling Canon City she seemed a lonely creature, but in reality she was far from lonely. She relived, over and over, the summer of her happiness with Satanta, wrapping herself in his blanket and remembering dreamily all that he had been to her. By late October his face was not so clear in her memory as it had once been; her body no longer echoed with his touch and she reluctantly acknowledged that his spirit had slipped away from her. The agony of missing him was gone and in its place came a new pain —emptiness. She loved him as a memory only, and as she entered this new phase of her suffering other memories crowded about and she once more thought of her father.

It seemed impossible to her that she would ever find him now, yet she had come West for that purpose. She wrote once more to Mr. McSweeney, saying only that she had lived with a Cheyenne tribe for a time and was now in Canon City, trying to earn enough money to make her way to California. She concluded by admitting that he had been right to scoff at her earlier protestation.

"I told you no one could hurt me again," she wrote, "and I was foolish. But I am older now, and wiser, and this time I can say with perfect confidence —*I am invulnerable.* I want only to know if my father is alive or dead and, if the former, to see him again. I remain, your grateful friend, Mara McQuaid."

She sent it off before she could regret her impulse. She knew there was no real reason to write to him. The terms of their agreement ended the moment she paid him in full. Still, he was the only human being on the face of the earth to whom she could write.

There was a dance at the mission one evening and Mara, drawn by the lively fiddling and sounds of laughter, went to stand in the crowd. There were reels and square dances and rollicking free-for-alls which reminded her of the hurdy-gurdy house. She watched, lips parted and cheeks flushed, while the girls spun and twirled with their partners. How innocent they seemed! Had she ever been like that—throwing herself into such girlish pleasures with whole-hearted abandon?

The music altered and she realized the fiddlers were trying to duplicate an Irish reel. They confused the rhythms so that what emerged was a cowboy's conception of the music of Ireland, but she was moved nonetheless. She found herself swept into the melee, helter-skelter, and the flutist—in a burst of inspiration—cut sweetly over the cacophony of the fiddles in a fair rendition of *Rakish Pat*. Mara threw back her head, put her hands to her hips, and showed them how it should be done. She danced her way through *Rakish Pat* and *Sean McKenna's Reel* and part of the jig called *The Road to Sligo* before she saw the crowd had swept back in a semi-circle to give her room. They were clapping good-naturedly, urging her on and applauding her nimble feet. Her hair came undone from the decorous knot at the back of her neck as she flew about wildly; she felt exalted and joyful while the music lasted and she was barely winded when the musicians exhausted their Irish repertoire.

A man she had seen about the town approached her, carrying a cup of punch for her. He was a thin, pale fellow, rather elegant for Canon City, with a drooping dark moustache and a slightly accented voice. "That was a rare treat," he said, handing her the punch. "You have always been so serious, Miss McQuaid, but then the Celtic blood warms to a reel, does it not?"

She accepted the drink gratefully but made no answer to his remark. When he asked her how long she planned to remain in Canon City she said only until she had earned enough money to go on to California. He looked amused.

"At that rate you will be an old woman before you see the Pacific," he said. "They cannot pay you much to stand in the draper's six days a week and sell bolts of calico to thrifty housewives, eh?"

"That is true," Mara sighed, "but I haven't much choice."

The man laughed, his lips drawing back in a parody of mirth, but all the while his eyes were studying her with a shrewd and calculating look. "Yes," he said. "I knew it, but now I am sure."

Mara stared at him in confusion and a faint warning signal went off somewhere in her mind. She could not imagine what he was about to say, but looked at him evenly, her face composed.

"I have thought for some time," he drawled, "that you were the model for my favorite bit of post-card art. When I saw you dance tonight I knew it beyond doubt."

Her head whirled and she barely restrained a gasp of astonishment.

" 'Hibernian Beauty,' " he said, relishing the

look of amazement the words brought to her face. "You are quite famous, you know, quite in vogue. Even—" he laughed—"in California."

"But that was in Chicago," she whispered, "a lifetime ago." She had a sudden chilling memory of Roger's prophetic, mad reaction to the innocent penny postal. "Hundreds of men are now free to stare at my wife's face for the price of a penny," he had said. Now it was true.

"Ah, yes," the man continued, "there are reproductions of your lovely face from here to New Orleans, Miss McQuaid. If memory serves, an artist has immortalized you above the bar in Carson City, too. No need to be modest. Beauty is beauty, my dear. Trade on it while you may. The only thing that put me off your trail was your—how shall I say it?—tragic air when you arrived here. 'Hibernian Beauty' had all her life before her, but you seemed in mourning. Until tonight, that is."

His eyes glittered as he surveyed her face; he looked like a man who had discovered gold where he least expected to find it. "It occurs to me," he said slowly, "that you are being wasted at the draper's. Have you any idea how much men would pay to gamble if a girl like yourself dealt the cards?"

Mara laughed aloud. "I don't know how to play cards! I have never played in my life."

"That's of no importance," he said. "I could teach you. Faro, poker—simple games, my girl, but what a deal of money men spend on them. And what a deal more if a beautiful girl represents the house, eh?"

Mara drew back. "I don't know your name," she said austerely.

"Oh, call me what you like," he replied. "I've got as many names as you have secrets, sweetheart. 'Round here I'm known as Jacques Chardin. Does that suit you?"

"You are French?"

He sighed. "When I'm Jacques Chardin, I am French," he said patiently. "It doesn't do to ask me too many questions. I suspect the same is true of you. Only consider this: We can help each other, you and I. At the end of six months you'll have enough to go to California in style, and I'll be a rich man. Dealing cards may not seem the most ladylike occupation to you, but then——" he laughed knowingly ——"there *are* worse things."

Mara knew that a year ago she would never have allowed such a conversation. The man was a rogue and probably a bit of a criminal as well, but he was so open about it she felt reassured on one score at least. Once rebuffed, he would never try to make love to her. She was worth too much to him in terms of money to risk it all for a few kisses. To test her theory, she allowed him to take her back to her boarding house. It had grown cool, and the mountains hung over them like a dark fortress, blotting out the feeble starlight.

At her door he took her chin in his hand and slowly lowered his lips to hers. She suffered his touch, her lips cold and unmoving, body rigid with distaste. He withdrew quickly.

"So," he mused. "The Hibernian Beauty is an ice maiden?"

"Yes."

"What a pity. Ah, well—never mind. It's better for business that way."

Jacques began instructing Mara the very next day. He came to her lodging-house, to the landlady's chagrin and disapproval, and asked the loan of the parlor. He produced several packs of unopened cards, rolled up his sleeves, and commenced the lesson.

Mara proved an apt pupil. She quickly learned to keep a neutral face and to calculate her chances without changing expression. She loved the feel of the glossy new cards slipping away under her fingers as she shuffled furiously. She mastered faro in an afternoon, but it was poker she liked best. "But I will only deal?" she asked plaintively. "I want to *play!*" Jacques produced a pile of copper slugs and proposed they play for sport, encouraging her to give free reign to her impulse.

At the end of an hour she had won most of the slugs. He grinned and reached into his pockets, counting out a pile of bills. "This is what you've won," he said. "Go and buy yourself some pretty clothes. I am heartily tired of seeing the great Hibernian Beauty dressed like a farmer's daughter."

She selected a gown of moiré silk in pale, lemon-yellow, and a blue confection with multi-colored ribbons piped round the bodice and sleeves. "Better," he said. "Now, what do you propose to do about the schoolmarmish knot at the nape of your pretty neck?"

By the end of the fourth afternoon of instruction she felt she knew all there was to know about cards. "Not so fast," warned Jacques. "Cards are never for sport alone, sweetheart. Still, I am pleased with your progress. You've taken to folding early on—it's the flaw of most women to hang-in for love of a worthless pair of kings."

Fingers awkward from lack of practice, she began to dress her hair as she had done in Denver. Sitting at her looking-glass she saw that the honey-glow of the sun was leaving her face, gradually fading. Her bosom and shoulders were still a shade lighter than her neck and face; thoughtfully, she powdered lightly to produce a more uniform effect. How was it, she wondered, her face could still appear so unmarked and innocent? All her sufferings, all her bliss, and nothing to show for it on the smooth mask which looked back at her in the mirror. Only her eyes, if one peered beyond the golden luminosity framed in the thick tangle of black lashes, betrayed her. They seemed to carry a warning, to flash a signal to the world at large: *Keep away!*

The settlement on the Grape River was little more than a clearing at the foot of the mountains. It was neither town nor village, but a place where men could come to drink, gamble, and debauch themselves to their heart's content. There were only four buildings—a two-story frame hotel, a saloon, a bordello, and Jacques Chardin's gambling house. Mara was stunned when she saw what the hours of training had been leading up to. She had imagined that she would sit in an elegant room, presiding at a baize-covered table, dealing cards to a group of discreet gambling men. Only the baize-covered table materialized.

Jacques' gambling house was a converted saloon, sold to him cheaply by the previous owner, who had fled to New Mexico to escape the wrath of his former wife, a prostitute who now made her home in the nearby sporting house. Jacques sold whiskey by the bottle only. There was no music, no bar, no loitering camaraderie among the men. Gambling was the business here, and it was pursued with a single-minded intensity which seemed almost grim to Mara.

"You are disappointed," said Jacques. "That is only natural. We're not here for fun, my pretty. Think only of the money."

To enter the gambling house, a customer paid five dollars. This entitled him to stay all evening if he so desired, but if he left to visit the saloon or sporting house he was obliged to pay again before re-entering. Jacques supervised the dice games, and a lanky, laconic man named Brice, the faro table. The largest section of the room was Mara's domain. Here there were a dozen tables, watched over by a trio of grim men whose names Mara never learned. She dealt stud at the largest of the tables and there was always a line of men waiting to sit down with the remarkable girl who represented the house. If a man wished to play a hand of poker with Mara herself, he paid a dollar for the privilege, win or lose. It was this practice which brought in the greatest revenue. Sooner or later every man who entered the place paid his dollar for the pleasure of playing with Mara.

Their jaws hung open with amazement and delight when they spied her, blooming like a white flower in the smoke and clutter of the room. Her little hands seemed to caress the cards as she expertly shuffled, slender fingers flicking out saucily as she dealt them 'round. The ripe, delicious swelling of her breasts above the top of the gown, the maddeningly sensual way she bit at her full lower lip when concentrating, the grave glow of her cat-like eyes when she announced sweetly that she would fold, or draw—all these exerted such a powerful fascination on the men that they no longer cared whether they won or lost.

"I am so tired," she told Jacques at the end of her third night. The gray dawn was creeping down from the mountains and she shivered in the wintry chill. "I thought the hurdy-gurdy house was exhausting, but this is worse. Here I must concentrate."

Jacques grinned as his hands counted a stack of bills. "This will cure your tiredness," he said, handing her the one-quarter of the night's take he had promised. Her winnings she kept free and clear.

"Yes," she sighed, "it helps . . ."

Mara came to know some of the regulars, although no words passed between them except the brisk dialogue of the gaming tables. There was a ginger-haired fellow who had made a great deal of money in tungsten who came often, staring at her with such proprietary lust she shuddered. Another admirer was fully seventy years old. One night he passed her a folded note, offering her fifty dollars if she would accompany him to the hotel across the road and stay with him for an hour. A cowboy named, improbably, Winston Chetworth, paid her a visit every Friday and always brought a crumpled bouquet of flowers which he dropped by her side with helpless adoration.

The only man she liked was a slender blond youth whom everyone called A.J. He had large, burning dark eyes and a sweet mouth which seemed to promise both tenderness and humor. His sandy light hair hung in his eyes, and he was forever pushing it away impatiently. He played very solemnly, concentrating all his attention on the cards, and when he won he was jubilant. Losing made him very angry, but he tried not to show it. This made him seem achingly young to Mara, although she reckoned he was only a year or two younger than herself, and she allowed herself to smile at him once or twice. He was the only customer she ever smiled at, and the only opponent she disliked winning from.

One night she drew two jacks and found herself holding a full house—jacks and threes. A.J. was nursing his cards intently, and when it came time to bet he shoved his entire pile of money between them. Mara met him and, sighing, showed her hand. The boy flushed, tossing his three nines aside disconsolately. He was used to strong language, but he could hardly use it in front of this lady whom he so liked and admired.

"Oh, turkey leg," he muttered, and then Mara laughed so hard that Jacques came to see what the trouble might be. She could not stop laughing, even when A.J.'s face clouded with embarrassment, and presently he laughed, too, the two of them gasping and turning quite red. It was the first time she had laughed aloud in over half a year, and it felt strange and wonderful to her.

"What is your name?" she asked A.J. when they had quieted.

"Adam," he said shyly. "Adam James."

There was nothing to do at Grape River but sleep, eat, dress, and prepare for the long night's work. She could not walk about the town, since there was only a dirt road which quickly ended in a single-track rut bounded by weeds and thistles. There was no one to talk to. The only other girls were prostitutes who resented her for earning as much, or more, than they did without having to sell herself. One of them, a buxom, red-cheeked girl called Daisy, had made this very clear the day after Mara arrived.

"What makes you so special?" she asked, curling her lip. "We're all the same here, sister, and don't you forget it."

There was frost on her window when she awoke one afternoon, and she could see snow lying thick and sleek on the mountains above her. She had a new fur-lined cloak, not so elegant as the one Roger had given her, but warm and pretty enough. It made her smile to think of the many garments she had left behind all over the country. She wondered if Lillian Hamm had taken her jewels and distributed her clothing to the other girls when it became apparent Mara was never going to return. She thought with pleasure of Michele and Sheila, of Diana and Dulayne and Gretchen wearing the hand-made gowns fashioned for her by the finest *modistes* in Chicago. And then—suddenly—she had a clear image of the emerald green ball gown she had brought with her from New York, crumpled in her cardboard valise.

The thought caused her to turn pale, and she sat abruptly on the edge of her bed, unpleasantly aware of the acceleration of her heart. It was not the green dress that caused her agitation, but the memory of he who had given it to her. How many times had she pushed the same memory down, trampled on it, refusing to acknowledge the potency of her reaction? She could think now of Satanta with love and the echo of longing, with affection tinged with pain, but the other—whose name she did not permit to be pronounced even in her inmost thoughts—stirred her whole being to violent hatred.

She pushed open her window to breathe great gasps of the frosty air and calm herself. She saw A.J. loping along, coatless, toward the saloon. Grateful for distraction she called down to him:

"Mr. James—you will catch pneumonia like that!"

He smiled up at her, looking both shy and pleased, and Mara saw he had a smudge of dirt on his cheek. She did not know why it should be, but the sight of him calmed her, made her happy . . .

That night a man entered the gambling house who had the precise opposite effect on her. People parted at the door to let him pass, and conversation ceased. Mara stared curiously as the stranger approached, shouldering his way through the room like an angry bull. Rarely had she seen a face which so repelled her, although she could not think why. His features were regular enough, and although the skin was coarse and reddened and his locks unkempt and greasy, he was far from ugly. He looked in some ways like a wild man. The blond hair, liberally streaked with gray, flowed to his shoulders, and his lips, framed in the massive beard, appeared unpleasantly red. She judged him to be somewhere in his forties; his body was massive and square, like a blunt instrument, and he wore fringed buckskin trousers and jacket, giving him the air of a mid-century fur-trapper. Even when he approached the gaming tables he kept his broad-brimmed, rawhide hat slouched low on his forehead. She did not expect him to be courteous, and the gravelly voice that issued from him came as no surprise.

"How much to play a hand with the little lady?" he asked peremptorily. He was grinning now, amused by Mara's discomfort. Jacques had come to stand near her, but to her dismay he treated the wild man with great respect. "A dollar a hand, Mr. Quentin," he said obsequiously, "and well worth it. I've trained her myself."

Mara watched while the man called Quentin pulled a huge roll of bills from his pockets and tossed them to Jacques. "Count it," he grunted. "I want her for the evening."

Jacques rolled his eyes and gestured feebly. "She is only a dealer, Mr. Quentin—Miss McQuaid is not, so to speak—" He nodded in the direction of the sporting house.

"I know she's not a whore," replied the wild man scornfully. "I wouldn't want to play cards with a whore, now would I?"

A titter ran through the room, but everyone stood well back, avoiding the man's wrath and watching curiously to see what Mara would do.

"If you are going to play poker with me," she said distinctly, "you will have to remove your hat."

Quentin fixed her with his pale blue eyes, studying her insolently and in some detail before he answered, "Deal the cards, Missy. Stud to start, draw when you've lost enough to learn some manners." Nevertheless, he removed his hat, placing it on his knee and sitting heavily opposite her. A large and wicked-looking hunting knife was strapped to one buckskin thigh. Truly, she thought, the man is insufferable!

They played for an hour with single-minded determination, winning equally. "Two-handed poker is a terrible pastime," he said, "but looking at you makes it all worthwhile." He smiled, as if he had delivered a pretty compliment, and openly studied her bosom. Presently he called for a bottle of whiskey and began to drink it, straight from the bottle. He wiped his mouth on his leathery hand and announced that it was time to play draw.

"But, Mr. Quentin," Mara said sweetly, "I am here for the novelty. Surely you'd have a better time playing with more partners?"

Quentin threw back his head and roared. "Leave the good times to me, Missy—I know what to do with them!" His humor seemed to please him inordinately, and he chuckled and gasped for some time, peering out at her from beneath his shaggy brows as if trying to coax a laugh from her. At last he tired of his sport and pushed back from the table, leaving his money and allowing his eyes to caress her intimately one last time. "I'll see you again," he grunted. "That's a promise. Next time wear black." He lowered his voice, bringing his crimson lips close to Mara's ear. "A white-skinned woman wearing black can make a grizzly bear roll over and beg," he whispered, and then he left as abruptly as he had come.

"Who was he?" she asked Jacques later. "I have never seen such a horrible man in all my life." Her very flesh still felt unclean from his hot glances, and she trembled to think of the innuendo in his coarse remarks.

Jacques evaded her glance, counting money with a preoccupied air. At last, he said casually, "That was Quentin, of course. Everyone knows Quentin in these parts. He's a peculiar man, bit of a legend, really. He fought on the Confederate side as a young man—they do say he comes from a good southern family—and when the South went under he came West. He made a pile mining the Comstock, but that's not the half of it." Jacques chuckled admiringly. "Old Quentin was born too late," he said. "He just barely had time to hunt buffalo before the big herds went, and then he hired himself out to the army as a scout. He's an Indian fighter without any Indians to fight, a fur-trapper fresh out of beavers to trap, and if I were you I'd tread carefully."

Mara was amazed. "Why should I give him another thought?" she asked disdainfully. "I do not like the man."

"Ah, but he likes you. He lives in the mountains above Grape River these days. He'll be back."

"When he comes he will have to find another partner." Mara blushed. "Can he not visit the sporting house instead of plaguing me? He'll find a warm enough welcome there."

Jacques sighed. "It is your reticence he likes," he explained. "That, and your voice. They say his first wife was Irish."

Mara was beginning to be more than a little annoyed. Jacques' air of wonder when he described the exploits of the odious mountain man was becoming wearisome. He had said that Quentin made money in the Comstock. She had a vision of filthy hermit-quarters somewhere in the forbidding mountains, where Quentin kept thousands inside a grimy mattress. That was the reason for Jacques' respect, and Mara shuddered. "Has he no other name but Quentin?" she asked.

"Percival," Jacques replied. "Percival Theophilis Quentin. Call him that at your peril."

# BOOK IV

## *The Good-Time Girl*

## Chapter Eleven

The next time Quentin came down from the mountains, he brought Mara a present. It was an exquisite boa of rippling black feathers, which he tossed on the table as if it had been a joint of venison. Mara regarded it with horror. It lay between them, lifeless and beautiful, and she wanted to push it from her and run from the room. Before she could reject his gift he was slapping piles of money down, shouting to Jacques that he wanted a proper game. "I'll have five men," he said, as if ordering dinner, "and Irish here can deal."

He looked around the room as if stalking game, pointing to the men he wanted at his table. "I'll have him for a fifth," he decided, indicating the door. A.J. had just entered.

"You don't look old enough to play with the big boys," Quentin joked, scrutinizing A.J. carefully. "Still full of your mother's milk, are you?" The boy flushed angrily and looked with mute apology in Mara's direction.

"I work in the sporting house," Adam said, "and I am eighteen years old. I played faro in my cradle, and poker before I could walk."

Quentin howled in appreciation. "Sporting house, is it? And what do you do there, laddie? Sing the girls to sleep?"

"I am the cook," said A.J. The laughter was so loud now that Mara felt sick with pity, but the blond boy grinned good-humoredly.

"Gentlemen," Mara said with a note of authority, "shall we begin?"

The game was a nightmare from start to finish. So long as the mountain man won all went smoothly, but when anyone bested him his pale eyes narrowed into slits of sullen fury. He accused one man of cheating, and when his victim blanched with terror he laughed uproariously and said it was only a joke. He lectured another on the futility of drawing for an inside straight, although the man had done no such thing. They humored him, out of fear and the suspicion that he was mad, and because he had so much money to be won. Only A.J. refused to bend to Quentin's whim, and because he was winning so steadily this made his position doubly dangerous. Quentin would look at Mara after each hand, his eyes caressing her so openly it made her flesh crawl. His large tongue licked at his red lips and once he winked at her, as if they shared a lewd secret.

There was one extraordinary hand of draw, toward the end of the ordeal, that charged the room with terrified electricity. Only Quentin and A.J. had stayed in the game past the third card. The mountain man raised the bet to a sum beyond the boy's means, but A.J. went shy and met him defiantly. His dark eyes were wide and shining, his lips parted expectantly. Mara half-prayed that he would lose; to win seemed too perilous under the circumstances. She held her breath as Quentin displayed a straight to the jack. Slowly, and with infinite relish, A.J. turned his cards to show a full house of aces and eights. The room was very silent for a moment, and then Quentin gave a great bellow and leaped from his chair, grasping the boy in his mammoth arms and lifting him into the air as easily as if he had been a toy. He was roaring with laughter as he turned to the room and made his announcement.

"The boy has got the dead man's hand! I'd sooner lose than come up aces and eights!" Then he picked up the discarded feather boa and draped it ceremoniously over Mara's bare shoulders. "Our little dealer is cold," he murmured. "Come, sweetheart, put on a smile. Don't you know what happens to grim-faced dealers?"

Numbly, Mara shook her head.

This provoked Quentin to a fresh outburst of hilarity. He stamped his feet and pointed to his hunting knife, wiping the tears of mirth from his eyes and stretching out a hand to touch her hair. "Why," he said, "she gets her ears cut off. First the right one, then the left."

Mara stared across the room at A.J. The boy was drained of color now. He picked his winnings up carefully and turned the unlucky aces and eights face down on the table. Then he sent Mara a look of purest sympathy. Quentin's courtship of her had begun in earnest . . .

He brought her fur pelts, and a gaudy bangle of paste and rhinestone she felt sure had belonged to another woman long ago. She didn't want to accept these gifts; indeed, she tried to return them each time he appeared, but the expression on his face turned so wrathful she didn't dare press the issue. Then, one night, he handed her a golden nugget as casually as if it were a fifty-cent piece. She held it in her palm gingerly, her eyes darting about the room to see who might help her. Jacques was occupied elsewhere and A.J. was nowhere in sight. Brice, the faro dealer, would only laugh at the foolishness of a girl who would refuse a golden nugget.

"I thank you," she said to Quentin carefully. "You are very generous, but I think there is something you fail to understand. I don't want your presents, Mr. Quentin. It makes me uncomfortable to accept them. I am an independent woman and I do not wish to change my status. Please take the nugget back."

His eyes clouded and then bleached of color, becoming as pale as the frost on the windows. He bent close to her. "There is no such thing as an independent woman," he muttered furiously. "You ought to be thrashed for saying such things, but——" he smiled at her in a grotesque parody of tenderness—— "I am fond of you. I don't want to hurt you." And then he caught her in his muscular arms and pressed her to his barrel-chest, his hands digging into her shoulders with incredible strength. His lips covered hers and she reeled at the fumes of whiskey, the unpleasant scratchiness of his beard, the wriggling of his tongue as he worked his lips against hers, forcing them apart. She kicked at him and twisted wildly in his arms, but he felt nothing. When he let her go he was breathing hard, looking proud and satisfied.

She ran to Jacques, eyes flashing, and cried, "You must bar Mr. Quentin from the premises! Please, Jacques—he is annoying me— Please!" But Jacques smiled uneasily and turned away, as if she had complained of a trifle.

Quentin came to her side. "I tried to be gentle with you," he said sorrowfully. "I have been very patient, little girl. My patience is at an end, now. You'll see—you'll learn gratitude."

"You are mad," Mara said between clenched teeth. "I owe you nothing. Nothing! Why do you pursue me? I've given you no cause."

"You've bewitched me," Quentin said with deadly seriousness. "All Irishwomen are witches and you're no different. This time you've picked the wrong man to work a spell on." His massive head came close again and he whispered: "This time you've tangled with the Devil himself." Then he laughed his booming, madman's laugh while Mara —sick with horror—ran from the room and out the door. The road was a solid sheet of ice and she stumbled and fell twice before she reached the safety of her room in the hotel. She locked herself in and sat, as she had once done in her bedroom in Chicago, sleepless and alert. When a tapping came some time later she picked up the china water pitcher and crept to the door. "Who is it?" she whispered.

"Jacques," came the reply. Weak with relief, she unbolted the lock and let him in.

"I've brought you some tea," he said consolingly. "I want to apologize for the behavior of that lunatic. I've barred him—he won't bother you again."

Mara sipped the tea gratefully. "I feel sorry for him," she confided. "He is so uneasy in his mind—so *unstrung*. But, oh, Jacques, I fear him. There is something inhuman in those pale eyes."

Jacques nodded and poured more tea for her. He was very solicitous, inquiring if she were quite warm and comfortable.

"I am so sleepy," she murmured. "I feel half-asleep right now . . ."

"Sleep, then. We'll manage without you tonight." And then he told her how proud he was of her, how quickly she had learned the lessons he had taught her. "I knew you would make me a fortune," he said.

But she was already asleep, her head pitched forward on the little table, her long lashes drooping over the drowsy golden eyes. Jacques smiled and touched the crown of her shiny head affectionately.

"Goodbye," he murmured. "Good luck, Hibernian Beauty . . ." And then he walked quietly from the room, leaving the door ajar.


Was she dreaming? The rough jolting motion under her—what could it be? For a moment she imagined she was at sea again, aboard the *Alberta,* but the movements were too abrupt and rattling. Neither was she on a train, nor on the back of a horse . . . Never mind, it was a dream. She burrowed under the blankets which wrapped her round, shivering, and sunk back into oblivion.

Later, when she wakened, all was silent. She seemed to be lying beneath a pile of blankets, and her toes and fingers tingled oddly. She could see flurries of snow drifting by the window to her right, and such a strange window it was—rough and uneven, curtainless and looking out on nothing but a wilderness of white. She turned her aching head to the left and suppressed a scream, for there—not five feet away, nursing a bottle of whiskey with his feet propped against the wall—sat Quentin. He seemed to be reading, absorbed in the pages of a thick, dark-bound book, and she smothered her sound of alarm and tried to lie calmly, feigning sleep.

"Good morning," he called cheerfully. "Are you hungry?"

She did not reply but lay as if paralyzed while he lumbered over to her side. His jacket had been removed and she saw, between the partially opened lapels of his woolen shirt, the thick, gray mat of hair on his chest. It curled out in little electric tendrils, as if trying to escape. "You would probably like a cup of tea," he continued. "I myself prefer coffee, but you Irish are great tea-drinkers." He chuckled.

Tea. Jacques had given her tea last night. It was the last thing she remembered. Quentin was busying himself near the immense, cast iron stove which gave out considerable warmth. He brought her a cup of strong tea and a tin plate upon which two eggs stared at her like baleful eyes. Her stomach convulsed.

"I told you," Quentin said proudly. "I knew you'd come to me."

"I did not come to you," Mara said tonelessly. "I have been drugged and brought here against my will. Even here, Mr. Quentin, men go to jail for such things."

He raised a bushy eyebrow quizzically. "Jail?" he said in a comical voice. *"Jail?"* He squatted by the side of the bed, fixing her with his pale blue eyes. "You are in my domain, you Irish witch. Mine. I am the law here." He laughed. "I rule this kingdom, Missy. There is nobody here but myself, and you."

She pushed the blanket aside angrily and then lay back with a groan. She was completely naked. Quentin had undressed her.

"I never put a lady to bed without making her comfortable," he said. "You were so cold, after our long journey. I warmed you and then I let you rest, just like any gentleman."

Mara regarded him almost with awe. The man was so changeable—so full of insane contradictions. At times she could hear the deep, slow cadences of the South in his voice, and then he sounded very like the southern aristocrat Jacques had said he was. At other times he seemed to be only partly human, like a creature who has lived alone so long that all traces of civilization have fallen away, leaving only the animal. "Where are we?" she whispered, clutching the blankets to her chin.

"In the mountains," replied Quentin. "In my cabin."

"They will come for me," she said desperately. "Jacques will send people to find me." Even as she spoke she realized it wasn't true.

"Jacques," he snorted. "Who do you suppose

turned you into a Sleeping Beauty? Your friend Jacques cares only for money, and I have given him enough to pay for losing you. *I bought you,*" he said proudly. "There was no other way."

"You can never buy me," she cried. "You may take me against my will to your miserable cabin and keep me here forever, but I would sooner die than be your—" She couldn't think of a word she could bear to use.

"Oh, die, die," he said wearily. "Anyone may die. It takes no special talent to die. You are here to learn to love me. Mark my words—before the month is out you will love me." His hand snaked out, taking hold of one long strand of hair. He caressed it gently while she lay, staring at him as if mesmerized by a snake. A thousand replies had leaped to her lips, but she was silent. It was not possible to argue with a madman. Quentin's heavy, callused hands moved softly over her cheeks, traced the line of her lips and then fondled the slender white column of her neck.

"It has been a long time since I've had a woman who wasn't a whore," he whispered huskily. He seemed almost to have forgotten her presence and talked on, heedless, in a quiet, ruminative voice, his fingers on her throat.

"I have had three wives, you know . . . three. The first came from Ireland—she had hair like yours, gleaming and coal-black . . . She died in childbirth, of course—such a sweet thing she was, no more than eighteen . . . The second was a Shoshoni, with eyes like black diamonds and long, long thighs, but, do you know, she turned to drink. A sad thing, that.

I had to let her go because she became so wild . . .
so violent! The third——" he laughed shortly, tapping
his fingers against the pulse in her throat— "the third
married me for my money in 1883, when I was in
the prime of my manhood. The prime! She thought
she'd get her hands on my gold, but I fooled her.
I waited until I was sure, you see, I didn't want to
act unfairly. When I knew she was a greedy, lying
bitch—knew it beyond any doubt—I locked her
from the house! All night long she beat her hands
on the door and called and called for me to let her
in. Her voice grew fainter and fainter and then—
in the morning—she was frozen . . ." He sighed.
"That was in Dakota, a long time ago." He looked
down into Mara's eyes, his sandy lashes flickering
as if to hold back tears. "I'm ready to love one last
woman," he said. "I always knew it would be
you . . ."

He turned the blanket down slowly, exposing her
white body and admiring it with his eyes. She lay,
every muscle coiled to attack, but he covered her
up again and told her to eat her eggs. "I can wait,"
he said. "Waiting makes it sweeter."

While Mara ate the eggs she looked around her,
determining the limits of her new prison. The cabin
was one spacious room, containing the enormous
stove, a rickety table and one chair, the bed on
which she sat, and very little else. The walls were
made of rough-hewn logs with bits of sod stopping
up the chinks. There were two windows, and a number of blankets and lengths of cloth hung everywhere to keep the draft out. Only one thing
seemed incongruous. There were rows of heavy,

leather-bound books neatly placed in parallel shelves above the table where Quentin had sat earlier, reading. Except for the expensive-looking books, the cabin was exactly what she would have supposed of an eccentric hermit. Two rifles and a shotgun hung on pegs near the door. Quentin saw her looking at them and clucked. "They are not loaded, Missy. Only I know where the ammunition's kept." And then he laughed his wild, secret laugh, for all the world as if he had said something devastatingly witty.

When she had choked down the eggs and swallowed her tea, he proposed to show her about his domain. His manner had altered again. Now he seemed a gentleman who courteously proposed a stroll around the perfumed gardens of a plantation. He even turned his back discreetly while she dressed in the buckskin trousers and shirt he threw to her. He had also provided her with high, heavy laced boots, a fur-lined jacket, and leather gauntlets for her hands. All of these were too large, and Mara pulled helplessly at the waist of the trousers, trying to keep them up around her slender frame.

Quentin saw her predicament and quickly stripped his own belt off. With the sharp point of his hunting knife he made a new hole in the length of leather and wrapped it around Mara's waist, pulling it snug. "I've brought all your things," he said considerately, "even that old Cheyenne blanket you kept in your room. For now, though, you'll be better off like this."

They stepped through the door and Mara gasped at the arctic frigidity of the thin mountain air. The sun had risen and made dazzling patterns on the snow, and she was temporarily blinded by the brilliance. Fresh snow had fallen, leaving a powdery layer over the hard-packed crust beneath, and Mara floundered, falling against her abductor with the very first step she took. He gripped her arm tightly and forced her on down the path toward the stand of fir trees at the bottom. "In a month we'll need snow shoes," he said calmly. "The winter has only begun."

A month! Mara thought if she remained in this desolate spot for a month she would be as mad as Quentin. The piercing wind cut through her layers of clothes and hurled the snow in fine flurries against her face. Already she was cold. "We are beneath the timber-line here," Quentin told her. He pointed far above, where the sharp trajectory of the mountain seemed to be leaning dizzily down, threatening to topple into the clearing. "Over that peak," he said, "there is a view worth more than gold. You can see all the way to the Continental Divide." She shivered at his words. For all she knew they were in a place where human beings never ventured. They could be five miles from Grape River, or fifty. He would never tell her . . .

The darkness came on so suddenly it was as if a huge curtain had been flung over the windows of the cabin. It could not be more than four in the afternoon, but already it was night. Quentin insisted that she watch him prepare their supper; from now on it would be her duty. He shredded dried meat from the larder and dropped it in a frying pan with onions and a thick, rancid-smelling grease; he stirred the mess until it bubbled and steamed, sending up a gamey odor that permeated the cabin. Quentin ate with relish, but Mara could not swallow more than a mouthful. She refused the whiskey he offered her, and they sat in silence while he rolled a homemade cigarette and smoked it with evident pleasure. Then he selected a book from his shelves and settled back to read, ignoring her. She sat quietly, wrapped in her Indian blanket, hoping he would forget her presence. She had tried to clear her mind of everything. It would not do to plot an escape until she knew more about her location, and any other avenue of thought might drive her into a fit of screaming, raging terror. She counted the chinks in the log nearest her, arranging them in patterns and trying to see the shapes of animals in the stains on the smoke-blackened ceiling. From far away, she heard the sound of a book snapping shut, the soft tread of Quentin's feet as he approached her. "It's time for bed," he said briskly, touching her shoulder.

He pulled her to her feet and the blanket fell away, dropping to the floor. His hands fumbled at the buttons on the too-large shirt, and she came to life, slapping them away.

"Don't touch me," she said evenly. "I will cook your supper and sleep in your bed if I must, but you may not touch me."

Quentin sighed, the way an indulgent husband might at a wife's little whims, and said, "Suit yourself, Missy, but take your clothes off." He unsheathed his hunting knife, then and held it up so that the sharp blade caught the light from the flames in the stove. He studied the blade as if it were an object of great interest, turning it this way and that. "Take off your clothes," he repeated. When Mara remained standing, rooted to the spot, he closed in on her, circling round her slowly, coming ever closer until he was inches away. Mara never took her eyes from him, but her hands unfastened the buttons of her shirt, stripping the cloth away and letting it fall. She tugged at the heavy belt but her fingers, numb with fear, would not work properly. The hunting knife came closer, closer, until the point was at her collar bone. Quentin moved his wrist with exquisite grace, and now the blade lay flat against the swellings of her breasts. She could feel the cold steel like the hand of death on her warm flesh; the blade was turned away from her, but he was playing with her, showing her how quickly he might turn it, plunging it deep into her until the blade ground into her breast-bone, cutting her life away as easily as it might cleave into a lump of butter. She tried to still the heaving of her breasts; each breath she took brought her closer to the knife—she saw it rising and falling as she gasped.

She grappled furiously with the belt, at last freeing the buckskin trousers and letting them slide down the length of her bare legs. "Lie down on the bed," he whispered. "It is time for you to learn to love me." She lay down obediently, her eyes still glued to the knife blade. Quentin shucked out of his trousers as easily as a snake sheds its skin and stood before her, naked and powerful. The thick pelt covered his legs as well as his back and shoulders and chest; his sex sprang from the furry groin, alive and rigid. He looked like a primitive creature, something that walked the earth eons ago, and with the knife still in his hand he threw himself beside the bed with a guttural cry. His callused hands traced over her body with a curious touch, as if he could not be sure she was real. He held the knife carelessly and once she felt the sharp point graze her thigh so quickly it stung only for a moment, like the bite of an insect. Blood sprang from the cut and he bent to suck it away, holding her thighs in his huge hands so that she could not move. She felt the mass of his long hair and beard tickling her body and squeezed her eyes shut, grinding her teeth and biting back the shriek of repulsion that threatened to rip from her throat.

He kneaded her breasts, crushing them in his hands and then suckling at her nipples like a hungry child. Her fingers swept the floor, searching for the cast-off knife. If only she could find it she would kill him, plunge the blade into his back and rob him of his life, but her hands closed on emptiness. When he battered his way into her body she cried out only once and then lay still. He mistook her stillness for compliance and gave a great cry of triumph, shuddering in the grip of his pleasure, and fell heavily down on her, pinioning her body beneath his massive limbs and almost suffocating her. When he raised his head some moments later, she spat full in his face. She no longer cared what he might do to her, or so she thought . . .

Her punishment came early the next morning. After they had drunk their tea and Mara had scrubbed the tin cups and put them away, Quentin looked at her sorrowfully. "I must teach you a lesson," he said. He forced her to kneel beside him, shaking his head sadly at what he had to do, and once more took his knife in his hands. She felt it glimmering close to her jaw and shut her eyes, preparing to die. She was thankful that the blade was so sharp—she would feel less pain.

He took the mass of her hair in his hand, sliding his fingers up and down one long tress as if to bid farewell to its silken beauty, and then he sliced it off. The glistening hair floated to the floor like something in a dream, and then he cut another strand, and another, until he had hacked all of her glorious hair, cropping her like a boy. She knelt in the mass of it, sobbing uncontrollably. For some reason it touched her more profoundly than his assault on her body. She felt ashamed, mutilated, and when he caressed her wet cheeks mournfully she made no move to stop him. Her spirit was broken, as he had known it would be, but only temporarily . . .

She never again antagonized him, or looked at him with defiant eyes. She prepared the food and hauled the water, hacking at the frozen ice in the little brook, and she suffered his caresses. She was biding her time, waiting to kill him. Waiting to kill him, but how? The guns were not loaded and his knife was always strapped to his leg, except when he slept. Quentin seemed to fall into oblivion with the same brutal swiftness that accompanied everything he did, but let her stir ever so slightly beside him and his arm clamped around her like a band of steel. She had imagined she might return with the water one day and fell him with the blunt axe she used to break the ice, but he was so much stronger than she that he could easily disarm her, and he was wary, like an animal, with a sixth sense. There was something else: She was not sure that she could bring herself to kill a man. When he violated her body she hated him with an intensity that knew no bounds, but later—the next day—the violence of her hatred had dimnished.

One day when he was out chopping wood she looked at his books, taking the volumes in her hands and studying them, turning the pages in astonishment. He had several books of the lives of Lewis and Clark, and histories of the great mountain men, Kit Carson and Jim Bridger. It was obvious to her that he had patterned his life after theirs, but having been born too late he lacked their purpose and dignity and had lapsed into madness. More amazing than the histories and books of adventure was the poetry. He possessed many books of eighteenth-century poetry, and the margins were thick with remarks and notations in his hand. He had underlined his favorite portions of the poems, and as she stood looking at them, alone in the cabin, she grew dizzy. How could she kill a man, however brutal he might be, when she had seen his secrets on the pages of a book?

Her days passed in a state of numb despair; her nights were worse still. He did not attempt to make love to her every night, but when his passion came upon him there was no turning it back. He mauled her in his huge arms, bruising her tender flesh and leaving her battered and breathless, wide-eyed in the dark beside him as she plotted her revenge. Tomorrow she would hurl the heavy water-bucket at his head and flee while he lay groaning and helpless in the snow. Or she would pry up every floor-board in the cabin until she found the supply of bullets and shoot him as he entered the door. And then to-morrow would come, and he was simply a middle-aged man who tried to be kind to her, but had the misfortune to be a lunatic. Then she would catch sight of her reflection in the panes of the window-glass and see a young girl whose hair hung straight to the ears, like a medieval page, and ponder on the sort of "lesson" he might teach her if she tried to take his life and failed . . .

"There's a blizzard coming," he announced one evening. "Won't we be snug then?" He sat holding her on his lap, absently stroking her back with one paw-like hand. "You are happy with me, aren't you?" he asked.

"How can I be happy when I am a slave?" she replied recklessly.

He thought about this for some time, and then he got heavily to his feet and went to the small cupboard in the rear. He returned carrying one of the dresses she had worn in the Grape River gambling house. "Put this on," he said gruffly. "You are right in what you say, Miss Mara. I have treated you too much like a servant."

He fetched a bottle of wine from his well-stocked larder and when she stood before him in the crumpled dress he expelled a long sigh of content and smiled. "This is how we should be in the evenings," he said. "Now we will drink a glass of wine together and be civilized." Mara felt more an inmate of

Bedlam than ever. The silk dress, here in the chilly cabin, her boyish hair and cracked and reddened hands, the grizzled man who lifted his glass to her like the gallant aristocrat he had once been—all of it made her want to laugh wildly, yet she dared not.

"Tomorrow I will kill a rabbit," Quentin said, "and we'll have stew. Then I shall teach you to use the snowshoes." He spoke with quiet pleasure, and Mara saw that he had lived so long alone that rabbit stew and snowshoe lessons seemed activities of monumental interest to him.

"Quentin," she began, "I should like to know more about you. Are you really from the South as people say?"

"I was born in Vicksburg," he answered, "so I suppose I am from the South. I have no interest in the past. If we are going to have a conversation we will talk about you. How is it you were not a virgin?"

The question stunned her, but she answered simply: "I have been married. Twice."

He stared at her in astonishment. "Twice? Lord, Missy, you've lived a lot in very few years." He stroked his beard. Several times he started to ask her a question, but clamped his lips together to stop himself. "Well, well," he sighed finally. "I don't care about your past, either." He led her off to bed then, and for the first time he was gentle with her. Perhaps it was the silk dress, or the effects of the wine, but his hands were soft and slow as they undressed her, and his movements almost tender. He cupped her breasts and bent his lips to them, his shaggy hair ticking her flesh, and he stroked her belly and thighs with his thick, callused fingers, taking his time, savouring the beauty of her young body as he had never done before. She felt her nipples rising helplessly and cried out for him to stop, but the old, familiar heat was enveloping her and she could not turn it back. She felt that she might burst through her skin and dissolve in a flame of pure desire—not for Quentin, but for the joy he made her feel with his questing, expert hands and lips. She could not allow it; she pushed at his chest and curled her fingers deep in the mat of his thick hair, but he thought she was urging him on and pulled her to him, going deep into her body with a single thrust. For the first time she was ready for him. Her mind could not accept it, but her treacherous body welcomed him eagerly, and this so excited him that he could not hold back and gave a great shuddering cry of fulfillment. Her own pleasure quivered, receded, and was gone, and she was so thankful she almost wept. If Quentin could make her feel the ecstatic pleasure she remembered dimly from the past, she would never forgive herself . . .

The next morning she went about her chores with a new air of determination. Quentin's horse whickered gently as she approached the stall in the lean-to. It still amazed her to realize that she had been transported here in a rickety wagon drawn by the beast who nuzzled at her hand now. It was impossible to guess how far she might be from civilization. She had once seen the view Quentin had pronounced "worth more than gold" and shivered just to think of it. It was impossibly lonely—a vast panorama of peaks and ridges that stretched for as far as the eye could see, cold and forbidding. That way lay certain death. She would have to take the horse and let him guide her down the near side of the mountain; even that might take days, but she would eventually reach a town or settlement. The problem was in getting away at all. Quentin was never far, even when he was out of sight.

She heard the crack of his rifle and knew that he was shooting a rabbit; soon he would bring it back, wringing the little neck and skinning the creature, leaving bright red blood in the snow . . . No, she must choose a time when he was further from her. If he caught her running from him she hadn't a chance. She knew he would kill her as easily as he had just killed the rabbit for their stew. It had begun to snow again, and Mara—who had once loved snow—cursed the thick flakes, the leaden sky, and the desolate, purple mountains. She leaned against the warm flanks of the horse, praying for a little luck.

Too late. The promised blizzard howled 'round them all that night, and by morning the snow was piled above the window-ledges. There was no escaping on horseback now. She had waited too long. Quentin saw her look of despair and mistook its cause. He took the snowshoes down from the cupboard, smiling cheerfully.

"I have two pairs of these," he said. "A man's life may depend on them in winter." They bundled warmly and pushed against the great drifts that had lodged against the door. Mara saw that if the wind had come easterly they would have been snowed in, but the drifts were only knee-high at the door.

In the back of the cabin they reached almost to the roof. Quentin showed her how to strap the great, awkward, webbed frames on her feet, and together they pushed off over the gleaming blanket of white. He moved easily, lifting his feet and placing them on the snow with the grace of one who has lived among the elements for years. Mara floundered, feeling great weights had been fastened to her ankles. Her legs ached and she was exhausted before she had gone ten feet. It was like the heavy, clogged gait of a nightmare, and she wanted to weep with despair. A plan had begun to come to her, but it could never work if she could make no more progress than this . . .

"Come inside, Missy, you've had enough," Quentin said paternally.

Mara laughed and feigned pleasure. "Oh, please," she cried, "it's such fun! Let me play awhile!" She was warm from the effort, and knew her warmth to be a dangerous illusion. It was bitter cold, the sort of cold that might freeze a man to death in less than half an hour if he didn't keep moving. She had improved and was making her way with reasonable speed along the great white banks. The trick was not to lift her legs so high, to relax the muscles of her aching thighs and become an efficient machine.

"Come inside," Quentin repeated. Her lesson was at an end.

That night she asked for wine, and when she had drunk a glass she giggled and climbed onto his lap, twisting her fingers in his beard kittenishly and pretending to be giddier than she was. This amused him so much that he drank several glasses rapidly, becoming flushed and jolly and bouncing her on his knee. When she asked if they might have another bottle he gave her a brief, suspicious look.

"When it goes there will be no more until spring," he said thickly.

She pressed her lips to his leathery cheek and swung her legs against his thighs. "Please," she crooned, "just for tonight."

Still, he looked doubtful.

She whispered then, in his ear, telling him how she had never thought she would come to love him until the night before, confessing shyly that he had brought her pleasure such as she had never known. "The wine loosens me," she murmured, "it helps me to overcome my reserve."

He smiled at that, remembering, perhaps, his Shoshoni wife, but he went to the larder and brought out another bottle. He didn't seem to notice that she drank only half a glassful and replenished his glass as soon as it was empty. He half-drowsed in the chair, caressing her breasts idly with gentle hands, and when she begged him to come to the bed he stumbled with her across the room and dragged her down beside him. She thought she had calculated accurately—Quentin was a whiskey-drinking man and could toss back shots all night without effect, but wine made him sleepy. He fondled her, murmuring that he would waken later and make love to her properly, and then he was asleep.

She lay beside him for a long time, hardly daring to breathe. At last she tested him, moving away from him slightly. No iron arm restrained her. He snored softly. She crept from the bed, moving only inches at

a time, sliding across the floor like a wraith. She
took his fur-lined jacket and cap, and his gauntlets
as well as her own. She filled her pockets with dried
meat from the larder, and poured whiskey into his
flask, corking it tightly and dropping it into one ca-
pacious pocket. The golden nugget he had given her
went, too, but she realized with despair that she
would have to leave her Indian blanket behind. She
couldn't hope to carry it, and her red shell necklace
—last remnant of her love for Satanta—lay in the
cupboard beyond Quentin's sleeping body. She did
not dare risk wakening him. At the door she picked
up both pairs of snowshoes, astonished at their com-
bined weight. Then she pushed lightly, dreading the
cold wind which might rush in and urge him back to
life, and the door opened. He had cleared away the
drifts and the door swung easily outward, soundless
on its freshly oiled bolts. The moon had risen, and
all around her lay the snow, smooth and deadly in
the pale blue light. She strapped the snowshoes on
quickly. Still carrying the other pair awkwardly
clasped to her breast, she set out along the high,
gleaming crests. Her heart beat so wildly she was
afraid it could be heard, like a drum for miles
around. She was free . . .

The burden in her arms became heavy very
quickly. She had no sense of balance. She tried
holding one snowshoe in each hand, but this dragged
her down and tired her wrists. When she thought
she had gone far enough, she plunged first one, and
then another, into the deep snow drifts. She bent
with effort and covered the frames in a shallow
grave. When the wind rose it would do the rest of

the job. Quentin could never follow her now. No matter how expertly he tracked, no matter how great was his animal strength and intuition—without snowshoes he would be helpless.

She rose to her feet, feeling the cold that encroached whenever she stopped moving, and pushed on. The night was still and windless; she must go as far as she could before it was light. Her body in its dark clothing made a perfect target against the expanse of white. She was terribly afraid that an hour's slow progress had brought her only a few hundred yards from the cabin. Already her legs ached, and for the first time she realized she might well have traded in a swift death at Quentin's hands for one that would be more lingering and cruel.

The dawn was coming up, or was it a trick of the mountains? She stopped, uncorking the flask and taking a long swallow of Quentin's whiskey; it burned at first but swiftly lodged somewhere at the center of her body, spreading a warm glow. Yes, the reflection on the snow was definitely rosy now, and behind the mountains at her back a pale, oyster-colored light was spreading. The whiskey gave her a second wind and she pushed off, trying to ignore the desperate tiredness in her legs, the pain tingling through her fingers. She clenched and unclenched her hands, trying to bring some warmth to them, but the bitter cold penetrated through the thick gauntlets and crept up through the soles of her boots. She was afraid to lose the circulation in her feet, both because she would no longer be able to walk very well and because she knew what could happen. *Frostbite.* The word was harmless enough, but she had heard the terrible stories of ordeal by frostbite in the Far North—toes and fingers breaking off, or turning black and falling beneath the surgeon's knife. Already her face was stiff, immobile. She thrust her chin down into the collar of Quentin's coat and put one foot in front of the other, forcing herself to think of pleasant, homey things—a birthday dinner for her mother back home in Ireland, at which she had been allowed to wear her Sunday dress . . . the way an old fiddler in their village had cocked his head when he played . . . Her mind was full of bright, warm images, and when she came to herself it was only to see, with despairing eyes—that it had begun to snow again.

She forced herself to eat a little of the tasteless dried meat and drink another swallow of whiskey. It was fully light now, but she thought Quentin would still be asleep, snoring beside the dying fire. She saw trees ahead, and beyond, a wilderness of white that stretched unbroken to the limits of her vision. At least she was moving steadily downhill, rising wind at her back.

Mara was dreaming on her feet, hearing snatches of conversation hum and buzz in her ears—or was she talking aloud? She tried to form a word and found that her lips would not move; a toneless croaking was all that emerged. She was thirsty, and bent to scoop up snow, holding it to her lips, feeling it burn against her face. Had she passed through the stand of trees now? Or were they still ahead of her? The sun was out in all its force, blinding her as it glared and dazzled on. Strange that it could be so bright yet give so little warmth . . .

Now there came a sharp new pain in the bottoms of her feet, as if she were walking on knives. The snow shoes dragged heavily, scraping along, grating . . . and then, with a heart-jolting swift flash of comprehension, she saw the reason why. The snow was only inches deep here. She had strayed out of the high mountains and on to a crude path of rocks and frozen mud, rutted and uneven, thinly covered with fine powder. It took a long time for her numbed fingers to unfasten the bindings of the snowshoes, but when at last she kicked them away she felt as though she had been set free from an instrument of torture. She thrust her hands inside the boots and massaged her deadened feet, wincing at the pain renewed life sent pulsing through her veins. She felt sure she could make it now, if only she could get up again, stumble to her feet and continue down the path.

Mara tried to run but found that she was no longer strong enough. So she plodded, desperately ignoring the sly voice that told her, over and over, how pleasant it would be to rest, to lie down in the snow and sleep for a bit. Once she thought she saw smoke on the horizon, but it was only a long spiral of eddying snow dancing in an air current. There was nothing ahead of her, nothing but the vast wilderness, and she had been a fool to think she could pit herself against it and win.

Either it was growing dark already or she could no longer see. She felt herself pitching forward, rolling downhill a little way, and coming to a halt, her head against a fallen tree. To rise again was an impossibility. The death she had tried to cheat seemed welcome now, and she sighed with content at the flood of warmth and comfort she felt coursing in her veins. It seemed almost like summer now—balmy and peaceful—and she let herself imagine that she was with Satanta again on the banks of the Arkansas River. She smelled the sweet grass and heard bees humming, but then it was not Satanta whose face loomed close but that of Roger—the early Roger, sitting on the wall in Mrs. Monahan's garden in New York. That garden became the garden in Mayo; the faces those of Padraic and Mary McQuaid. She was safe with those who loved her.

She was sinking into euphoria, sucked down into the depths of her happy delusion, when something nagged at her—like a dog nipping at a coat sleeve—dragging her from her bliss and back to the deadly reality. "Help me," she moaned. "Don't let me die here. *Oh, Desmond . . . Desmond, help me.*"

A.J. was hauling wood for the brothel kitchen, as he did every Monday afternoon. He cursed softly under his breath, for it was a job he hated at the best of times. Today it was bitterly cold and he had gone several miles up into the mountains with the horse and cart. He was heartily tired of Grape River and liked to escape it occasionally; the quiet and peace of the mountains made even hauling wood less loathesome. Now that the Irish girl had left, gone back to Canon City he'd been told, there was no one he cared about in Grape River. The whores were quarrelsome and teased him constantly, and the men at the gambling house were just as bad now that Brice had taken over. Jacques Chardin had disappeared at about the same time Miss McQuaid did—A.J. couldn't imagine that she fancied Jacques, but he often wondered. It wasn't only the girl's beauty that had touched him. There was a sadness in her eyes, a certain mournful dignity he thought he understood. She was an orphan, like himself; she had to take care of herself.

He was actually thinking about her when his mongrel dog came running up, whimpering in an ecstasy of righteous alarm. The dog dashed off again and ran back to A.J., barking frantically. A.J. sighed. The dog, like everything else in his life, was a bit silly. He took alarm at everything, quivering and whimpering at all sorts of imagined perils. Still, A. J. followed him to a small clearing off the path and sucked in his breath when he saw the figure lying quietly in the snow. He whistled softly and bent down.

At first he thought it was a boy. The cap had fallen away and A.J. could see the spill of glossy black hair against the snow, cut bowl-style like his own. He turned the figure over gently and gave a loud cry of amazement. Her face was so white it seemed all life had drained away, but when he bent to her he could see that she was breathing shallowly. She was alive.

"Jesus," he whispered, trying to warm her in his arms, "Oh Jesus, it's *her*." He didn't know whether to rub her hands or leave them alone, or if he should waken her and make her walk. Everything he'd ever heard or read about what to do in such cases blurred together in his mind. He got her on the cart and urged the old horse toward home, still holding her close to him. Her eyes opened sightlessly once. She stared at him but did not know him.

"It's Adam, Miss McQuaid," he whispered close to her ear. "You're going to be all right now. You're safe."

## Chapter Twelve

A pair of fumed-oak doors, massive and well-polished, marked the entrance to Leonie Underwood's parlor-house which stood on O'Farrell Street in the Tenderloin District. Through these doors came politicians, high-ranking police officers, society bloods, and—occasionally—minor members of the noblest houses of Europe. Everything was orderly and pleasant. A neatly capped black girl answered the door, took a gentleman's coat and tall silk hat, and settled him with a glass of champagne. Then Mrs. Underwood herself would make a discreet appearance. Talking and joking with the visitors, she would hold a consultation, nod wisely, and send for two or three of her girls. They were all young and beautiful, all elegantly dressed and well mannered. When the gentleman had made his choice he would disappear to one of the bedrooms upstairs for an hour or two. If his tastes ran to the exotic Mrs. Underwood could always arrange for a special "show" in the third-floor gallery. All sorts of unusual needs were catered to here, but voices were never raised. There were no fights or brawls—for that sort of entertainment a man had to make his way to the Barbary Coast's seamy red-light district. Nothing could have seemed less like a house of prostitution than Mrs. Underwood's establishment, which was precisely what made it the most elegant bordello in San Francisco.

Ten girls worked at the O'Farrell Street parlor-house. Each one was fresh and youthful and each had some special claim to distinction. Belinda was from a very good family and could amaze her clients by speaking in perfect French and discussing art and poetry. Nini, on the other hand, had worked her way up from a low dive through sheer ambition and pluck. She looked as sophisticated as Belinda, but it was whispered that some of the tricks she'd picked up on Pacific Avenue would bring a blush to the cheeks of a cow-yard whore. All the girls were skilled at pleasing men. Nine of them were available for sexual favors ranging from the plain to the fantastic.

The tenth was Mara McQuaid.

On a warm evening in May, 1895, Mara sat before her looking glass, preparing for an important evening. She was to attend a ball in an elegant Nob Hill mansion, and every detail of her costume and make-up had to be perfect. She wore a low-cut gown of black satin which was so simply cut it might have seemed plain on another woman. The material clung to the lines of her body like wet ink, moulding her full, high breasts so they seemed to be offering themselves, like ripe fruit, to be plucked. Clusters of white silk roses twisted about the voluminous hem so when she twirled in her partner's arms she would appear to be moving in a cloud of flowers.

Her hair had grown out now so that it reached her shoulders. She could not arrange it in the elaborate coiffures she had managed when it hung halfway down her back, so she simply brushed it and let it hang straight in a shining curtain of gleaming black silk. People turned to stare at this unheard of hairstyle, indignant at first, and then admiring. Her hair curved like a bell, moving when she moved, floating around her slender neck and emphasizing the burning whiteness of her skin.

She needed no make-up—the sooty black eyelashes and golden eyes could not be enhanced by artifice—but tonight she brushed the minutest film of sparkling powder on her face and bosom, and colored her cheeks so delicately that the result was unnoticeable to all but the most practiced eye. On one hand she wore a square-cut emerald, the gift of an admirer. She brushed scent on her bosom and shoulders, fastened a white silk rose in her hair, and nodded, satisfied.

It was the eve of her twentieth birthday, and tonight she would mingle with society women as if she were one of them, rather than the inmate of a brothel. It was understood that she would not sleep with her escort. Her beauty and companionship was all she had to sell. Occasionally one of her clients chose to ignore the terms of the arrangement, believing that he alone might rouse the passions of this strange, cool courtesan. He was always disappointed.

This evening's escort proved to be a young, handsome Englishman, a stranger in San Francisco whose impeccable family connections had won him an invitation to the Mattheson ball on Nob Hill.

"May I fetch you some champagne, Miss McQuaid?" His eyes glowed at her, trying to conceal the astonishment he had felt steadily mounting all evening. He treated her as he would the daughter of a duke, but Mara sensed there would be trouble. He was too young and earnest to accept the fact that she was not for sale.

"Yes, please." She smiled at him, returning ever so slightly the pressure of his gloved hand. Poor boy.

"It's a smashing party," he said, toasting her for the fifth time over the rim of his glass. "And you—if I may say so—are the loveliest girl here."

Again she smiled. The ballroom was festooned with mauve orchids. Clusters of them were twined in the chandeliers, and at regular intervals whole baskets of petals were flung over the railings of the gallery onto the dancers below. Little boys dressed in satin liveries and wearing towering powdered wigs handed round the trays of champagne. It was rumored the hostess was serving a whole roast suckling pig later. Mara sighed. It seemed a great waste of money to her, and the hostess—a newly rich railroad widow—was surely a fool. When her young Englishman introduced her around she amused herself by calculating how many people knew she was from Mrs. Underwood's—there were at least five men present who knew her, but they kept carefully proper expressions when they came face to face with her. It was all a great bore, and she wished for the evening to end.

Just as she had known, the English boy insisted on asking her about herself. On the way home in the carriage he stammered out question after question. "It's only that—well, I mean, you're so lovely, Miss McQuaid—" He gulped miserably. "I didn't expect you to be so—"

"Unlike a tart?"

He blushed furiously.

"But I am not a tart," she said kindly. "I am here to provide you with companionship in a strange city."

"But why?" he asked desperately. "You could do anything—you could be married." He spoke as if marriage were the highest form of achievement.

"I have been married," she replied. "I do not wish to marry again. I enjoy the company of men, but I prefer to keep a distance. They have not always treated me kindly."

When they reached O'Farrell Street he tried to take her in his arms. "You drive me mad," he whispered hoarsely. "Damn it—*I* would treat you kindly." She let him brush her lips with his and then turned away, ringing for Jane, the maidservant. She thanked him politely for a lovely evening and wished him a safe trip back to England if she should not see him again. The Englishman shook his head in despair. He had paid fifty dollars for the pleasure of escorting this maddening girl to the Mattheson ball, and now it was over. Who could have dreamed it would be such a painful experience?

Mara undressed slowly, sitting at her dressing table and brushing her hair with languid movements. All around her the house hummed with its secret activities. If the police captain were here tonight, two of the girls would be dancing together in the gallery, clad only in their chemises. He liked to watch girls dance together. That was all he asked. Vivacious Louisa was probably sipping champagne in her room at this instant, clad only in her long black stockings, telling her Wednesday night client the racy stories he longed to hear. Mara closed the windows of her room, even though the air was warm and fragrant. She didn't want to hear the amorous moans and shrieks of Nini, who became quite carried away sometimes, and screamed to her clients that she'd never had such a man . . . never dreamed a male organ could be so huge, so stiff, so tireless . . . ! Nini confessed it was all a fake, but Mara hated the sounds anyway.

Sometimes, in the discreet stillness, she imagined she could hear the myriad bedsprings squealing with their human cargo, bouncing up and down joyously beneath their burden of sweating, grunting, lusting men. She shuddered, reaching for her lace peignoir. For a moment she caught sight of herself, naked, in the mirror. Her body was like a slender white flame, punctuated by the sable hair above and beneath. Her breasts rose so invitingly, the nipples gleaming like pink pearl, and her thighs rubbed together gently, gently, as if issuing a mute invitation. She looked as if made for love, designed especially for the pleasure of men. Mara laughed bitterly. How many times had she said she was through with love, through with men? This time she meant it. Even Mrs. Underwood had realized that Mara was serious . . .

"Bless me," the madame had cried when Mara first came to the house on O'Farrell Street, "if it isn't the Irish girl!" She had grown quite pale with wonder, peering at Mara to make sure it was indeed the same girl who had disappeared from Denver a year before.

"It's really you! I thought I'd seen a ghost, dearie. Why, we all thought the Indians had you! I left Denver not long after you were taken from that train. 'Ow did you find me here?" The questions came tumbling out, and Mara, smiling at the madame's remembered warmth and enthusiasm, quickly sketched in the less lurid details of her life since she had last seen Mrs. Underwood.

"Old Lil Hamm was fit to be tied," chuckled the madame. " 'Er piano player concussed and 'er best 'urdy-gurdy girl taken off by an Indian! She threw a bloody fit!"

"And Caleb?" Mara inquired eagerly. "He recovered?"

"Well, that was a bit sad," Mrs. Underwood said. "Lil confided to me that he felt quite *responsible* for what happened to you. He went off looking for you, quite broken-'earted he was, too—but you'd vanished, and nobody's 'eard of him since." She leaned forward confidentially. "I wouldn't be surprised if he wasn't in San Francisco," she said. "The whole world's come West, dearie! There's so much money to be made 'ere, for them who doesn't mind a bit of fun."

She rang for some tea then, giving her instructions to the maid in the flawless English she used most of the time, and sat back regarding Mara shrewdly. "You're prettier than ever you was," she sighed. "Just lovely, duck. Do you remember 'ow shocked you was when I said what line of business I was in? Lord, that seems a long time ago."

"I am no longer shocked, Mrs. Underwood. I have worked as a stud-dealer in Colorado, and I traveled west with a boy who served as cook in a brothel there."

Mrs. Underwood's eyebrows lifted meaningfully. "That's nice, dear. Your young man, is he?"

Mara laughed. "I owe him my life," she said. "Adam found me lying half-frozen in the snow and saved me. He is a lonely boy, and very dear. I sold a gold nugget and brought him West with me, but no—we are only friends. He wants to go to Alaska and prospect for gold." She smiled indulgently.

"And you? What do you want?"

Mara took a deep breath. "As soon as I heard you were here I wanted to come work for you. I have been in San Francisco for a week. It has taken me all this time to gather my courage."

"Courage? Why, duck—I'm delighted! A beauty like you? The day I turn you down is the day they put me out to pasture."

"Please," Mara said urgently, "let me explain myself. I feel I can tell you things—intimate things—and you will not scorn me. I trust you." And then Mara, sitting very straight and reciting like a child in school, told the madame how she had come to feel as she did about men.

"I was ravished by a man I trusted," she said in a low voice. "I cannot bear to speak of him, even now. Then I married a man who seemed the soul of kindness, only he turned into a madman, torturing me night and day with his lunatic jealousies, demanding the name of the one who had taken my virginity. When I left him he killed himself . . . The Cheyenne who took me as a wife was all the world to me. I know now that I loved him only with my body, loved him for the pleasure he made me feel. I couldn't even speak to him, you see—the man was a mystery to me and I to him—yet when he abandoned me I thought I would die . . . Just when I had begun to feel alive again I was sold to yet another man, as if I were a slave. He kept me in a mountain cabin—taking me whenever he wanted me. I was afraid of him, of his knife—the knife that cropped my hair . . . I was running from him when Adam found me, half-frozen and nearly dead, and brought me back to Grape River. I was lucky, they said, to be alive at all."

Mrs. Underwood was looking shocked and a bit disbelieving.

"As God is my witness," Mara cried, "it is the truth! I swear it. I want nothing to do with men. I do not want their arms around me or their bodies close to mine or their terrible violence anywhere near me."

"Then why, if I may ask, dearie, do you want to come work in a sporting 'ouse?" The madame's eyes were curious, yet sympathetic.

"Because," said Mara, "yours is a very special establishment, I've been told. Men *like* me, Mrs. Underwood—indeed, they seem to come unstrung in my presence. There are plenty of girls to sleep with them here. Mightn't some be willing only to talk to me—to have me for a companion? I do not hate them; only their lust." She was close to tears now, and felt that she was pleading. She tried to calm herself, but all that had brought her from New York to San Francisco weighed so heavily upon her that she was unable to check her emotion. "I would be safe here," she said piteously. "I would be protected. I would do anything for you, Mrs. Underwood. I could deal cards, or help the other girls with their hair . . ."

Tears trembled on her lashes, and Mrs. Underwood stretched out a comforting hand. "There, duck," she said softly. "I'll take you in. Why, it dresses the place up just to have you near. Besides—" her eyes had taken on the shrewd expression again—"what you say makes sense. Why not give 'em an ice maiden for a change? Lord knows I've enough spit-fires and passion-flowers and everything else you could name . . ."

And so Mara took her bags from the hotel on Market Street and moved into Mrs. Underwood's that very day. That was in January, and in the four months she had lived in the O'Farrell Street parlor-house she had become the most sparkling harlot of them all. If she was a cheat, then so be it.

She lay in her comfortable bed, caressed by fine linens and covered with a satin quilt, safe from the terrible demands of the world. Strange, she thought sleepily, that the only place that offered her protection from men should be a bordello . . .

In the morning the girls visited one another, rising near noon and ringing for their breakfast, tripping up and down the long halls in their lavishly feathered peignoirs and trading stories. Mara liked the girls at Mrs. Underwood's. She had feared they might be contemptuous of her for refusing to do what any good whore did, but they were easy-going and tolerant.

"What I think," Rebecca had said, "is that everyone's different. I like to dance on tables and have a fellow pour wine on my body and lick it up—well, fine! Mara likes to be admired and courted and then turn them away at the last moment. Fine, too! We're just like the men, aren't we? Something different for each of us." She was a pretty blonde girl from the peninsula who had come to the O'Farrell Street house when she was seventeen; she still looked like a fresh-faced farmer's daughter and was a great favorite with the men.

"No," said serious Bianca, who had a reputation as a thinker, "it's not that simple. Mara feels too much, so she has decided to allow herself no feeling at all."

Mara allowed them to formulate their theories, smiling impartially at all of them, lending her jewels and listening to their stories with frank interest. On the morning of her twentieth birthday Nini and Louisa came in, yawning and giggling, to tell her what happened the night before.

"Monsieur LaPortier came last night," said Nini breathlessly. "Do you remember him, Mara? The little man with the drooping moustaches? He is nearly seventy, you know." She giggled.

"He was in San Francisco when Lola Montez used to do her wicked spider dance," continued Louisa. "Last night he conceived a great passion to have me recreate the spirit of Lola Montez. Mrs. Underwood had to go fetch a quantity of rubber spiders, and then I had to stuff them into my stockings and—" she stood in the center of the room, grinding her hips and belly sensuously—"let them fall out all over the place!" She collapsed on the bed, weak with laughter.

"Afterward," shrieked Nini, "he got an enormous erection—la!—it was *prodigious* for such an old party—and he carted Louisa off to bed crying 'Viva Lola!' "

"Poor old dear," crooned Louisa. "He's sweet, really."

Mara laughed, too. Sometimes the stories were not so pleasant, but Monsieur LaPortier and his spiders cheered her for some reason.

Mara had a letter from Adam, posted from Seattle. He was on his way to Alaska, and full of high hopes. She read and re-read it, cherishing the simple, friendly phrases. Except for the girls at the house, he seemed her only friend in the world. Mr. Mc-

Sweeney did not precisely count as a friend, but she wrote to him anyway, stating that she had found work with Leonie Underwood in San Francisco and that she was content. It was not a lie. She felt at ease, relaxed. She thought San Francisco the most beautiful of cities, and delighted in walking or riding up its steep, sunny streets, reveling in the golden hills, the sparkling waters of the bay, the dash and elegance with which the native San Franciscans dressed. The city had its darker side, its sordid history, too, and Mara avoided the Barbary Coast region. She had heard of the lawlessness and terror which held sway in saloons like the Whale. There, too, were houses of prostitution very far removed from the comfort and luxury of Mrs. Underwood's parlor house. The bordellos of Broadway and Stockton, Washington and Montgomery Streets were little more than crib-houses—filthy tenements where girls serviced dozens of men in one evening and the police would not come near for fear of being cut to ribbons.

Nini had told her about the life of a crib-girl, and Mara felt weak with pity and horror. She had heard of the slave-girls from China, sold into prostitution when they were twelve years old, arriving like a shipment of cattle and sent straightaway to waste their young lives in a haze of opium, venereal disease, and depravity. If such a girl became ill, Nini said, she was sent to a "hospital" where she either starved to death or took her own life. Nini was full of stories of the bad old days, although she had not yet been born when sailors were drugged with Mickey Finns, dropped into a pit behind the bar of some

Barbary Coast saloon, and shanghaied 'round the
Horn. One of Louisa's steady customers, respectable
and rich now, in his fifties, had only half an ear. He
told the girls it had been sliced away in a fight on
Pacific Avenue. Such things were common.

Mara wanted nothing violent or sordid to touch
her. She lived a life of privilege in the upper Tenderloin. Her clients took her to Nob Hill parties, or
private suppers on Russian Hill, or to the theatre
and opera. Tonight she would go with Jack Grady,
a friend of the mayor's, to a small gathering of politicians and their lady friends on Mason Street. All
the men had wives who stayed at home; all of them
were polite and affectionate to their paid companions. Only Jack Grady, a tall, heavily built Irishman
with black brows and gimlet eyes, would return to
his wife unsullied . . .

Grady lit a cigar and slung an arm around Mara
in the casual, fatherly way she liked. "Jesus, sweetheart," he said, lifting his fifth bourbon to his lips,
"you get prettier every time I see you."

"If you drink much more, Jack, you won't be
able to see me anyway." Mara smiled. It was not her
place to nag, and she spoke teasingly.

"I've been turning something over in my mind,"
Grady said. "I like you, Mara. I admire your spirit
and I'd like to do something for you." He put down
his drink and regarded her seriously. "What would
you say to setting up housekeeping? I could put you
in a little place of your own—I can afford it—and
you'd see no one but me. I would come to you as
often as I could . . ." His voice trailed off and Mara
saw that he was in earnest. Laughing, easy Jack

Grady wanted to keep her for himself, and he hadn't even slept with her.

"Of course," he added, looking flustered, "I'd expect you to loosen up a bit. Damn it, Mara, you can't be a chaste whore all your young life. Better to be my little sweetheart, eh?" He was flushed with eagerness and embarrassment, his knuckles white with the effort of making his proposal. Mara felt sorry for him.

"Thank you, Jack," she replied. "It can't be."

He accepted her decision and never brought it up again. Only when he had brought her back to O'Farrell Street, near dawn, did he make an oblique reference to his feelings for her. "Make haste, sweetheart," he said hoarsely. "Find the man you're pining for and give yourself. It doesn't last forever . . ."

As Mara made her way along the dim gallery to her room she heard the soft sounds of weeping behind Bianca's door. The girl cried softly, helplessly, and Mara knew she was alone, giving voice to an abiding sorrow that never left her. Of all the girls, Bianca was the most mysterious. She was highly intelligent, thoughtful, and almost stern in her refinement. Mara tapped at the door and when there was no answer she let herself into the dim room on impulse and went to Bianca. She sat on the side of the bed and touched the girl's hair lightly, comfortingly. Bianca turned over and Mara could see, beneath the ravages of tears, that her eye was blackened and her face bruised and puffy.

"Who has done this to you?" Mara asked indignantly. "You must tell Mrs. Underwood and have him barred!"

Bianca caught hold of Mara's hand and squeezed frantically. "No!" she hissed. "Don't tell anyone. I can cover it—I can bathe my face and look as good as new tomorrow."

"But, why?" Mara saw to her horror that Bianca's lips was cracked and bleeding.

"I saw Maurice," the girl whispered wretchedly. "We quarreled."

Maurice was Bianca's lover, the only man who did not pay for the privilege of using her body. Mara had seen him once. He was an oily-looking young man with two gold teeth and furtive eyes. She could not understand why a lovely girl like Bianca should care for such an unsavory fellow, but Bianca claimed that Maurice was all the world to her.

"He loves me so," sobbed Bianca. "That's why he hits me. It proves he cares for me, don't you think, Mara? He wouldn't beat me if he didn't love me." She was smiling tremulously now, her eyes soft with the memory of Maurice's violence, sure that every blow he gave her was proof of his affection.

"That is not love," said Mara. "Oh, Bianca, leave him. He might kill you one day."

"What would you know about it?" the girl cried. "You're as cold as ice, Mara. Everyone knows it! At least I can feel for Maurice. You keep yourself to yourself and feel nothing. Nothing! I pity you."

Mara sighed and went to her room. She was the last person to help poor Bianca, and she knew it. She thought of what the girl had said, tentatively placing her hand on her breasts, as if it were a lover's hand. Her flesh felt warm, alive; it slid like silk beneath her trembling fingers. Was she cold? She knew that Rebecca and Nini sometimes slipped into bed together, kissing and caressing each other like schoolgirls, making love to each other with the tenderness their clients lacked. "You should try it, Mara," Nini had said to her one day. "A woman is gentle and slow—not like a man." But Mara had smiled and turned away. She saw no harm in it, but the thought did not rouse her. "I am done with all love," she reminded Nini. "It doesn't matter to me."

Now she slipped beneath the coverlet and lay silent and wakeful. Thoughts of Bianca's destructive passion merged with images of Jack Grady and the other men who paid to have her on their arm. It all seemed so futile, yet even as she told herself this she became aware of a stirring in her body. It was gradual, tentative, as if coming from a long distance away. She was restless and warm, and when she turned to find a more comfortable position her legs seemed unmanageable and awkward. She touched her thighs, as if to still them, and lay back, breathing heavily. She wondered if she could be coming down with a fever, and lay still so that her trembling body might calm itself. The last thing she thought of before falling into a troubled sleep was what Jack Grady had said to her:

"Find the man you're pining for and give yourself."

Later she was to ask herself if she had any sense of foreboding the night Jack Grady took her to a private card party. It was a hot evening in early

September; the sun burned low and sullen all that day and the closeness continued long after dark. She dressed with special care, for despite the gimlet-eyed politician's proposal to keep her he remained one of her favorite escorts. Four months had passed since he had asked her to be his mistress, and he had never broached the subject again. He was easy-going and jolly, and he treated her like a lady. The night before, she had gone to supper with an intense Frenchman who had insisted on grappling with her at the door; she was looking forward to the evening with Grady. They understood each other.

Since it was so unseasonably warm, she chose a summer gown of watered silk. It was a bright green, sprigged with white flowers, and clung to her like a second skin. Her hair had grown down below her shoulders now, but something made her keep it in the simple, straight line which was so unusual and striking. She went to meet him in the parlor with a light heart and a smile on her lips. No, nothing had prepared her for what was to happen . . .

The men who had gathered in the posh club on Market Street had brought their mistresses, and the vast room echoed with laughter and gaiety. Champagne flowed, and the women, rosy beneath the glow of the cut-crystal chandeliers, draped themselves over the gaming tables, urging their men on and occasionally playing a hand themselves. A great cheer of welcome went up when Grady entered, for he was a popular man in gambling circles, and a number of the men smiled at Mara. Some had been her escorts on other evenings.

The greatest excitement seemed to be at the

poker table near the back, where a knot of women had gathered around one player, watching him intently. Mara could see that he had amassed a great pile of money. While she watched, a slender girl with golden hair and dark eyes touched his shoulder for luck, her white fingers lingering on the man's dark coat. Someone handed him a goblet of champagne and he turned slightly to take it. She saw only the line of his jaw and cheek, but something in the brief impression seemed familiar, disturbing. The way his dark hair curled at the nape of his neck, the set of the shoulders, even the way he tossed the champagne down, made her heart beat rapidly. Grady had taken her arm and was propelling her forward, but she hung back, reluctant. The women had closed around the winning player now, obscuring her view of him, but she did not want to go any closer. She felt almost dizzy with premonition and clutched Grady's arm desperately.

"What is it, sweetheart?" He bent to her with concern, but then someone hailed him and he called back and Mara was being carried along through the crowd, closer and closer to the man she dreaded.

"I have here," Jack shouted jovially, "a lady who deals stud poker with the best of them!" The men cheered and winked, and as Mara watched, the dark-coated player turned in his chair, scanning the room. She fell against Grady, going as pale as death and giving a little cry of despair.

It was Desmond.

He had not seen her yet and she struggled with all the strength at her command to compose herself. She lifted her head proudly, placing a hand on her bosom to calm the painful jolting of her heart. In the moment before he caught sight of her she studied his face, drinking it in with desperate eagerness. The dark, satanic face was as she remembered it, vivid against the gleaming white of his tall collar. His glittering eyes beneath the black brows still pierced through a room, glowing like blue hell-fire, striking straight to the core of her. The sensual lips which mocked and taunted were soft and relaxed; even while she looked he smiled at the golden-haired girl, laying his dark long hand on her arm, wooing her with his eyes. She seemed to sway toward him, and he grinned, his black lashes lowering, his teeth flashing white in the Saracen face. He had not changed, although two years had honed him yet finer, had added to his lean, coiled body a quality of steel. He looked more dangerous than she remembered, and she feared that the hatred rising in her would choke her with its violence. Her only triumph had been in seeing him first.

Someone had refilled his glass, and he was lifting it to his lips when he caught sight of her. She smiled, curving her mouth in an exquisite gesture of scorn, while his eyes widened with shock. His hand trembled violently and then, with a sharp, spasmodic motion, his fingers tightened and the glass broke in his hand. The ladies gasped with shock to see the blood gush from his wound. The entire room was silent now, curious. The blonde girl bound Desmond's hand in her lace handkerchief while he sat, not noticing, his eyes still on Mara.

"Who is he?" Grady whispered.

"A very distant relation of mine," Mara said. "A cousin I have not seen in more than two years."

Together they advanced on the table. Grady held Mara's arm in a proprietary gesture and smiled around. The men greeted him and made room for Mara when Grady announced she would deal. Desmond was trying to compose himself, but for once in his life he could not produce the raffish grin. His face had drained of color.

Mara nodded to him formally. "Mr. O'Connell," she murmured, acknowledging him. Then she sat at the table, took the cards in her hands, and shuffled expertly. Jack Grady proudly explained that she had dealt stud in Colorado. "My little friend knows what she's about," he said. Desmond smiled shakily, accepting another glass of champagne and lifting it to her in a mock salute.

"Good evening, Miss McQuaid," he said. *"Slainte."* Then he downed the entire glass and asked for another. As soon as Mara began to deal his luck turned. He played recklessly, as if he no longer cared, and before half an hour his winnings were gone. Mara kept her face a perfect mask of indifference. When he threw in his cards and pushed back his chair she did not even look up. She didn't have to see him to know that he remained in the room; she could feel him as surely as if he were touching her. She marvelled at her own ability to function smoothly, to smile and deal and call the combinations in a clear voice. The men adored her, paying her compliments and congratulating Jack Grady on his infernal luck, protesting when she said she had had enough of dealing.

She and Grady strolled through the room, sipping their champagne and laughing together. When Desmond approached them they halted, smiling politely, to hear what he might say.

"I beg your pardon," he said to Grady in his low, soft voice. "I don't mean to intrude, but I must speak to Miss McQuaid. We are cousins."

Jack Grady stood aside, his friendly face wreathed in smiles, but Mara laid her hand on his arm. "Why, Mr. O'Connell," she said airily, "this is a social gathering. We must not bore Jack here with our dull family affairs. If you will come to me tomorrow evening at my lodgings I will see you then."

"I will," said Desmond humbly.

She gave him the address, named a time, and turned away. He left immediately, walking through the crowded room without a backward look.

When Desmond approached the fumed-oak doors on O'Farrell Street it was nearly ten o'clock. The little maid who let him in gave him a curious look and asked if he would see Mrs. Underwood.

"I have come to speak to Miss McQuaid," he said. Jane nodded, but before she could speak Leonie Underwood entered the parlor.

"Well," she said appreciatively, "what 'ave we 'ere?" She eyed Desmond as if he were a particularly tasty morsel at a banquet and cocked her head knowingly. "I know what you want," she said, winking at him, "I 'ave just the girl for you."

"I have come to speak to Miss McQuaid," he repeated.

"Ah, they all want Mara," the madame chuckled. "Such a beautiful girl. You do understand her terms?"

Before he could answer, Mara entered the room. "Oh, Mrs. Underwood," she said brightly. "I see you have met my cousin."

The madame twittered at her mistake, laughing merrily and begging them to use her private parlor for their talk. She ushered them to the back of the house, clucking maternally, and left them alone.

Desmond could only stare in amazement. Mara was wearing a Chinese robe of black silk which fastened across her breasts, leaving tantalizing gaps through which her white flesh could be glimpsed. Her hair hung straight, swinging silkily about her shoulders and glinting in the light. She sat on a plush chair and rang a bell, inquiring what he would like to drink. When the maid appeared she called for champagne. "Do sit down, Desmond," she said. "You seem so ill at ease."

"Mara—" his voice was husky and he passed a hand over his eyes. Then he recovered. "You have cut your hair," he said conversationally.

"Someone cut it for me," she replied, "against my will." She laughed. "So many things seem to be done to me against my will!"

He blanched then, but continued to lounge in his seat, legs thrust straight out as she had seen him so many times. When the champagne arrived he sipped and seemed to gather strength.

"*Slainte*," said Mara mockingly. She felt full to bursting with the sweet triumph of her revenge. Desmond knew he was in a sporting house, knew beyond a shadow of a doubt what she was. She did not intend to tell him that a mere technicality prevented her from being a true whore. "How do you like my new home?" she asked sweetly. "It is nice, is it not?"

His eyes grew black then, his breathing more ragged. "I have looked for you for two years," he said at last. "Not a day has passed that I didn't think of you, wherever I was. Not a day, not a night."

Mara laughed. "Roger was better at tracking me than you," she said. "Perhaps you have heard what happened?"

He nodded. "It was in Colorado that I lost your track," he said pensively. "They told me you had been taken by Indians. Do you know what I did, Mara? Do you know what I did when I heard that you had been stolen from a train by the Cheyenne?"

"Oh, let me guess," she crowed. "You went searching for me—is that it?"

He was silent.

"You were not successful, were you?"

"I wept," said Desmond evenly. "I did not want to live."

"I, on the other hand, discovered what it *was* to live. Did they tell you, Desmond, how tall and straight my Cheyenne husband was? Did anyone inform you? The newspapers could hardly know of our wedding ceremony. How shocked they would have been at the thought of it!"

"Stop, Mara." He was pleading now, trembling uncontrollably.

"Very well. I will change the subject. Do you remember Kathleen Daly? I hardly suppose you will have forgotten her. She came to Cripple Creek one

Christmas, pregnant and homeless. Her child was born dead."

"That was not my doing, I swear to you. I never touched Kathy once we docked in New York. Poor girl—I am sorry."

"Ah, yes, you are always sorry, are you not, Desmond? Apologies fall so easily from your lips. But I think we have strayed from the important subject. I have reconciled myself to the fact that my father is dead. If it is so, you must tell me."

Desmond shook his head. "I know no more about Padraic than I ever did. It is all a great mystery. Your family has a wondrous talent for vanishing from the face of the earth."

"Well, then," Mara said, making as if to rise, "I suppose that is all we have to say to each other. I thank you for coming to see me."

"Mara." He spoke her name as if it were the tolling of a bell. "Mara—you cannot stay here. Let me take you away; let me take care of you. I no longer care what you've done, what you are." He looked as he had done when he knelt by her bedside in New York—the blue eyes luminous with love and suffering. She savoured the sight of him for as long as she could, bathing him in the light of her golden gaze.

"What very peculiar ideas you have, Desmond," she said finally. "I have no wish to go away with you. I am happy here."

And then he was hurtling from his chair, crossing the room to her in two long strides and pulling her violently into his arms.

"I have traveled the width of America to find

you," he grated. "I have endured a life a dog would revile, and for what? *For what?*" His voice rose to a shout. "To find a *whore!* Any man with the price may have you—any pig of a man can take what I would have given my life for . . ."

"But, Desmond—you have already had me! Surely you've not forgotten so soon?"

She thought he would strike her, but he withdrew his hands from her as if she had burned him. When he spoke his voice was broken, anguished. "I wish to Christ you were dead," he said, "or I were dead. You've poisoned my life, you lying, whoring bitch. I did you wrong once, because I thought I might lose you and I couldn't stand it . . . And you loved it, Mara, you were blind with passion for me . . . I thought it had something to do with me. With *me!* And all along you were only a little whore, like a dog in heat, with no heart and no soul—" His voice trailed off in a sobbing gasp of misery and despair.

Mara felt a pain so acute she wanted to scream, but no sound would come. She tried to whisper his name, but her lips were frozen.

He stood staring at her, as if to memorize her forever. Gradually, through an almost heroic effort, he regained some of his arrogant composure. Before he left her he even smiled a ghost of his old, mocking grin.

"Goodbye, Mara McQuaid," he said. "God knows I hope we never meet again."

When he had gone she ran to her room and bolted the lock with trembling fingers. She could not breathe properly; her breath came in great painful gasps and she clawed at the neck of her robe with desperate fingers. She fell back on the bed, plunging her hands into her hair and writhing uncontrollably. Her lips opened on a silent scream and then she was sobbing as if her heart would break, crying out his name and pressing the pillow to her lips to still her wails of anguish.

It seemed to her that the sweet revenge she had waited for so long might, after all, be the death of her.

## Chapter Thirteen

The saloon was called the Sailor's Haven. It perched precariously on a slanting waterfront street, near the teeming port, and it became almost a second home to Desmond O'Connell. The city of Seattle lacked the glamor and beauty of San Francisco, but nothing could have induced him to stay in the place where he had last seen Mara. Knowing that she was there, lost to him behind the oaken doors on O'Farrell Street, was a torment; still worse was the certain knowledge that he would see her about town, on the arms of men like Jack O'Grady. Desmond had headed north immediately. There were vague but exciting rumors of gold drifting from the high, arctic regions of Canada and Alaska, and he thought of earning enough money at cards to make his passage to the Far North.

Tonight he sat in the Sailor's Haven watching the world go by, nursing a whiskey and prolonging the exquisite moment when he would choose a bed-mate for the evening. Every sort of human being alive and of an age to drink passed through the Haven's seamy portals. There were Russian and Finnish sailors, Portuguese fishermen, Scandinavians who toiled in the vast shipyards, Indians, Chinese, and Irish card-sharps like himself. There was also a never-ending supply of willing women, women of easy virtue who would be his for a smile. No whore had ever asked him for money yet, and most of these girls were not even whores. They were simply the restless women who dwelt at the edges of civilized America, infected by the rumors of Alaskan gold and only too willing to fall into the arms of a handsome gambler. Desmond craved a different partner every night. Drink helped some, but only the flesh of women made him forget, for a while, the heartless girl whose face still haunted his dreams.

He was fascinated by a girl from Sitka and made love to her once or twice each week. She was part Indian and part Russian, and had the dark skin and eyes of a Chilkat and the blonde hair of her Siberian father. Her name was Sonia, and when he smiled at her she came to his side immediately, laying her hand on his thigh and moving her fingers suggestively. He left with her, going to her room on Front Street. She poured him a tumbler of whiskey and sat watching him, her dark eyes sombre and alert.

"Come, sweetheart," he said. "If you look so melancholy I will think you want me to leave."

"I can't help it," Sonia said. "You are a strange man, Des. You make love like an angel, and then you ignore me. Is it because you found me in a saloon?"

He sighed and took her on his lap, stroking the

heavy blonde hair. "I do not ignore you," he soothed, tracing the line of her high cheek-bones with his fingertip.

"Let me come and live with you," she said all in a rush. "I would take such good care of you." She began to remove his belt, slipping her hands inside his shirt and trailing her fingers over the smooth, hard flesh, scratching him with her pointed nails so that he shivered slightly with arousal, his lips softening and parting as he bent to her.

"I can't bear to be parted from you, Des," she moaned. "I love you."

"Love! There is nothing to love but this," he said, loosening her gown and rubbing his hands over her warm, wriggling little body. She was solidly built, with a well-muscled back and high, hard breasts. It excited him to feel the way her body rippled under his hands. "Nothing but this," he repeated, nuzzling the rigid nipples she offered him, allowing his body—his body, which never failed him—to plunge him into blessed forgetfulness.

Sonia was easily aroused and took her pleasure quickly, almost like a man. She was fierce, and bit him hard, subsiding into an exhausted sleep the moment she was satisfied. Desmond lay with her head on his arm and stared at the ceiling, drinking from the bottle of whiskey beside the bed. He thought of other women, other couplings, to take his mind from that which obsessed him . . .

There was Betsy, a good-natured blonde whose delight it was to torment him with her little pointed tongue until he laughed and pleaded with her to put him out of his misery . . . . There were Johanna

and Gunilla, Swedish sisters who ran a dance hall on
Front Street and shared him lovingly between them
. . . And Janet, daughter of a rich ship-builder, who
had sent him a note at the Haven, carried by her
Chinese maid. He had tumbled the maid, but left
Janet to those who wanted to deal with society
virgins. He wanted no trouble; only to forget.

The very act of love was treacherous, because
although he lost himself in it, the aftermath made
him think always, and with agony, of Mara. Her
face would appear to him so clearly it was as if she
were in the room. He would see again the sable
hair and white skin, the cat's eyes and lovely, curving lips, the ardent body so maddening in its inno-
cently slender voluptuousness . . . He would remember how she had clung to him, her body shaking in
tremor after tremor of ecstasy, calling out his name
in fear and helpless pleasure . . . the feel of her, the
taste of her flesh, the sweetness of her hands on his
back, her legs twining around him . . . He would
grow weak with longing and groan in misery, remembering . . .

When she had disappeared he had gone out of
his head with grief and disbelief, terrifying Brigid
with his ceaseless questions, bursting into Constance
Burkhardt's Fifth Avenue mansion and threatening
to kill Roger Winthrop if he were responsible, at
last going to McSweeney with murder in his heart.
He had fought with two of McSweeney's bodyguards,
emerging bloody and battered but undaunted, reeling on his feet and demanding to know—as her only
relative—where Mara had gone. "To Chicago," Mc-

Sweeney had said, grinning at Desmond's reckless-
ness, but he had given him no address. He arrived
penniless in Chicago and began to look for her, taking menial jobs when his luck at cards was bad. He
stoked furnaces and loaded beer barrels on a truck
for a southside saloon; he stalked the streets of the
city by the lake like a man possessed. When he saw
in the papers that Mara had married Roger Winthrop, he went on a binge and stayed drunk for a
week. When he came to his senses he realized he
could do nothing. She was married, probably happy,
and he had no right to interfere. Still, he stayed in
Chicago, close to her if she should need him. And
then she had flown, and Roger—poor devil—had
shot himself, and once more Desmond had no clue
to her whereabouts. He thought she would head
West, and so did he . . .

He lay in the dark, Sonia's warm body close to
him, pulling on the whiskey bottle, reliving the terrible months of his journey west. The job in Omaha
with a rancher who wouldn't believe an Irishman
could ride well until Desmond had shown him. An
Irish cowboy, the rancher joked, who looked like
he ought to be on a Mississippi paddle-wheeler. He'd
played cards with the other roustabouts and avoided
the advances of the rancher's wife, and when he had
enough money he took a train as far as North Platte,
only to be shot at by a maddened little Welsh tailor
who accused him of cheating at cards. The bullet
wound was superficial, but then he had fallen ill with
influenza and been nursed by a plump widow until
he was well enough to repay her kindness in the only

way he knew. By the time he'd made his way to Denver, Mara had disappeared again, only this time it seemed she might be dead.

He had told her that he wept when he heard, and he cursed himself for giving her that pleasure, but it was true. He had gone with the man, Caleb, into the foothills of the Rockies on horseback. Together they had searched until the day when both of them—haggard and half-starved—admitted sorrowfully there was no further reason to look. He drank a silent toast now to Caleb, wherever he was, and wondered which was worse—to have believed Mara dead or to know that she was very much alive, and available to every man but him. The first had dulled his soul with grief, while the second gnawed at his heart so remorselessly he was never free of the pain.

He rolled over and caught Sonia in his arms, shaking her awake. Her eyes flew open in astonishment, but then she moved against him in the special, lazy way she had, and soon enough he was finding sweet oblivion in her warm, giving body . . .

"Please, Jack," Mara pleaded. "You have ways of finding people when they vanish. You could find him for me."

Jack Grady regarded his long-time friend with astonishment. He had never known her to plead for anything before, had scarcely heard her raise her voice. Now she clutched at his arm like a demented thing, her huge eyes burning with purpose. He had accepted her frigidity because he was so fond of her and he could satisfy his body elsewhere, but now she had come to life. Like the ice maiden who melts into a pool of fire, his little Mara was in a fever, and after all his patience it seemed *he* was not the cause. He smiled a trifle sardonically.

"I thought," he said, "he was only a cousin. You told me you would discuss dull family affairs with him. You didn't even seem to like the fellow much."

"I hated him," cried Mara passionately, "perhaps I still do. But, oh, Jack—I must find him. I'm afraid he's left the city."

"He is a gambler," said Jack with a tone of flat finality. "If he is still in San Francisco he can be found."

"Thank you," she whispered. "You are so good to me, Jack. I only wish I had given you more."

"It's not too late," he said, taking her hand in his. And then, as Mr. McSweeney once had done, he struck a bargain. "What will you give me if I find your worthless cousin for you?" he asked.

"I will give you anything you ask for," she said.

"No," sighed Grady. "I don't want you like that. If a woman isn't willing there's no pleasure in it."

Tears spilled down Mara's cheeks and she shook with silent sobs. "I do not understand myself," she said. "I have never been so unhappy in my life."

Two weeks had passed since she had crumpled Desmond with her unrelenting scorn, and she was sick with fear and remorse. And yet what did she fear? That she would never see him again? That he would harm her, or harm himself? It was not so simple. Her fear spread over her whole body, turning her skin icy and making her shake with chills. She told Mrs. Underwood that she had caught cold, and lay in her room, silent and taut with the strange misery she could not comprehend. Then had come a new madness. She had leaped from bed one day, dressing quickly, and flown out onto the streets, searching for him there. She followed strangers, if they were tall and dark, hurrying furtively after them until they turned and she could see they were not Desmond. She began accepting the invitations of her clients once more, solely in the hopes that she would see Desmond at a supper-party or the theatre. Once she saw the blonde girl who had bound his hand in her handkerchief; she was turning into a building on Turk Street, and Mara followed her.

"I am sorry to trouble you," Mara said, her cheeks flooding with crimson. "I believe you know my cousin, Mr. O'Connell?"

The girl stared at her for a moment and then smiled frostily.

"Oh, yes," she said with a trace of a French accent, "you are the girl who deals the cards?"

"My name is Mara McQuaid. I work for Mrs. Underwood on O'Farrell Street. I hoped you could tell me where I might find my cousin."

"The tall, dark man who cut his hand? Black hair and blue eyes—a lovely combination I always think. You're out of luck, my dear. I never saw him before that night, and after *you* came in he never looked my way again. Pity!"

Mara mumbled her thanks and turned away, but not before the girl had called out mockingly: "No doubt I'll see you again, Mara. We share the same profession."

It was then that she had gone to Jack Grady, entreating him to find Desmond for her. Even while he complied with her wishes, she could not rest. She took to combing the sordid saloons of the Barbary Coast, searching for him in the ugly, ramshackle back rooms of places she had avoided in her early days in San Francisco. She dressed in her elegant, expensive clothing—she had no other—and made a strange figure among the drabs and toothless hags who nodded over their gin or sat, lost to the world, in an opium dream.

On a foggy, chill evening in October she found herself in a dive on Montgomery Street, threading through the unwashed bodies that lined the bar, her fear subdued by the terrible need to look for Desmond. A Russian sailor caught at her as she went by, smiling beerily and trying to draw her onto his lap, his rough hands snagging on the satin of her hooded cloak. She sought out the bartender, who looked at her as if she were a vision from another world.

"Please," she said. "I am searching for a man; he is my cousin. He is Irish, and very tall, and plays cards a good deal . . ."

Her voice trembled at the futility of it. The barman laughed and mumbled something about how many a husband hid from a wife on the Barbary Coast. "You'll get no help from me," he jeered. "You look well-fixed—leave the poor bugger in peace."

She turned away, stumbling in her haste to leave, and was almost at the door when she heard a gay, soaring laugh rise from the clamor of the crowd and a familiar voice cry out: "Keep your hands to yourself, Karl, you wicked thing!" She turned, following the voice to its source and beheld a round blonde girl with flying curls who perched precariously on a sailor's knee. Before she could think she had cried out the girl's name in amazement and pleasure.

"Kathy!"

Kathleen Daly looked up, furrowing her brow and cocking her head. She had been enjoying her flirtatious games with the sailor and was annoyed at the interruption. She slapped Karl's hands away and peered through the smokey gloom, and then she saw Mara and her jaw dropped open in sheer astonishment. She flew across the room, calling to her friend and tripping on her trailing, tattered skirts in her haste to reach Mara. She caught her in her arms, whirling her around, kissing her cheeks, and squealing in delight.

"Mara, Mara!" she cried. "I thought never to see you again!"

"Come away with me, Kathy—we cannot talk here."

*"Mon dieu—pourquoi pas?"* But Kathy made her goodbyes to the sailor, kissing him affectionately, and allowed Mara to lead her away.

"O'Farrell Street?" said Kathy, raising an eyebrow. "Posh address!" She giggled. Kathy had not changed, although she had grown stouter and was not so well-dressed these days. She grew solemn when she realized that the building Mara took her to was a sporting house.

"You?" she asked softly. "Oh, Mara—I cannot believe it. Why should you sell yourself? Even I am not a—prostitute." She said the word apologetically.

"When I ran away from John I had no clear idea where I was going. I only knew I could not bear to live my life with him. I came West, and then I discovered I was going to have a baby——" Her voice faltered.

"I know," said Mara. She told Kathy about her encounter at Cripple Creek. "I am so sorry," she said.

"The child was John's," Kathy whispered. "Of that there's no doubt."

Mara longed to confide in Kathy but could not bring herself to mention Desmond. It would be a great cruelty to Kathy, who clearly had no knowledge of his whereabouts. And so she listened while Kathy prattled on about Karl, the sailor who was mad keen in love with her.

"He is *formidable!*" Kathy confided. "He can make love for *days* without tiring! I shall probably marry him——although of course I can't, because John and I are not divorced." She laughed. "*Quel horreur.* My parents pay me to stay away, you know, so I shall never starve! I'm exactly like a remittance man, my dear; so long as I never set foot in Cork again they are satisfied." She looked at herself in Mara's mirror, frowning. "I'm much the worse for wear," she said wryly. "But you, Mara——you are lovelier than ever. Do you remember the night at Delmonico's when that funny man gave you his card? Everyone looked at you, because you were so beautiful."

Now was the time to talk to Kathy, to confess to her and be comforted as once——long ago——she herself had comforted her friend. But it was impossible.

Kathy had wept for Desmond and Mara could not reopen the wound. The moment passed, and Kathy did not inquire. She was being considerate, discreet. One did not ask a friend who had become a prostitute the reasons why.

"Once you gave me a beautiful gift," Mara said. "Will you allow me to do the same for you now?" She took the emerald ring from her jewel box and slipped it on Kathy's finger. Kathy protested, crowed with delight and said that Mara was much too generous, but she took it.

"You must not worry about me, Mara," she said seriously. "I am happy as I am. I was never intended to live a respectable life as a proper little wife in Cork—I was always a wild girl, *ma foi!*— why do you think my Papa was so eager to marry me off? I am content now; I wish you could be as happy as I."

"I do not think I was intended to be happy," said Mara. "Some of us must be sad or there would be no way to judge joy."

Kathy looked at her with concern. For a moment it seemed she might say something important. Desmond's name, his presence, hovered in the room palpably. Then she turned, promising to come again, to visit Mara often. Her voice was thick with sorrow when she bade her friend goodbye.

Mara never saw her again.

Life at Mrs. Underwood's had soured. The day after Kathy's visit, Bianca tried to kill herself. Mara never forgot the long, wailing scream that came when Jane discovered Bianca, pale and unmoving, lying across the bed. The girl had taken poison, and although she lived the doctors said she had permanently injured the lining of her throat. Bianca would never speak again.

Jack Grady came to Mara with the news she dreaded—Desmond had indeed left San Francisco. He was, Grady said, in Seattle. Mara counted the money she had made in her months at the house on O'Farrell Street, found it was more than she had even imagined, and told the kindly madame that she must leave.

"Oh dear, oh dear," snuffled Mrs. Underwood, "first poor Bianca and now you, my dear. I shall miss you ever so much, but I've never stood in any of my girls' way. Where will you go, Mara?"

"To Seattle."

"And why Seattle, dear?"

"I must," said Mara. She could not have told Mrs. Underwood her reasons, even if she understood them herself.

On a snowy morning in December, Desmond wakened with a feeling of profound disgust. He had played faro in a back room near the shipyards until nearly dawn, and when ever-patient Sonia had crept to his side, begging him to come back home with her, he had turned her away brusquely. It was the first night he could remember in Seattle when he had slept alone. His head felt fuzzy and thick; his eyes burned and he cursed the long hours in smokey rooms that were so necessary to his goal. His luck had been bad, and now it would be too late to book passage North until the spring. The Bering Sea was frozen, dangerous; even the inner passage would be unnavigable for months. He threw back the covers and strode to the small, chipped washstand, where he poured a pitcher of icy water over his head and shoulders, gasping with the shock of it and toweling himself briskly until he began to come awake. He pulled on his trousers, took a long slug of whiskey from the ever-present bottle, and stared glumly out at the snow. There came a tapping at his door, and instantly he was alert. He went for his shirt, but a desperate voice called softly:

"Let me in, Mr. O'Connell. Oh, hurry, please!"

The girl who slipped through the door and ran into the room was no more than eighteen. She wore a brown cloak and prim bonnet, and her face was alive with distress. It was Janet Trevelyan, the shipbuilder's daughter. Desmond stared at her in amazement.

"What is it, Miss Trevelyan? What are you doing here?"

Janet removed her cloak, revealing an equally prim brown dress which buttoned up to the chin, and sank down in the room's one straight-backed chair. Her eyes moved over Desmond slowly, taking in the wet dark hair, the smoothly muscled naked chest, the genuine alarm in his startlingly blue eyes. She smiled.

"I wanted to see you," she said slyly.

"You should not have come here," Desmond said.

"I sent you a note." Her tone was accusing now. "My maid brought it to you at the Haven. You never answered."

Desmond rubbed his jaw; then he smiled wryly. "You have come for an answer?"

The girl nodded. The note had been simple and alarmingly straightforward, stating that she wished to meet him, and since she could not come to the Haven he must come to her. She had included her address, and signed it imperiously: "Janet Maria Trevelyan."

Desmond sighed. She was a remarkably pretty girl, with smooth fair skin and quantities of auburn hair cunningly looped at the nape of her neck. Her brown eyes were wide and innocent, but something dangerous burned in their depths when she looked at him. She was trouble.

"Here is your answer," Desmond said. "Dear Miss Trevelyan—your parents would not be pleased at any association with a man such as I. I am not in the habit of corrupting wealthy and innocent young ladies. I am a man of few principles, it is true, but seducing virgins is not my line—"

"And how do you know I am a virgin?" she pouted.

"I have not finished," said Desmond. "If you will not think of yourself, then think of me. You can land me in a deal of trouble, Miss Trevelyan, and trouble is what I wish to avoid. Yours in all sincerity, D. O'Connell."

Her lips parted. "You are so beautiful," she whispered. "I think you are the most beautiful man I have ever seen . . ."

"I thank you," said Desmond grimly. He reached for his shirt, but Janet cried out so sharply he froze in his tracks.

"You had no such scruples with my maid!" she said scornfully. "Lin never tells me anything, but I saw it in her face. You made love to her, and yet you refuse me—it's not fair!"

"Your maid is not so innocent as you," Desmond said gently, "and yet more important—she does not have a papa who would see me ridden out of Seattle on a rail."

"My father wants what I want," said Janet. "He would not despise you for being Irish."

"That's uncommonly good of him," said Desmond with disgust. He walked to the door and stood beside it. "Please leave me now. I have an appointment."

"With a tart? Or playing cards? What do you have to do that is more important than making love to me?"

Desmond opened the door and Janet gave a little shriek. Her hand had flown to her throat and she began, very slowly, to unbutton the first of the dozens of jet clasps that held her dress. Desmond shut the door quickly. "Devil take you," he said, laughing. "Please, Janet. Look—I will kneel to you and beg you to leave. If that does not work I will have to throw you out." He came to her and got on his knees, bowing his head in mock supplication.

She reached out and touched his hair, curling her fingers in the dark, damp locks and sighing with pleasure. "Throw me out, then," she said. "I will make such a noise you'll never be able to live here again."

"Then," said Desmond patiently, "I shall move." The girl's hands had moved to his shoulders now;

her warm little fingers caressed his bare chest. "You are so smooth," she murmured. "Kiss me, Desmond. If you kiss me I will leave."

Her lips were soft and very pink, like crushed rose petals. Desmond brushed them gently with his own lips, barely touching her, and rocked back on his heels. "Now go," he said hoarsely. The girl had aroused him, as she had known she would, and she smiled in triumph.

"I cannot leave now," she whispered. "Someone might see me coming from this house who knows my father. I must wait until it is dark."

Desmond hauled her to her feet, bundling the cloak around her, and propelled her to the door. She kicked and squealed, fighting him every step of the way, and when he set her down she lifted her chin and looked at him defiantly. "You may as well do as I say," she hissed. "If you don't, I'll tell everyone you attacked me. I'll shout it from the rooftops and you'll be put in jail."

The words were childish, but Desmond knew she meant them. She was quite capable of avenging herself in that manner. "Why do you want to ruin me?" he asked curiously.

"I want to love you," she replied. And then she placed her hand on his body with all the finesse of a woman many years older and more experienced. Slowly, slowly, she caressed him, sighing with pleasure at his arousal. "Do you see?" she whispered. "I would learn very fast—I would be an apt pupil, my love . . ."

And Desmond, reeling on his feet with the power of his desire, thought that for all Janet's boldness she was innocent—as innocent as Mara once had been. He saw again Mara's face, flushed with desire as it had been in his cabin at sea, and heard her crying

*"Please, Desmond . . . Oh, love . . ."*

He gave a soft cry of despair and, with trembling hands, shoved Janet through the door. It was the first time in his life he had ever denied himself the pleasure of a woman's body.


The back room at the Antlers Hotel was packed. A.J. had heard of the game through his friend Bill, who worked at the Seattle *Times-Intelligencer* as a junior reporter. As he had expected, the players were mainly newspapermen—easy-going, hard-drinking chaps who played to relax rather than to make money. Adam thought he'd have a good night of it. He alone needed to win, and in his experience need spurred a player on more effectively than anything else. There was only one other man who seemed, in A.J.'s view, to be a professional gambler. He was an intense, dark-skinned Irishman who dressed with casual elegance and kept to himself. He drank a good deal, but when the other lads joked and made sly allusions to the women they knew, the Irishman merely smiled and retreated into himself.

After an hour's play A.J. had won only twenty dollars; the Irishman was faring slightly better, but under his professionally impassive expression Adam detected a certain desperation. Once, when his flush in hearts lost to a full house, he cursed softly in a language A.J. took to be Gaelic. Occasionally Mara had sung him a song in Gaelic during the long days of her recovery, and A.J. warmed at the thought. He loved her like a sister, and never failed to write her a note each week. She replied, of course, but never said much about herself. A. J. was determined to win enough so that he and Mara could both travel north and search for gold. It would be a glorious adventure . . .

One of the newspapermen was bringing out a sheaf of postcards, passing them around and commenting lewdly on the attributes of the women who posed in black stockings and tight bodices, or clothed in racy French can-can drawers.

"For my money," said the man to A.J.'s left, "there's more passion in *this* than in a dozen of those posturing chippies." He withdrew from his folding purse a penny post-card and looked at it affectionately. " 'Hibernian Beauty,' " he murmured, "the finest portrait of a young girl ever produced." He laid it on the table and A.J., who had seen the postal many times, smiled his approval.

"I agree with you," he said happily. "The young lady is even lovelier·than her picture. I know—she is my friend."

Even as he spoke his voice faltered, for the Irishman had reacted so peculiarly to the sight of Mara's portrait that the entire table quieted with curiosity. The color had drained from his face and he flung one hand up over his eyes as if to blind himself.

"Blinded by beauty!" joked the man to A.J.'s right.

The Irishman now stared helplessly at the photograph, his eyes riveted to Mara's face as if he could not tear them away. He looked haunted, thought A. J., as if he had seen a ghost.

"Have you never seen it?" inquired one of the men. "It's quite famous."

But Desmond had scraped his chair back from the table and was on his feet. "Deal me out for a time," he said unsteadily, and walked toward the door.

When A.J. found him he was standing motionless on the long hotel verandah, staring out at the snowy streets.

"I beg your pardon," said Adam politely. "Do you know Miss McQuaid?"

"She was my cousin." His voice was flat.

"Why do you say 'was'? Mara is still alive—she lives in San Francisco. I have just written to her this evening."

The man gave a short laugh. "All men know my cousin," he said bitterly. He looked at Adam closely. "And all boys, too, it seems."

A.J. flushed. "I will warn you not to say anything about her that might anger me," he said. "She is like a sister to me. We traveled together to San Francisco. I—I saved her life, you see, and she is very dear to me."

The Irishman rounded on him then, gripping at his arms like a madman, his face terrifying in the dim light. A.J. stood his ground, feeling a profound pity for this strange, violent man.

"How saved her life?" The whisper was hoarse and passionate.

"It's a very long story," said A.J. calmly. "I will tell you if you like." And then he and Desmond sat on the steps of the verandah, impervious to the cold, and Adam related the story of Mara's fantastic abduction and escape. When he told of finding her half-dead in the snow, the Irishman ground his fists against his eyes as if trying to erase the image. "You see," said A.J., "she had suffered so much she wanted only peace. She told me she wished to be away from men for the rest of her life."

"And do you know where she lives now?" Desmond asked softly.

"On O'Farrell Street," said Adam.

"What sort of house is it?"

"Oh," said Adam vaguely, "a boarding house, I believe."

The man smiled briefly, but said no more about Mara's lodgings. He took Adam's hand and wrung it painfully. "If there is ever anything I can do for you, you have only to ask," he said. "Never mention to her that you know me, though. It's better that way."

"But why?" asked Adam in astonishment. "Aren't you fond of her?"

"Oh, very fond," the man replied, laughing oddly, "but she does not care for me."

They returned to the gaming tables. Adam played seriously, amassing a good pile of money before another hour was out, but the Irishman was careless and lost everything. He drank continuously, and when the blue-eyed barmaid bent to whisper in his ear he grinned and nodded. Before very long he disappeared altogether and never came back that evening.

Janet Trevelyan lay sleepless in her bed night
after night. She had gone twice more to Desmond's
room, but never found him in again. She suspected
that he slept with his chippies and tarts in their
quarters, to avoid her. She relived over and over
the moments when his lips had touched hers, when
she had felt his hardness stirring under her persuasive fingers. Nobody had taught her how to seduce
a man. No man had touched her; except for the
polite clasp of an escort's hand on the dance floor
she had never known what it was to feel a man's
flesh against her own. The skin of Desmond's chest
had been so smooth and hard and warm . . . No
doubt he had thought her a wanton, but the truth
was that her behavior astounded her as much as
it did Desmond. She was obsessed by him. From the
first time she had seen him, striding along one of
the crowded downtown streets, coat open to the
wind, she had been consumed with passion. She
knew he was a gambler and a rake, but these qualities only made her want him more. The thought of
his black lashes lying tangled on his cheeks while
she caressed him made her quake with longing.

She had always been a good and obedient girl,
her parent's jewel. She was their favorite, having
been born to them late in life, and they had lavished
on her everything within their power to give. In
return she had loved them dutifully. She was cheerful and affectionate at home; a model student in the
school for young ladies that perched high on a hill

above the port. She had never lacked for anything; consequently she never asked for anything. Now she wanted Desmond with a single-minded passion that bordered on mania, and Desmond had rejected her. It was unbearable for her to think of him at large in Seattle, romping in bed with tarts who did not love him as she did, smiling his slow smile while they writhed beneath him. If she couldn't have him then why should they? Her torment would be eased if he went away where she would never have to see him again. So she told herself when she went sobbing to her father with her tale of woe.

Tears streamed down her face when she confessed, with a maidenly blush, that a gambling man named O'Connell had taken advantage of her. She watched her father's stricken face while it changed from sorrow to outrage to hatred. "It's true, Papa," she said piteously. By this time she believed her own story.

By 1897, the port of Seattle would be so clogged with ships determined to make their way to the Klondike that it would seem a scene from bedlam. But in the last month of 1895, the gold was still a vague rumor. Only hardened prospectors who had mined in every camp from the Dakotas to Cripple Creek made the long voyage. Occasionally they would be joined by visionaries who sensed that the dream of gold would become a reality, or men with nothing to lose who found themselves on the run. In December the sea lay clogged with ice, and even the most desperate to escape Seattle could not book passage.

Nobody knew where Desmond had gone, but that he had been obliged to leave was common knowledge. It was a juicy scandal, and the men in the Front Street saloons never tired of chewing it over. Old man Trevelyan had sworn out a warrant for his arrest, threatening that he himself would horse-whip the filthy scoundrel to bloody ribbons if ever he came face to face with him. At the Antlers one wag laid a wager that the women of the town had helped their darling to escape.

When Mara arrived in Seattle the town could talk of little else, for the Trevelyans were one of the most important families, but she was yet ignorant of the affair and only knew that she was once more beginning again in a strange city. She chose a room in the Royal Hotel, far from the humming life of the waterfront, and sat motionless amid her trunks and boxes, paralyzed with the immensity of her decision.

What would she say to Desmond when she encountered him? The thought of facing him, of looking into those glittering, contemptuous eyes, was almost more than she could bear. She knew only that she must see him once more—whether to beg his forgiveness or be free of him forever, she did not know.

She sent a note around to A.J. and then, smiling at the ritual, penned her customary letter to Mr. McSweeney. She didn't even know if he were still alive, but she wrote to him as one clinging to an ancient custom. She was tired from her long ride on the Union-Pacific, but she knew it was useless to sleep. Her body had once more betrayed her. Ever since her encounter with Desmond she had been restless, physically. The months of indifference, the long evenings spent in the mechanical flirtatiousness so necessary to her success with Mrs. Underwood, had left her empty. The most supreme irony was her new awakening, her body's hunger. Now that she was no longer in the business of pleasing men she longed for love. It was all Desmond's fault. She pressed her arms close to her body, shivering, and looked out on the white streets below her window. A tramway was plying up and down the steep hill, and she drew in her breath at the sight of a tall, dark man boarding the car. He moved with Desmond's easy grace, but he was not Desmond.

Adam was oddly restrained when he came to her. His face glowed with joy at seeing her again, but when she explained that she had come to find her cousin the boy looked away in embarrassment.

"What is it, Adam?" Her face was vivid and highly colored tonight. Her eyes blazed in a way A.J. had never seen before, and she moved about restlessly in her room, pacing the floor like a caged leopardess.

"I have met your cousin," A.J. said slowly. "We played cards together one evening and talked of you."

Mara's cat-like eyes widened and she caught her breath. Adam dreaded telling her but plunged in before her look became so rapturous he could not bear it any more.

"Mr. O'Connell is not in Seattle any more," he said quickly. "He left three days ago."

"Where has he gone?" Mara asked. "Where is he?"

"Nobody knows," Adam said. "He left town—abruptly. There was a reason—I do not like telling you, but you'll hear of it soon enough. A Mr. Trevelyan, who owns the largest shipyard in Seattle, has sworn out a warrant for his arrest."

"But what has he done?" Mara's voice rose alarmingly.

"They say he seduced Trevelyan's daughter," Adam mumbled. And then, seeing Mara's face, added quickly, "I do not believe it. There are many who claim the girl lied out of jealousy because he would not—"

"You needn't say anything more," said Mara icily. "It is no doubt true. My cousin has always been a blackguard. He cannot see a woman without wanting to make love to her." Her voice trembled then and she seemed on the verge of tears.

"Please, don't be sad," Adam pleaded. "I liked Mr. O'Connell—he is all that a man should be. It is not his fault if women run after him."

And then the tears which had been welling in Mara's eyes stopped. She felt the old hatred of Desmond returning. What was she but yet another woman running after him? He had seemed undone in San Francisco; he had told her that he had loved her all these years and suffered the torments of the damned when she disappeared. Yet he had been forced to leave Seattle a few scant weeks later because of another woman.

"Desmond has never cared for anyone but himself," she whispered. "He is the most arrogant and worthless of men."

"He told me you did not care for him," said Adam grudgingly.

And then, to his astonishment, Mara became frenetically gay, decking herself with jewels and insisting they dine in the Royal's best rooms. "God knows it is not San Francisco," she cried cheerfully, "but here I am and I must make the best of it." Her gaiety seemed so forced that Adam felt afraid for her. Even when she had lain, half-frozen in the snow above Grape River, he had not feared for her as he did now.

# BOOK V

## *Queen of the Klondike*

## Chapter Fourteen

Mara's reputation had traveled with her. The Pacific coast was a much smaller place than she had dreamed. It seemed almost that the wanderers who plied their way from San Francisco to Seattle to the Yukon and back again were riding the same treadmill. Each of them seemed sure that riches and glory lay just around the next corner—that on the next trip he would stumble into a frozen river and find it lined with nuggets of gold.

She saw men she had known in San Francisco. Occasionally a familiar face would haunt her until she realized with a shock she had last seen it in the hurdy-gurdy palace in Denver. Men whispered about her, telling each other that the Irish girl had been the highest-priced whore in the Tenderloin—a moody beauty with a mysterious past. Some maintained that she was uncontrollably passionate, while others scoffed that all the world knew the Hibernian Beauty was cold as an Alaskan glacier. Each man tried to find out for himself, and each was turned away cheerfully.

Nobody knew how difficult it was for Mara to rebuff the men who swarmed around her. Her restless state had continued until she felt at times that she might burst. Her blood sang dizzily when she felt their hot eyes on her, and she trembled with desire when she was touched. One night, when she and A.J. dined together, she returned to her room and made a decision. People would think her notorious no matter what the truth was. Very well, she would become as infamous as possible—as infamous as Desmond had been.

With the desperate gaiety that so alarmed A.J., she walked into the Antlers one evening and announced that she would be pleased to deal for the newspapermen. They cheered and toasted her, their eyes roving triumphantly over the white breasts so daringly exposed in her flame-colored gown.

The Antlers had a proud new acquisition—an oil painting of a naked woman which shimmied and undulated with suggestive movements. One of the men showed her how it was accomplished by means of a bellows placed behind the painting; he roared with laughter and let his hand drop to her bare shoulder. He was fat and fifty, and even so she shuddered.

She visited the dance hall operated by the Swedish sisters, and persuaded them to let her masquerade as a working girl. She whirled in the arms of manifold partners, her head spinning and heart pounding with delight. Johanna and Gunilla were pleased. On the nights when Mara came, their take was twice as much as usual. They didn't understand, any more than Mara did, her true reasons for becoming a fixture in the waterfront night life. The truth was that she had to be near the people Desmond had known —his women, the women he had made love to. When they dropped his name in tones of fond memory she felt a choking sensation, a desire to fly at them in fury. But it was better than not hearing his name at all.

"Are you really his cousin?" Gunilla asked her.

"Yes—the infamous O'Connell is my cousin," replied Mara with a laugh.

Gunilla rolled her eyes. "Such a man he was," she giggled.

And then Mara would pry, ever so gently, and hear the things that tormented her so.

"It wasn't true about the Trevelyan girl," Johanna said thoughtfully one evening. "These rich doxies are all alike—they get hysterical when a man turns them down."

"And why would he turn her down?" Mara asked, holding her breath.

"I only know," Johanna said slyly, "that he was with me and Gunilla the night she said he ruined her. *Ruined* her!" She snorted scornfully. "It would have done her the world of good, *ja*, Mara?"

On the last night of the year, Mara found herself hoisted to the bar at the Haven by a dozen willing hands. She had drunk three glasses of champagne and stared about in giddy delight at the sea of faces looking up at her.

"Dance for us!" shouted a drunken editor from the *Times-Intelligencer*. "Dance in the New Year, Mara!"

They began to clap rhythmically so that she could not even hear the discordant clamor of the off-tune piano, and gradually her body began to move with the rhythm. At first she merely swayed, her hips weaving gently beneath the cloth of her satin gown, but as the men's clapping grew more insistent she raised her arms above her head and let her entire body undulate in a long, shivering movement that seemed pure invitation. She mimicked the movements of an Irish reel, but so slowly that every gesture took on a new meaning. She threw her head back, feeling her hair cascade down her back, and smiled with sheer sensual joy.

There was a man who watched with particular fervor—a blond giant of a man she had seen night after night. He had flat, sea-green eyes and always wore a broad-brimmed miner's hat jammed down on his thick hair. His name was Ivor, and some said he was Finnish, others Russian. Mara danced for him, catching his eye as she swayed her hips and arched her back, offering to him alone the body reflected in each man's gaze.

When it was over several fights broke out, but Ivor threaded his way through the brawling men like a mighty ship in full sail and lifted her down from the bar in his bear-like arms. She felt her body brush his as he set her on her feet, and she shivered with anticipation.

"Miss Mara," he said simply, "do you have a lover?"

"If I told you I did not would you believe me?"

Ivor's green eyes washed over her slowly, like sea-combers on a tropical beach, and then he said:

"It is not safe for you to be alone. I will protect you."

"Yes," she whispered, mesmerized. It seemed eons before they were in her room. He had wrapped her in a thick robe in the carriage and then turned from her, never speaking. Mara was stunned at the force of her desire and shocked at what she knew she was about to do, but when they entered her room there was no turning back.

Ivor played with her as if she were a doll, taking up her hairbrush and letting it slide through the long tresses with an air of wonder. She watched raptly in the mirror while he fingered the diamond necklace at her throat, examining it like a curious child. It occurred to her that he was simple-minded, but she wanted him with a force that had nothing to do with his mind.

"Pretty," he said gruffly, sliding her dress from her shoulders with infinite care and planting his huge hand on the white swellings of her breasts where they rose from the black silk chemise. When she stood before him in her chemise and black stockings he fingered the rosettes of her crimson garters wonderingly. His touch was amazingly light for such a giant of a man. He lifted her to the bed and made her stand before him while he stripped the chemise away, his fingers cupping her breasts so lightly she seized his hands and pressed them to her hungry flesh. Her knees were giving way with the power of her desire and she fell against him, moaning. Patiently, he stripped away the stockings, leaving her bright garters on, and bent his lips to her thighs.

She lay back, feeling tears of joy and ecstasy spilling down her cheeks, her body pulsating in blissful abandon, her arms catching at him as he covered her slender form with his massive body. She was crying out wantonly, begging him to hurry, twining her fingers in the shaggy mass of his white hair and arching her hips to meet his thrust. She felt him deep inside of her and then he was moving savagely, wonderfully, pushing her before him on a flooding of pure sensation. She grasped for it, gasping and writhing beneath him, but it fled before her, eluding her and vanishing. Ivor gave a huge cry of delight and collapsed on her, sated. He held her in his arms, biting gently at her neck and panting. Mara stared at the ceiling, her eyes wide with despair.

She had felt nothing.

From that day on Ivor was accepted as her lover. He protected her from the advances of the wilder men and walked by her side like a bull mastiff, guarding her. She discovered that he was neither simple-minded nor a miner. He was a merchant seaman, with a wife and three children in Helsinki, who was not interested in talk. Even with Mara, to whom he seemed utterly devoted, he rarely spoke. He continued to adore her body, rousing it with his enormous, gentle, hands and then making love to her tirelessly, with single-minded ardor. It was not Ivor's fault that Mara felt nothing, and she lay beneath him, night after night, hoping that it would be different. When he returned to his ship in February after an early thaw, he bade her goodbye with his customary stolidity. He took her hand, shaking it formally, and gave her a bottle of cheap scent. Mara saw, to her amazement, that his sea-green eyes were full of tears. She kissed him lightly and watched him walk away from her forever. She marvelled at the fact that she would soon be twenty-one, and knew no more about men than she ever had . . .

A.J. clung to Mara with loyalty, even though he disapproved of her wild behavior and could not understand her attraction to Ivor. When the silent Finn returned to his ship, Adam came to her with a proposition.

"There is nothing for you here," he said solemnly. "Soon the ice will thaw, Mara. We could go north then, up the inner passage! I have enough money for my kit now, and you could sell your jewels—think of it, Mara—gold!"

She smiled at his enthusiasm.

"It would be such an adventure . . . and we are young and strong! Please, Mara . . . I can't leave you here—" He blushed, considering the wisdom of what he was about to say. "I am sure we would find Mr. O'Connell," he mumbled hurriedly. "I feel certain he's in the Yukon. Where else can he have gone?"

"I don't in the least care if I ever see Mr. O'Connell again," she said haughtily. She rose and paced the room as she so often did these days. Then she went to her jewel box and counted the money which she kept there. Her wild Seattle spree had diminished it, but she was still far from poor. She turned to Adam, frowning. "What you say is true," she murmured. "There is nothing for me in Seattle. I don't care about gold, Adam, and I have had enough adventure to last me a lifetime. All the same——" she smiled at him—"I will go with you."

He grinned in sheer delight. "I knew you would," he said. And then he unfolded a large map and began very seriously to chart out their passage to the Yukon.

They sailed in April, leaving Seattle for the unknown aboard a refurbished steamer called the *Sitka Star*. Mara remembered the ill-fated Atlantic crossing on the *Alberta* and was glad that she and A.J. had chosen the Inner Passage. Those who went the all-sea route had an easier time of it, but the journey from the Gulf of Alaska to the Bering Sea and on to the headwaters of the Yukon was 4,200 miles or more. She had heard of one group of stampeders who set out from Seattle and were on board ship for six months before they reached their destination. For better or worse, she and Adam would sail the Inner Passage to Dyea, and then take the overland route. He had warned her of the dangers of the passage through the mountains, but she would simply deal with that when they came to it. For now she wanted to be moving, traveling again, looking for a new life.

The noise on deck was fearful. Horses in their cramped stalls whinnied and kicked in terror, and the caged sled dogs howled ceaselessly with long, mournful notes that made her flesh creep. Every available inch of space on deck was taken—there were even tents pitched in some of the life-boats.

She and Adam were perched on a large bale of hay, and Mara could not help laughing at the madness of the venture.

"It's pandemonium," she whispered. But Adam was watching the port of Seattle slip steadily from view and smiling absently.

She regarded him with affection. Like the other men on board, A.J. was infected with more than the lust for gold. All of them felt they were embarking on the adventure of their lives—that whatever lay in wait would test their true mettle as men and provide them with stories for their old age. A.J.'s eyes were almost reverent when he spoke of the Yukon.

Mara sighed. There were several women on the *Sitka Star,* and it seemed to her they were far less mystical about the voyage than the men. There was a red-faced, cheerful Dane who said she was planning to bake bread and sell it at ten dollars a loaf to miners, and a timid minister's wife who looked terrified at the blow fate had dealt her in posting her husband to the savage Arctic. The rest of the women clearly belonged to the profession Mara had abandoned in San Francisco. Their mission was clear enough; they were cheerful, rough girls who smiled at the men as if rehearsing for the main event when they reached the Yukon.

The cabin Mara shared with A.J. was close and cramped, and both of them spent as much time on deck as possible. Mara began to be entranced by the beauty she saw slipping by as the *Star* made her way up the Passage. The sea lay green and still, awash with pieces of floating ice, cupped between

the western islands and the foothills to the east. The
shoreline was forest, thick and unbroken, and it
seemed to her that the dark trees might have stood
like this since the dawn of time.

They passed Indian villages, where the savage
totems had been placed looking out to the sea. The
minister's wife gasped in shock at the sight of the
grotesque and beautiful carvings, and her husband
patted her arm absently. Mara found them lovely—
like ancient gods guarding the primeval forest.
Equally lovely were the ornately carved Indian
canoes which occasionally passed them. Their pad-
dles moved so silently the canoes shot by on a plume
of silver spray like something from a dream, leaving
the *Star* to plow her way along like a clumsy sea
monster in their wake.

One afternoon as she sat dreaming on deck a
swarm of porpoises broke the water, leaping glee-
fully about the ship. "Look!" she cried to A.J. "See
how beautiful they are!" Adam looked at her and
thought how much more calm she was now. The
terrible tension seemed to have left her. He didn't
know if she was happy, but the manic gaiety was
gone. She seemed to be waiting for something to
happen . . .

At Wrangell some of the men bought whiskey at
the trading post and sat up half the night, singing in
drunken voices that made the dogs howl in protest.
Mara heard laughter on deck and knew that the girls
had joined the revelers. They were going North to
sell their bodies to sex-starved miners, and they
were more honest than she. She had pretended to be

a courtesan and denied herself to the men who paid
for her company; then, when the full flood of desire
had returned to her, she found it could no longer be
satisfied. It seemed a cruel joke. She'd told A.J. she
never wanted to see Desmond again, but she acknowledged wryly that it was all she wanted in the
world. At least she was moving toward him now.
Part of the new-found peace she felt came from the
belief that she would be near him again. No matter
how vast the new territory might be, she would find
him . . .

They passed Sitka, the one-time Russian capital,
and everyone cheered. Between Sitka and Juneau
there was nothing but dense cedar forests and awesome glaciers plunging straight down to the sea.
Mara was once again suspended in the beauty of it,
lost in a dream of wonder. When the *Sitka Star*
anchored well off-shore in the mountain-bound
harbor of Dyea, she was almost sorry the voyage
had come to an end.

Nothing had prepared her for the chaos of landing. Goods were ripped free of their moorings and
thrown overboard to drift in on the tide. The terrified horses were swung into slings and lowered into
the water, where they were left to swim for shore.
A.J. and Mara crowded into a leaky scow with
six others and floated to safety amid the whinnies
of frightened horses, the shouts of men trying to
corral their lumber, and the floating bales of hay.
The tide was on the turn and the waters moved
swiftly. Mara watched with horror while a vicious
fight broke out on the beach between two men who

had both grabbed the same limping, pathetic horse and seemed about to pull the unfortunate animal in two.

As soon as they had reclaimed their possessions on the gray tidal strand, A.J. took her arm and helped her to stumble up the dismal beach toward a rough trail. "Stay here," he said, "while I bargain." She watched while A.J. approached one of the Chilkat Indians who stood looking on with what almost seemed to her amusement. "How mad they must think us," she thought. "Gold-crazed fools arriving with so many supplies that we can't even move them by ourselves." She saw the problem. If they left some of their gear on the strand it would surely be stolen by the time A.J. returned for it, but they had refused to pay $200 for one of the spindly, sickly horses that were being palmed off on the credulous back in Seattle. "We cannot take a horse where we're going," Adam had told her grimly. "We would only have to abandon it once we reached Chilkoot Pass."

The Indian arrived at a satisfactory arrangement and advanced silently, strapping a harness to his broad back and lifting over a hundred pounds of their gear with an effortless movement. He motioned for a woman whose face was smeared with a black, oily substance to stand guard over the rest. "Why are the women painted black?" she whispered to A.J.

"For beauty's sake," he said. "No doubt they think you very ugly indeed."

Mara laughed. Her spirits had risen the moment they left the chaos of the hideous landing, but they began to sink a bit once she caught sight of Dyea. It was merely a tent-town; past the rows of tents a single boardwalk thoroughfare ran through the mud. Beyond were the mountains. Their Chilkat guide returned for the rest of their supplies and the goods were redistributed. Mara carried fifty pounds of food-stuff on her own back, glad that A.J. had made her purchase ugly, stout walking boots. In her boots and mackinaw, her raven hair coiled beneath a cap, she might have been a boy. She felt safe and protected. Her beauty could not lead her into trouble here—there were more important things to deal with in the wilds than the transitory passions of men and women.

Her exhilaration carried her through the perilous, boulder-strewn crevice that was Dyea Canyon. It did not daunt her to realize that she and A.J. would be dining on beans and bacon later, sleeping huddled on the floor of Sheep Camp, part way up the pass. Hardship, she thought, was what she needed. She had lead a soft, pampered life for so long—ever since she had escaped from Quentin—that she had forgotten what it was to grapple with more elemental things. Or so she mused, gazing up at the notch in the mountain they would traverse. She could understand why horses were unable to cross the Chilkoot—it was too steep, too sheer. Lifting her face toward its heights, she suddenly remembered a childhood visit to the Moher Cliffs, in Ireland. It had been cloudy, the mist hanging low so that when Padriac lifted her in his arms and let her peer down the cliff wall she had seen only the swirling vapors. Then, with heart-stopping precision, a ray of sun had picked through the clouds and she had seen—so far below it seemed something from a nightmare—the lashing of the sea. She had shivered, withdrawing in terror.

She felt something of that primitive fright now. The notch looked evil. A towering glacier dominated the whole pass—far up on the face of the rock she could see a thin line of backpackers, struggling along in a single-file column, like ants assaulting a mound of sugar. The snows had not melted further up. A.J. told her there were steps hacked from the ice and she laughed incredulously.

"How will we haul our supplies up in one trip?"

"We won't," said Adam grimly. "The guide and I will make three trips—you will only have to climb it once."

She never forgot, for the rest of her life, what it was like to feel the winds whipping around the face of the pass, lashing at her as if to pluck her away and send her whirling to her death. If she looked up there was the impassive, shining mass of the glacier, glowing with refracted light and making her dangerously dizzy. They moved slowly, inching along under the burden of their packs, feeling carefully with the toes of their boots before setting their feet down on the perilous, slippery snow and ice.

When they rested at Sheep Camp, more than halfway up, Mara looked around at the barren floors where exhausted climbers slept, shoulder to shoulder, on tattered blankets. She was thinking that she could not possibly sleep in such circumstances when she fell into a profound and dreamless slumber.

They completed the ascent the next morning, and

some of Mara's exhilaration came flooding back when they reached the top and she saw, panoramic below her, a long trail leading to the shores of a sapphire lake. After the ascent of Chilkoot, nothing could daunt her again. The encampment on Lake Lindeman where Adam built their makeshift boat seemed a paradise to her. Once she had thought the mountains of Colorado beautiful. Now she thought nothing could be so lovely or so grand as the icy mountains and thick forests, the deep blue lakes and roaring rivers, of Northern Canada. Adam taught her to use the rifle and she shot a ptarmagin for their dinner one night when they were camped above the Whitehorse Rapids. The light held for hours, the long day dying finally in a pale languor.

"At mid-summer it will be light nearly all the time," said A.J.

Mara went to him, taking his serious face between her hands and kissing him on the cheek. "I am happy, Adam," she said. "For the first time in so long I am happy."

They saw two caribou swimming in the river one night, their proud heads outlined clearly in the pearly dusk. It was Mara's twenty-first birthday, and she could not have asked for a nicer present. It hardly seemed possible to her that she had been away from Ireland for more than four years. Her mother was dead, her father, God knew where, and she had lived many lifetimes since the day she boarded the *Alberta* for the New World.

Adam, as if reading her mind, said, "Do you ever think of Mr. O'Connell, Mara?"

She stiffened. "I think only of pleasant things," she said.

"He told me if there was anything he could do for me I had only to ask," said Adam slowly. "I told him I saved your life once—it was for that he thanked me. Nothing else."

Mara took up a twig and traced patterns in the dirt thoughtfully. "Mr. O'Connell knows how to charm people," she said. "He can be very persuasive, but you must never trust him."

"Why do you dislike him so? What harm has he ever done you?"

Mara looked at him oddly, opened her lips as if to speak, and then thought better of it. She had never opened her heart to Adam, close as she felt to him. He was even younger than she, and more than anything she sought to protect him. He had been on his own since he was eleven years old and worked in a brothel until they had fled to San Francisco together—surely nothing would shock him. And yet she knew instinctively that the truth of her relationship with Desmond would hurt him. She kept her silence.

The next day they shot the Whitehorse Rapids. It was infinitely more dangerous than scaling Chilkoot Pass, yet Mara felt wild with happiness as she and A.J. whirled through the deadly foam, narrowly escaping the boulders that would have torn their little boat to shreds and sent them to their deaths. She screamed her laughing defiance into the white-water mist, collapsing in helpless giggles when the danger was past. A.J.'s face was white and set; he understood the danger better than she. "I sometimes think you Irish are all mad," he said. "You cry at trifles and laugh at death."

"And what are you?" Mara asked. "Where did your parents come from?"

Adam hung his head. "I don't know," he said.

As she and A.J. moved north, Mara realized she did not know what the gold would look like. She vaguely pictured broad shimmering bands stippling the rocks beneath the surface of the water, or nuggets strewn along the pebbly beaches like so many golden eggs. All during the month of May they stopped along the river and dipped their pans, and all she discovered was that panning for gold was backbreaking work. The deceptively blue and tranquil water was freezing cold—in these subarctic climes, even in mid-summer it would never be warm. Legs freezing, Mara would leap from the shallow water and massage her cramped leg-muscles furiously until she felt steady enough to plunge back into the icy shoals and work her pan again. Then her fingers would freeze and she would repeat the process, smiling ruefully at Adam. "I do not think we'll become rich this way," she said.

Eventually, they found gold as fine and lacy as sifted flour along the banks of a tiny, unnamed streamlet that rushed into the Yukon at Thirtymile. Ten miles further, gold as coarse as sand showed in their pans. Always, though, it was a tiny amount. Two hours of labor might yield a dollar's worth. Still, she was fascinated by even the smallest grain. A.J. had told her that clever bartenders in the gold camps collected dust beneath their fingernails when they raked in the drinker's money. At the end of an evening they might be ten dollars richer! Fantastic—the lure it had. She had made twice, ten times as much money for twirling in the sweaty arms of one of her partners at the hurdy-gurdy palace—fifty times as much for appearing with Jack Grady at a Turk Street soiree, but it was not the same.

Despite freezing toes and a repetitious diet of ptarmagin stew and beans, despite sleeping with only a blanket roll between her body and the hard ground, she was happy. The summer foliage was magenta and gold, the mountains crimson and emerald. The air she breathed was so pure and unsullied it sometimes made her giddy. And the sun, the Arctic sun, burned down upon their tent until nearly ten at night. As the summer moved toward its blazing zenith, she moved north with A.J., content to let him take her where he would. The civilized world had never seemed so far away or so unimportant. Only news concerning these northern provinces meant anything, and this they gathered from the occasional wanderers who passed them, going up or down the Yukon.

"Go to Indian Creek!" a party of grizzled men might shout as they spun by in hide canoes, or: "Try the Big Salmon—surface bars there!" Once they met a strange man who beached his craft and sat with them at their modest supper, for all the world as if they had issued him a formal invitation. He seemed half-crazed to Mara, yet she did not fear him. It was the isolation of his life that had given the evangelical glaze of lunacy to his faded eyes, and she and Adam treated him kindly.

"They do say Parson's taken leave of his senses," the man said, picking his teeth with a bit of willow twig. "Anglican Church sent him up to Indian Creek for a spell and it were the gnats—the gnats and skeeters—did him in. Sent him 'round the bend."

"How long have you been in the Yukon?" Mara asked.

"Two years," said the man. "Been up above Indian Creek, and crossed over to Alaska. Been to Quartz Creek, too. The gnats and skeeters is what gets to you."

He left as suddenly as he had come, thanking them with formal politeness for their hospitality.

"Oh dear," said Mara, "we won't become like him, will we, A.J.?"

And for the rest of the evening A.J. made her weak with laughter by leaping around the campfire and shouting "gnats and skeeters" until she had to beg him to stop. "Actually," said the sobered Adam, "that geezer is probably very rich. He'll head back for Seattle and spend all his money on a spree. Then he'll be back." There was a visionary look in his wide, dark eyes as he said this, and Mara realized she could easily envision Adam losing himself in the wilds. For the first time a tiny thread of discontent crept into her feeling of well-being. She had begun to look forward to the far off Fortymile, where there would be some amenities. Roughing it was all very well, but she wanted a warm bath. Above all she wanted to wear something other than the long skirt, shawl, boots, and mackinaw which had become her only costume. Or so she told herself. Above all, she wanted to reach a settlement where she might have news of Desmond. From the moment she allowed herself to admit it, she grew impatient.

Occasionally they stayed in Indian villages, and there was invariably a white man who had married an Indian woman and settled with the Indians, becoming more like them every day. In a tiny settlement where two rivers branched she watched while three squaws tossed a portly German—once from Pennsylvania—in a blanket. The women shrieked with laughter as their captive's heavy body thudded into the blanket like a swollen caterpillar falling from a tree. They offered to toss A.J., too, but he blushed and shook his head.

Later the man from Pennsylvania offered them a dram of whiskey and some advice. "Go to the Thron-diuck," he told them. "It flows into the Yukon some hundred miles above where we are."

The word as he pronounced it emerged like the gasp of a man being strangled.

"What is it?" asked Adam. "How do you say it?"

"Thron-diuck," said the squawman. "Klondike to you. Finest salmon river in the world."

"But gold?"

"Who can say?"

It was mid-summer when they passed through the moose-pasture called Dawson. Neither of them could know that in two years' time Dawson would be flooded with tens of thousands of stampeders eager to mine the richest gold field in the north. For now it was simply a cluster of tents perched along make-shift roads laid out across the mud. They were headed for Fortymile.

When Mara saw the group of primitive cabins that marked the remote settlement of Fortymile River, her heart sank. She had been expecting some of the gaiety of a Cripple Creek, and found instead a desolate village of murky, fetid dwellings whose windows were made of tanned deerhide, cotton cloth, or—in one case—rows of pickle jars chinked with moss. Here the men mined in narrow shafts, keeping fires going throughout the night, even in July, to soften the permanently frosted ground to the point where a pick could be thrust in.

"I didn't expect it to be so grim," she told A.J. sadly.

"There are ten saloons along the main thorough-fare, and an opera-house," he replied. But even A.J. looked a bit daunted.

They pitched their tent, and while he went to the saw-mill to bargain for wood, Mara wandered the ugly, rutted streets. She found contrasts so strange they seemed miraculous. There was a French dressmaker next to one of the most primitive saloons, and a store which dispensed *pâté de foie gras* and tinned plum pudding. The roads were fairly empty at this hour, for most of the men were huddled in their airless, smoking mine shafts, but the Husky dogs and Malamutes ran everywhere, baying and searching for food. She had seen cakes of soap tied in the crotches of trees outside the town; now she saw them lashed to the roofs of cabins. She shook her head in wonder, thinking that at last she had truly come to the ends of the earth.

"They place them high up so the dogs won't eat them," said a voice close at hand. "I can see you've only just arrived. Don't be discouraged—it's not so bad here as it looks."

Mara turned and saw a girl of about her own age, dressed in the ubiquitous mackinaw and boots of the Yukon, smiling tentatively.

Mara smiled back. "It is more primitive than I had imagined," she said. "My friend and I have been on the river for two months or more. I was foolish enough to think Fortymile would offer—distractions."

"Distractions?" The girl lifted a delicate brow. "Gold is the chief distraction here." She was a slender girl with a lively, inquisitive face and long, smooth hair of a pale strawberry shade. She was certainly pretty, but something in the cast of her features set her apart from the dance hall girls and fortune-seekers Mara had become accustomed to meeting.

"I am called Mara McQuaid," said Mara, who suddenly wanted nothing more than to talk to this calm, pleasant girl. She had been alone so long with only Adam for company that she felt shy and ill at ease.

"I am Veronica Gannett. I am a journalist."

"Do you mean you actually write for a newspaper?" Mara was astounded. She had never met a woman journalist before, had never dreamed a girl might make her living writing.

"I write for several," said Veronica. "At present

I'm doing a piece on the gold camps for a magazine in New York." She smiled kindly. "You mustn't look so confused," she teased. "I know it's unusual, but it suits me. My father was a journalist for *Harper's* —he made the path easier for me."

"Do you live here alone?"

"Quite alone," said Veronica emphatically. "And you?"

"I am traveling with a friend. He is like a brother to me. We've been through much together."

"Perhaps I could use your experiences in my story," said Veronica eagerly. "The whole point is to show the vast variety of people who come from all over America to the North—do you know there is a man here who has never seen a railroad? He has kept one jump ahead of the railroads since the 'seventies. Finally there was only one place left to go." She laughed. "We are all misfits here," she said. "It is a mistake to think that everyone in the Yukon seeks gold only. Many of us simply want to be left in peace—to be alone."

Mara pondered her words. "But not you, surely? When you have finished your writing you will go back?"

"Yes—I've my career to think of," said Veronica. "But I haven't seen nearly all there is to see yet. Come, let me show you around the town, such as it is."

Veronica pointed out various notables to Mara, sketching in their histories in a low voice. "Do you see that man just leaving his cabin?" she would murmur. "He is called Cannibal Ike because he likes raw moose meat." Or, "The man who owns this saloon grew an enormous, black beard to cover up his scars. He tried to cut his throat one day, and nobody discouraged him. Here we do as we like." Veronica also explained to her the codes by which the miners lived.

"Nobody goes hungry here, or we all go hungry," she said succinctly. "There is an unspoken law, and all men obey it. Fortymile may be primitive, but there is a sense of honor. If one man discovers gold some miles away, he spreads the word. Hoarding is unthinkable, and so is theft. Any man in need may use another's cabin, so long as he replaces the kindling he has used."

"Why only the kindling?"

Veronica looked at her gravely. "It is summer now," she said. "During winter a man's life may depend on how quickly he can light his fire."

Veronica took Mara to her own cabin. Her furniture was fashioned from the stumps of trees, her cutlery of tin, and above the red hot sheet-iron stove a pan of fermenting dough had been placed. "Sourdough," said Veronica, wrinkling her nose. "You will get used to it soon enough." She had a stack of papers which had arrived in late May, and Mara read them eagerly, astounded at how much had been going on in the world during her absence. England and Russia seemed on the brink of war, Queen Victoria was feeling poorly, and another play by Henrik Ibsen was scandalizing New York.

"How far away it seems," sighed Mara. "I have lived in New York, and in Chicago and Denver, San Francisco and Seattle—and I can barely remember what it was like to wear silks and scent and dine out."

"Do you miss it?"

"Sometimes," said Mara. "But I've also lived with the Indians, and in a mountain cabin scarcely more luxurious than this—I seem to miss nothing." Her expression belied her words, and her new friend shook her head sagely.

"A woman like yourself, simply drifting from place to place—why?"

But Mara became taciturn then, and leafed through the old newspapers listlessly. She could not bring herself to tell this wonderful and self-sufficient girl that she was searching for the very man whose brutality had set her adrift to begin with. Veronica would only laugh at her. She did ask in a casual and dismissive way if Veronica had ever run across a gambler called O'Connell.

"No," the girl said. "What does he mean to you?"

"Nothing," said Mara.

She and Veronica Gannett became good friends, although the journalist was impatient if she was interrupted at her work. She spent hours covering long rolls of coarse, yellow paper with her fine small handwriting. "I shall never get it right," she sighed, and once—before Mara and Adam's astonished eyes —she rolled a homemade cigarette and smoked it fiercely, staring past them with a rapt and visionary look.


Adam had built their cabin in record time, and he and Mara now slept in a log structure chinked with alpine moss, separated from each other by a tattered curtain. Water, at least, was plentiful, and Mara bought a large tin tub and reveled in a hot bath, lying back in the comforting water and dreaming. When the water grew tepid and forced her out, she dressed in one of the good gowns she had so laboriously hauled over the Chilkoot Pass. It was a simple dress, cut well and of a becoming pale blue color. Her hair, which was now well below her shoulders, she rolled into one of the elaborate coiffures she had worn before Quentin had put an end to such vanity. When she was ready she thrust aside the curtain and walked to the door, leaning on the rough wood and looking longingly toward the lights of the main thoroughfare. Adam was working his claim with pick and shovel five miles away; she knew she ought to help him, but for the time being she was fed up with hard work and dirt beneath her nails. It would not be lady-like, she knew, to enter one of the saloons unescorted. It might even be dangerous. On the other hand, she and A.J. were running out of money and the short summer was nearly at an end.

She laughed at herself. What was a woman who had lived in a bordello doing, worrying about the propriety of things? She took her mackinaw down from the peg by the door, wrapped her head in her shawl, and picked her way over the hardened mud toward town.

The owner of the saloon called the Northern Lights was to tell his cronies, over and over in years to come, of the night the black-haired Irish girl approached him for a job. It bowled him over, the way she walked in as if she owned the place, and demanded to see the man in charge. Bold as brass, but refined, too—and such a good looker!

"What can I do for you, my lovely?" he'd said, winking at Big Alf Porter, who stood leering a few feet down the bar.

"I deal stud, or faro," the girl had replied in her clear, light voice. "My partner and I are not having much luck, and I need a job. I have worked in Grape River, San Francisco, and Seattle—I am sure you will find me acceptable."

"Oh, sweetheart," moaned Alf and his partner Jim Shaw in unison—"you're acceptable to us!"

The girl had smiled with a certain aloof professionalism and waited, head high, for the owner to make a decision.

"Well, we'll try you out, Miss," the owner said, almost choking in glee at this stroke of good fortune. "Can't do fairer than that." It was exactly what he'd been looking for—an ankle to put his rival next door to shame. The girl went right to work, sitting decorously at a table in the back and seizing the deck of cards as if they were long-lost friends. By eleven that night the Northern Lights was packed to overflowing with men who'd come to see the beauteous new dealer. The current star of the traveling review at the Opera House was furious; it was the first night since she'd come to Fortymile that found her taking a back seat. Everyone else was happy, though. Even Veronica Gannett, who had come to see what all the ruckus was about, pressed her nose to the saloon's front window and grinned admiringly.

By midnight, when it was still light, the proprietor

of the Nugget, next door, came in to concede defeat.
From that moment on, until the time Mara left
Fortymile, the Northern Lights was the most popu-
lar saloon in town.

"I suppose it's all right," said A.J. dubiously, "if
it makes you happy."

"It's very independent of you," said Veronica,
"but why must you work so hard? You and Adam
have plenty of money now."

Adam was bringing almost ten dollar's worth of
gold dust from his claim each day, while Mara
earned three times as much sitting in the Northern
Lights. "One can never have too much money," she
told Veronica, "in a town where a gallon of milk
costs twenty dollars."

Veronica was worried about her friend. Mara
bought daring dresses at the French *modiste*'s and
thought nothing of paying twelve dollars for a book
of poetry she fancied. And always, always, she
worked through the night. The men, so eager to
court her at first, discovered that she was unavailable
to them in some mysterious way and treated her with
sorrowful respect. Only once did she receive a letter,
posted six weeks before from New York; she laughed
oddly and told Veronica that it was from a "bene-
factor" she wrote to from time to time.

Mr. McSweeney's letter had been short and to
the point.

"I've sent two men after you, Missy, in the time
since you've been gone. One paid to find you and
the other fought. We all know what happened to
the first one—but what of the fighter? Give him my

regards if you should ever see him again. If I were not getting so old I would come to join you in the Yukon and try my luck.

Yours faithfully,
James J. McSweeney

Mara read Mr. McSweeney's letter as she sat on the banks of the river, far from the clamor of the town. All around her the frosts of late August were turning the salmonberry bushes a bright crimson, and the pale sun shed little warmth. Where, indeed, was the fighter? She had been so sure Desmond would head north, but once more he eluded her.

Veronica had told her about Circle City—"the Paris of Alaska"—whose reputation for wickedness was unparalleled. For all its racy gaiety, the Paris of Alaska was near the Arctic Circle and even more remote than Fortymile. If she and A.J. were to go there they would have to start out at once, before the snows came. Rumors of a stupendous find on the Klondike had filtered up and down the Yukon, but the smart money at the Northern Lights held it was a hoax. Mara deliberated for a long time, gazing out to Liar's Island and wrapping her shawl tightly around her, shivering at the mere thought of what winter would bring. When she returned to the cabin she had made up her mind.

"Adam," she said. "Let us go to Alaska. Our luck may be better there."

And A.J., sick to death of the airless mine shaft on the Fortymile, agreed.

## Chapter Fifteen

Circle City lay 170 miles northwest of Fortymile, on Alaskan soil. By the time Mara and Adam reached the Paris of Alaska it was mid-September; they were only one jump ahead of the Arctic winter.

If Fortymile had looked strange and primitive to her, Circle City might have been a medieval engraving depicting Hell. Here the river spilled over the Yukon Flats, meandering sluggishly across the Arctic Circle. Huge columns of smoke rose from the ever-burning fires and hung in a dark pall over the settlement. On the outskirts of the town log caches on stilts kept supplies from the ravenous dogs. In spite of the music halls and theatres and Opera House, in spite of the twenty-eight saloons Circle City boasted, it seemed grim indeed.

With her earnings from the Northern Lights, Mara took rooms at the hotel built by Jack McQuesten, the founder of the town. She was looking forward to the luxuries of a warm bath and good food, anticipating these modest pleasures with an almost childish eagerness, when Adam came to her. He wore the obsessed and zealous expression she had learned to dread.

"Mara," he said in a low, intent, voice, "I have decided to go on to Fort Yukon before the heavy snows come. I must go soon, but I'll be back within the month."

"But why?" she was incredulous. "We have only just got here."

"If I stake two claims, we can work the one at Fort Yukon when the thaws come next spring."

"But I don't want to go to Fort Yukon," she all but wailed.

"You won't. It's much too arduous for you. I'll go alone, as soon as I've staked us here." He spoke so firmly that Mara stared at him, realizing as she did so that her friend was no longer a gangly boy. The two years since they had left Grape River had both refined and hardened him; A. J. was now a man who must make decisions and abide by them. She had no right to hold him back.

"I will worry about you," she sighed, "but if you must go, you must."

As soon as he had staked their claim and charged her with the duty of tending the fires once each day, he bought a sled and dogs. He rigged a blanket, sail-like, to catch the wind, and packed his supplies. He was itching to be off, and as she watched him slowly disappear into the Arctic twilight, she felt her throat constrict. She was proud of him, and afraid for him, and very much alone.

The first night she took supper in the hotel's riotous dining room, she was approached by so many men she could barely eat her meal. They asked if they might escort her to the Opera House, or to the Music Hall, and each time she replied courteously and coolly that she preferred to be alone. She wondered if they thought her a prostitute, and later, in her room, she examined her face in the mirror. She was searching for signs of hardness, for some coarse shadow or decadent gleam, but she found none. Her cheeks bloomed vividly in the creamy pallor of her face, and her eyes burned golden in the dim light. She did not look wanton, but she saw that she was obviously lonely—the men who approached her saw only a young girl aching for love. She remembered a song which warned maidens to take love while they could. Without love, the lyric said. *Be she ever so lovely she'll wither away . . .*

The next day she rented a sled from the trading post and hired a guide to take her to A. J.'s claim. It lay five miles off in the center of a muskeg swamp, bristling with stunted spruces, and as the guide urged the Malamutes over the snow she studied his every move intently. From now on, she planned to make the trip herself. She feared the dogs, but saw that they were necessary. Indeed, without them, there would be no way to travel from Circle City to the long, straggling row of claims. Already her lashes were frozen together and her bones ached from the cold.

When they reached the claim she sank a pick into the still-frozen earth, testing it. If she did not tend to the fires it would take that much longer to crack the ground in the spring. She stoked the flames, feeling her fingers numb in the fur-lined gauntlets, and when she was satisfied she instructed the guide to return with all speed. She did not relish a daily trek here, but she felt the least she could do for A. J. was to tend his fire.

Gradually, her days assumed a pattern. In the perpetually falling twilight it was impossible to tell what time it was, which made it all the more essential to keep to a schedule. Otherwise she might sink into that deep melancholy the miners called Arctic madness, and become as daft as poor old Billy Shepherd, who roamed the streets of the town bent double over fifty pounds of old newspapers.

In the morning she breakfasted, reading the month-old papers it was possible to buy from Charles Ryder's shop. Then she went to the shop itself, where she bought a book or browsed through the periodicals. Charles Ryder was a gentle, well-bred man originally from Virginia. He stocked complete sets of Darwin, Huxley, Carlisle, and Ruskin, as well as popular novels and adventure stories. Nothing amused Mara so much as to see a burly miner, mackinaw shedding snow and mud, jaw bristling with beard, tramp in and select a volume of Victorian poetry, paying in gold dust.

"It helps to keep us sane," Charles Ryder told her. "Even at the ends of the earth, men must read."

Once he had shyly shown her a yellowing copy of "Hibernian Beauty" which he kept in a private album at the rear of the store. "I knew who you were the moment I saw you," he said.

"I am afraid it will pursue me for the rest of my days," Mara laughed.

"I consider it a work of art," Ryder said solemnly. "You should be very proud."

The warm, drowsy atmosphere of the bookstore was so seductive that she had to force herself away at noon. The afternoon was entirely dedicated to the long sled-trek and the tending of the eternal fires. She had bought her own sled and dogs, and once more she began to worry over money. It seemed to her time to find work, but Circle City was more sophisticated than Fortymile. The novelty of a lady dealer would hardly be so great in a place where Princes of the Yukon strode from music hall to saloon each night, their necklaces of golden nuggets proclaiming their wealth for all to see.

The evenings were the hardest. She could hear the jangling clamor rising from saloon and dance hall, mixing with the baying of the dogs and the wild laughter of women and men who heeded the old song, taking love while they might. Only Mara seemed alone.

She took herself off to the theatre one night, which proudly advertised a production of *Hamlet*, starring Constanze Bougenier, the French tragedienne, in the starring role. Mara watched, entranced, while the tall, divinely slender Bougenier, dark eyes burning across the footlights, held the audience in thrall. Nobody believed she was the Prince of Denmark but not a soul in the theatre cared. When the actress took her curtain calls she was showered with a storm of golden nuggets thrown from the loges onto the stage. With a superb gesture, she kicked them aside as if they were so many hen's eggs and bowed deeply. "She is almost as magnificent as

Bernhardt," said a man sitting behind Mara to his companion. Mara felt almost giddy with pleasure. The crude opulence of the theatre, the gaiety of the crowd, and—above all—the illusion of warmth and civilization defying the deadly cold of the Arctic night, had gone to her head. When she saw Charles Ryder, she asked him to take her to one of the less infamous saloons.

"With pleasure," he said, his face lighting up. And so began her friendship with the cultivated bookseller. She felt he was the only man in town who would understand her need for friendship without trying to make love to her, and for a long time he proved her right. Every evening they sat in one night spot or another, surrounded by gaudy prostitutes and carousing men, earnestly discussing books and life. If he wondered at her casual taste for champagne and expensive clothing, he wisely did not comment. At least a week went by before he began, very delicately, to question her about herself.

"You say your father simply disappeared?" he asked. "In what year did you come to America?"

"It was 1893," said Mara, "in the spring. I remember it was very warm for April." She felt almost nostalgic, remembering the sultry heat that framed her memories of New York.

"Your father—had he strong political inclinations?" Ryder seemed unusually intense. He had never interrogated her before, and Mara was curious.

"Father? No. At least, I don't think so. He came over from Ireland a year before we did. He'd had news of a legacy, you see, and we had become very poor. A solicitor wrote to him that an uncle of his had died in Schenectady—a very distant relation. That's what made it so surprising—that Father should be mentioned in the will. It was all a mystery. At any rate, he wanted to make a fresh start in America. My mother and I went to join him, after he wrote us to come, only she died at sea . . ."

"And you were alone?" Ryder's face brimmed with sympathy.

"No—not quite. A cousin traveled with us. He took charge of me."

"He must have been very close to the family to make the journey with you."

Mara's eyes widened. She was not prepared to speak of Desmond, but once she was given the opportunity, she found she could not stop.

"Mr. O'Connell," she said slowly, "was not closely related by blood. He came from Galway, the youngest son of a man related to my mother by marriage. I did not meet him until I was fifteen, and then he simply appeared in our village one day and announced that he was going to live there. His parents had died, you see, and he had been on his own for some time."

"Had he a trade?"

"Desmond?" Mara laughed. "Oh, no. Desmond was very grand, or thought himself so. He rode a horse superbly, and played cards a great deal. He'd been spoiled, you see. He was very . . . handsome, and quite charming, and all the village girls lost their heads over him. My parents took to him immediately. I remember it made me quite angry."

"And why was that?" Charles Ryder asked gently.

"He was arrogant." Mara listed the catalogue of Desmond's sins with great relish. "He was conceited, and reckless, and thought he was God's gift to the world. Why he stayed in Mayo I'll never know." She sat forward. "You asked if my father was political. It was Desmond who was political! You never heard such wild assertions about Irish independence, Irish supremacy! Desmond spoke Gaelic as well as English, and he swore one day we'd see the return of a free Ireland."

"And where is he now?" asked Charles Ryder. His voice was very soft.

"I do not know," Mara replied. "I rather thought he would come North, along with the rest of the world." Her voice was unintentionally wistful.

Soon after, Ryder told Mara he was uncommonly tired. He took her back to her hotel and pressed her hands warmly at the portico. He had one last question. "What was your father's name? His first name?"

"Padraic. Padraic McQuaid." Something in his expression alarmed her. "Surely you didn't know him?" she asked.

"No, no—I was only curious." Charles Ryder smiled at her with his sad and knowing eyes, and took his leave. Mara lay awake for a long time, pondering their conversation. The talk of Desmond had deprived her of her sleep. The mere act of mentioning his name would have been enough. She felt the blood racing in her veins and cursed herself for a fool as she tossed and turned in the narrow bed. When at last she fell into a fretful half-sleep, it was only to dream . . .

She was in Mayo, in the kitchen of their house. She had come home from school and was in the act of lifting her heavy satchel of books to the peg near the door when her mother's voice called out:

"Mara, this is your cousin Desmond, come from Galway!"

And there, lounging at her mother's kitchen table with an infuriating air of belonging, sat a dark-skinned boy of twenty years or so, regarding her insolently with eyes as blue as cornflowers. She stared back at him, trying to match his arrogance, and felt herself drowning.

*"Dia's Muire Dhut,"* he said, bidding her hello in Gaelic, and then—as the dream-Mara searched for a reply—he became the Desmond she had seen in San Francisco, snapping the champagne glass in his hands at sight of her . . .

She awoke with a heavy feeling of premonition and went to the window, scraping away the thick frost and peering out. It was dark, but the little clock she had bought told her it was mid-morning. She dressed quickly and ran up the street to Charles Ryder's bookshop, hardly knowing what it was she expected to find. The look on Charles' face made her feel she was still dreaming. He gazed at her with sorrowful eyes, and before she could say a word he was leading her to the back of the shop.

"What is it Charles?" The atmosphere of doom had become so thick she wanted to shake him by the lapels until he laughed and poured her out a cup of strong coffee; at the back of her mind she understood only too well that she was about to discover something unpleasant.

"Dearest girl," said Charles, settling her in an ancient leather chair that gave out clouds of dust, "I have something for you to read. When we spoke last night it all began to come clear for me, but I wasn't sure. I returned to the shop last night, and found what I was looking for." He handed her a periodical magazine, dated August, 1893, which had been folded back at a certain page. "I am so sorry," Ryder murmured, "but you had better know the truth."

Mara stared at the title of the piece, which was written in bold black letters at the top of the page. "NEW FENIAN MOVEMENT REVEALED!" blared the title, and underneath, in smaller letters: "Irish Zealots Come to Grief." She was confused suddenly, because it seemed that the article could have nothing to do with her, or anyone she knew. She began to read, conscious that Charles had left her to attend to some customers. The first part of the article was a short historical lesson on the background of the militant Fenian Movement, of which Mara had heard. Every schoolchild in Ireland knew that the Fenians had organized underground in America almost half a century ago. Their ill-fated attempt to invade British-owned Canada in the 'sixties, led by the dashing Civil war veteran John O'Neill, was something her father had talked of often. "Bloody daft plan," he used to say, shaking his head in disbelief mixed with reluctant admiration. "Can you imagine a few hundred boyos thinking they could take Canada? And even if they succeeded, bloody England wouldn't liberate us." Still, politicians had courted the Fenians and at the height of their power it was estimated they numbered 45,000 strong. It had all been a long time ago, but Mara read on obediently, her cold fingers trembling as she turned the yellowed pages.

> This reporter discovered, in December of 1892, that rumors of a new Fenian movement were strong in certain Irish strong-holds of New York City. Diligent inquiries turned up an amazing story, no less amazing because it repeated so accurately the earlier failures of a group of deluded patriots . . . The new Fenians had abandoned the grandiose plan of invading Canada, and were occupying themselves with the more serious intention of shipping arms to Ireland from the Maritime provinces . . .

> The zealots had rendezvoused frequently in Buffalo, where the headquarters of the movement were established. To Buffalo, in the late winter of 1892, had come three undercover government agents, instructed to infiltrate the movement and make arrests. They reported that the Fenians seemed equally comprised of native-born Irish Americans and recent emmigrants. The Canadian government had been alerted, and on the evening of a proposed gun-run to the border, fifty Royal Mounted Police had been waiting.

> It is estimated that ten men escaped in the ensuing panic. Five were arrested and are currently serving prison sentences. Only three of the misguided revolutionaries attempted to shoot their way free, and all were killed in the gun battle, dying instantly. Because each member of the movement used a false name,

the identities of the slain men were difficult to obtain, but recent information has cleared the ill-fated affair, burying doubts once and for all. The slain were Thomas Dooley, 25, of Buffalo; Gerald O'Rourke, 32, of New York City, and Padraic McQuaid, 49, late of County Mayo, Ireland. It is to be hoped that their unfortunate ends will serve to discourage those patriotic Sons of Hibernia who still believe that violence can cure the ills of the world."

Mara read the last paragraph over and over, seeing her father's name leap up from the orderly lines of print as if it had been written in fire. *Late of County Mayo* sounded in her brain like the tolling of a bell. At last she laid the magazine down and stared, unseeing, toward the front of the shop. How could it be possible? Her mind could not grapple with the image of her father, torn apart by gunshot, dying alone and unknown for principles she had not even known he believed in. What had happened to him in the months in New York to make him join such a movement? Or had he always been a revolutionary, nurturing in secret bright, outrageous plots she and her mother never dreamt of? He had been dead before they ever docked in New York, before they set out from Liverpool . . . How little she had known him, after all.

"Rest in Peace, Father," she thought. "I am sorry you died in exile."

When Charles Ryder came to her she was quite composed, dry-eyed and calm. Only her extreme pallor betrayed her. He knelt by her side, taking the magazine from her hands. "Mara, my dear," he murmured, "don't hate me for being the one to tell you. I would have given so much if it weren't true. Is there any doubt?"

"No," said Mara. "No doubt at all. I am glad I know the truth."

Charles poured her a glass of sherry and took her hand in his. "Let me take care of you," he said softly. "I have fallen in love with you, Mara. I would be the happiest man in the world if you would marry me."

But Mara seemed not to have heard him. She lifted her head and said to no one in particular: "He was the best of fathers."

That night Mara went to the dance hall and requested an interview with the proprietor, a blowsy blonde woman who was said to drive the hardest bargain in Circle City. She was led to the offices in back, where Mrs. Turner, swathed in diamonds, was going over her books.

"I don't need any more girls," she said without looking up. "I've got more than I need right now."

Mara removed her shawl and said in precise tones, "Look at me, Mrs. Turner. You have no one like me."

The woman studied Mara, chewing on her lower lip and nodding in agreement. "You're right," she said. "Modest, too."

"I am sorry if I sounded immodest," said Mara glacially, "but I would very much like the job."

"Need money, do you?"

"Probably less than most of your girls. I have some money. I want the job for other reasons—I promise you I will work as hard as if I were starving."

"Well, now, ain't that fine?" Mrs. Turner volunteered what passed, with her, for a smile. "I'm curious, though. Why would a well-fixed beauty want to work in a dance hall? You'd make twice as much peddling your pretty hide."

"I have already tried that, in San Francisco," said Mara in level tones. "I want to be obliged to work very hard, so that by the time I fall into bed I can sleep."

"In that case, dearie," said Mrs. Turner, grinning, "you're hired!"

Mara went directly to the dance floor, threading through the crowd of rough, good-natured girls and approaching the bar. The men turned to look at her, appraising her greedily. They didn't understand that she was for hire, and merely stood looking, jaws ajar with bewildered lust, at the slender, black-haired beauty who had wandered in. "Well?" said Mara. "Will no one dance with me?"

Instantly there was a sort of stampede in her direction, and she found herself gripped in the arms of a lean, black-bearded miner who beamed with delight at his good fortune. He clomped around the floor with her, his hands heavy on her back, proud to be the first man to dance with her. It was not so unlike the hurdy-gurdy palace, she thought, except that Mrs. Turner charged a dollar in dust for a dance, and took exactly half of each girl's earnings. A trio of grim, silent men carefully weighed the dust in scales and made notations in leather-bound books;

if any girl tried to cheat Mrs. Turner, she was put on the street without a second chance.

The black-bearded man relinquished Mara and she found herself clasped to the enormous chest of Yukon Joe Jenkins, a legendary man who boasted that in ten years he had been south of the Chilkoot only once. "What's yer name?" he bellowed above the noise. When Mara replied he misunderstood and strained her yet closer. "You and me—we'll get along fine, Mar'gret," he murmured. Her nose told her that Yukon Joe had not bathed for weeks, but she smiled gamely and allowed him to twirl her into the piano. "Sorry!" he cried, lifting her up and completing the dance so that she hung five inches from the floor. Her next partner was a young, morose man who confided that it was his first time in the dance hall. He held her carefully away from him, but he looked so deeply into her eyes she was afraid he would have a seizure. She welcomed each new partner eagerly, glad for the remembered pain of aching feet and trampled toes. If she could dance her way to honest exhaustion she would attain her goal, which was simply not to think, to remember, or to care . . .

By the third night she realized that the other girls resented her. She was so much the star attraction that their wages were falling off. "Look here," she said to one of them, "what if we pooled all our earnings? Then we could share equally at the end of the evening."

"Wouldn't do no good," the girl replied glumly. "Mrs. Turner likes to know how well each of us is doing. Me—I've only made five dollars all night."

Mara gave her five more, but the girl was not appeased. "It's not fair," she said. "We're all ordinary, good-time girls—we like a laugh and a dance and we need the money. Then *you* come along and turn all the men's heads and suddenly *we* ain't good enough."

Mara sighed. The girl, who was sallow and flat-chested, was trembling with righteous indignation. When Yukon Joe came lumbering up, Mara said, "Please dance with Rosie, Joe—I have a fierce headache." But nothing mollified the other girls. Night after night they slanted poisonous glances in her direction, and night after night the men thronged in, waiting patiently to hold Mara in their arms.

She had succeeded. Each morning, when the dance hall closed, she fell into bed so weary and numb that sleep overpowered her instantly. She still took the sled each afternoon to the desolate site of A.J.'s claim. The constant fires had done their work and the earth seemed softened sufficiently to begin digging. It was in these solitary moments, kneeling alone beside the fire, that her mind whirred with questions. She wondered if Desmond had known of her father's activities—if he had lied to spare her feelings or was as ignorant of Padraic's death as he had pretended. And what of Mr. McSweeney? She found it impossible to believe that he had not known, at least by the time she had written him from San Francisco. Most immediate—where was Adam? She feared he had become snowed in at Fort Yukon, or worse, that he had set out for Circle City and met with disaster. Always, running beneath the current of her tortured thoughts, was the longing for Desmond. She remembered the cruel things she had said to him in San Francisco, and the look on his face when she had taunted him. Only her gruelling evenings at the dance hall kept her sane, and she silently blessed the rowdy, lecherous miners for distracting her from her pain . . .

Charles Ryder entered the dance hall one evening, seeming stiff and ill at ease. His eyes, when they caught sight of Mara, were sorrowful. He pulled her to a corner where the noise was less fearsome, and said, without preamble, "This is monstrous! I cannot bear to see you working in a place like this. Please come away with me—I will take care of you as long as I live. I want to marry you, Mara—" his words tumbled out; he stammered in his misery.

She turned him away as gently as she could. She understood his pain but could do nothing to remedy it. Not for the first time, the world seemed a very cruel place.

As the winter deepened, the citizens of Circle City seemed desperate in their search for gaiety. One night Yukon Joe went on a "spree," as he called it, and managed to demolish three saloons in four hours. He entered the first swinging a huge club and shouting his intentions to the delighted crowd. When he had flung the cordwood for the stove into the air, jumped into the water-barrel, opened the beer-tap and smashed the whiskey bottles, he drove everyone before him with his club and repeated the performance up the street, until he passed out. Mara was astonished to hear people referring to Joe's "spree" in approving tones; he had reimbursed each saloon-keeper for his fun, and everyone was satisfied.

A man who lived alone in a cabin on the flats set his dwelling on fire and almost perished running through the cold for help. The men who came to his aid whooped about in the flames and then all of them settled down for a week-long drunk. An eccentric chap called Zachary took to leading his pet moose into saloons and demanding drinks for the creature. The town had gone mad, and Mara was very glad that Mrs. Turner inspired as much fear as she did. Nobody would dare to rampage through the dance hall, but plenty of men dreamed of it wistfully.

When it was announced that Constanze Bougenier planned to sell one dance to the highest bidder for charitable purposes, the town went wild. Yukon Joe was said to be planning an offer of one hundred dollars.

Mlle. Bougenier entered at approximately midnight, clad in a long, sweeping cape of black sable. A reverent hush settled over the dance hall as she removed the cloak to reveal a simple gown of black satin. She wore no jewels, which served to heighten the austerity of her beauty. She stood immobile before them, waiting for the bidding to begin.

"Fifty dollars!" howled Yukon Joe, starting modestly. Bougenier's lip curled with scorn.

"Seventy-five!" bellowed an elderly miner with white whiskers . . .

"One hundred!" called Bobby Platte reluctantly.

The bidding escalated until Yukon Joe's offer of three hundred dollars stood supreme. The sum hovered in the air for a moment, and then Bobby Platte shrugged and announced, "Five hundred."

In the end, Yukon Joe triumphed and, for the

sum of seven hundred fifty dollars, was allowed to trample the toes of the fourth-greatest actress in Europe. To the accompaniment of the piano he shuffled round and round the floor, his enormous arms clasped firmly about the exquisite form of Constanze Bougenier. Everyone was silent. When the dance had finished, the actress announced that she would donate her fee to the town's only hospital.

Yukon Joe gave a great whoop of laughter, beating his palms together happily.

"I fail to see the humor," said Mlle. Bougenier in her deep, thrilling voice. "The hospital is essential, is it not? Only this morning a party of men have been admitted, suffering from exposure. I cannot imagine a worthier cause." Then she stretched out a long white arm for her cloak and swept off, stalking through the room like a lioness.

Mara had heard the curt exchange and was filled with foreboding at her words. She ran to her, catching her at the door. "Mlle. Bougenier," she asked, "the men who were brought to the hospital—where were they found?"

"I only know," the actress replied, "that they were coming from Fort Yukon."

Mara had never been to the hospital before. The Episcopal Church had donated the money to build it, and the small, two-story wood building sat proudly at the edges of the settlement—proof that Circle City had all the comforts of civilization.

A solitary nursing sister sat in the dim receiving hall, reading a month-old copy of the Seattle *Times*-

*Intelligencer.* She looked up in surprise as Mara ran breathless through the door, her gaudy yellow gown rustling improbably beneath the mackinaw. The sister had seen odder sights than Mara, however, and she inquired mildly as to what she might do.

"The men who were brought in this morning—the party from Fort Yukon? Is there a boy among them, a Mr. James? He is tall and blond, about twenty."

"Mr. James is with us, yes," said the sister. "He is doing very well, indeed. Some of the other men were not so fortunate."

"I must see him," Mara cried, her knees weak with relief. "He is my partner—please!"

"Very well, but I must ask you not to tire him. He has had quite an ordeal." She took Mara up a flight of bare plank stairs and led the way to a square room at the end of the corridor. Inside, by the flickering light of an oil lamp, Mara could see A.J. lying on a bed, his eyes closed. He looked very young and pale and she gave an involuntary cry of distress.

"He looks much better now," the nurse observed. "You should have seen him before I shaved him."

Mara approached the bed and A.J.'s eyes opened slowly, focusing on her with difficulty. When he saw her face clearly he smiled and held out a feeble hand. "Don't worry," he whispered, "I'm fine—I'm going to be good as new. I'm only tired."

Mara bent to hug him, smoothing the lank blond hair from his forehead. "I only just found out," she said. "Oh, A.J., I've been so worried about you."

"We ran into a blizzard," he murmured, "and lost some of our food."

"Hush," Mara said, "don't talk now. I'll come to you tomorrow, when you're stronger."

She was at the door when his hoarse whisper came to her. "Mara!" He sounded frightened, urgent. "Mara—there were four of us. I don't know how the others are . . ."

"I'll find out," she promised.

"You don't understand," he moaned. "One of them is Mr. O'Connell—Desmond—they won't tell me if he's all right . . ."

The name exploded in her mind like a white star and she clutched at the doorframe, afraid she would fall. The nurse's words rang in her ears: *Some of the other men were not so fortunate.* Mara ran into the corridor, stopping at each room, peering into the gloomy interiors desperately. A man lay silently two doors down, but she could see that he was old and gray. The rooms next to his were empty.

The last room was lit, like Adam's, by an oil lamp. The eerie white light elongated the shadow of the cross which hung over the bed where Desmond lay, as silent and motionless as death. His hands were bandaged, lying lifeless outside the coverlet. Mara knelt beside him, staring at his face. He was almost unrecognizable. The fine, dark skin was drawn and pale, and he had a two-week's growth of beard. His black hair was matted and wild. Only the dark lashes, splaying peacefully across his cheeks, looked untouched. Except for the slight rise and fall of his chest, he might have been dead.

"Desmond," she whispered, "oh, Desmond . . ." But he could not hear her. She felt a hot, choking grief that was nearly overpowering, and then she was weeping, her tears spilling over's Desmond's ravaged face, weeping as if her heart would break. She put her hand on his cheek and was surprised to find it warm, and then fresh sobs burst from her because she wanted so to touch him, to bring him back to life. She kissed his bandaged hands, and rocked back and forth in her anguish, begging him to recover, to be well and strong again.

She was still sobbing when she encountered the nurse in the hall. "Please," she cried, "you must tell me what's wrong with Mr. O'Connell. He is so still —he seems to be dead."

The sister sighed. "He is very weakened," she explained. "It is possible that he will lose an arm."

"No!" It was a scream, and the nurse took Mara by the hand and ordered her to compose herself. "Listen, my dear," she said, "one of the other men has already died from exposure and the fourth will almost surely lose a leg. They were older than Mr. O'Connell, and not as strong. We have every hope that he will recover, but I cannot promise you anything."

And then, despite Mara's protests, the nurse ordered her away and told her to come back in the morning. "You can do no good here," she said kindly. "Go and sleep."

Mara sat up all night in her room, staring in dumb horror at the darkness outside her window. Images of Desmond came to torment her: Desmond riding horseback along the strand in Mayo . . . Desmond leaning with lazy grace in the doorway of his cabin at sea, holding her in his strong arms all through the gale . . . pulling her to him with brutal desperation that night in New York . . . She could not bear it if he should lose an arm. That he might die seemed so dreadful to her that she dared not even think it. Finally, when she could weep no more, she bathed her swollen eyes in freezing water and prepared to wait the long hours until she could return to the hospital . . .

The night nurse was just leaving when she arrived. "He is awake," she said, "but he is in pain." She patted Mara's arm encouragingly. "That's a good sign," she whispered, "and Mr. James is doing splendidly."

They had shaved him and tidied him a bit, but her heart sank when she saw him, all the same. His blue eyes regarded her blankly, without emotion. He turned his head on the pillow to look at her, but that was all.

She knelt beside the bed. "Desmond," she whispered, "please say you know me."

A ghost of a bitter smile touched his lips. "I would know you anywhere," he said. The words were without affection.

She began to weep again, telling him how she had discovered him last night, how she had been forced to go away by the nurse. "Let me stay and take care of you," she pleaded. "I know you'll be well, soon— you are so strong—and the suffering will pass . . ."

Desmond's face was blanched with pain, but he managed to utter a soft laugh that was so mocking Mara felt as if he had struck her.

"This is all most touching, Cousin," he whispered. "You cry so well! Have you decided to go on the stage?"

"You have every right to hate me," Mara cried, "but I am so sorry for all I said to you in San Francisco. I swear I didn't mean it, Desmond. I have regretted it so bitterly . . ." She stretched a hand out to him, to touch his hair, and he narrowed his eyes.

"Don't touch me," he said with surprising strength. "Don't ever touch me!" The look in his eyes was one of sheer loathing, and Mara felt the very earth drop away beneath her. She stared at him, speechless, and his eyes blazed back at her, alive with hate. Somehow she managed to get to her feet and walk from the room. She could not imagine how she might bear this new grief. She remembered Desmond, shaking with the fury of his anguish that night in San Francisco. *"I wish to Christ you were dead,"* he had cried, *"or I were."* He had suffered then as she was now, and he had emerged from his grief to find that he hated her. She wondered if she would be so lucky.

Adam was released that afternoon and Mara brought him to her room, feeding him delicacies from the hotel dining-room and making him lie on her bed. Her eyes were so swollen from weeping that A. J. regarded her wonderingly. He had never seen her so, and yet he was obscurely glad to learn that she could grieve. "Are you weeping for Mr. O'Connell?" he asked gently, and when she nodded he was satisfied.

Adam himself was in a curious state—partly horrified at the death of one of his companions and the threatened mutilation of the others, and partly elated at having escaped. He couldn't stop talking—the words tumbled out wildly. "It was like a nightmare," he would say, "the kind where things happen over and over. When the snows caught us we were coming down Birch Creek, or so we thought, and then somehow we headed for Rampart by mistake . . . One of the dogs turned on us and we had to shoot him . . . The reason I am so much healthier than the others is pure accident—I fell and struck my head on the ice, and I was lying under the robes on the sled for two days while the others slogged it . . ." Mara laid her hand on his head and soothed him, feeding him glacéed fruits and begging him to be calm, but a kind of fever had possessed him.

"I fell in love at Fort Yukon," he said suddenly. "You will meet her in the spring—her name is Nadine and she is a missionary's daughter. It's funny, isn't it, Mara? That a bawdy-house cook should love the daughter of a Holy Joe?" She made him drink some sherry, and he quieted temporarily, only to begin again. "Wasn't it odd, meeting Desmond at Fort Yukon? Dear God, I hope he will be all right. He wanted to come with us, to stake a claim at Circle City—how is our claim, Mara? Did you keep the fires going?"

And Mara told him that the ground was almost soft enough to dig in, and while she spoke to him in a soft, lulling voice he fell asleep as suddenly and deeply as a child.

Mara stole from the room and went to the hospital, where the sister told her that Desmond was much the same. Then she went to the dance hall, where her tear-stained eyes were much remarked upon, and danced so wildly and with such an abandoned gaiety that even Yukon Joe could barely keep up with her. Her hair slipped from the pins and flew about in disarray; her gown slipped down from her shoulders under the dragging weight of her partners' hands. When she saw herself in the dimly mottled glass behind the piano she wondered who the frantic looking creature could possibly be, and then she saw it was herself—a perfect slut. She gave a low laugh and her young partner gathered her closer in his arms and murmured against her cheek: "Come home with me tonight, sweetheart—I'll give you a loving to remember!"

She broke away from him abruptly, horrified at the jolt of feeling his words had given her. He followed her, taking her arm roughly, and then Bobby Platte came roaring up to inquire what the trouble was.

"Is he annoying you, Princess?" Bobby's red face was even redder and Mara saw that he was quite drunk.

"She didn't finish her dance with me," the young man shouted indignantly, reaching out again to paw at her.

Instantly, Bobby dragged the boy away and flung him against the piano, his huge fists balled and ready for a fight. Rosie gave a scream so shrill that everyone's eyes flew to the center of the room, and then they were all pressing around, urging the fighters on, eager for blood. The boy lurched to his feet and hurled himself on Bobby Platte, who outweighed him by fifty pounds, seizing him by the throat and carrying him backward to the floor. They rolled over and over, coated with sawdust and cursing in thick grunts, and Rosie screamed again when Platte caught his fingers in the boy's hair and banged his head on the floor. "Go for the eyes, lad!" shouted someone, and the underdog managed to free a hand and then it was Mara's turn to scream, as she saw Platte's eye come bulging from its socket like a veined and rotten fruit, drooping onto his cheek as if it would pop out and go rolling across the floor. "Stop it," she shrieked, "Stop it!"

Yukon Joe came to her worriedly, slinging a heavy arm around her shoulder. "Hush, now," he said kindly, "they're only having a bit of fun."

As if by magic, Platte's eye popped back into its socket and then the two combatants were on their feet, bruising their bare knuckles in wild swings at each others' faces. There was no clear winner, and by the time the two men staggered to the bar, arms flung about each other, everyone agreed that the boy had won his right to finish the dance with Mara. She shrank from him, but Rosie's voice hissed at her: "You started the trouble, Miss Icicle—now give the boy what he paid for." And so Mara, shivering with exhaustion and horror, let the bruised and bloody boy stumble about the floor with her for two more minutes. His lips were swollen and puffed, but he managed to tell her, haltingly, that he would fight a dozen men for her.

Adam was still asleep when she returned to her room. She took a blanket, wrapped herself in it, and lay on the floor. Sometime later, when Adam was preparing to go to the hospital, he looked down at

her and shook his head sadly. Her hands were
clenched in fists, even as she slept, and the lovely
face was grieving. There was a trickle of dried blood
on her neck. She had not removed her satin gown,
and he could see that it was ripped. Mara had told
him that Desmond did not want her near him, and
he knew the reason why. He had never known two
more obstinate people than Mara and her cousin,
nor two more passionate. His own love for Nadine
was a gentle, happy thing. He could not imagine
making her suffer—the very thought was repellent to
him. But Desmond and Mara, he feared, were
capable of killing each other in the blindness of
their love.

He planned to plead with O'Connell when he saw
him, to beg him to unbend and show some sign of
kindness to Mara. He rehearsed his words all the
way to the hospital, planning how best to appeal to
Desmond on Mara's behalf.

But Desmond could neither listen nor speak. He
lay in a fever, his blue eyes glazed with pain and
bewilderment, while the little daynurse bathed his
head in cool water. She put her finger to her lips
and shook her head at A.J. "The other man is
dead," she whispered, "and Mr. O'Connell has pneumonia."

## Chapter Sixteen

"Oh, how he fights!" The old nurse in charge spoke with almost fierce admiration. "You can tell, you know—even when they're barely conscious. Mr. O'Connell wants very much to live. He'll pull through if I'm any judge."

"And the danger from frostbite is past?" Adam couldn't bring himself to mention the threat of amputation.

"Oh my, yes, and thank God for it. It would be a cruel pity to mutilate a magnificent young man like Mr. O'Connell. We've only the pneumonia to worry about." She smiled reassuringly and studied Adam shrewdly. "Mr. James," she said after a moment, "I am worried about the little black-haired dancehall girl. She comes here every day—so distraught she is—and begs for news of him. She is so tragic, poor thing, and yet it seems he will not allow her near him. I find it most perplexing."

"They are cousins," said Adam warily, "and they

have quarreled. But surely you might allow her to
see him? He will not know the difference."

"So you might think," the nurse replied. "And
yet, when he is lucid, he has only one thing to say
to us. 'Don't let her come near me,' he gasps. Now,
the strange thing in this—when he is delirious he
changes his tune. He calls for her over and over. It
is heart-rending." The nurse's eyes gleamed. "Do
you understand what I am saying, Mr. James?"

"Yes."

"And yet I cannot allow her to go to him. She is
in a very precarious position. If he does not come
to the crisis soon, I fear she'll crack to pieces. Then
we shall have them both here, together."

A.J. went straight to the dance hall, where he
discovered Mara with a long line of eager partners
waiting. He studied her face, looking for signs of the
cracking the nurse had warned of. He found them.
It seemed to him that she had never looked so beautiful. Her golden eyes were enormous in the small
face, made brilliant by the tears she had shed. Her
suffering bathed her in a luminescence that made
her almost painful to behold. Everything seemed
wound so tightly that the slightest jolt might shatter
her fragility. He went to her, ignoring the impatient
cries of the men who were waiting, and drew her
aside.

"The nurse says she is sure he will get well," he
told her. "There is no need to worry about his . . .
arm anymore."

She watched him intently, as if he held the power
of life and death over her.

"Mara, the nurse says he wants to live. He is a ...ghter."

She nodded. Mr. McSweeney had called him a ...ghter, too. "Have you seen him?" she asked.

"Yes—he didn't know me at first, but then his ...yes cleared and he called me by name. He will be ...ell, Mara. I know it."

She turned away then, and slipped into the arms ... her next partner. The last thing he saw was the ...an's hand, red and coarse, against the delicate ...hiteness of her shoulder.

When the crisis of his illness came, Desmond ...ught it as the nurse had predicted. His labored ...eathing filled the room; his body arched helplessly ...d then more strongly, as if he were wrestling with ... demon. The youngest nurse was in tears. "He is ...ish," she said piteously, "we must call a priest." ...t the old nurse in charge laid her hand on the ...rl's arm and said only: "Wait."

Gradually Desmond's breathing grew more calm ...d he lapsed into a tranquil sleep, his features ...ooth and free of pain. When he awakened they ...ought him a glass of barley water and he drank it ...gerly, pausing only to lift the glass in a toast.

"*Slainte*, ladies," he said cheerfully.

By the end of the next day he was ravenous, but ...re was a new problem. The young nurse ran to ... superior with crimson cheeks. "I can't bathe ...m," she cried in an agony of embarrassment. "I ...nnot bathe such a man as that."

"The more fool you," replied the older woma[n] taking the basin of soapy water from her hands.

"Now, ma'am," Desmond said warily when t[he] determined nurse entered his room. "I am perfect[ly] capable of bathing myself." But when he tried [to] sit up he fell back against the pillows helplessly.

The old nurse bathed him as tenderly as if he ha[d] been a child, and Desmond—who had never know[n] a moment's modesty—lay meek beneath her hand[s,] blushing as hotly as a virgin. The nurse enjoy[ed] her task, and thought enviously of the little dan[ce] hall girl. Surely, now that her charge was better, [he] would go to her.

When she heard that Desmond had recovere[d] Mara's gratitude and relief were so profound th[at] she could not speak. She was training herself for [a] new ordeal—that of forgetting him. Or rather, sin[ce] she could not forget him, of resigning herself to [his] hatred. She wondered how much he would reme[m]ber, her stomach churning as she recalled how s[he] had wept by his bedside, pleading with him to f[or]give her. She dreaded seeing him, but until the th[aw] there was nowhere else to go. They would both [be] forced together in Circle City for the remainder [of] the long, dark winter, and every chance encoun[ter] would be a torment to her. Already people me[n]tioned him. If she trusted the gossip she heard [at] the dance hall he had a steady stream of visit[ors] bringing him food and whiskey and newspapers a[nd] sweets.

"Where are all the women in this town?" roar[ed]

Yukon Joe one evening. "All gone to the hospital to have a look at that blasted Irishman!" He wheezed with laughter over his joke, and Mara felt her throat swell with pain.

"He was so thin," A.J. said wonderingly, "but they've fed him and pampered him and now he is almost back to normal."

"Is it true he is visited by women?" Mara asked primly.

"Oh, no," lied A.J., "only the nurses."

The fearful jealousy she felt heightened her beauty, and every night one man or another swore his undying love for her. Sometimes they were drunk, and occasionally dead sober, but always she smiled glacially and said: "Do not waste your time. I am incapable of love."

She heard that Desmond had gone to live with a singer from the music hall, and then that he was sharing a room with one of the actresses in Mlle. Bougenier's company. Both rumors proved to be false.

She saw him from her window one evening, as she was preparing to go to the dance hall. She sank to her knees and watched, breathless. He was walking slowly up the street, alone, and he appeared to limp slightly. He wore the high boots, mackinaw, and broad-brimmed hat that was Circle City's only winter costume, and it was too dark to see his face. Then he passed beneath a gas flare in front of a saloon, and Mara saw him fully. She almost gasped at the difference between the wasted, pale Desmond she had last seen and this healthy, blooming creature beneath her window. His dark skin glowed and the hair beneath the hat was glossy and black as ever. She trembled as wave after wave of desire assailed her; so potent was the feeling the mere sight of him aroused in her that she sank back from the window in dismay. How could she ever face him?

When she looked again, he had gone.

That night the men in the dance hall could talk of nothing but the Klondike. Fresh rumors had circulated in the past week and even Yukon Joe had begun to believe them. "Carmack!" he shouted. "I knew Carmack five years ago. Who'd believe him then?"

"What is he talking about?" Mara asked Bobby Platte. Bobby explained that George Carmack, a notorious failure of a miner, had discovered gold last August on Rabbit Creek, a tributary of the Klondike. At first nobody had believed his find to be of much importance, but the rumors were too numerous now to be ignored.

"Gold as thick as cheese," Bobby murmured longingly. "They call it Eldorado."

A great pall of envy and dissatisfaction hung over the dance hall. The men grumbled and cursed. Nobody in his right mind would try to make it to the Klondike now, in mid-winter, but how they longed to be there. "We're all in the wrong bloody place!" shouted Yukon Joe.

A.J. refused to listen to the rumors. Every day now he took the sled and went to his claim, tunneling down into the softened earth until he had fashioned a miserable shaft some ten feet deep and three feet wide. Once Mara went with him and watched, appalled, while he burrowed down into the smokey crevasse. Everywhere the constant fires burned in the mid-winter gloom, and she thought again how like a scene from Hell it was. She had come to hate Circle City, and everything about it. She wanted only to leave.

She passed Desmond in the street one evening and thought she might faint. She saw him from a long distance away and took care to hold her head very high in anticipation of the inevitable moment. She gave thanks for the heavy mackinaw—at least it covered her trembling body and hid her accelerated breathing from him. Her breast rose and fell alarmingly, but her face was calm.

He stopped a few feet from her and touched his hat in a polite salute. His eyes were unreadable.

"Good evening," she said. "I am so glad you are recovered."

"Yes," he said, "I am recovered." He made no move to walk on.

Despite her resolves, her eyes were drawn to his as if magnetized. They stood, staring at each other helplessly. He was the first to speak, and his voice was so soft it was barely audible.

"Where are you going?"

"To the dance hall. I am employed there."

He smiled. "So I have heard. You cause no end of trouble."

She felt as if she were drowning. They had resumed their old roles, it seemed. She was once more the pesky girl-cousin who tried his patience. "The work suits me," she said airily.

"There is no need for you to work in a dance hall," he replied.

"Ah, but I enjoy myself," she said, She forced a little smile. "You know how fond I am of the company of men."

She saw by the darkening of his blue eyes that she had scored, and seized her advantage. "If you will excuse me," she said, "I must be going. Good evening, Cousin."

He refused to move and she was obliged to walk around him. She felt his nearness like a physical blow, but he made no move to touch her.

"Des O'Connell is living with the young nurse who took care of him," one of the other girls giggled that evening.

"He ain't," observed glum Rosie. "He's stayin' with Daisy from the gambling house."

"You're both wrong," said Mara, who could not bear to hear another word about him. "He shares a cabin on the flats with my partner, Adam James."

"That may be," said Rosie, "but does he *sleep* there?"

When Mara turned on them indignantly they quieted, but she heard them snickering behind her back. They had waited for a long time to have their revenge on her and now they took it eagerly. They knew only that he was her cousin and believed she bridled at their remarks because of blood-ties. She shuddered to think of the torments they might devise for her if they knew the truth.

"I saw yer cousin at McQuesten's saloon," a girl called Nancy trilled. "He had a girl on each knee— one blonde and one dark."

Mara pressed herself so desperately to her next partner that he grew inflamed and tried to kiss her, burrowing his bristly face against her throat and seeking desperately for her lips. She twisted away, but not before his dry lips had pressed against her own for the barest second. For the first time she went to the bar and asked for a drink of the awful watered-down whiskey Mrs. Turner dispensed.

"Maxine from the opera gave your cousin a whole bottle of brandy," a voice hissed close to her ear. And Mara, beleagured beyond endurance, went to Mrs. Turner's office and announced that she was quitting.

"Not for two weeks you ain't," her employer said grimly. She searched for a piece of paper in the depths of her messy drawers, fishing it out with a triumphant grin. "Two week's notice," she said, pointing to the place where Mara had written her name.

"And another thing," she called out, as Mara was leaving. "If there's any more fights over you I'll charge you for the damages."

It was shortly after two in the morning when Desmond entered the dance hall. The girls called to him and he grinned at them, but he did not want to dance. He stood quietly at the bar, tossing back whiskey and watching Mara in the mirror. She was being pawed by a large man who labored under the delusion that he was a graceful dancer. He bent her body in his arms, swooping and gliding as he drove her before him across the floor. At the finale, he put his huge hands around her slender waist and lifted her high into the air, whirling her around so that her skirts billowed out and the men had a satisfying glimpse of her long, elegant legs. They stamped and cheered and Desmond passed a weary hand over his eyes. "Christ," he said to the bartender, "give me another."

Mara, deep in the center of the crowd of dancers, did not see him. The other girls were laying bets on what Mr. O'Connell might do, but to their immense disappointment he bought a round of drinks for the men at the bar and then departed, alone.

The next time she saw him she was struggling with a heavy parcel she had bought at A. J.'s request. It contained two gallon jars of paraffin and numerous cans of tinned food. She had just left the store and was on her way to the hotel when Desmond appeared, walking along beside her as casually as if they had strolled together every afternoon for the past week.

"That parcel is too heavy for you," he said politely. "Let me carry it." She slanted a look in his direction and saw the mocking expression she had always hated. It seemed to her that he was toying with her, playing at cat and mouse to pass the time.

"I can't allow you to carry it," she said coldly. "Please, leave me alone. I have nothing to say to you."

"Then I am the only man in Circle City who cannot approach you," he said. "I will have to pay a dollar and dance with you, it seems."

"Ah, but that is impossible," she said. "You have forbidden me to touch you, so how can I dance with you?"

Instantly she regretted her words. Desmond stood in her path now, his eyes burning with wild triumph.

What she had said was as good as an admission of love.

"Mara." He spoke her name so gently it was like a caress. "Mara—you must understand why I spoke as I did. When you came to me I thought I was destined to be a cripple. I knew they were waiting, waiting to see if my arm was dead. For God's sake, Mara, they would have cut my arm off! Could I have said, 'Yes, yes, Mara—stay by my bedside—watch while they hack away at me! Watch while I die! And if I should live, think what you have to look forward to—a lifetime with a cripple!' " He was breathing harshly; a tiny vein throbbed at his temple. "And so I told you to go away, and not to touch me. Oh, God—above all things not to touch me."

They were so close she had only to move a fraction of an inch to feel him against her. She yearned for his touch so acutely that she gripped her heavy parcel with all her strength to keep from swaying toward him. Desmond clenched his hands at his sides, and did not take his eyes from hers.

"I do not forbid you to touch me," he said. "In fact, I long for it." His blue eyes were luminous, as she had seen them before. He was pleading.

She thought of the hatred in those same eyes when he had looked at her in the hospital, and she thought of the dozens of women who had fallen victim to him, believing what he told them because his words were like honey. "Please, Desmond," she whispered wretchedly. "I cannot believe anything you say. I think you want only to destroy me. Please—go away and leave me in peace. You will find consolation soon enough—you always do."

"Don't do this," he begged. "We have tortured each other long enough, Mara. Do you want to drive me mad?"

He stretched one trembling hand out to her and she shrank back against a doorway.

"Don't ever try to run from me," he said savagely. "Not ever again. I will follow you everywhere. You'll never be rid of me." And then he turned and walked swiftly up the street, his boots striking hollow notes against the snow, and she was alone.

That night she dressed as carefully to go to the dance hall as if she were preparing for her wedding. She did not ask herself why she made such preparations; she was beyond thought and obeyed her instincts as surely as an animal. She bathed and perfumed her body, and brushed her hair until sparks flew in the dim room. She chose a dress of emerald green, very like the one she had owned so long ago in New York, and coiled her hair so elaborately that even Kathleen Daly would have approved. She studied herself for a long time in the glass. Something, she knew, had to happen, or she would lose her senses. For better or worse, she was ready.

The men were almost afraid of her that night, for she was nearly regal to them in her beauty. They handled her gently, as if she were fragile as glass, and many of them did not approach her at all.

When Desmond came in at midnight she neither blanched nor colored. Her face remained composed, a perfect mask as unreadable as it was lovely.

Desmond paid the men at the scales and walked to her, holding out his hands. "I have paid my dollar," he said without expression. "I fear you will have to dance with me."

She nodded graciously and put her hand in his, and then they moved across the floor to the strains of what the pianist evidently considered a waltz. He held her lightly, decorously, without attempting to press her to him. She felt his warm fingers on her back, the smooth muscles of his arm beneath her own fingers, and with all the strength at her command she forced herself to appear tranquil and graceful, pliant and heedlessly gay, in his arms. Her heart hammered and her pulses reeled, but only she knew it. She was counting off the minutes, hoping with frantic desperation that the dance would end before the knocking of her heart pushed her to her knees. Only she and Desmond could appreciate the ordeal—to the others they seemed an elegant couple, well-matched in their grace and beauty, enjoying the simple pleasure of a dance.

She threw back her head and looked at Desmond, acknowledging the contest. Without missing a step he smiled grimly back, his jaw clenched with the effort of holding away from her, his eyes misted and brimming with terrible emotion. Both of them began to tremble, and just as she feared she would fall against him like a dumb, pleading animal, the music ended. He let go of her abruptly, bowed, and left the dance hall as suddenly as he had come.

She was alone for the rest of the evening; nobody came near her or asked her to dance. The most insensitive souls in the hall understood, if only dimly, what it was they had seen.

When an hour had passed she took her cloak and shawl and left, not bothering to collect her wages. Not even the deadly cold outside could soothe her burning flesh. When she had almost reached the hotel, she heard her name called: *Mara McQuaid!* And then again, the words piercing the silent night like arrows, echoing with eerie persistence. *Mara McQuaid!* It was a strangely formal sound, and she turned and saw Desmond, standing far up the street, calling her as if it were an invitation to battle. He came toward her slowly, and when they were almost face to face he said: "You will invite me to your room."

Her eyes widened and she shook her head. "No," she whispered.

"Ah, but you will," he breathed. And then he withdrew his hand from his pocket and she saw, glinting dully in the gaslight, the gun which he pointed at her breast.

So that was what she had prepared for, she thought. Desmond was going to kill her. She laughed, and it was a surprisingly light-hearted sound. "Why must you kill me in my room?" she demanded. "Shoot me here, in the street, if you must."

He grinned. "That won't do," he said. "The dogs would eat you." He thrust the gun at her and she began to walk toward the hotel, leading the way for him, the gun at her back. They passed through the small knot of incurious people who milled about in the receiving hall, and up the flight of stairs to her room. She opened the door with a steady hand and he followed her, kicking the door shut and walking to the window. "Light the lamp," he said. "I want to see you."

Calmly, she obeyed. Then she stood in the center of the room, facing him.

He studied her face, his blue eyes soft with love and longing. "I have never seen beauty," he said at last, "except when I have looked at you, Mara. From the first moment I saw you, in your mother's kitchen, you were all the beauty in the world to me." He gestured with the gun. "Take off your cloak," he said.

She undid the clasps and let it slide to the floor in a heap. Her breasts, above the green satin of the gown, rose and fell beneath the scrutiny of his eyes.

"I have loved your body, too, my Mara, but not as I would have wished to. You are the only woman I have ever taken by force, and I have been punished a hundred times over for it—with guilt, and grief and longing that you could never imagine." He laughed. "I would sooner suffer the torments of frostbite all over again than the pain of dancing with you tonight." He held out his hand; the gun lay on his palm and he offered it to her, the handle toward her hand. "Take it," he said.

She took the gun from him, feeling the metal, warm from his hand, with a kind of joy. He removed his coat and stood expectantly before her.

"And what will I do with it?" she whispered.

"Shoot me," he replied, "and have done with it."

"And why must I shoot you?"

"Because I prefer a swift death to a slow one. It is better than dying little by little for love of you."

She placed the gun on her dressing table, laying it down with infinite care. Then she walked across the room to him. She lifted her hand and slowly, slowly, her fingers trembling, touched his cheek. His eyes closed at her touch and a flood of color rose in his face. "Hold me," she whispered, "hold me, Desmond." And then his arms came around her and he was murmuring her name, kissing her wet cheeks and eyes and pressing her so fiercely to his body that she felt she had melted and become one with him. Her hands flew over his back and shoulders, she caressed him hungrily and felt all of her body flaming with the passion that his slightest touch had always roused in her.

"Desmond," she cried, "I love you so . . . I have never stopped . . . I tried so hard not to love you . . ." And then his lips were on hers, so sweet and soft her own lips parted to drink him in, until he could be gentle no more and kissed her with a wild savagery, his hands like hot brands on her back, his maleness hard and throbbing against her thighs. She took his hands and placed them on her breasts; he knelt before her and pressed his lips to the place where her aching flesh swelled above the gown. Then he freed her, gently, from the emerald green satin, his hands and lips a sweet torment at her breasts. She plunged her fingers into his thick black hair and held his head to her, feeling her nipples bursting beneath his tongue. "Desmond—" she pleaded—"make love to me now or I will die . . ."

He lifted her up and carried her to the bed. She was trying to unbutton his shirt, to feel his hot, smooth flesh, but he laid her down and then knelt beside her, stripping her stockings away and planting kisses on her thighs, her knees and ankles. He drank the sight of her in as if he could never have enough. She held her arms out to him and he set her on her feet again so that he faced her. She unbuttoned his shirt, slipping it from his smooth shoulders and pressing her lips to his chest, feeling the tremors that went through him at her touch. Her hands strayed to his belt and he gave a long, shuddering sigh. She fell back on the bed and watched while he undressed, marvelling at the lean, hard beauty of his body. When he lay beside her she pressed herself to him, crushing her breasts against his chest and twining her legs with his, feeling as if a thunderbolt had struck her. His hands were everywhere, tracing fire across her thighs and belly, brushing her breasts with exquisite tenderness, until she cried for him to take her.

She felt him move away from her and reached out desperately, but he was loosening the pins from her hair, watching it cascade down and then catching the tresses and pressing them to his lips. He gathered her in his arms and whispered, his voice harsh and breaking with passion, "You will never doubt that I love you?"

"Never."

And then his body was covering hers and she could feel him, proud and surging, thrusting into her and driving to the core of her. All the pain of the last

three years fell away and there was only the miracle
of Desmond, filling her with a pleasure so great i
seemed impossible. It mounted and mounted unti
she grew afraid, clinging to him frantically and calling his name, and then she was swept up on the
fierce tide of it, drowning in it, falling away . . .

He lay as he had done in New York, his head on
her breast, his hands plunged into the wild mane of
her hair, murmuring words of love, but this time
the tears spilling down her cheeks were those of
joy.

She thought that perhaps they might go to Eldorado together, or to Fort Yukon with Adam when
the spring came. It didn't matter where they went,
so long as they were never parted again. There
would be time enough to tell him about her father,
time to write to Mr. McSweeney and report that
she had found the fighter. There was so much she
had to tell Desmond and to learn from him; the
cruel years of their long separation had to be
bridged and put to rest. But for now she wanted
only to lie close to him and feel his heart beating
against hers.

He took her in his arms again, still trembling with
his need for her. Instantly she came alive to him, joy
mounting in her as she pressed close to his body.
Her dark lover; her Desmond. Suddenly she had a
thought so terrible her eyes flew open with the shock
of it.

"Desmond—was the gun loaded?"

"Yes, my love." He smiled. "I have always been
a gambler."

"But what if I had shot you?"

"It would have been a great pity," he said. "A terrible waste." And then he was kissing her again, and there was no more talking.

# This
# Outlaw
# Heart

*Rosetta Stowe*

More romantic than SHANNA, bolder than SAVAGE SURRENDER, here is the story of a passion as stormy—and as enduring—as the sea. It is the story of Jeanette Verlaine—lovely, yearning, unfulfilled—fleeing a Santo Domingo slave uprising and a cruel marriage accompanied by her handsome black maidservant, Bliss. She falls into the hands of a fierce privateer, Jamie McCoy, with whom she discovers the deep tides of her own sensuality.

All too soon they are violently separated and with Jamie presumed dead, Jeanette weds a wealthy English sea captain, is captured by Malaccan brigands and enters into a strange three-way relationship. In an explosive finale, she's brought together with the love of her life—the one man who can, with the sword of love, tame her outlaw heart.

# WILDFIRE WOMAN

## Marianna Spring

Here is the big romantic novel of an insatiable passion that raged across two worlds—for every reader who thrilled to LOVE FOREVER MORE.

Lovely, innocent Emma LaMarque Otis, untouched by passion, fled the Old World for the New, to escape the vengeance of an all-powerful Lord, only to find herself betrayed, ravished and shamed—hostage of the raging wildfire emotions one mysterious man has wakened in her blood.

From a Beacon Hill mansion to a New York pleasure house, from a frontier cabin to a Paris hideaway, from a privateer's deck to a London gallows, Emma Otis survives all dangers except the one that lurks in her own secret heart.